Murder
AT AVEDON HILL

P.G. Holyfield

Dragon
Moon

WWW.DRAGONMOONPRESS.COM

ACKNOWLEDGEMENTS

As most of my friends and listeners know, this has been a long and life-changing process for me. I'd like to take this opportunity to thank some (but certainly not all—I wish I could!) of the people who have made this novel possible:

FOR THE INITIAL WRITING OF THE NOVEL:

Errol Pinto for providing an initial audience for my fiction on the NWVault website. Beta readers Scott Neilson and Matt Sanner, thank you for saying "More action!" To my dad, Ron Holyfield, for the wonderful cover art for the original cover of the self-published version of the novel. Thanks to James Hazelett for the icons of the *Children of Az*. I love that when people think of the Land of Caern, they always see these icons in their mind. And most importantly, thanks to my wife Liza for keeping me focused until the first true iteration of the novel came to life.

FOR THE PODCAST OF MURDER AT AVEDON HILL:

The decision to podcast MaAH as a full-cast audio drama was a blessing and a curse. A blessing because of the great people that helped bring this story to audio life: the voice cast, my assistant producers, the musicians who allowed me to use their work, the artists who helped fans visualize what goes on in my crazy mind. The quality of the audio production and the energy that went into it was what built the podcast audience, and the size of that audience, combined with a good story, helped to convince Gwen Gades at Dragon Moon Press to take a chance on an unpublished author such as myself. The curse, you ask? That production of the podcast novel took two years to complete.

But I must take a moment to thank those who helped me most during this time: Mur Lafferty, Philippa Ballantine, Evo Terra, Matthew Wayne Selznick, Matt Wallace, Christiana Ellis, Rich Sigfrit, J.C. Hutchins, Scott Sigler, Seth Harwood, Chris Miller, Rick Stringer, Leann Mabry, and the man that took me under his wing back in 2006 and has been nothing but a giving friend ever since, author Tee Morris.

Praise for P.G. Holyfield and

Murder
AT AVEDON HILL

"P.G. Holyfield creates a realm rich in culture and lore, and then shatters its sweet innocence with a murder that begs to be solved. This is *Name of the Rose* set in Narnia, and a terrific ride for any fan of mysteries."
– Tee Morris, author of the *Billibub Baddings* mysteries

"P.G. Holyfield is now firmly planted on my radar as a target that must be destroyed."
– N.Y. Times Bestselling author Scott Sigler

"With *Murder at Avedon Hill*, P.G. Holyfield creates a mysterious world full of twists and creatures worth diving into, headfirst!"
– Mark Yoshimoto Nemcoff, author of *The Art of Surfacing* and the Parsec Award winning *Number One with a Bullet*

"One of the best podcast fiction writers out there. Listen to this book and you'll never turn back!"
– Seth Harwood, author of the *Jack Falms* crime series

"I've always thought a good whodunit needed vampires, monks and gods. P.G. Holyfield has created an engaging world that both fantasy and mystery fans will enjoy."
– Mur Lafferty, author of *Playing for Keeps*

"P.G. Holyfield has created a textured world full of intriguing details, a canny protagonist who is both approachable and sympathetic, and a powerful, dreadful antagonist; MaAH is a believable fantasy mystery that entices from the very start!"
– Sam Chupp, author of *Heart of the Hunter*

ISBN 978-1-897492-10-9

Dragon Moon Press

Printed and bound in the United States
www.dragonmoonpress.com

FOR THEIR CONTINUED SUPPORT DURING THE EDITING OF MURDER AT AVEDON HILL:

Podcasting has been a blessing, and the friendships that have been forged over the last four years have been nothing short of life-saving, especially this last year. Thanks to Patrick McLean (the most creative man I've ever seen), Chooch and Viv, the Breakalls, my extended GRD family, the guys at DRS, Tabitha Smith, "The Picks," Nathan Lowell, Christof Laputka, and most of all to my team at Dragon Moon Press: Gwen Gades; the force of nature and wonderful art director Alex White... and to everyone who enjoys this novel: you can thank my editor Gabrielle Harbowy. She taught me how to be a better writer. Thank you, Gabby.

And because it must be said... Thank God for Ali.

DEDICATION

To my family.

PROLOGUE

Too much the heavens weep for the maiden lost,
o'er nothing and everything, considering the cost.

—2nd Collected Prophecies of Iberian, Book 1, Verses 245-246

GRETTA PLATT SAT ON a well-crafted stone bench in the southern quarter of the open courtyard. The courtyard was her place of refuge, a sanctuary from the hustle and bustle of her position as Housemistress of Avedon Manor. She still worked, as was her way, writing in a large journal that rested in her lap. Gretta wore a simple linen dress; the powder blue material lay tight against her legs, allowing her to easily balance the bulky yet lightweight journal. Gretta owned many dresses that exhibited her beauty, but she always chose function over elegance.

Anyone would have described Gretta as the most beautiful girl in town—with the possible exception of Sarah Tremaine, who might well have been the most beautiful woman in all of Caern. Gretta's golden locks and topaz-flecked gray eyes were enough to turn any man's head, but her position as Housemistress kept the men in town from staring longer than they should.

Gretta raised her eyes from her journal and spied Mount Olviar to the northeast. The architecture of the central courtyard and the surrounding manor never ceased to amaze her. Hundreds of years of ivy growth, the ancient oak trees around which the manor had been constructed, the Lantis mountain range filling the horizon just above the nearly-hidden courtyard walls—one could easily forget they were enclosed by stone and mortar.

Gretta sighed. Her gaze wandered left, to a spot high on the courtyard's windowless northern wall. *How did it come to this, Lord Avedon? Mother would know what to do.* Gretta blinked and looked away, directing her thoughts back to day-to-day events.

The sun had fled to the west, escaping the Grozhian skies above, but the lanterns Gretta had installed in the courtyard allowed her to enjoy the gardens well into the evening. Gretta took a moment to dip her quill into the inkwell on the bench to her right. At the top of the blank page, she began with the date: *24 Arjunate, 505 AI.* She read aloud as she wrote. "Talik wants to meet with me about bringing a carnival to town this winter. He thinks it will attract visitors to Avedon Hill and to his inn, and give the townspeople something to enjoy while the Pass is closed for the season." *Az help me… the man just doesn't get it.* Gretta turned to a new page.

"Father Jorrus wants another audience with Lord Avedon, to convince my lord to take his warnings more seriously." *Not now, Jorrus. You chose the wrong time for one of your rants about undead threats rising in Caern.* Gretta shook her head and continued writing.

After a time, she turned the page. "Jilly asked me to go on a picnic with her to our grove east of town." *Has it been long enough?* She sighed. *Should I chance it?*

Gretta heard the snap of a twig in the distance. She instinctively turned toward the noise, watching for movement in the meticulously landscaped garden. Now she heard only the water flowing through the fountain to her left and the breeze rustling the ancient oaks. *The wind carries all sorts of sounds over these walls…*

She stared for a time at the trees and tall shrubs cared for so lovingly by the manor's groundskeeper. When viewed from the only balcony window that overlooked the courtyard, the trees and shrubbery formed intricate patterns. Her mother had once told her that the patterns represented Az and his Children, but no matter how long she stared at the gardens from above, she couldn't see them.

Gretta gazed at the few remaining leaves twisting on their branches, clinging to their last moments of life. She shivered. *Winter is nearly here again.*

The sound forgotten, Gretta turned back to her journal. "Herrjarr's reputation has grown. He again seeks permission to sell his wares to shops in Ellyonne and Taxx." *Impressive, Herrjarr—in less than ten years you've surpassed your master's craftsmanship.* Gretta sighed. *Maybe it's time to send the blacksmith on his way. Give Ollus an opportunity to run the smithy.*

The young Housemistress turned her thoughts to the problem that rested most heavily on her mind. *Oh, what am I going to do with you… what if Marrissa is wrong about—*

Something grabbed Gretta's right shoulder and yanked her back off the bench before she even had the chance to wince. Her journal flew out of her grasp and hung briefly in the air, spinning proof of the strength of the attack.

Gretta's muscles tensed, expecting the tug from behind to be followed by a hard landing on her back. Instead, she found herself pulled high into the air, abruptly stopping a good six hands beyond her own height. She tried to turn her head to look at her attacker, but all she could see was the ground quickly approaching her face.

Gretta hit the courtyard floor, her chest and face striking hard against the cold dirt; at the same time, her journal landed on the opposite side of the bench with a flutter of pages. A moment later her quill fell to the grass. Only the inkwell remained upright and undisturbed on the stone bench.

But Gretta didn't have time to notice. A strong hand reached around her head and clamped her mouth shut. *No, this isn't happening!* Gretta struggled, but with a speed beyond her understanding the unseen figure was on top of her, knee in her back, driving her chest once again into the dirt. Gretta pulled at her attacker's arm. She tried to bite the hand holding back her screams, but her assailant's vise-like grasp squeezed harder until Gretta's vision blurred from the pain. Realizing she didn't have the strength to pull her assailant's arm away, Gretta clawed at it, digging with her nails, but this only seemed to intensify her attacker's resolve.

With all of her waning strength, Gretta flailed her legs. A foot connected with her attacker's torso and thigh, but the blow elicited no sound.

Something solid struck Gretta on the right side of her neck; pinned as she was, the blow threatened to separate Gretta's head from her body. Her stunned surprise turned to pure confusion. It felt as if she had been hit by a hammer—but no blunt weapon she had ever seen could maintain contact with its target in a manner such as this. It was as if the weapon had attached itself to her neck.

She had no time to consider the possibilities. Gretta's head began jerking to and fro in uncontrollable spasms. The convulsions were brutal. Each time her head jerked back, she felt as if the back of her skull was touching her spine, and she expected to hear the bones within her neck snap. In moments the violent paroxysms spread, racking her entire body. But from this impossible position Gretta could see the downside-up face of her attacker.

No! You!?

Gretta heard what she thought was the click of snapping teeth and felt an immediate rise in heat on her neck. Something sharp and jagged tore through her flesh. Immediately, her arms and legs lost all feeling—in a matter of moments her convulsions ceased, and she slumped limply forward against the earth.

While her body failed her, Gretta's mind still thrashed in the throes of fear. Her consciousness screamed, but Gretta could not find her voice; her senses retreated, seeping out of her like water from a cracked glass. Her sight was the last to go, but soon enough darkness edged into her field of vision. As shadows overcame her, the last thing Gretta saw was a leaf: falling, twisting beautifully as it traveled from its lifelong home to the cold dirt of the courtyard floor.

No... not like this—

Gretta Platt's murderer stood over her—remarkably unbloodied, but shaking in near-ecstasy from the power of her innocent blood.

I trusted you.

Retrieving Gretta's journal, the figure looked once more upon the Housemistress's corpse.

I now have what I need… to destroy them all.

Confident no one had overheard Gretta's failed struggle for life, the figure stood quietly for a time, breathing in the mountain air. A raise of a hand extinguished the nearby lanterns, wrapping the courtyard in a blanket of darkness.

That's better.

Slowly, the figure exited the courtyard. *We'll see each other again very soon, Miss Gretta.*

Part I

THE TEARS OF ARTUS

1
ARRIVAL

Elai sits unmoving at the entrance of his great mountain.
Elai, just like his earthly home, is never what he seems.

—Old Inarran proverb

Many locations in the Land of Caern have inspired volumes of history and commentary. There are places where great wars have been waged, alliances have been forged, and discoveries have been made; places where great leaders and historical figures lived and worked and battled and loved... and died. Places whose names live on in the thoughts and memories of all the people of the Land.

Avedon Hill is not one of those places.

Nearly five hundred years ago, a miner named Gaelen Avedon was granted permission by the Ossur dwarf clan to begin mining at the base of Mount Olviar. Twenty years later the Avedon Mining Company had built a tunnel and road through Mount Olviar to the northeastern edge of the Lantis Mountains, a range of peaks that stretch for hundreds of leagues. The Olviaran Pass, as it came to be known, was the Avedon family's only claim on history. Traveling by horse, it had previously taken twenty to thirty days—two to three weeks—to make the journey around the Lantis Mountains. The Olviaran Pass cut travel time by at least a week. The settlement built around the southern entrance of the Pass became known as Avedon Hill, and a member of the Avedon family had always watched over the town and its inhabitants.

Through the centuries, Avedon Hill had never grown beyond the fortified walls of the original settlement. It was home to few townspeople and tradesmen, and travelers, mostly merchants, were welcomed to stay and visit before making the journey through the Pass, though rarely would a trader choose to remain longer than a night in the quiet hamlet. Avedon Hill was a footnote; a town not often considered even in regional political circles, and certainly not a place written about in history books.

It was here that Arames Kragen now found himself. More importantly, it was here that Arames Kragen now found himself on the wrong side of some particularly tall town gates.

In his younger years, Arames Kragen had served the Land as an Aarronic Advisor—one of the more renowned Advisors of his day. But Arames had retired to a more hermitic life before he had even turned forty. Now fifty-three, Arames was respected in certain circles as a scholar and an interpreter of prophecy.

A brisk mountain breeze threatened to dislodge Arames's thinning hair. Once full and auburn, it was now becoming more of a grayish white. Arames's eyes still held a youthful quality that belied his years, but as he eyed the town walls, the skin around his eyes wrinkled from the smile that had been the trademark of his youth. He stood quietly, slowly shifting his weight from foot to foot. Arames was not a large man, but years of training had focused his skills. In his day, he had been considered formidable in battle. No physical attributes, however, would allow Arames Kragen to bypass the gate of Avedon Hill.

In two weeks, Arames was scheduled to chair a religious discussion of the 3rd Collected Prophecies of Iberian at the Grozhian capital of Kith-Karn. Before he had started on his journey, Arames had sent word ahead to his cousin, Red, who had moved to Avedon Hill almost a year before. Usually only those willing to pay a goodly sum were granted use of the Olviaran Pass, but Arames hoped his cousin would be able to help.

"Arames, sir, should we seek the gatekeeper?" Arrin Perti, Arames's traveling companion, was a young man nearly twenty years of age. His face was a theatre of emotions, currently a mix of impatience and fatigue as he shifted the weight of the heavy load on his back. Arames trusted that Arrin would one day develop the ability to conceal at least *some* of his feelings from public consumption.

Arrin Perti stood more than a head taller than Arames, and still had a year or so left of growth. The half year of exercise and training with Arames had brought out more of the angular facial features of the Perti family—the high cheekbones, the way his square jaw cut back from chin to neck at an upward angle. Arrin's shoulder-length blond hair was pulled into a pony-tail, the customary style of a page or valet. He dressed the part as well, with well-worn pants, vest, and cloak. Even the shirt he wore was more yellow than white.

Arames always traveled by foot; as a member of the Aarronic Order, he owned little in the way of possessions, and certainly no horse. The sun hadn't yet reached mid-morning, but the two men had been walking since before dawn without rest. Three cykes had passed since dawn, and judging by the sun's position in the sky, they had six more before the sun set to their southwest.

"No, we have arrived at the exact time I indicated in my letter. If Red received it, he will meet us here."

"Why is the gate even closed? Doesn't a town like this want travelers?" Arrin dropped his packs and flopped down onto the largest one, crossing his legs in front of him.

"There could be several reasons. There might be trouble from the brigands that likely make camp in some of the forests along this road... or maybe there have been wild animals wandering into town looking for food. More than likely, the gates are closed simply because the Olviaran Pass is used much less this time of year..."

"Have you ever used the Pass?"

Arames suspected that Arrin already knew the answer to his question. It was sort of a game—a day wasn't complete until he tried to get a story out of Arames about his past. "Yes, once, although Avedon Hill was the exit during that particular trip. Let us just say that I did not seek permission to use the Pass that time, and it was not a pleasant journey."

"Was this when you worked for my grandfather?"

Arames smiled. "Arrin, as I have stated many times, an Aarronic Advisor serves the Land, not its rulers."

"Yes, sir." Arrin frowned; it seemed the lad had hoped to hear a story about his own family.

Arames managed to hide a smile. "Yes, Arrin, the only time I passed through this part of Grozh was as ambassador for your grandfather. I am sure one day your mother will tell you all about it."

Arrin caught the playful tone in Arames's voice. He knew that eventually he would hear the story straight from Arames—another test of patience from his teacher. "Sir, is that your cousin?"

The gate had opened without so much as a creak. An older man slipped through the gap and it immediately closed behind him. Tall and gaunt, the man made his way slowly toward them with a slight limp, favoring his right side. Arames, walking much faster, met the man more than halfway to the gate. Arrin stood, following quickly so that he could be at Arames's side when the two men began speaking.

"Red? Is that really you?"

"Ah, the great Arames Kragen." Cousin Red extended his arms outward as if to say 'Here I am.' The hair that had given Red his moniker was still thick but tinted with gray. "Yes, this is me in all my glory, cousin. The years haven't been as kind to me as they have to you, I'm afraid."

Arames kept his hands folded inside the sleeves of his robe, not expecting an embrace. "What is wrong with your leg, cousin?"

Red shook his leg a little. "Eh, just age pains, I guess. I get around well enough to do my job."

"What work is that?"

Red smacked his lips together before speaking. He smelled of drink, and it looked as if he had been wearing the same clothes for several days. "I work at the inn, washing dishes and bed linens. I sometimes take over the kitchen for the innkeeper." Red looked over at Arrin. "You got a servant now, Arames? Or just a special friend?"

Arrin's face reddened, but he managed to hold his tongue.

Though the Aarronic Order stood on the premise that a group of lawful men and women could make a difference even in a world filled with chaos and uncertainty, many did not especially like Aarronic Advisors, even when they were family. For some, the dislike was born out of fear. Only a few within the Order achieved the rank of Aarronic Advisor, chosen to act as counselors to one of the many leaders across Caern, and the monastic training of an Aarronic Advisor often resulted in the development of certain mental abilities that caused discomfort for a great many people. For others, it was a byproduct of jealousy. In the almost three hundred years since the Aarronic Advisors had begun their work, many leaders had grown dependent on them as counselors and diplomats.

Red's attitude, however, was directly tied to what he considered his life's greatest failure. Red Karlsson had at one time traveled to Thorn's Way seeking to become an Aarronic Advisor, but he had not passed even the initial test that would have gained him entry as a student of the Order. His younger cousin Arames was accepted and eventually rose to the rank of Advisor; it was a blow from which Red Karlsson had never truly recovered. The fact that Arames had retired many years before meant little to Red.

Arames fully realized that his cousin would not readily help him; he spoke carefully, not wishing to completely eliminate the chance of aid. "Red, this is Arrin. He has been my student for some time now. And since you are here, you must have received my letter—and you also know we need access to the Olviaran Pass. Will you help us?"

Red ignored Arames's question. "How long has it been since we last saw each other, cousin?"

"Some fifteen years. It was your mother's funeral. You refused to speak to me even then. I only knew you had moved to Avedon Hill because your sister Ellidel still writes to me every season."

"Fifteen years, and now you show up needin' something?" Red turned his head to the side and pursed his lips, staring at Arames from the corner of his eye. In spite of himself, a smile leaked onto Red's sour face. "Ellidel is good at that, isn't she?"

"Red, I thought time might have softened your views of me and what I have done with my life. I certainly hold no ill will toward you. We were good friends when we were children."

Red closed his eyes, remembering something from his youth, or possibly deciding what to do next. He opened his eyes and smacked his lips together again. "Fine, cousin... you win. I wanted to tell you to bugger off, but I guess I'm just too old for this. Being a complete ass isn't as easy as it used to be."

Arrin, not knowing the history between Red and the Aarronic Order, couldn't help himself. "I doubt that. You seem to be pretty good at it."

Red laughed. "Ha, that's a good one, *boy.*" Arrin nearly responded, but Arames brought one of his hands into view and motioned for him to stop.

Arames still searched his cousin's eyes. "Red, can you help us?"

Red looked back at the gate and sniffed loudly. "As I said, I wash dishes. Even if the town wasn't shut down, I don't have the pull it takes to get you access to the Pass."

"Shut down?"

"There's been a murder. Gretta Platt... worked at Avedon Manor. Good looking girl, only a few years older than your boy Arrin here."

"But why has this closed the town?"

Cousin Red shrugged. "The constables ruled out the only three merchants passing through town at that time, which means someone here must have killed the girl." Red looked back at the gate. "I'm sure Cletus is up in his roost watching me as we speak, making sure I don't hobble down the road."

He turned back to Arames. "But even more important, Lord Avedon has closed the Olviaran Pass—on both ends, as I understand it. Even if I could get you into town, you can't use the Pass." Cousin Red stuck out his hand and waited until Arames took it in his. "I wish you luck. I told Cletus about you. Maybe you can convince him to open the gate for you."

Arames shook Red's hand. "We will come see you after we get settled at the inn, if we do not see you there."

Cousin Red ended the handshake and bowed his head slightly toward Arrin. "Young sir... knowing my cousin here, I'm sure we'll meet again soon. Good day to you."

Arrin returned the nod. Red limped back to the town gate. Arames placed his hand on Arrin's arm to keep him from hurrying to their packs. "Let us give Red a moment to speak to Cletus on our behalf. We will approach once Red has gone on his way."

Arrin returned to his perch on top of the larger of his two packs. He snorted. "Probably a good idea."

Arames pulled out an apple. As he began cutting slices for them both, he took a moment to study the town walls. The oak trunks reached fifty feet in height, and the pitch-treated wood showed little wear even after four hundred years. The wall was at least six tree-trunks deep, and the beams tapered to sharpened points along the top of the wall. Interspersed between those wooden spikes were metal pikes and sharp metal wire jutting out in all directions, creating a deadly option for anyone foolish enough to attempt the climb. Arames recalled that there were platforms along the inside of the wall and spy holes for archers.

Once the apple was gone, the monk and his student stood before the town gates. Not seeing a tower or guard station, Arames raised his voice and hoped he was heard. "Cletus! Hello...?"

A gruff voice answered from the other side of the wall. "What!? Who's there?"

Arrin spoke up. "Good morning, sir! We seek entry to your town. We would like to stay at your inn."

They heard a small laugh. "My town? My inn? Oh, my town's actually a few leagues south of here. You can go there if you like."

Arames sighed. "Cletus, sir, we would appreciate entry into Avedon Hill."

Again they heard a snort of laughter. "What's the magic word?"

Arrin scowled and muttered to himself, "Oh for the love of Iberian—"

Arames, however, was unfazed. "Please, sir. May we enter?"

"No... just go away." This time Cletus's apparent mirth could not be contained with a snort. Peals of laughter erupted from behind the town gate.

"Cletus, please come out and speak to us face to face. We have business with Lord Avedon."

Arames and Arrin heard some short curses from the other side of the wall. "Hold your horses, sonny. I'll be down in a moment."

Arrin turned to Arames. "Business with Lord Avedon?"

Arames looked over to his young student. "Watch, Arrin. This could be fun."

Arrin returned a glare that left little to Arames's imagination—and had nothing to do with fun.

Ruler of the Known World

The beggar pulled off his hood. Baron Towford gasped. "King Leonid!"
The king held a knife to his enemy's throat. "Never underestimate the forgotten man,
Baron. It will be your undoing, one day—possibly today."

—The Tale of the Peasant King

Cletus, muttering muffled curses on the other side of the gate, kept Arames and Arrin waiting. Apparently, speaking with the two of them face to face was a great inconvenience. Finally, a small door hidden within the left side of the town gate opened toward them.

A large man, presumably Cletus, squeezed through the door. The town's gatekeeper was dressed in what might have been called a uniform—at one time. But the garb was well past worn, and the man standing before them seemed not to care. Cletus looked to be around forty years old, with the arms of a warrior; Arames surmised that Cletus had served in the Grozhian army. The man's belly was not the result of a long army career, however. Cletus weighed nearly as much as Arames and Arrin combined, and as he stepped toward them Arames could hear the strain of his leather belt. A greasy face gave the impression that Cletus may have been interrupted mid-meal—his full beard held remnants of at least two kinds of meat.

Cletus eyed Arames suspiciously; his first glance had already dismissed Arrin as a simple retainer. Arames was dressed in a black robe, its hood pulled back over his shoulders. The robe's border of gold- and silver-threaded bars indicated his current status within the Aarronic Order.

Cletus sighed audibly. "Well, what's so important?"

Arames bowed his head slightly. His arms were folded in front of him, hands hidden in the folds of his robe. It was his normal stance, giving him access to several hidden pockets while suggesting the appearance of calm passivity. "Good morning, Cletus. My name is Arames Kragen. This is my student, Arrin. We require entry into—"

"Require, eh? We'll see 'bout that." Cletus took a stick of packed tobacco from a pouch at his side and gnawed off a large chunk of it. Spit and saliva leaked out of his mouth and down to his chin. The tobacco explained more about the condition of the man's facial hair—it appeared that at least half of what he spit never made it to the ground. Cletus chewed and spoke at the same time; as a result, what he said was hard to follow. "Whut is yer business with," spit flew to their left, "Lord Avedon?"

"Cletus, I am traveling to Kith-Karn to attend a conference. We need access to the Olviaran Pass, and I understand Lord Avedon has closed it completely."

"Yes 'e has. An' since 'e's closed it, you won't be needin' to come into town, neither."

Arrin, red-faced, spoke up. "Gods' sakes, man, don't you see who this is?"

As large as Cletus was, he was still forced to look up at the taller and leaner Arrin. Cletus furrowed his brow, and then slowly lowered his gaze to the ground, spitting a large wad of tobacco directly onto Arrin's left boot. "Boy, you think monk robes make a difference to me?" Arrin started forward but Arames used an arm to bar his advance. Cletus's speech became much clearer. "Your precious order has never found Lord Avedon or his ancestors worthy of an Advisor... not that the Avedons would have accepted one."

Arames guided Arrin back a step, forcing Cletus to focus only on him. "Excuse my young friend, Cletus. I am a good teacher, but only time can overcome the impatience of youth."

Cletus glared back at Arrin. "Time, and maybe a swift kick in the ass."

Arrin, nearly apoplectic, stormed off toward his bags. Six months before, he might have drawn a weapon by now. Instead, realizing he was no help to Arames, he concentrated on being ready to go when the time came, whether it was through the town gates or not.

"Cletus, the boy does have a point, though. I am sure that your Lord Avedon would not appreciate you turning away a representative of the Aarronic Order."

Cletus smiled a tobacco stained smile. "You see, Sir Arames, that's where you're wrong. If I don't let you in, Lord Avedon never knows I turned you away." Cletus turned and pointed. "You see this gate?"

"Of course."

"This gate has been the doorway to Avedon Hill for over four hundred years. No army has ever breached it—not that any has tried. No thieves have ever found their way over or around it, other than the merchants and peddlers that use the Pass as their trade route. It only needs one guard, and that's me. No one enters or leaves this town without my say so. I'm relieved for a few hours here and there so I can get a bath and a good meal at the inn. Otherwise, I'm always here. I even sleep in the guard station most nights. For you and your friend, right now, I am the ruler of the known world." He spat another wad of wet tobacco onto the ground, but away from Arames.

Arames looked into Cletus's eyes. The monk's gift at reading people was one that many Aarronic Advisors developed over time, and it was useful in situations such as this. There was intelligence in Cletus, no matter how he attempted to hide it. "Why are you just the gatekeeper here?"

Cletus stopped chewing. "Just?"

"It is the way you speak, sir. Your speech changed when you goaded my student into anger; you have a quick wit. Unless you have simply managed to irritate everyone in Avedon Hill, this gate does not appear—at least, to me—to be where you belong."

Cletus smiled. "What I am is what I am. I choose to do what I do freely, sir, which is much more than most people can say for themselves. You look to be a good man, Sir Arames. Cousin Red vouched for you, even though I could tell he don't like you much. But it doesn't change the fact that Lord Avedon has closed the town, and you haven't given me reason to disregard his orders." Cletus no longer slurred his speech in the least, and he also stood a little taller now, as if even the way he carried himself had been part of a character he had played.

Arames would not be taking anything at face value in Avedon Hill.

Despite Cletus's statements, Arames sensed a door had opened slightly. "Tell me about the woman who was killed. Gretta Platt?"

Cletus squinted. "Ah, Gretta. Gretta Platt was the Housemistress of Avedon Manor. She took care of the manor and everyone in it. She also served as a secretary to Lord Avedon. Handled his schedule, that sort of thing."

"Her death seems to have hit Lord Avedon pretty hard."

"Yes, you'd have to say that. He and most of his family have been holed up in mourning for nearly a week now."

"My cousin told us the few visitors in town had been cleared of the murder, leaving only the townspeople as suspects."

Cletus spat again into the grass. "Your *cousin*—are you saying that Cousin Red is actually your cousin?"

Arames raised an eyebrow, surprised by the simple question. "What do you mean?"

"Cousin Red has always called himself that. Hell, some people around here probably think 'Cousin' is his first name."

Arames grinned. "Ours is a large family. He has so many cousins around Yew that he probably just found it easier. Back to the point, though: who is investigating Gretta's murder?"

"Head Constable Louis was, but he hasn't had much to work with."

"Do you work for Constable Louis?"

"No, I work directly for Lord Avedon, just as the constables do."

Arames sighed. "I have had some experience with this sort of thing. I might be able to help Lord Avedon discover who is responsible."

"Hmm... with the town closed, my job is a whole lot easier. I don't have to think as much. I just don't let anyone in or out. I can sleep at my post or do whatever I want to, now can't I? Maybe I don't want you to find who killed her."

"I do not believe that, Cletus."

Arrin had returned with their packs, but to Arames' relief he knew not to interrupt.

"Yes, of course I want to find out who did this. Gretta Platt was a wonderful girl. There aren't many like her in the world, I know that well enough."

"Is there a Lady Avedon?"

"No, Lady Avedon died in childbirth seven years ago, along with the child." Cletus looked at Arames for a moment. "And no, there was no romantic relationship between Lord Avedon and Gretta Platt, if that's where you were going."

"No, not at all—just trying to understand the landscape."

"Look, Sir Arames, I've enjoyed our little conversation here, but again, I have my orders." Cletus turned to walk back to the gate.

"Cletus, wait. How about this? I have no gold to offer—"

Cletus snorted. "Of course not. No riches on a member of the Aarronic Order, eh?"

"Well, I have enough to stay at the inn and make it to Kith-Karn, but certainly not enough to bribe anyone. But I think I do have something that you might appreciate, and it will give you enough of a reason to explain why you let us into town."

Cletus turned back to face Arames. "I'm listening."

Arames turned to Arrin and whispered something under his breath. A shocked look crossed the younger man's face. Arrin, after a brief struggle with his own emotions, opened his pack, pulled out a package and gave it to Arames. Arames untied the cord holding it closed and pulled out a smaller leather-bound package the size of a book. He looked at it for a moment and then held it up in front of him. "This is pipe tobacco from Arien. I am sure you understand its worth."

Cletus's smile broadened. "Yes, I do."

"I give you this, and you let us in. And if someone asks, I convinced you that we are here to offer trading rights to Lord Avedon on behalf of the governor of Arien, and this tobacco is just a sample of what we have to offer. By tomorrow, you should not have to worry about that being a lie."

Arames handed the package to Cletus, who held it up to his nose and sniffed deeply. A rumble of a laugh erupted from the large man, and his belly shook. "Fine. Sir Arames, you win this round. Go north along the main road. Take the first good road east and you'll reach the inn. Talik Bere will be probably the only welcoming soul you'll meet in Avedon Hill."

"Thank you, Cletus."

"I'm sure we'll meet again, monk. You'll be heading back through these gates once you realize you're not going to meet Lord Avedon. You remember I said Constable Louis didn't have much success in his investigation?"

"Yes?"

"The constables have been relegated to guard duty outside of Avedon Manor. Lord Avedon must not have been pleased with their efforts, and it hasn't left them feeling very... generous."

A few moments later, the secret door sealed behind them. The two men proceeded down a wide, empty dirt road lined with quiet small shops and houses. All the homes and businesses looked to be at least a century old, constructed using thick oak beams, with walls and foundations a mix of wood and stone, and all seemed to have been recently whitewashed. Some buildings, had walls reinforced with iron bands.

Arrin had a smirk on his face. "Arames?"

"Yes, Arrin?"

"I apologize for making the situation more difficult than it needed to be." Arames shrugged, indicating the past was just that. "I do have one question, however."

"What is it?"

Arrin asked, "Do you feel like you've broken any vows by lying to Cletus?"

Arames stopped to look at a sign that pointed the way to the town's inn. "How exactly did I lie, Arrin?"

"About representing the governor of Arien..."

"Arrin, I did not lie. I simply gave Cletus something he could pass off as a lie so that he will not be reprimanded for granting us entry. I told Cletus nothing less than the truth. Now, come on. Let's find this inn and get some lunch. Oh, yes, and by the way—"

"Yes?"

"Sorry about your tobacco. I know how much it meant to you." A last smile crept across Arames's face as he clapped the younger man on the back. "I will pick up some more for you the next time we are in Arien."

Arrin knew he would never see his tobacco replaced. "You realize it would probably cost Cletus his life savings to buy that much?"

"And as a result, Cletus will enjoy that tobacco more than you ever would. Remember, Arrin, possessions do not define who you are."

"Tell that to my father, Arames."

"Oh, I did, many times. I hope you listen better than he did."

Warm Welcomes

Sometimes you must turn friend and family against you in order to protect them.

—Father Isaac, Brotherhood of Arjun

MONK AND STUDENT FOLLOWED Cletus's directions until they stood before a small inn. "Hmm... 'Avedon Hill Inn, Talik Bore, proprietor.' Original name, eh, Arames?"

"Straightforward, at least." They had passed what appeared to be an antique shop and a tailoring shop, but had not passed a single person.

Arrin turned his head, surveying the empty streets, then pulled the door open. "Maybe everyone is in mourning?"

"A possibility, to be sure." Like the rest of town, the inn was a testament to inactivity, although Arames heard sounds and saw light around the edges of the door behind the bar. The interior of the inn spoke to its function as the town's primary meeting place. There was an open area with tables and booths and a small raised area on one side of the room that could be used as a stage. On the opposite side of the room there was a bar, a door that more than likely led to the kitchen, and a set of stairs.

Arames reached the bar and was about to ring a large bell that hung over it when a smaller version of Cletus burst through the door behind the counter. He barely reached Arames's chin in height, but a girth that might once have been well-distributed was now centrally located in a midsection barely covered by a stained apron. A deep laugh of warm greeting erupted from the man.

"Ho, good sirs! Welcome to the Avedon Hill Inn. Talik Bore, innkeeper, at your service."

"Good morning, Talik. We would like to get a room, if possible, and a hot meal as well."

"Of course, of course! I see Cletus is letting people into our fair town... I didn't know Lord Avedon had lifted his restrictions."

"Not quite the case, I am afraid. We have business with Lord Avedon, but he has not opened the town."

Arames pulled out a few coins but Talik pushed his hand away, ushering the two men over to the booth nearest to the bar. "No need for that right now, sir monk. I see by your robes that you are trustworthy folk. Let's get you some food and refreshments. How does a nice mug of ale sound? I brew it myself right here at the inn."

Arames declined the ale, noting the time of the day. The two men moved to a nearby booth, and a short time later a young lady approached with a tray of sliced bread and cheeses. After only a few moments, Arames had realized that while it was apparent that Talik loved to hear himself talk, it was more efficient to ask questions of the more reserved Leilah, the inn's only maid and waitress. Leilah had a pleasant face and black hair that reached her waist, a common length for Grozhian women.

"Leilah, how long have you worked here?"

"Four years now, Sir Arames."

"You do not need to call me sir, Leilah."

Leilah's eyes widened. "No sir, Sir Arames sir... I have been told stories of the monks of Aarron since I was a child in Callas." She lowered her eyes to the ground. "I'll be calling you Sir Arames." Arrin smiled at his teacher in amusement.

Arames pursed his lips for a moment, but did nothing more to dissuade her. "Is Cousin Red here?"

Leilah was surprised by the question. "Red? No, he doesn't come in until tonight. Why do you ask?"

Arames smiled. "Red actually is my cousin." Leilah laughed, more at ease.

After some continued pleasantries, Arames asked, "Leilah, did you know Gretta Platt?"

Leilah's face lost some of its color. "Y-yes, sir. Everyone knew Gretta. She was just a few seasons older than me." She looked around nervously. "Excuse me, sirs, but I should get your room ready." Leilah curtsied and hurried away from the table.

Arrin leaned in. "This is a very strange sort of town."

"I have not seen anything that would force me to argue against that point, Arrin."

From behind the bar, Talik watched Leilah scurry off. He approached the table, towel draped over his arm. "Did Leilah do something wrong?"

"Absolutely not, Talik. I simply asked her about Gretta Platt."

Talik furrowed his brow. "Gretta... why did you ask about her?"

"We were told of her murder, and wondered why her death has effectively closed your town."

"This is a small town, Sir Arames. Everyone knows each other. The Platts have been here since Avedon Hill became Avedon Hill. Everyone knew Gretta Platt. She wasn't just the Housemistress. She was a part of this town, and she'll be sorely missed."

Arames sensed that Talik felt strongly about what he was saying, but there was more to it than that.

"But the closing of the town and the Olvieran Pass must hurt your business, does it not?"

Talik shrugged. "It's only a couple of weeks before the Pass would have closed for the winter... but yes, this hurts me more than most I usually have around five guests a week, even when the Pass is closed. Traders still travel around the Lantis Mountains during the winter, and this is a good place to stop along the way. I'm sure Lord Avedon will open the town gates again soon." The innkeeper smiled. "Let me ask you, Sir Arames. How do you feel about carnivals?"

Arames and Arrin found they were too hungry to be rude. While they ate, Talik rambled on, mainly about increasing the number of patrons at his inn. Talik also confirmed that if they wanted to meet with Lord Avedon, they would have to bypass the constables guarding the manor gates.

<hr />

After they finished, Leilah led them to their room. A short time later, the two men left the inn and started north. To the west they saw more residences and places of business, and structures that seemed to serve as both. The primary streets were unpaved yet well-maintained. A hill in the distance rose to a plateau, and whatever lay beyond was cordoned off by iron gates.

"Any of this look familiar to you, Arames?"

"I believe that fence is a more recent addition. It has been a long time. These buildings look the same, except for that one." Arames pointed toward a temple along the road to the manor's gates.

"Do you want to go to the manor?"

"I want to stop by Red's house first. Let us check that house over there." Arames pointed to a dilapidated structure near the temple. "That could be it."

Arames knocked on the door of the small single-level home. It was the first house they had seen that had not been recently white-washed. Arames heard some rustling inside, followed by a short period of silence.

The door whipped open and a blinding light blazed forth from the entryway, as bright as the sun on a cloudless spring day. Arames fell back a step. The monk didn't need to look over to know that Arrin covered his eyes with an arm, but Arames also knew they were in no danger—he recognized the light as the unnatural radiance of a holy symbol. It could only harm those with reason to fear the power of one of the immortal Children of Az.

Arames attempted to look past the light at the man summoning it, but he could only make out a long beard and a pair of intense eyes—and then the light dissipated.

The man at the door was dressed in a long white nightshirt. He looked older than Arames, with a face so wrinkled that it nearly hid a scar that ran from his left cheek to underneath his ear. It was the face of someone who had lived a hard life. The man's long white hair went in all directions, possibly the result of being awakened, but most likely due to the use of his staff.

Arrin had only removed his sword a third of the way from the scabbard strapped tightly to his back. He kept his hand behind his head, trying to make it look like he was scratching at the back of his neck as he quietly slid his sword back into the scabbard, but judging by the way the cleric glared at Arames, Arrin had not been noticed at all.

"Who are you? Why do you knock on an old man's door?"

Arames bowed. "Apologies, Father. My name is Arames Kragen. My student and I were looking for my cousin Red's house, and we mistook your home for his."

The old man's eyes widened in recognition. He lowered his holy symbol to his side, no longer brandishing the staff as a weapon. He looked at the monk's robes. "Kragen, eh? You are no longer an Aarronic Advisor?"

"No, Father. I am retired many years now. I only represent the Order in an academic capacity."

"Hmm..." He pointed over to the east to a small group of buildings. "Red's is the last house, past the stables on the right."

"Thanks, Father—"

"Jorrus... Father Jorrus."

"Father Jorrus, why did you feel the need to call on the spiritual power of—" Arames studied the symbol at Father Jorrus's side. It had been carved out of a dark, almost black wood, and had a leather-wrapped grip long enough for the staff to be wielded two-handed. "Arjun, the Protector?"

Father Jorrus looked from Arames to Arrin. The priest seemed confused by the question, as if he had already forgotten how he had greeted them. He raised his free hand and pointed at Arames. "There is evil here in Avedon Hill. You can never be sure what will greet you at your door..."

Arames asked, "You refer to the murder of Gretta Platt, Father?"

Father Jorrus made a scoffing sound and waved his hand. "Regrettable loss, she was. Gretta was a casualty of war that did not need to be. There will be more losses here; be sure of that, monk."

Arrin spoke up. "What do you mean, Father? Do you know who killed Gretta?"

Father Jorrus had a wild look in his eyes. "Devils come and devils go, boy! And I'm tired of making them go. Are you here to help me?"

Arrin cocked his head. "Help you?"

"The undead are here, boy. The battle nears... and I need help." Father Jorrus grabbed Arrin's forearm, shaking it vigorously. "Ah… you are one who can serve me well."

Arrin pulled his arm away from the priest's grasp. Arames interjected, "There are undead here in Avedon Hill?"

"Can you not sense them? They are here, to be sure."

Arames shook his head. "No, I am afraid that power is beyond me."

"Power… you don't need any power to know it. You just need to look for them. Come back when you can truly see, Arames Kragen." Before they could ask anything more, Father Jorrus stepped back and slammmed his door shut.

Arames took Arrin by the shoulder and turned the perplexed youth away from the door, guiding him down the road toward the group of buildings that Father Jorrus had indicated. Arrin finally found his voice. "What just happened?"

"I am not quite sure. From the holy symbol and his manner of speech, Father Jorrus must be an undead hunter, or at least was at one time."

"He just seemed crazy to me."

"There are many reasons why people act the way they do. Let us not judge him without understanding more."

Cousin Red's home was more of a shack than a house. The hay-thatched roof was in dire need of repair, and the one window near the door had two broken panes. Arames knocked on the door. "Red?"

Red called out for them to enter. They found him in the only room, sitting in a chair. He had a bottle in his hand and the place was littered, mostly with empty glasses and clay ale-pots. "Sorry I didn't have time to clean up the place. You can see why I didn't invite you to stay here with me." Red lifted the bottle to his mouth and drank deeply. "I trust Talik was happy to see you?"

Arames nodded. Arrin did his best not to make eye contact with Red, but the older man noticed. "What's wrong, Arrin?" Red's challenging tone caught the youth's attention. He waited until Arrin locked eyes with his. "Listen here, boy. I am poor. I work at an inn in the middle of nowhere. When I'm not working, I drink and I sleep. I'm old, and I don't have the energy to keep this place any better. I work for what little money I have, and maybe someday I'll be able to build me a better house. Not everyone can have what you have, Arrin Perti…"

Arrin suppressed a gasp. Red watched his expression, then continued. "Yes, I know who you are. I am not my cousin's equal, but I know my royal family when I meet them."

Arames stepped forward smoothly and took the bottle from Red's hand. He smelled it. "Is this Talik's ale?"

Red smiled. "Yes. The innkeeper has his faults, but he does brew a fine ale."

Arames drank from the bottle. "Very nice." He forced Red to focus on him. "I am sure you understand—my student's identity is best kept secret."

Red took the bottle back. "Of course. Even though no one in this town would care that a prince of Yew travels unprotected through its lands, this is still Grozh."

Arames moved closer, standing over his cousin. His eyes, almost always an extension of a smile, bore down on Red with a fire all their own. "Red Karlsson, that is enough. Yew and Grozh have not been at war for almost thirty years. And you know Arrin is not traveling unprotected..."

Red sat up straighter in his chair, as if he were twelve and had just been chastised by his mother. "Forgive me. Old wounds never heal, just like they say. You know I would never do anything to betray the royal family of Yew, no matter how I've acted toward you and the Order."

Arames's smile returned and he patted Red on his shoulder. "I know, cousin. Tell me, why are you even here? Why did you leave Yew for this place?"

Instead of answering, Red stood up and began cleaning the room, as if he had suddenly noticed his surroundings. After a moment, Arrin joined him, picking up bottles and jugs off of the floor and placing them in a box Red had moved to the center of the room. At first Red seemed horrified to have Arrin's help, but the look on Arrin's face made Red grudgingly accept his aid. A short time later, Red had relaxed enough to continue the conversation.

"I was in Liza's Choice a few years ago. I met this man by the name of Jaden Koss. He was an old storycrafter who had once worked for a duke near Kaelin's Perch, but when I met him he was down on his luck, much like me. One night we were drinking and he told me this story of a woman who came from a town called Avedon Hill. He said he spent a glorious week with her nearly twenty years before, and she was only after one thing—she wanted to get bumped."

Arrin interrupted. "Bumped?"

Red snapped his fingers, trying to think of another term. "Teemed." Arrin's face didn't change.

Arames interjected, "She wanted a baby, Arrin."

Red slapped himself on the leg, amused by the prince's naiveté. "Yes. He never learned her name, but it was obvious she was wealthy and certainly beautiful, so he obliged her." He looked at Arrin's reddening face. "Or at least he did his best. After that week, he never saw her again. Anyways, Jaden gave me the impression, without really saying it, that he thought there was treasure here. He said he was going to move here and try to strike it rich. Since I was such a good drinking companion, he said I should come with him."

A wistful look crossed Red's face. "Then Jaden got himself killed in a bar fight, before sharing any of the details he had in his damned head. Even though he had died, I decided to come here anyway. I thought if I looked hard enough, I might find what he kept hinting at—maybe strike it rich."

Arames asked, "You had no luck discovering what Jaden's secret treasure was?"

"No. The only riches here must be controlled by the Avedons, of course."

"I am sorry, Red."

"Eh, it was just an old man trying to hang on to one last dream. I know it may not look like it, but I have been happy here. I've got good ale, a job working for a decent man, and there are a lot of good people here—although some are a bit strange..."

Arrin snorted. "I hadn't noticed."

Arames nodded. "Tell me about Father Jorrus. We just met him, and he seemed... less than lucid."

"Jorrus, eh? He used to run the temple, but he spent most of his life in Inarra with the Brotherhood of Arjun. About a year ago he began 'seeing' the undead behind every tree and gravestone. Lord Avedon finally sent word to the Priests of Caern and they eventually replaced him about three weeks ago with a young cleric, Father Holt Livasdawn."

"But Father Jorrus remained in Avedon Hill? And he is not *apostae*?" Religious sects used the word to signify a cleric who had been expelled from the priesthood.

Red shrugged. "He remains a priest—just, without a temple. He stays in his house during the day, but he spends most nights in the town boneyard, convinced that an evil presence threatens us here."

"And Gretta's death seems to indicate that he might be right."

Cousin Red sighed and cleared his throat. Arames raised an eyebrow; Red appeared to be choosing his words very carefully. "Arames, there is a rumor that the circumstances around Gretta's death—that they are less than easily explained."

Arames cocked his head slightly to his right. "Circumstances?"

"Two days ago I was on my way to the inn and Constable Louis was questioning Father Jorrus and Father Livasdawn at the temple. I overheard Father Jorrus shouting something about Gretta being the victim of an undead attack, and that people had better start listening to him before others began falling prey, too."

Arames thought for a moment, but didn't ask any more questions. "Red, thank you. Arrin and I must gain an audience with Lord Avedon. This is quickly becoming more than just a stop on the way to Kith-Karn."

⚜

The two men left Red's house and proceeded up the hill toward Avedon Manor. In doing so they retraced their steps past the stables, where three men were now at work. One, a teenager, cleaned a stallion with two brushes; the horse seemed very pleased with the young man's efforts. The teen waved a brush in greeting as Arames and Arrin passed by. Arrin thought Arames might stop to talk to the young man, but he only waved back and continued toward the manor gates.

A man's voice—presumably Father Livasdawn's—carried through the temple walls as they passed. Unlike the other buildings in town, the temple had three levels, culminating in a great bell tower larger than Red's home.

As they continued up the path, Arrin caught his first sight of Avedon Manor. The path beyond the manor gate wound its way up at a consistent incline until it reached a large grove of trees. Many of the trees had to be three hundred hands high; the path must have angled up even further, because the manor perched above the tree line.

Arames had remarked that Avedon Hill was a unique town, built on a plateau near the base of Mount Olviar with mountain cliffs wrapping around the town like a blanket. Now Arrin understood that Avedon Manor was as unique as the town itself, built directly into the side of the mountain, more castle than manor house. The two-story fortress had been constructed from large blocks of stone, most likely pieces of the mountain removed during early excavations.

"That's a manor?" Arrin quipped.

Arames smiled. "Quite the home, is it not?"

As they approached, they saw three figures on the opposite side of the gates: a mustached and bearded man wearing a blue fringed vest, sitting on a chair; a short, sandy-haired man laying on the ground, his head propped against a nearby tree; and a tall, dark-haired man wearing a leather shirt, sitting on a rock near the tree. The fence was about sixty hands high, but the finger-width iron bars were spaced a hand apart, allowing easy speech.

The older man on the chair had an official air about him, especially compared to the other two. His hat, blue felt with a folded peak, confirmed this to Arames; it marked the man's position as the town's garrison leader. Arames assumed he must be Head Constable Louis. The man sitting on the rock kicked the third man awake. They remained by the tree while their superior addressed the two visitors.

"Stop right there. That's close enough. You are the monk and servant Cletus let through the gates this morning." Constable Louis pulled at his close-cropped brown beard as he spoke, eyes focused on Arames.

Arames bowed his head slightly. "Yes, Head Constable Louis. I am Arames Kragen. We desire—"

Louis raised his hand. "Hold. I don't know how you managed to get past Cletus. I'm sure Lord Avedon will take that up with Cletus personally. I don't care who you are or who you represent."

"Constable, I am certain Lord Avedon will want to hear what I have to say—"

"And again, I don't care. Unlike Cletus, I follow my Lord Avedon's orders. Unless, of course, you have a letter of introduction?"

Arames knew where this was going, and played along. "Letter of introduction?"

Constable Louis smirked. "You understand the Rules of Entreatment as well as anyone, Advisor. If you represent the governor of Arien, as you claim, show me a letter from him and I'll introduce you to Lord Avedon myself."

Cletus had provided information to the constable more quickly than Arames had anticipated. "I am afraid I do not have such a missive from Governor Rheon." Arames quickly considered the door that Constable Louis had inadvertently opened. "But I am sure I can find someone in Avedon Hill who could provide us with a letter of introduction, to satisfy the Rules of Entreatment."

It was clear that Constable Louis hadn't expected this turn of events. "Like who?"

Arrin spoke up. "Talik Bore, or the temple priest?"

Louis studied Arrin for the first time. "Certainly not the innkeeper. And Father Livasdawn hasn't been at Avedon Hill long enough..."

"Then whom should we seek?"

The constable scowled, upset that Arames had placed him on the defensive. "You expect help?" He grunted. Arames supposed it was his version of a laugh. "I'm sure Lord Avedon will open the town in a few weeks—although by that time the Olviaran Pass will be closed for winter." The other constables laughed.

Arrin could not contain himself. "Is guard duty your cup of tea, Constable?"

Arames's eyes flashed over to his charge. Constable Louis smiled. "I do what my lord requests of me. I know my place, boy."

Arames countered. "I think what my young friend is asking, in his own way, is why are you not investigating the murder of Gretta Platt?"

Head Constable Louis lowered his eyes, but only for a moment. "At this time, Lord Avedon's will is for me to protect these gates."

Arames responded, "So you have said, Constable Louis. So you have said. We shall fulfill the Rules of Entreatment and return with a letter of introduction. Until then, good day to you."

Arames turned and walked back down the hill. He waited until he was out of range before speaking. "Arrin, if you cannot control your sarcasm, either remain silent or return to the inn. I grow weary of covering for your emotional outbursts at every turn."

"Yes ... sir."

"Well, luckily for us, that went well."

Arrin laughed. "You call that 'well'? I'm surprised he didn't escort us to the town gates."

Arames stopped walking. "I am sure he wanted to. But he gave us an opening by calling on the Rules of Entreatment. Louis correctly surmised we are not here representing the governor of Arien, but he cannot take back his offer. I believe he is a man of honor. When we bring him a letter of introduction, he will be forced to take us before Lord Avedon."

"So, what now?"

Arames smiled. "Now? Now we get to know the townspeople a little better."

Arrin crinkled his nose at the thought. "The inn is growing more appealing by the moment. Maybe I can get Leilah to draw me a bath."

Arames slapped the tall young man on his shoulder. "No, this will be good for you. I'll let you do most of the talking."

GODS AND THE UNDEAD

Kalin will turn her back on the Abyss, and Artus will not know himself.
The dead will appear, and Doppin will dance with glee.

—3rd Collected Prophecies of Iberian, Book 2, Chapter 1

ARAMES AND ARRIN STOOD before the opening to the main temple sanctuary. The two men could see lamps burning along the interior walls; a partially exposed ceiling left several stone and marble benches unprotected from the elements, but the altar at the back of the temple seemed shielded from all but the worst weather.

Arames led the way to the rear of the sanctuary. A set of stairs most likely accessed the temple's bell tower, but Arames ignored these for the moment and called through a door partially hidden behind the altar—a door that likely opened to the offices of the temple.

"Father Livasdawn? Anyone there?"

A few moments later a man emerged. He was much younger than Arames expected. On top of that, he was a small man, and his white robes had not been tailored to fit his size. He ran his hands through his blond hair and bowed slightly before the monk and his student. "Good day to you. Your faces aren't familiar to me. Are you visitors to Avedon Hill?"

Arames answered with a question of his own. "You are Father Livasdawn?"

"Yes. And to answer your next questions, I'm twenty-four and neither of my parents are of dwarvish descent."

Arames bowed in return. "I apologize, Father. It wasn't my intent to be discourteous." Arames introduced himself and Arrin. "We spoke earlier to Father Jorrus. He told us you have only been here a short time?"

"Three weeks now. I'm still learning who everyone is, and trying to get things in order here at the temple."

"Father Jorrus didn't stay on until you were transitioned?"

Holt Livasdawn shook his head. "Oh-h no, you misunderstand. Father Jorrus was a great leader here, and was instrumental in getting this temple built. He just hasn't had the time to work with me since I arrived."

"I heard he is busy at night, patrolling the town's ... cemetery?"

Livasdawn looked at the temple floor for a moment. He massaged three fingers of his right hand with his left, and Arames could tell the man's breathing had quickened a bit. The cleric moved over to one of the benches and sat, motioning for the two men to join him. Arrin remained standing but moved near. "Father Jorrus was an undead hunter for the Brotherhood of Arjun for many years. He believes that undead walk the Land in greater numbers each day, and that their presence is growing in and around Avedon Hill. But he and I haven't spoken much these last few days. He's found me... lacking. Too inexperienced."

"Did he retire on his own, or was this a move initiated by Church leadership?"

"I'm sorry, Arames, but I'm not at liberty to discuss that, even with a member of the Aarronic Order."

Arames nodded. "Of course, Father. Does he feel this undead threat has something to do with the death of Gretta Platt?"

Father Livasdawn hesitated. "What do you mean?"

"It seems that Gretta Platt's death has affected everything and everyone here. Lord Avedon has closed the town and the Pass because of it. My friend and I seek use of the Olviaran Pass, and in order to gain access to the Pass we must first speak to Lord Avedon. We have learned that we cannot gain an audience with Lord Avedon until we receive a letter of introduction from someone in town."

Father Livasdawn thought for a moment before speaking. "Well, I can tell you that there are some questions around how she died. Constable Louis didn't provide much in the way of details, but apparently Gretta lost a great amount of blood. Yet there wasn't blood, or at least much of it, where they found her body."

"Father Jorrus believes it was an undead attack?"

"A vampire attack, yes."

"Have there ever been any vampires in Avedon Hill?"

"To my knowledge, no. But Father Jorrus thinks there are, and as you said, he spends his nights searching for them."

Arames asked, "What do you think about Gretta Platt's death, Father?"

"I only met Gretta twice. She was a very intelligent woman, with too heavy a heart for someone so young."

"Was she involved with anyone in town?"

"Involved?—oh—not that I knew about. Again, I only met her twice, and her personal life was not our topic of conversation."

Arames stood. "Thank you for your time, Father Livasdawn. I know you must be busy. We will see ourselves out."

"I wish I could help you with your letter of introduction, Sir Arames. I'm afraid Lord Avedon would not accept a letter from me... it'll be some time before I've earned his respect on that level."

"Thank you, Father. If I may, though...?"

"Yes?"

"Why was this temple dedicated to Az and not to Iberian?"

"Part of me believes it was so I could be sent here, since I am a priest to our Holy Father Az. But it was primarily because Father Jorrus refused to allow a temple to Iberian here."

"He wanted the temple dedicated to Arjun?"

"Of course. To care for followers of Arjun at his own temple had to have been his life's goal. But the Grozhian High Priest refused, as you might expect. Because of the Olviaran Pass, this thoroughfare requires a temple with the widest possible appeal—and a temple to Arjun did not meet that requirement. The compromise, of course, was to build a temple to Az, Father to all his Children, including Arjun and Iberian."

"What about the old temple? It has been many years since I have been through Avedon Hill, but I remember another temple."

"Yes. On the western edge of town there was a temple to... well, to Artus, Sir Arames. It hasn't been used for many years. There is a legend that an incarnation of Artus lived somewhere near Avedon Hill."

⁂

"You were quiet, Arrin," Arames said as they left the temple. "You are not angry at me, are you?"

Arrin rolled his eyes. "I didn't want to cause any problems. You know how I am with my tone."

"I still need you thinking and asking questions. You are a second set of eyes for me. I'm not as quick-witted as I used to be." Arames turned southwest, to a part of town that they had not yet visited.

"Ha. That's a good one. Where are we going?"

"There are merchants in the center of town... hopefully we will meet someone who will help us."

"Arames, what did Father Livasdawn mean about the temple to Artus? I've heard my mother speak of Artus, but I never learned much about him."

"How can you not know about Artus?" Arames shook his head. "Where to begin... You might say that some of my fundamental problems with the Priests of Caern began with their treatment of Artus."

Arrin sighed. *Lesson time.*

"The initial followers of Iberian grew into what we now know as the Priests of Caern—"

Arrin added, "Iberian, an incarnation of the Prophet, one of the Children of Az."

"Yes. As you know, Az is the Father, the Creator. But as such he could not walk the Land, and it saddened him so that he cried... and from his tears, his Children were born."

Arrin interjected, "The Ten Who Walk the Land..."

Arames smiled. "Well, historically speaking, The Ten that became the Eleven that became the Ten Who Walk the Land."

"What?"

Arames laughed. "As you know, before Iberian lived, now almost five hundred years ago, each race—dwarves, elves, and humans—had its own pantheon of gods. Studying the myths of the Old Races and the New, Iberian discovered too many similarities to ignore. All of Caern's races have myths around a mother or father god of creation. They all have myths concerning their creation god's children. In every race, these children came to represent some facet of the parent deity—magic, war, trickery, love, and so on.

"Each race also had similar oral and written histories: legends of the Children—gods who chose to live on Caern as powerful yet mortal beings in order to affect the events of the world. They also shared similar stories of the near-destruction of Caern during ancient times by these Children. Iberian proposed that in fact there is only one pantheon of Caern. He called this theory—"

Arrin interrupted. "The Principle of Inclusion?"

Arames nodded. "The theory changed the way all the races viewed religion so deeply that our very calendar is divided into the eras BI and AI—before and after Iberian. It stated, for example, if the Child of Magic was born into a dwarf clan in the mountains of Inarra, he or she would be born as a dwarf. Iberian used the collected stories of all the avatars to build a timeline, proving his theory that only one avatar of the same Child ever lived in Caern at the same time. He developed a single pantheon that crossed all the races, naming the Creator god Az—the beginning and the end—and within this pantheon he named ten different Children of Az."

Arrin asked, "So, what does this have to do with Artus?"

Arames raised a hand. "I am getting there. When Iberian first defined the Children of Az, he only named ten... and the Prophet was not one of the ten."

Arrin raised his hand, mimicking his teacher. "But Artus was?"

"Yes. Artus was the Child of War. There are legends of avatars of Artus in every race."

"I thought the Warrior was Kalin or Arjun, depending on the story."

"That is how it is taught now... but in Iberian's day there was a distinction between Artus, the Child of War; Kalin, the Child of Destruction; and Arjun, the Child of Protection. Many of the incarnations of Artus are now seen as incarnations of Arjun or Kalin. I am sure Iberian would not be pleased to see how things have changed in his Church. Many legends depict Artus, Kalin and Arjun fighting alongside or against each other."

"But why? This doesn't make sense."

"No, it does not, does it? It will in a moment. How is it rumored that Iberian's life ended?"

Arrin nodded. "It's said that Theuroik Ironblade arranged his death."

"And what is Theuroik Ironblade known for?"

Displeasure crossed Arrin's face. He felt like he was visiting his younger brother's history class. "Theuroik Ironblade led the armies of man against the demons from the Outworld, in what we now call the War of Man. Along with the elf-Queen Elisia Llewellyn and her armies of the Old Races, and with Iberian and his bands of demon hunters, Theuroik is said to have prevented the destruction of Caern."

"Theuroik Ironblade..."

A look of understanding replaced Arrin's displeasure. "Artus, the Child of War."

"Yes. Iberian claimed that Theuroik was an avatar of Artus, even though the two men privately hated each other. One of the reasons that many of the prophecies of Iberian remain secret to this day is that he wrote long passages about Theuroik as the embodiment of Artus."

Arrin finished his thought. "And after Theuroik had Iberian killed, the Priests of Caern not only revoked mentions of Theuroik as an avatar, they also removed all teachings of Artus, altogether?"

"Exactly."

"Okay, I understand that well enough. But what about Iberian? How did he become a Child of Az?"

"Iberian was not the first prophet in Caern's history. But his great works, his part in the War of Man, his bringing together of the Old Races and the New, were indicative of one with divine powers. It was not long after Iberian's death that his followers, now known as the Priests of Caern, collected legends of some of the great prophets of Caern and named the Child of Prophecy as one of the Children of Az. It was only fitting that they name this Child Iberian.

"Even though the Priests of Caern have struck the name of Artus from their own canon, Artus was still worshipped extensively across Caern, especially by the remaining dwarven and human barbarian clans of western and central Inarra. Only in the last century has the open worship of Artus come to an end. Most temples to Artus were converted to temples of Arjun, Kalin, or even Iberian."

Arames concluded his lesson: "So what began as the Ten became the Eleven, and the Eleven became the Ten."

The two men made their way toward the town circle. "Where first?"

Arrin smiled. "The bakery. By the time we're done there I'll be hungry for pastries."

Hemming, the baker, looked to be around forty years of age, with an engaging smile and bushy eyebrows dusted with flour. The smells wafting through were a delightful welcome.

"Well, well—what have we here? A cleric and his forest guide, perhaps? What can we do for you today? Cakes? Bread? Here... have a sample of wilderberry tort while you decide." Hemming pulled out a tort and cut it in half, giving the pieces to Arrin and Arames. "Is Lord Avedon allowing people into town now? If so, I have to get to work." It didn't look as if Hemming could bake any more than he already had.

The baker's happiness gradually wore away as Arames explained that the town gates were still soundly shut. "I was hoping Lord Avedon had started to put this all behind him. Gretta's death was such a waste."

A woman around Hemming's age came through the door from the back of the bakery. "Yet our lives must go on. Come now, Hemming. We have to get this order done for the manor. Are these gentlemen done yet?"

"My wife, Dally. What can I box up for you? How about a pie? I've got six kinds right over here."

Arames answered, "Just a couple of the torts, Hemming, thank you." Arrin looked over with an unsatisfied expression, obviously wanting more.

Arames Kragen explained their situation and their need for a letter of introduction. "Ah, I see now why you are here. I'm afraid I can't be of much help to you—unless you think some cakes and pies might get you through the manor gates."

Arames smiled. "Having met the Head Constable, I would have to say no." He thought for a moment. "What about the butcher?"

Hemming barked a short laugh. "You'd have to write it." He moved over and began filling a basket with round, fluffy pastries. "Caasz knows his Olviaran Whitetail, but he never had time for his letters."

They thanked Hemming for his time and left the bakery. Arrin tore fiercely into his tort, as if venting his frustrations on it. "What are we going to do? No one here is going to help us... either they're scared of Lord Avedon or they just don't care."

Arames stopped before a small house. It was a white-washed one-level home like the rest, but this one was surrounded by large gardens with many varieties of plants and herbs. There was a sign above the front door: "Marrissa, town herbalist."

"All we can do is keep trying. I think we need a doctor..."

THE TROUBLE WITH MOTHS

"The Priests will get their wish, and the magics will fall.
Kaelee's stitch, Iruna's thread… The Tears in the Fabric will flow freely."
"May Az ease our suffering at the hands of the Tourim."

—High Priest Kallan, of the Sisters of Kaelee

ARRIN PERTI PEERED AT Arames, unfamiliar with the term. "Doctor?"

Instead of approaching the herbalist's door, Arames sat down on a bench facing the nearest garden. Through the door they could hear someone moving around. He motioned for Arrin to sit beside him. Arrin suspected Arames wanted to gather his thoughts before meeting another less-than-helpful townsperson. Also, Arames never passed up an opportunity for a lesson.

"What can you tell me about the nature of magic, Arrin?"

Arrin sighed. "Exactly how long are we going to be sitting here?"

"I am attempting to answer your question, young prince of Yew. What do they teach now at Castle Pen on the subject of magic?"

When Arames had served as Aarronic Advisor to Arrin's grandfather, King Renoir—at that time, still Prince Ren—he had been the sole instructor of all of the children at royal court. Now, the royal family fell under the tutelage of the resident clergy, leaving only the arts of war and political strategy to the resident Aarronic Advisors.

"The source of all magic is Az. Divine energy and its shaping are the only acceptable uses of magic."

"Which means?" Arames's face was a calm mask, but Arrin could hear a subtle change in his tone.

"Which means that the use of magic is controlled by the Priests of Caern?"

"Yes. But we both know there are other types of magic. What are they?"

"There's druidic magic. It still flows from Az, but it uses the Land itself as a conduit. Druids tap into it and use it to protect the Land."

"What else?"

"Well, there are the powers displayed by Aarronic Advisors..." Arrin answered, but Arames clearly expected more. "Abilities developed during the years of training as an Advisor."

"How does this differ from druidic magic?"

Arrin answered, "It's more of a mental discipline. You use the energies within yourself and around others in ways that normal people cannot."

"Good—let us move on. What else?"

"There is sorcery."

"What do the Priests of Caern say about that?"

"That it comes from the Outworld—and from the demonspawn that inhabit it. That its use is what brought about the War of Man five hundred years ago, and what threatened the destruction of Caern thirty years ago during the last war between Yew and Grozh."

Arames sighed. "And what have you yourself learned about sorcery?"

Arrin looked down at the ground. "There have been great wizards in Caern's history, mostly from the Old Races... *Let them one day return to us.* Most humans that developed magical abilities became proficient at item-crafting, but rarely did they show the aptitude for spell casting that the Old Races were known for. I know it's an energy that can be used for both good and evil, and that it comes from Az just as all energy comes from Az."

Arames smiled. "Good. I wanted to make sure you understood that distinction. The Priests of Caern have worked very hard the last thirty years, cementing the idea that the use of magic by those other than clergy is a dangerous thing."

Arrin finished the thought. "Solidifying their power as the only 'legal' users of magic."

"Yes. As a result, most druids can only be found deep in the woods of Grozh or Inarra. As for wizards, most have died or have hidden their secret so well that they would not even recognize each other if they sat in the same room. And those who do still live in the open..." Arames pointed at the herbalist's sign, "use titles such as herbalist, item-broker, and potion maker."

"So Marrissa is a sorceress?"

Arames stood and approached the door. "I do not know. She might be a simple seller of potions or a charm maker. She may, like most who have the ability to sense the river of magic, lack the ability to *dip* from those waters, simply because she never had the opportunity to learn how to use her talents. Or she may possess great power, but due to the times we live in, must hide here as an expert of flowers and herbs."

"And the term *doctor*?"

"It is ironic. In the old Church, the clergy used to call eminent theologians doctors. At the same time, it was used as a name for a practitioner of folk magic or medicine, to distinguish a clerical healer from one who uses potions and herb magic. Now we use it for someone who is forced to hide his or her abilities from the Priests of Caern." Arames opened the door and walked in.

"Hello—anyone here?"

Arames's query was answered with the sounds of metal crashing and glass breaking from across the room. "Treygh's jaws have you!" The curse didn't appear to be directed at Arames, but at some vials that had broken and others that were rolling across the floor in several directions.

Arrin moved swiftly forward and gathered three small bottles before they fell from the landing that separated the two halves of the room. The lower half of the shop contained a sitting area and a few books placed on a stand in one corner. The area was rather clean compared to the upper half of the room, where tables were covered with jars, vials, mixing bowls and various items for measuring, separating, and mixing ingredients.

Shelves along three walls held at least a hundred bottles. Most were filled with dried ingredients, but others contained liquids of varying color and opacity. Herbs hung from suspended lines between shelves. Arames recognized several—lungwort, feverfew, lemon balm, and marjoram among them. Sheep horns hung from pegs on the shelves. Arames guessed that these were used to store preparations made by the herbalist.

The work area looked as if it had been hit by a storm.

Marrissa's arms were filled with glass vials. She stared at the two men standing before her in confusion, her mouth hanging open, until the unsteady vials started to slip. The herbalist turned away and placed them on one of the tables as carefully as possible. Then she walked back and held her hands out to Arrin, palms up. When he stared at her without comprehension, Marrissa stomped her left foot and shook her hands impatiently. Arrin gave her a smile and was about to speak, but she snatched the bottles from his hands and stormed away.

Once she had ensured the vials' safety on the table, she finally regarded her visitors. They still stood on the lower level, and she made no move to join them. "Good morning, gentlemen. I am sorry, but this is a very busy time for me. Is there something you need?"

Arames stepped forward. He bowed and unfolded his arms, holding his hands out in front of him. "Marrissa, my name is Arames Kragen. I and my student Arrin are visitors here. We were hoping you might be able to help us gain an audience with Lord Avedon."

Marrissa threw up her hands and walked away from them, toward one of her tables. "Lord Avedon? Avedon has closed the manor. I can't do anything for you..."

she turned back and looked at Arames. "Artemis, was it?"

Arames took two steps forward and then jumped gracefully up to the raised landing, his robes covering his legs in such a way that he almost seemed to have levitated up to join her. Marrissa's eyes widened and her hands went to a symbol of Iberian that hung from her belt. Fear washed across her face, but Arames's calm look seemed to put her at ease after a moment, and it quickly passed.

Arrin moved to the stairs, but didn't climb them. He didn't want to alarm the woman further.

"Arames..." corrected the monk.

From the sound of her voice Arames believed Marrissa was a little younger than himself, but the lines around her eyes made her look older than her probable years. Marrissa's hair was black but streaked with thick sections of white. Her dress looked like a hand-me-down from another time—thick, dark purple fabric, lined on the edges with various common gems. Its many patches seemed to be holding the garment together.

"We know that Lord Avedon has closed his manor. We need a letter of introduction from someone in town—someone who can vouch for us."

"Ah, I see." Marrissa walked around one of her work tables, placing additional distance between herself and Arames. "I don't know you—" she looked over the mess on the table before her, "and I am far too busy to get to know you."

Arames sensed something in the woman's voice. He pressed on. "Marrissa, you look tired. What's wrong?"

Marrissa placed her hands on the table in front of her. Her fatigue was visible now, overshadowing any fear she might have had moments before. "That isn't your concern. I'm working on—" She stopped, as if she hadn't meant to say even that much.

"A potion? From your supplies... your merchandise, it appears you are very good at your work. Why is this particular potion giving you trouble?"

"I never said anything about a potion."

Arames shrugged, but didn't move. Marrissa looked into the monk's eyes for a moment, then sighed. Arames could feel a door opening for them.

"I lack a prime component for the potion," Marrissa admitted.

Arrin spoke for the first time. "Maybe we can help you."

Marrissa gave Arrin a tired smile. "Young man, I doubt that."

"What is the potion for?" Arames asked.

"Again, none of your concern."

Arames nodded. "True enough. We apologize for the inconvenience. We will leave you."

Arames ignored Arrin's quiet snort. He turned toward the steps that led to the lower half of the room, but did not move to them. "But, my student is right. We might be able to help you. If I had to guess... this is something no one else in town can help you with."

Marrissa's eyes moved from Arames to Arrin and back again. "What do you mean?"

"Only that everyone we have met thus far seems too busy with their own lives to help anyone else. We are stuck here with nothing to do until we can meet with Lord Avedon. We can help you, if it is something that is within our power."

"Oh. I see." Marrissa only took a moment to weigh her options. "Fine. You need a letter of introduction?" The two men nodded in unison. "I need a King's Head moth."

Arrin ran his hands through his blond hair. "A moth?"

Marrissa sighed even more heavily, as if explaining would take too much effort. "Not just a moth... a *King's Head moth*."

Arames asked, "Is there some sort of merchant that sells them?"

"Merchant? If I could buy one, I wouldn't need you, would I? No, you have to find them. There's a series of caves east of town where the King's Head lives. They like the cool air there during the summer. The problem is, they die off in the winter. I've been out there twice in the last week but I've had no luck. They started dying out nearly a month ago. But powerful potions make use of the King's Head moth. And I need one." She paused. "I'm taking a risk just telling you this."

Arames nodded. "I am not an agent of the Church, if that is your worry."

Arrin interjected, "At this point you could be making poison for all I care."

Arames smiled at Arrin's enthusiasm. "Marrissa, we will find your moth. I am sure you have a great need if you are allowing us to help you. I trust that you are doing good work. We shall return as soon as we can."

⁂

As they walked, Arrin swung the small cage Marrissa had given them. It was about the size of a lantern, made of wire mesh that would easily hold live insects. "Finally, something to do. Do you think we'll encounter some animals or bandits? I need some excitement."

The older man laughed. "Excitement... I see."

"You hid something back there. You said that no one in town would help her because people wouldn't make time. There was something more."

"I believe she cannot ask for help. While I believe that she is doing nothing *wrong*, there is a reason she could not tell us about the potion—and it had nothing to do with us being strangers."

Cletus met them at the town gate with a laugh. "Leaving so soon?"

Arames acted as though he liked the gruff gatekeeper. Arrin, who still had a stain from Cletus's tobacco on one of his boots, did not share his mentor's enthusiasm toward the man. "We are not leaving for long," Arames said. "We have a little side trip to make. I do have a question, first."

"Yes?"

"You mentioned Constable Louis had been relegated to guard duty because his investigation was unsuccessful."

Cletus nodded.

"How long was he given to investigate?"

"Four days, I believe—time enough to question most of the townspeople. He had trouble connecting anyone to the murder, so he began talking to the Avedon children, against Lord Avedon's wishes."

"You said earlier that Lord Avedon's wife died in childbirth—" Arames pulled out a small ledger just larger than his hands and opened it to a page. Arrin realized that Arames must have written some notes while he had unpacked at the inn, "—along with the child. How many children does Lord Avedon have?"

"Five. Richard is the oldest. He's eighteen, I believe. Edvard is the next male in line. He's sixteen, maybe. Carin is the oldest daughter, who's seventeen, Jon is fourteen, and Julienne is ten."

"Thank you, Cletus. How far are the caves to the east of town?"

He raised an eyebrow at the mention of caves, but answered without a question of his own. "You should be able to get there and back in two cykes or so. Take the first true left-hand path leading up into the foothills. You'll eventually see the caves from the path."

Arames squinted up at the sun. *Two cykes for travel, plus time to search the caves—we should make it back in time for our next meal.* "You will let us in when we return, correct?"

The guard laughed. "Why not? I'm already in trouble with Constable Louis. I'm sure I'll eventually hear about this from Lord Avedon, but until then I have some of the best tobac in all of Caern." With a wink, Cletus moved to open the gate.

Arames and Arrin continued east along the same road that had brought them to the town. Arrin felt uneasy as they traveled. He half-expected an attacker to spring from the trees that lined the road. As a result, he now kept his sword belt strapped around his waist. Arames, who apparently did not share his fears, spent much of his time cutting pieces of apple and eating them as they walked.

They reached the path without incident; the narrow trail wound its way north into the foothills of the Lantis Mountains. To the northwest, Arrin could see Mount Olviar. The mountains ran their course across the entire horizon. For the first time, Arrin realized how difficult it must have been for Lord Avedon's ancestors to carve a path through the mountains... and how important it was to gain access to the Pass.

An apple and a pouch of walnuts later, Arames and Arrin found themselves in front of a cave. There were several other cave entrances around them—some at the base of the small mountain, others too high up to access without climbing.

"What are these caves?"

"I do not know. Most of those entrances do not look natural. Possibly the same miners that built Avedon Hill worked in these mountains as well. Or maybe they are old enough to have been built by dwarves. The Ossur dwarf clan is still supposed to live in several areas of the Lantis Mountains, although to my knowledge they do not interact with humans at all."

They entered the nearest cave and moved down a long passage until they found themselves in a large cavern. Most of the chamber's open area was taken up by a pond. A soft green glow rose from the water, illuminating the cave so brightly that there was no need to light a torch.

Arrin was surprised. "Some sort of plant life? Algae?"

"I am not sure." Arames bent down and looked in the water. "Some sort of sediment." As they moved further into the cave they saw that the walls glowed in areas as well. "It appears that as the walls erode, the rocks end up in the pond, and they give off this light. Interesting..." Arames found several stones intact at the edge of the pond and picked them up, studying them in the palm of his hand. They glowed brightly, smaller versions of the mineral deposits jutting out along the walls of the cave. He poured some walnuts out of the leather pouch at his belt and placed the rocks inside. "You never know when you might need a little light."

There were no signs of animal life within the cavern—no tracks, no droppings, no bones. The two men made their way around the pond to an opening at the opposite end of the cave. It opened to a path that wound its way up and then split in two different directions. Arrin asked, "Do you think all of these caves are connected?"

"A lot of them, most likely. If Marrissa can safely navigate through these caves, hopefully we have little to worry about. Let us continue."

They proceeded up the path and took the right-hand branch. It continued on, past several twists and turns until it let out into another open area, with a smaller but deeper pond. There were some signs of life in this cave. Small animals, dogs possibly, had at one time made their home here, but the signs were old. They backtracked and headed down another branch of the corridor. It eventually opened into another cavern.

There was a much smaller pool of water in this area, and very little light. Arames pulled out the stones he had collected and placed them inside the small cage from Marrissa, then held the makeshift lantern above his head. The light from the rocks did not illuminate the area very much, but did allow them to walk safely down to the center of the cave. The ceiling here was much higher than in the other caves they had searched. Again, there was little sign of animal presence.

Arames bent down and studied the ground near the edge of the water. "Well, we might have answered one question..."

"What is it?"

Arames picked something up from the ground and stood up. He held open his hand and showed his discovery to Arrin: a moth—a very large and very dead moth.

"Is it a King's Head moth?"

Arames studied the white insect. "See the black patch on the moth's back? I guess to some, those markings look like a crown. So yes, I believe it is."

"Great! Let's get back to town, then." Arames didn't look pleased, however. Arrin asked, "What's wrong?"

Arames held up the cage he was using as a lantern. "I do not believe Marrissa would have given us this to carry around a dead moth."

Arrin crinkled his nose. "Oh. Well, should we keep looking, or take this to—" The look on Arames's face silenced Arrin. His right hand instinctively went to the sword hilt on his hip. He whispered, "What is it? Do you hear—"

Arames interrupted Arrin with a kick to his chest that sent him backwards to the ground. Before Arrin could catch his breath, a large, dark mass flew over his body and landed on his teacher. Arrin drew his sword and was on one knee in little more than an instant, but he knew he did not have time to help Arames. Blood rushed to his head and pulsed at his temples. Without seeing, Arrin sensed there was something else behind him. No longer silent, growls of more than one wolf echoed in the cave. Arrin jumped to his feet to meet the threat, a smile etched on his face.

<hr/>

Arames had not felt the wolves' presence until it was almost too late. His anger at not having sensed the danger, however, did nothing to delay his action. The outline of the wolf leaped through the air at Arrin's exposed neck. As Arrin fell below the arc of the animal's attack, surprise glinted in the wolf's eyes, bright in the light of Arames's makeshift lantern. From the edge of his consciousness, Arames could sense the beast's surprise turning to pleasure as it closed on its second target.

Even in darkness and at his advancing age, Arames was a more formidable opponent than the beast could have anticipated. Jaws expecting flesh found only air; claws expecting to rend skin from bone met only cloth.

While Arrin turned to face the two smaller wolves now poised to attack, the larger beast and Arames fell to the ground in one blurred heap. Arames's robe was a better defensive weapon than any shield the wolf might have encountered. It was sewn in such a way that Arames was able to grab its sides and roll with the great wolf's attack, engulfing most of its enormous form with layers of material.

The wolf snapped its jaws in several different directions in an attempt to taste the flesh it could so clearly smell. Arames had used the beast's lunge to his advantage; even with the wolf entangled partially in his robes, Arames had gained leverage and had his feet against the beast's side. Teeth nearly found muscle and tendon, but by the third jaw-snap Arames was able to push off his own back, using his feet to propel the wolf. The momentum of the wolf's thrashing, aided by the kick, sent the monster some three body-lengths away and into the stone wall of the cave.

Arames rolled fluidly until he was on his feet facing the large beast, dagger in one hand, sai in the other. He had defended himself successfully against the wolf's first attack, but now Arames found himself winded, breathing heavily and staring in amazement at the sheer size of the animal before him. The beast was at least twice the size of the wolves Arrin faced on the other side of the cave. Arames also sensed an intelligence in the beast; it focused its eyes first on Arames, then on the battle between Arrin and the two wolf companions, and then back to Arames, clearly assessing the situation.

The beast snapped its jaws, spitting out the black silk that it had ripped from the monk's robes. The soft light produced by the lantern, now on its side on the ground, gave the wolf a greenish hue. The beast growled once, reared back on its hind legs, and whipped its head from side to side. As Arames tried to slow his racing heart, the beast fell back on all fours and howled, prepared for its next attack. By that time, Arames realized he was not facing a wolf at all.

<hr />

Arrin Perti was in his element. He had been trained since the age of eight to defend himself against both man and beast. While the darkness should have evened the battle to some extent, Arrin exulted as if he were an untouchable foe. Where Arames waited for an attack, Arrin launched his own. The wolves, accustomed to defensive prey, had no idea how to counter the charging threat. Before they could recover, Arrin barreled into the beasts. The two wolves had placed themselves too close to each other; the single charge left one wolf dead in an instant, sliced from chest to neck from Arrin's own bite—a longsword he had named Wildfire.

The second wolf attempted to rise up to meet the human with paws and maw, but Arrin crashed sidelong into the animal before it could reach its full height. Both man and beast fell to the ground. The wolf flipped to its feet before Arrin had a chance to do so, but found itself facing away from its intended meal. The blade entered one of its back legs as it turned toward its prey. It was a glancing blow with little strength, but it was enough to allow Arrin to reach his feet and wait in relative safety for the wolf's next attack. It came, and was met with a slash of steel that threw the animal back. The wolf attempted another charge, but instead collapsed in the pool of water at the center of the cave. It tried to raise its head out of the water but failed, unable to put weight on hind legs nearly severed by Arrin's blade. Shock overwhelmed the creature; its heart stopped beating in moments—before it even had a chance to drown.

Arrin turned to find Arames, his robes tattered, facing the largest wolf he had ever seen. The beast howled, and Arrin knew he would not be able to reach Arames before the wolf charged.

But the beast did not attack Arames. Instead it leaped over the pool and escaped down a passage that led deeper into the caves. Arames, still panting, dropped to his knees on the cavern floor.

"By Az, what WAS that?" Arrin shouted as he ran over to his teacher.

Arames regained control over his breathing and was soon back on his feet. "We should go. We will talk later."

Arrin retrieved the lantern. It took them both to find the carcass of the moth, which had been knocked from Arames's hand during the initial attack. After placing the moth in the cage, they exited the way they had come, down the passage opposite the one the beast had taken. Both breathed more easily when they saw sky again. The sun had traveled further along its daily journey, but it was only a cyke past midday; they still had at least four cykes left until sundown. They were halfway back to town before Arames spoke.

"If I had to guess, I would say that was a moon-beast."

"What?! They're not just stories?"

"There is much in Caern that is not 'just stories.' I have seen moon-beasts before, but never that large. And I have never seen any that traveled during the day, even in the darkness of caves."

"Are you injured?"

Arames glanced down at his tattered robe. "Only my clothing... and my pride."

"Thank you for saving me back there."

"I am upset that it even got that close. I did not sense its presence until it was almost too late."

Cletus raised an eyebrow at Arames's robes when the two men returned, but apparently knew when it was unwise to ask questions. They went directly back to Marrissa's shop, bypassing the inn and a fresh set of clothes.

⸻

"Of course it has to be alive. You should have known that, monk."

"I thought as much, but I wanted to be sure. The weather has turned. It is too cold for us to find a live moth."

"Well, you had better get out there and keep looking. This potion requires a live King's Head moth, and that's what I require if you want that letter of introduction."

Arames sighed. "Of course, *doctor*."

Marrissa started. His reference to magical powers was not lost on her. "Watch yourself, monk. You don't understand of what you speak."

Arames led Arrin to the door of the shop. He paused to brush off some of the dirt from his torn robes. "Oh, I understand full well, Marrissa—full well. We will return with your moth."

⸻

The encounter at the cave had left both men drained. They took a break from their search and returned to the inn. Following a short meal, Arames ordered Arrin to rest for a cyke, enough time for Arames to gather his thoughts and prepare for their next excursion.

"So, relegated to searching for small winged creatures? Not exactly saving the world, is it?"

Arames shifted his focus from Arrin's resting form, moving his gaze to the man who had spoken.

"We all play our small part in the cycle, Gareth. Except for you, of course."

Gareth Beckwin laughed. "I'm playing my part as well, Ari—keeping you on the path."

Arames closed his eyes. It didn't matter if they were open or not—Gareth wasn't really there. "It has been a while. What, a year?"

"Don't ask me, Ari. You are the one who has conjured me."

Gareth Beckwin, while he had lived, had been Arames's best friend. They had arrived at Thorn's Way on the same day, and had been tested as a pair by the Aarronic Brotherhood, as was their way. The testing process ensured the two men were worthy of inclusion in the Brotherhood, and the process linked them for life, another goal of the Testing.

What Arames had not realized at the time was that the link between a tested pair did not end at death. Gareth had been with Arames since his death twenty-nine years before. "I did not conjure you. Feel free to move on to your rightful place by Thorn Twoblade's side."

"What, and just sit around until the end of the Age? How boring would that be?"

Arames believed that Gareth was only a manifestation of his conscience. Even so, the visit pleased him. He opened his eyes to make sure that Arrin still slept. Gareth sat in a nearby chair. He hadn't aged a day, and still wore the green and brown uniform that he had worn as an Advisor for Duke Olandis Pell. It was the same uniform Gareth had worn the last time they had seen each other. "You look well."

"And you look weathered. Your years in seclusion did you no favors. You still have some brown left on that head, though."

Arames smiled. "I miss you, old friend."

Gareth lost his own smile. "Old friend—I died too young to become your *old friend*." Gareth Beckwin had lost his life at the hands of an assassin's poisoned blade.

"Well, to me you are."

"What?" Arrin's voice filled the air, breaking Arames out of his reverie. "Who are you talking to, Arames?" Arrin's eyes were still closed; he was only half-awake. Arames looked back, but Gareth was gone.

"Just thinking aloud. It is time to get moving."

Metamorphosis 6

"You will see Ursala everywhere.
She lives in the minds and hearts of every animal you meet."

—The Return of the Children – Yew children's tale

So, what now?"

They walked in a northwesterly direction, into a part of town they had not yet visited. "The library here has become one of the finest in this area of Grozh, if my information is correct. Maybe we can find something there to help us with our search."

Arrin dragged his feet as he walked; frustration tinged his voice. "We should talk about the moon-beast. You said you had never seen one that large before?"

"No, there was something different about this one. It was huge... and intelligent."

"Legends say that moon-beasts were once men. Is this true?"

Arames shrugged his shoulders. "Some say it all started with a transformation spell that went terribly wrong, leaving a druid somewhere between wolf and man. Others say moon-beasts are creatures that found their way here through rips in the fabric between Caern and the Outworld. Moon-beasts are also called *Treygh's Children*. I have never seen one that large, or one that runs with other animals."

"Is it true that you become a moon-beast if you're bitten by one?"

Arames shook his torn robes again to show Arrin the damage from the attack. "I think this beast's only goal was to kill us. As for the legend, I can only say I have not seen it for myself. But it has been twenty years or more since I last ran into one of these beasts. I am far from an expert on them."

This area of town was no different than the rest of Avedon Hill: places of business intermingled with small homes. To the west, near the town wall, a building that had to be the abandoned temple to Artus was nearly concealed by trees, brush, and weeds. Only its small bell tower escaped the years of unabated plant growth. Turning to the south, Arames and Arrin finally discovered the library.

As they approached the library's door Arames sighed. Arrin smiled, interpreting it as a sound of longing. "You like books a little too much."

"You know, I believe I miss the library at Castle Pen more than I miss the royal family."

"I don't doubt that."

They walked though a large door into a small alcove. At the other side of the entryway was a short set of stairs that led down to a large open area. The walls of the main room were lined with shelves completely filled with books. Several large chests and boxes around the room held parchments and scrolls, and there were tables in the center of the floor as well, each with its own small collection of books or parchments.

One of the walls had a small desk that was closed off from the main floor. Behind the desk was a smaller alcove and a set of stairs that most likely led down to a basement. There was a sign on the desk that read "Ring bell for librarian."

Before Arames could use the small hammer to ring the bell, the door at the bottom of the stairs opened. A woman glided gracefully up the stairs with little effort or extraneous movement. Her dress fully covered her feet, creating the illusion that she traveled without moving her legs. Arames wondered what type of training she must have had in order to walk in such an agile manner.

The woman's eyes sparkled as she reached the top of the stairs. She actually clapped her hands together in excitement once she had come to a stop at the edge of the desk. "Oh my, what have we here?" Her porcelain features were accentuated by black hair. It was obvious from her complexion that the woman rarely left the dimly lit library. Her nearly lineless face made her appear young, but to Arames her eyes held a wisdom that belied her years.

"My name is Lane—Lane Niccols. What can I do for two strangers to Avedon Hill?" She curtsied slightly, in apparent recognition of Arames's position.

"Arames Kragen, madam, and this is my student Arrin. We were hoping you might be able to help us. Do you have any texts that detail the fauna of this region?"

The librarian raised an eyebrow. "An interesting request, Sir Arames... are you looking for something in particular?"

"Well, possibly. We are searching for locations around Avedon Hill where certain animals might be found."

Lane's eyes brightened and she smiled at Arames. "Oooh, a hunt, is it? Give me a moment."

"Thank you so much, ma'am." Arames was smiling as well.

Arrin suddenly felt like he wasn't even in the same building as Arames and Lane. Arames didn't move at all until the librarian had left through a door at the bottom of the stairs. "It appears there are more books downstairs."

Arrin suppressed a joke and looked around the library's main sitting area. "It's too dark in here."

"You get used to it. This lady cares deeply about her books. Light, heat, water—these can all damage books over time." Arames indicated the light fixtures hanging above the open room. "Notice the lights—the openings of the fixtures only allow a small bit of air, keeping the flames very low. If those lamps fell to the floor, the flames would extinguish before anything could be damaged."

Arrin feigned a yawn. "Very interesting, sir."

"If I had been at Castle Pen while you were growing up, you would have spent a lot more time inside. You do not appreciate the written word as you should."

"Well, if Castle Pen had a librarian that looked like Lane Niccols, maybe I would have spent more—"

"I think I have what you need right here." The librarian had returned without either of them noticing.

Arames and a blushing Arrin turned back to the desk, where Lane held a rather dusty and aged book with bindings that were frayed on all sides. She wiped off the cover with a soft hand brush. "This is *The Linus Compendium*. Linus lived in Avedon Hill around two hundred years ago. He collected a lot of information about the flora and fauna of the region. If this doesn't give you what you need, I have other books that we can try." She handed the book to Arames. "Be careful of the spine. The hinge is tearing. I'll work on it now that I see how badly it needs mending."

"Of course. I think this might be just what we need." Arames opened the book and scanned carefully through the pages. "It is more of a diary, divided by year. It begins in the year 326 A.I."

Arrin, put off by the thickness of the book, wandered over to sit at one of the tables to wait. There were books stacked on the table, their titles marking them as tomes on history and religion. "How many books do you have here?"

Lane watched Arames intently while she answered. "There are two hundred and thirty-seven books on this floor, and around six hundred more in the basement. Not including the unbound manuscripts and scrolls."

"How long has this library been here?"

"Fifty-seven years. Only about a hundred of the books in this library actually belong to the town. The rest are from my own collection."

Arames asked, "And how long have you been librarian here?"

"Seven years now. I love it here... Quiet, but still on a trade route so that I can add to the collection."

Arames mulled over the numbers. "That is very impressive. There can be only three or four other libraries in all of Caern that have larger collections."

"Five, actually. I'll never be able to surpass the library at Thorn's Way, but the other four are in my sights." Arames nodded at the reference to the library shared by the Priests of Caern and the Aarronic Order—the largest in the known world.

Arrin put his feet up on the edge of the table. "Good luck with that."

Arames stopped his scanning and concentrated on one particular page. He looked up at Lane and indicated the table where Arrin sat. "Do you mind?"

Lane nodded. "Of course not. Just bring the book back when you are done, Sir Arames. I'll be downstairs if you need me."

"Thank you so much."

Arames brought the book over to the table. He knocked Arrin's feet from the surface in mock anger and sat down. "Rude."

Arrin smiled. "What did you find?"

"Well, we would be working with two-hundred-year-old information, but there is a lake to the south of Avedon Hill around which one can find examples of most of the animals and plants in the region. This Linus fellow seemed to concentrate most of his scientific efforts there."

"How exciting..."

"His work may have just saved us a lot of time."

"Does he specifically mention the King's Head moth?"

"Twice, that I have found. He mentions its medicinal purposes, but nothing specific about the potions it can be used in. And he has a drawing of one here." Arames pointed to the open page. It was definitely the same moth they had found earlier that day. A diagram on the opposite page detailed its metamorphosis from larva to moth.

"Sounds good to me. Let's find this lake."

Arrin waited outside while Arames thanked Lane again for her help. Arames brushed the dirt from his robes as they walked back to the gate. Arrin commented, "Quit smiling, would you?"

Arames exaggerated his smile even more. "Lane Niccols and I have something in common, young Arrin. It is nice to find that in a person. While I am certainly not here to pursue the fairer sex, it is nice to have met someone who shares similar interests. As for you, I am sure you will one day meet someone that you feel an immediate connection to..."

"Yes, and she had better be the daughter of a duke or a count, or it won't mean much, now will it?"

"Come. We have more walking ahead of us."

"You and your vows. We need horses." Arrin had over thirty horses of his own, all quartered quite comfortably at the royal stables of Castle Pen.

Luckily for the two men, Avedon Lake was nearer to town than their morning walk had been. True to Linus's old research, there was plenty of animal life in the forests surrounding the lake. The lake itself was very large—Arrin guessed it would take at least a day's travel to circle it—but in only a short time, they found a small swampy area off of the lake that gave them what they needed... in a manner of speaking.

For the second time that day, they found moth carcasses; but in this case there was less certainty as to species. Exposure to the elements and to other insects had all but done away with the distinctive markings. As before, they found no living King's Head moths. Arrin was about to scream when he made a discovery of his own. "Arames, what do you think about this?" He pointed to three caterpillars crawling across a downed tree trunk that lay across the ground. Several butterflies and other types of moths fluttered nearby.

Arames inspected the creatures. "Their markings match the drawings in the book, I believe."

"Caterpillars in the winter, though? I thought caterpillars appear in the spring."

Arames gave his student a nod. "Normally, yes. But according to Linus's book, the King's Head moth's lifecycle is different. They are born as caterpillars during the fall. They burrow into the ground and live through the winter in a state of hibernation. Then in the spring they crawl out and eventually become moths."

"Marrissa said she needed a live King's Head moth..."

Arames nudged several carcasses with his fingers. "Well, as you can see, the changing season marks the end of their life cycle. We must give this a try."

They gathered up the three caterpillars and hurried back to town. Marrissa was initially displeased. "I ask for a moth and you bring me caterpillars?! Are you both daft?"

Arames pulled one of the caterpillars out of the wire mesh cage and placed it on the table in front of Marrissa. "Look at the markings. This will become a King's Head moth. All of this year's moths are dead. This is what you've got to work with."

Marrissa looked at the caterpillar for a moment. Then her eyes widened and a small gasp escaped her mouth. "Ah!" she exclaimed, running over to a shelf that held several books. She pulled one down and shuffled through some pages. She eventually stopped on a page and scanned it... then scanned it again to be sure.

She came back, book in hand, and slammed it on the table. "This might just work. There is a potion that might speed up the caterpillar's metamorphosis. If it works, I might have a moth in two or three days!" In an instant, Marrissa had hope again, and she became a whirling dervish in her lab, rushing around, pulling down bottles of reagents and other supplies.

"Marrissa... if this meets your needs, as it apparently does, do you have something for us?"

Marrissa looked up and stared at them with a dumbfounded look on her face. She blinked twice... and then snapped her fingers in recognition. "Ah, yes... here you go!" She pulled a small scroll out of her pocket and threw it in their general direction. "I don't know what you plan on getting out of this. Lord Avedon isn't going to open the Pass for you."

"You could be right. But this will get us a step closer to our goal. Thank you, Marrissa."

Marrissa did not hear Arames's response. She was already hard at work. The two let themselves out.

They headed directly to the iron gates surrounding Avedon Manor. "If Constable Louis is a man of his word, this will get us an audience with Lord Avedon."

"And then what?"

"The law of supply and demand applies not only to trade, but to people as well. We just need to learn what Lord Avedon needs, and show we can get or do it for him. If we succeed in that, then he should give us what we want."

"What if he doesn't want anything? What if he just wants us to leave him alone?"

Arames put a hand on Arrin's shoulder. "Then, young prince, we will have to find a way to change his mind."

Avedon Manor

7

Walk into the mouth of the lion, and live the life Az has offered you.

—Theuroik Ironblade, The Battle at Ohme

Monk and student made their way east toward the manor gates, walking by a general store and a theatre along the way. To the north, before they reached the turn that would lead them to the gates, they passed a small cemetery. The graveyard was well cared for, and Arames soon saw why: Father Jorrus. The cantankerous priest walked the consecrated grounds, pulling weeds and cleaning up as best he could without the benefit of landscaping tools. The priest paused his work at various graves, stopping to pray.

As Arames slowed down to watch, Arrin grabbed his arm and hurried him along toward the manor gates. "Come on, Arames. Let the crazy man care for his graveyard."

"Yes, of course." Arames didn't tell Arrin that Father Jorrus was doing more than gardening. He was calling on Arjun to protect the souls of those buried in the cemetery. Father Jorrus was worried about far more than the murder of one inhabitant of Avedon Hill.

Their second approach to the manor gates greatly resembled the first. The gates were locked, and through them Arames and Arrin could see Constable Louis. This time, however, the two other constables were not with him.

Arrin had promised not to let emotions control him as they had when he had first met the constables, but if Arrin's first question was any indication, Arames still had a lot to worry about. "So, Constable Louis, where are Shem and Lem?"

If Arames hadn't been so angry, he might have laughed. Shem and Lem were the names of the two lackeys that always seemed to serve human incarnations of Doppin, the trickster god of Caern. Constable Louis got the reference, but didn't respond to the jest. "What do you want now?"

Arames pulled out the letter that the herbalist Marrissa had written, and handed it to Constable Louis. "You said that a letter of introduction would get us a meeting with Lord Avedon."

The Head Constable stared incredulously at the missive in his hand. "I don't believe it." The two men waited while Constable Louis read the letter. He snarled once, and then turned to walk up the path. "Wait there!"

A short time later he returned with one of the other constables. "Tanner, stay here until I return." Constable Louis unlocked and opened the manor gate and ushered the two men inside. Constable Louis started up the path toward the manor, not waiting to see if the two men followed.

Arames quickened his pace until he walked alongside the Head Constable. Louis looked over and pursed his lips in disdain. "Again I find myself in the bad graces of Lord Avedon."

"Bad graces?"

"I had to explain to Lord Avedon that you met my ultimatum, and that he had to meet with you or my word would be broken."

Arames responded truthfully. "It was not my desire for you to cause your lord displeasure."

"No, I'm sure it wasn't. Maybe this will be what Lord Avedon needs."

Arrin interjected, "You hope we can help Lord Avedon snap out of his depression?"

Louis smiled. "No, I hope he'll focus his anger on you instead of me. Maybe I'll get to jail you for the winter—or at least forcibly remove you from town."

"Constable, we all want the same thing here—for us to be on our way. We just want it to be through the Olviaran Pass."

"Of course, sir monk." They reached the end of the path that opened to the front of Avedon Manor. It was more a castle fortress than a home. Not only did it serve as the home of the Avedon family, but it also was the entrance to the Olviaran Pass: the middle of the two-story front wall was interrupted by a great square gate, large enough for land transportation of any size. Two small doors flanked the gate, one on a side, and two thin windows interrupted the wall above the gate in a way that made it resemble the mouth of a great lion.

Instead of approaching the great metal gate that controlled the entry to the Pass, Constable Louis directed the two men to a small door on its left. They entered a large foyer with marble floors. Four granite columns supported a vaulted ceiling that did not match any architecture they had seen in the rest of town. Portraits of the Avedon family lined the walls. "Wait here. Blake Weathertop will see to you momentarily."

"Weathertop?" Arames asked.

"The butler. He will take you to Lord Avedon."

Constable Louis disappeared through the door at the end of the corridor. When they were alone, Arrin spoke. "So, now that I see where we enter the Pass, how exactly did you come through it twenty-five years ago?"

Arames walked slowly down the corridor, stopping to study the various family portraits. "As I said before, your grandfather was doing everything in his power to avert a major war with Grozh at the time. As a result, I was sent into Grozh as an ambassador of sorts. On the way back, I was forced to hide in a trunk at the bottom of a cart that traveled through the Pass.'

"Doesn't it take a week to travel the Pass?"

"I did not stay in the trunk the entire time. Regardless, it was not a pleasant trip."

The door opened at the end of the corridor and an older man approached them. He was dressed in the garments of a servant for a wealthy Grozhian family: a blue woolen doublet lined with linen. "Good day to you. I am Blake Weathertop. I hope Avedon Hill is treating you well?"

Arames smiled. "Very well, thank you. The inn seems very nice. We were sorry to hear of the death of your Housemistress."

Weathertop's eyebrows rose slightly. "Yes, a tragedy. But we will survive. If you're ready, I will take you to Lord Avedon." Without waiting, he turned and walked back through the door through which he had just come.

The two men lagged behind, just out of earshot of the butler. Arrin whispered, "Looks like you said the magic words again."

"Yes, apparently I did. Arrin, you know how important it is that you do not bring Lord Avedon's attention to yourself. He is Grozhian royalty, such as it is, and frankly I do not know where he falls politically." Even though there had been peace between Grozh and Yew for twenty-five years, there were still many on both sides who were eager to instigate conflicts—and the northern nation of Inarra would certainly profit from any conflict between the two southern provinces of Caern.

Arrin bowed, half in jest. "I humbly submit to your wishes, Sir Arames. I will stand three paces back and to your right."

Arames ignored the youth's sarcasm. "Speak only to me and not directly to Lord Avedon. That should keep things from getting out of hand." Arrin checked his back, ensuring his sword was hidden from view beneath his backpack and cloak.

Blake Weathertop turned back to the two men. "Please, Lord Avedon is a busy man."

Arames bowed his head. "Our apologies, sir." They entered a second corridor with many doors along its length. The butler led them toward the large pair of doors at the end.

They followed Weathertop into the great hall. The ceiling was over thirty feet in height, with balconies along either side so that those on the second floor could view the activities below. A massive octagonal table was surrounded by twenty large wooden chairs. At the back of the great hall was a raised dais, and there were six chairs, nearly thrones, located on the platform. A man sat in the largest of the chairs, speaking to another standing beside him on the dais. The man he addressed wore a chef's uniform, complete with hat. The two men were having a heated exchange.

"What do you mean we have no oyster stew, Roland? I want OYSTER STEW!"

The chef was wringing his hands together in fear. "L-Lord Avedon, sir, Miss Gretta was supposed to place an order with her contact in Nallia. You know I don't have anyone who can get me oysters this time of year. I don't know if she placed the order or not, before..."

Lord Avedon stood up suddenly in a rage, but the anger seemed to slip away from him just as quickly. The ruler of Avedon Hill slumped back into his chair. "Go. See what you can do with your own contacts... please."

Chef Roland bowed deeply and left Lord Avedon's side, nearly running down the dais stairs. He made his way quickly out of the hall without once looking over in the direction of the butler and his guests.

Blake Weathertop stepped forward and spoke loudly and clearly. "Lord Avedon, presenting Sir Arames Kragen, member of the Aarronic Order, and his valet."

Lord Avedon waved them forward. He appeared slightly younger than Arames, but did not look well. His reddish, graying hair was unkempt, and his garments looked like he had been wearing them for days. It took them some time to work their way around the large table and approach the dais. Arrin remained several paces behind Arames as the monk touched chin to chest, and then continued his bow more deeply from the waist. "My Lord Avedon."

As Arames straightened, he saw that Lord Avedon held the letter of introduction in his hand. "Arames Kragen... your name is not forgotten even in this part of the world. You are still retired, I see?" Lord Avedon remarked, nodding to Arames's robe and the border which signified his rank.

"Yes, Lord Avedon. I have retired twice, in fact, from the position of Aarronic Advisor. But I still serve the Order in an academic capacity."

Lord Avedon appeared to lose interest about halfway through Arames's statement. "I see you tricked Constable Louis into getting this audience."

"Tricked, sir? We only met his requirements as quickly as we could—"

Lord Avedon waved him off. "It matters not. You are here now. So, what is it you want?"

"Lord Avedon, we only seek entry to the Olviaran Pass. I have a conference at Kith-Karn—"

"No!" Lord Avedon threw the letter to the floor. "The Pass is closed. You may leave now."

Arames reflected for a moment before speaking. "I am very sorry for your loss, Lord Avedon. From what everyone has told me, I can only assume that Gretta Platt was a wonderful woman." Invoking Gretta's name would either push Lord Avedon over the edge, or bring him back to a place where Arames could reach him. It was a chance he had to take.

Lord Avedon opened his mouth and raised his arm, pointing at the door from which they had entered... but nothing came out of his mouth. He closed it, opened it again... and then slumped back into his chair.

"Yes, she was." Lord Avedon gestured toward the door through which the flustered chef had exited. "And as you can see, she was integral to running this household."

"Lord Avedon, why are the constables not investigating the murder?"

A spark lit Lord Avedon's eyes. "Because they were looking in—" he paused, and changed course. "That isn't your concern."

"But it could be... if you wish."

Lord Avedon pondered Arames's statement. Again he opened his mouth, but his thoughts were somehow getting lost on their way to becoming speech. He closed his mouth and waited for Arames to continue.

"We can investigate this murder for you. We will discover who killed Gretta. As I understand it, you already know it has to be someone here in town—"

Lord Avedon nodded, as if he was reluctant to be the one to put that conclusion into words.

Arames shifted his arms within the sleeves of his robes. "Unless you believe Father Jorrus?"

Lord Avedon raised his head to meet the monk's gaze, then shook his head from side to side. "Vampires? No, I don't believe that. No matter how it looks, Avedon Hill is not under siege by creatures of the dark." He stood and began pacing across the dais, rubbing his face. He paused once, looked over at Arames, and then started pacing again. After a moment, he raised a finger, as if an idea was rising to the surface. Soon enough, he stopped and turned to face Arames. "True... this could work..."

"Come again, sir?"

"You're outsiders... you could do this."

"Outsiders?"

"Constable Louis and his men were not negligent—Louis especially—but their judgment is clouded. We are a small town, Sir Arames. Less than fifty people call Avedon Hill home."

"So few?"

"It isn't exactly the most inviting location in Grozh—hard winters, little chance for employment or fending for one's self here as a farmer. Many people pass through, but only a few love it and remain—like the Platt family..."

Lord Avedon was getting off track. "You were saying," Arames asked, "about the constable's judgment?"

"Yes. The head constable is close to nearly everyone in town. He was not equipped to deal with this investigation. I doubt anyone living in Avedon Hill could be. You, however, are not burdened by such ties."

"True, my lord. I only know one person here in town... my cousin Red."

Lord Avedon smiled for the first time since they had entered the great hall. "So it's true. Cousin Red actually does have a cousin."

"That seems to be the running joke. I am glad something still makes people laugh here."

Lord Avedon grunted non-committally. "Red had no contact with Gretta that I know of, so that shouldn't be an issue. Here is what will happen: You will discover who murdered Gretta. We will show everyone that this was a crime of human nature and not some evil, demonic plot. Then I will grant you access to the Pass."

"Thank you, Lord Avedon. We are at your service."

"Yes, that will do nicely." Lord Avedon had a gleam in his eye. "I hereby grant you temporary constabulary powers. You will still answer to Head Constable Louis as needed, but you have the authority to do what you need to carry out your investigation."

"Yes, sir."

"Your first order of business will be to see the courtyard. Louis will meet you there."

Arames furrowed his brow. "The courtyard?"

Lord Avedon sat back in his chair. "It's where Gretta's body was found. She went there almost every evening. It's where someone sought her out and took the light of her life, snuffing it out like a candle." There was fire in his voice.

"Was any evidence found in the courtyard?"

"You'll see for yourself. Only Gretta's body has been removed, to prepare her for burial. Go now. Walk through the double doors at the rear of the hall. A guard will direct you from there."

Arames turned to Arrin, and they both started toward the doors. After only a couple of steps, Arames stopped and turned back to Lord Avedon. "We will need to see the body."

A quick breath escaped Lord Avedon. "Very well. I will send word to Gloria Platt, Gretta's mother, for permission for you to enter Gretta's mausoleum."

"Gretta's mother lives here in Avedon Hill?"

"No. She moved away after she retired as Housemistress eight years ago. She was on her way here to visit her daughter, and instead had to attend her funeral."

"And Gretta has been your Housemistress ever since her mother retired?"

"Yes."

"Who will be taking over Gretta's duties?"

"I'm giving Gloria some time, but I'm hoping she will resume her duties until we can find a suitable replacement."

"I see. Thank you, Lord Avedon."

They turned toward the doors, but Lord Avedon stopped them. "One more thing, Sir Arames..."

"Yes?"

"My children are not suspects in this matter. Speak to them only if you must, and do nothing to cause them more grief. Am I understood?"

Without missing a beat, Arames again lowered chin to chest. "As you wish, Lord Avedon."

The guard on the other side of the double doors must have heard everything that had gone on inside the hall—he immediately gave the two men directions to the courtyard. "How many guards work here in the manor?"

"Six, Sir Arames. Two are on duty at any one time."

"Just two?"

"Yes. Shifts were changed for a while so that four of us were here at all times, but Lord Avedon ordered us back to our normal schedule this morning."

Arames had more questions, but they could wait. He thanked the guard and started down the corridor.

"Leave his children out of it?" Arrin had successfully kept his mouth shut during the audience with Lord Avedon, but could not contain himself any longer. "The most logical suspects are going to be people who had access to the manor and the courtyard."

"Yes. We must take care not to cross whatever lines Lord Avedon draws for us." Arames smiled. "Until we have to, of course."

"Well, it looks like we're on our way."

Arames stopped a few steps into a long hallway and turned to Arrin. "Maybe you should return to Thorn's Way. I am supposed to be taking you to a religious conference at Kith-Karn, not investigating a murder. Your family might be less than pleased."

Arrin laughed. "I think not. Like you've said many times, I need life experiences, not to be sheltered at royal court. I've learned more today than over the last season living with you, Sir Arames."

"Yes—maybe you have, at that. Well, as long as you continue to observe before taking action, you will be fine."

Arames and Arrin continued down the long hallway, their voices drifting out of range of the ear that rested against the wall of a hidden corridor—a dark passageway that ran parallel to the more public hallway. The figure moved quickly down the dark stone path, traversing secret passages so familiar that light was not required, following to perhaps hear more of their conversation. But another had been waiting silently just around the corner... and moments later the eavesdropper lay unconscious on the stone floor.

"What in Az's name were you thinking? If you were discovered—" The new figure paused, alert for the sounds of movement or voices, and then dragged the unconscious form down the corridor as quietly as possible, back into the darkness.

THE COURTYARD

"Do you plan on beating them over the head with your book?"
"Theuroik, if they get past my men and my mace, then yes!"

—Iberian and Theuroik Ironblade, before the Battle at Ohme

Odd..." said Arrin. He paused before a set of glass double doors that led into an open courtyard surrounded by four walls.

Arames stopped. "What is it?"

"From the outside it appears that the front of the mansion is the opening to the Olviaran Pass. Yet if my sense of direction is correct, this courtyard is in the center of the manor."

The monk smiled. "Very attentive, Arrin. If recollection serves me, the Pass angles downward immediately after entry and then works its way northeast through the mountains. I believe the courtyard rests directly on top of the Pass, at least partially."

Arrin looked troubled, as if he was having trouble visualizing the tunnel, but he trusted his teacher's words and nodded.

Inside the courtyard, they were both immediately struck by the seamlessness of the area. Arrin commented, "This is incredible. If I didn't know better, I would think I was outside in one of the gardens at Liza's Choice."

The famous gardens of Liza's Choice had been planted on the site of the most pivotal battleground of the War of Man. The courtyard of Avedon Manor was not an apt comparison in terms of beauty, but Arames nodded—it captured the illusion very well. The architecture, the ancient oaks and centuries of landscaped plant growth masked the walls and windows of the courtyard... it was easy to forget that one remained inside the manor's walls.

"A perfect place for Gretta Platt to escape the troubles of the day... so beautiful, so inspiring... also a fine place for someone to catch her defenseless and end her life." Head Constable Louis stepped out from behind a grouping of trees. He smiled. "I see you convinced Lord Avedon to keep you around. I don't know how you did it, but as always, I accept his decisions, no matter how... questionable... they might be."

Arames joined the constable under the trees. "You were listening to our conversation with Lord Avedon?"

"Of course. How else could I have gotten to the courtyard before the two of you?"

Arames pulled his hands from his sleeves and held them out in a supplicating manner. "Constable, I know I am threatening your position here. But my only desire is to find out who murdered this young woman and gain access to the Olviaran Pass. I hope you are able to work with us. I assure you, we can help each other."

Constable Louis shook his head. "You are an amazing man, Kragen. You have the ability to disarm people, just through conversation. It seems you always get whatever you want in the end."

Arrin spoke up. "Most of the time, anyway."

Arames lowered his hands to his side. "Although not usually when dealing with the impetuousness of youth."

Arrin rolled his eyes. "If you say so, sir."

"Can you truth-read, Sir Arames?"

Constable Louis's question caught Arames off-guard. "Somewhat. I can sense emotions in many, and recognize when people are trying to deceive me, but I am not as gifted in truth-reading as many in the Order."

"So, what are your strongest gifts, then?"

Arames smiled. "Possibly a topic of conversation for some later date. Where was Gretta's body found?"

Constable Louis led Arames over to an intricately carved stone bench. There was a small spot of dried blood on its seat. On the ground in front of the bench there was another small, dried bloodstain, slightly larger than the first.

Arames nodded. "As Father Livasdawn said, not enough blood. Could some sort of blow have caused her death? Did she have any broken bones?"

Louis shook his head again. "There were two small puncture holes in her neck, and there was bruising around the wounds. She had no broken bones. And when she was buried, she had more bruising on her face, arms and chest. As far as we could tell, most of the blood had been drained from her body. If she bled out—and the wounds certainly could have allowed for it—there should have been a lot more blood around her body and on her clothing."

"And there was not? I mean, on her clothing?"

"No, Sir Arames. A small stain on her dress, but no more than you see here."

"And how do you feel about the idea that a vampire killed Gretta Platt?"

Constable Louis shrugged. "I know they're supposed to exist, but I just don't consider it a reality until I see proof. The marks could have been made by teeth,

I guess, but this courtyard is not exactly easy to get to. My guess is that someone with access to the manor got into the courtyard, killed her, and then made it look like a vampire attack."

Arames Kragen surveyed the bench closely as he spoke. "Well, I can tell you vampires exist, but the ones I have seen were little more than walking dead... certainly not capable of devising some sort of plan to gain access here, kill Gretta, remove evidence, and then escape. Although I have heard tales of vampire masters that can walk among the living with ease."

Arrin asked, "Can one recognize vampire masters by sight?"

Arames shrugged. "Unless you find one walking outside during the day, probably not. Vampire masters are sensitive to sunlight, but are not damaged by it. And then there is their smell."

"Smell?"

"I should rephrase—their lack of smell. Supposedly, they emit no odor." Arames thought for a moment. "Does anyone in town keep indoors during the day?"

Louis chuckled to himself. "Sir Arames, this is a town of mining families, even if these mountains haven't been actively mined in three generations. I believe that fear is all that's kept them from moving into the caves of Mount Olviar centuries ago."

"Are the mountains dangerous?" Arrin asked.

"No, I meant the fear of being confused with the dwarf clan that lived here before us." The constable smiled at his own joke. "To answer your question, few here could be called outdoor types. Kell, and Lonne Garrett—the town's farrier. And the farmers on the outskirts of town."

"What about the children?" Arames asked.

"Of the Avedon children, Jon is the most active outdoors. He is a great horseman, even at fourteen. Of the others.. Shane Olivet works at the stables with Lonne Garrett. Jilly Hemming, the baker's daughter, spends a lot of time outside. Gretta loved being outdoors, herself. She would go riding outside of town two or three days a week.

"Some of the farmers have children. But most of those families rarely venture into the town proper, except to deliver produce or buy supplies. All of those families have been cleared, by the way. There was a party the night Gretta was killed—end of the harvest season, a great bonfire, the blessings of Arjun to get us through the winter months, and all that. The men and women from the farms were all accounted for."

Arames walked a slow circuit around the bench. "Lord Avedon said that nothing had been moved in the courtyard?"

"As far as I know. And it hasn't made Kell—the groundskeeper—very happy, to be sure. Lord Avedon has forbidden him to even water the flowers until we find Gretta's killer."

Arames bent at the knees to study the ground around the bench. The dirt was scuffed with the markings of several boots. "Who found her? Kell?" Arames pulled out his book and pen, and began taking notes.

"What is that?" Louis pointed at the pen.

Arames smiled. "I do not own many things, but this is special to me. You see... this glass ball, here, holds ink. The pen disperses drops of ink through a tube to the nib, but only when I press it to the paper."

"No bottle? No dipping?"

"I can write for hours without having to refill the glass ball."

"That is quite the tool." At Arames's expectant look, Louis cleared his throat. "Lord Avedon found Gretta's body."

"Lord Avedon?"

"Yes. He said he had been looking for Gretta to ask her about something, and since she came here most evenings, he came here to find her. When he entered the courtyard, he said, he found her on the ground by the bench and called out for guards. Constable Ulrich was on duty that evening. When he arrived, Lord Avedon was sitting on the ground, here..." Louis indicated an area just to the left of where the body had rested. "He was holding Gretta's right hand, crying. The bite marks were on the left side of Gretta's neck."

"Who was the last person to see her alive?" Arames edged around the stone bench in slow circles as he spoke, looking closely at the ground for any signs of evidence.

"The killer, I would guess..."

Arames smiled. "Very good, Louis, but you know what I meant."

"Yes, of course. She met with Lord Avedon just before sundown. Both Ally Morr and Brianna Ray saw her after that in different areas of the manor—"

"And they are?"

"The two maids. No one admits seeing her after that."

"And how long after the last maid saw Gretta was her body found?"

"Almost two bells."

Arames thought for a moment. "That reminds me. I have not heard a clock-ring or temple bell since our arrival."

Constable Louis nodded. "Another of Lord Avedon's restrictions. The Temple to Az has a wonderful set of bells, but they will not be rung until Lord Avedon ends his grieving."

"Did Gretta have any appointments scheduled that evening?"

Constable Louis moved away from the bench and led them to a stone bird bath nearby. "Funny you should ask that..." He reached into a pocket and pulled out a leather pouch, handing it to Arames. "The pouch is mine. I just used it to keep what's inside a little safer."

Arames Kragen opened the pouch and carefully pulled out a scrap of paper, about the size of Arames's hand. It was very thin, thinner than any paper Arames had ever used himself. He wondered how many pages of it could fit in a bound volume. A jagged tear and two straight edges indicated that the piece had been a corner of a larger page; as a result, the words, written in a curved script that suggested a female hand, didn't make complete sense:

> *have to meet with HA*
> *know what this is about, and I really do*
> *right now.*

"HA?" Arrin read over Arames's shoulder.

Constable Louis replied, "No one in town has the initials HA. But if this indicates a meeting with someone the evening she died, then HA might be our killer."

Arames carefully returned the scrap of paper to the leather pouch. "I will keep this with me, if you do not mind." Louis nodded. "Is the paper from a diary?"

"Gretta kept a schedule book, along with accounting journals and such. I found many books in her office but none with paper like that." Constable Louis led them to a flowerbed that lined one wall of the courtyard. "You can look at Gretta's office when you have time. There is plenty to read there, if you so desire."

Arrin spoke up. "Well, if Gretta had her journal with her when she was attacked, the killer must have taken it. The paper you found must have been ripped from the book?"

Constable Louis nodded. "That's my theory. I'm sure that book has been destroyed by now, if the killer thought it might implicate him." Louis dropped into a crouch. "The other item of possible interest is here."

Louis retrieved a small, curved piece of metal from the edge of the flower bed and handed it to Arames. It was the length of Arames's hand. One end of the curve had been sharpened to a point. The other end appeared as if it had been broken off of something larger. It was dirty, except at the unsharpened end. "No blood on it..."

"No, but if it was part of something else... it's just that the holes in Gretta's neck could have been made by the pointed end of something like this."

Arames smiled. "Interesting. It is certainly worth exploring, especially when we examine Gretta's body."

Arames and Arrin spent a good deal of time walking around the courtyard. There were several areas where footprints were visible in large numbers; Louis confirmed that the courtyard was a popular place for visitors and household alike, and that did not include the many people who had walked the site once Gretta's body had been discovered.

In one corner of the garden, Arrin came across a small metal grate set into the ground. Grass grew over its edges, but it was not hidden. Rust covered the iron bars—it appeared that it had not been opened for years. The grate had no handle, so Arrin grasped one of the bars near the edge closest to him and pulled, but it did not budge. Constable Louis approached as Arrin knelt to look through the metal frame. "That leads down to the Olviaran Pass. It was used by workers at one time, but as you can see, it's been locked for years—probably a century or more. Some people began using this entrance to bypass payment for usage of the Pass, the story goes, so it was permanently closed."

"What about secret doors, secret passages?" Arrin Perti had grown up at Castle Pen, one of the oldest and largest castles in all of Caern, and was familiar with the features of aristocratic residences. "Are these four doors the only access to the courtyard?"

"Unless someone figured out how to get onto the roof of the manor without being seen." Arrin looked up, studying the walls. One could lower a rope rather easily from the open roof. Louis continued, "But it would be near impossible for someone to get to the roof from the outside. If they got past the manor gates, the only access to the roof would be from the front of the manor, which is always lit and patrolled. And as for secret passages..." Louis smiled. "The manor has its secrets, but Lord Avedon would have to be the one to share them with you."

As if the use of his name had summoned him, Lord Avedon entered the courtyard, accompanied by Constable Ulrich. The five men met at the bench where Gretta's body had been discovered.

"I sent word to Gloria Platt, Gretta's mother," Lord Avedon said. "She is at Gretta's mausoleum as we speak. I believe Kell is with her."

"So, Gretta was not buried in the cemetery we passed on the way here?"

Constable Ulrich had a strained look on his face, as if Arames had spoken blasphemy, but Lord Avedon was non-plussed. "Our family has its own family cemetery, underground, at the end of a set of catacombs we built generations ago. The Platts, though not of our bloodline, have always been considered a part of the Avedon family. Many of the former Housemistrisses have chosen to be buried in the Platt mausoleum, even ones who have retired and moved away."

"Of course, sir."

"Ulrich will take you through the catacombs. I would send you without escort, but people have been known to lose their way." Lord Avedon turned to leave, but paused when he saw Arames's notebook. "I see you take notes. I like that. When you find out who perpetrated this abomination, I expect you to turn over your notes to me... I would not want to execute someone in error."

It was the first time Lord Avedon had spoken of retribution. He left the courtyard the way he had entered. Louis turned to follow, but Arames pulled him aside, out of earshot of the others.

"Louis, you know I have to ask the question."

"Ah, and I was just beginning to like you. So ask it."

"What were you doing the night Gretta Platt was murdered?"

Louis paused. "I apologize, Sir Arames, but I can't say. I was in town, but I was far from the manor. You'll have to trust me, for now."

Arames watched Louis intently while he answered. He did not sense that the head constable was lying, but there was great unease behind his evasiveness. "For now, I guess that will have to do. We will speak more, I'm sure. I plan on leveraging your knowledge of the townspeople, where possible."

"I will be here at the manor or at the garrison if you need me, Sir Arames. Lord Avedon has seen fit to release me from standing watch at the manor gates..." Constable Louis bowed and left the courtyard.

Constable Ulrich indicated the door opposite the one through which Arames and Arrin had entered the courtyard. He spoke to Arames, ignoring Arrin completely. "Are you ready, sir?"

Arames nodded. "Yes, I believe so. Let us go meet the grieving mother." He scanned his notes as he crossed the courtyard to follow the constable.

Who is 'HA'? Could a vampire master hide him or herself in a town without being discovered? What was Gretta's true role here at the Manor? Housemistress... it seems such an ill-fitting title.

THE AVEDON FAMILY PLOT

"A mother should never have to bury her own child."
"Balin, stop crying. You could outlive your future great-grandchildren."

—The Return of the Children, Yew children's tale

CONSTABLE ULRICH LED ARAMES and Arrin down a long hallway of well-crafted stonework, toward the back of the manor. The only non-stone walls Arames had seen were the painted plaster of the great hall. There were several heavy wooden doors leading off of this particular hallway—as had also been the case with the other hallways he had seen. Arames had noted a lack of windows and open rooms. He also had yet to see stairs leading to the upper floor.

"Constable Ulrich, may I ask you some questions while we walk?"

Ulrich kept his eyes facing forward and grunted non-comittally. Arames took the sound as acceptance.

"How close were you to Gretta Platt?"

Ulrich opened a door and led the other men through. Arames and Arrin found themselves outside again, this time at the rear of the manor. Even though Avedon Manor was seemingly built into the side of a mountain, the grounds to the north of the manor were made up of at least three acres of manicured lawn; beyond this, the mountain began its sheer ascent into the sky. The rocks of the steep cliff also wound their way around the property, preventing any entry to the back of the manor from the sides. It was a well-designed fortress, to be sure.

Arrin whispered to his teacher, "Remind me to come here if I ever need protection and Castle Pen is not available."

Constable Ulrich turned to face them. "I knew Miss Gretta about as well as anyone who worked here would. We spend every third shift here at the manor, so there is always a constable here if Lord Avedon needs us."

"Was Gretta romantically involved with anyone here at Avedon Hill?"

He shook his head. "No, I wouldn't think so. A Platt never marries anyone from Avedon Hill."

"Why is that?"

Ulrich shrugged. "I don't know. I just know that the Housemistress has always been a Platt, and that they always come to Avedon Hill from the west—it's like they have a contest for all the Platt girls, wherever they come from, and the winner gets to be the next Housemistress—but the Platts never marry anyone in Avedon Hill or raise their children here."

Arames nodded. "I see." It was customary for aristocratic families in Grozh to bring in people to work for them from outside areas, to protect them from courtly politics, but Arames did not consider the Avedons to be at that level of Grozhian society.

"Ulrich, Louis told us that you answered Lord Avedon's call when he discovered Gretta's body. What else can you tell us about that night?"

Arames didn't have to use any of his abilities to sense Ulrich's relief; apparently speaking about the murder itself was less stressful than talking in general about the Platts. "I relieved Constable Tanner at evening bells. I was eating dinner in the great hall, as I do when I am on duty here. I didn't see anyone but Avedon staff or family. I heard Lord Avedon yell just as I was finishing my meal. I wasn't sure where the shout came from at first, so I ran up the stairs to the second floor. That's where the Avedon family sleeps, and so I thought the shout might have come from there. I saw Ally Morr in the second floor hall. She had heard the shout as well. And then Richard came out of his room."

Arames looked at his notes. "Ally is one of the maids... and Richard is Lord Avedon's oldest son?"

"Yes. From their confusion I knew I was in the wrong place. I ran back downstairs and checked several rooms before discovering Lord Avedon in the courtyard. I found him at Gretta's side, holding her hand. He was crying... very upset."

"Had you ever sensed any romantic connection between the two of them?"

"I don't believe so. She was so young... but I have no way of knowing for certain."

"How much time had passed between his initial shout and when you entered the courtyard?"

"Well, I ran the whole way, only pausing for a moment at the top of the stairs... not long at all."

Arrin asked, "Even though you went the wrong way at first, you were the first person to enter the courtyard after Lord Avedon?"

"Yes. With the stone in these walls it is hard to determine where voices are coming from. Sometimes you can be walking down a hall and hear someone speaking upstairs. On this occasion, the only other people downstairs were in the kitchens, and they came into the courtyard after me."

"What about the guards? The one we spoke to outside of the great hall said there were at least two on duty at all times."

"One was back here as part of his rounds. The other was in the kitchens. Apparently he was flirting with Brianna Ray."

"Brianna Ray is the other maid?"

"Correct."

"One more question... do you remember anything before or after the murder that struck you as strange? People visiting the manor, arguments between Gretta and anyone... anything at all?"

"I've been trying to think of anything, Sir Arames, ever since this happened... anything that would help." Ulrich paused for a moment. "But I can't think of one person that would hurt Miss Gretta."

Arames could sense that Ulrich was measuring his words. He placed a hand on Ulrich's left shoulder. "We're going to figure this out. Maybe I can ask the questions you could not, or possibly trigger something that you had completely forgotten about..."

"Yes sir... I hope so. We should keep moving." Ulrich led them toward an ancient-looking tree. In its shade, a set of stone stairs led down to a grated metal door. Ulrich pulled out a set of keys as he started down the stairs, and unlocked the door. The metal shrieked against stone as it opened. Two torches hung in sconces just inside the door. A few moments later the three men proceeded into the underground catacombs, with Ulrich and Arrin carrying torches.

It was a maze, pure and simple. The stone passages would branch off every so often, not only laterally but also in degrees of elevation. Ulrich led them up certain passages and down others, took some branches to the right and others to the left—Arames lagged behind more than once writing the directions in his notebook, then rushed to catch up. There were simple markings on some of the stone walls; others were smooth and clean.

"What purpose does a set of catacombs like this serve?" Arrin asked.

"These tunnels are at least as old as the manor itself. They lead to the Avedon family plot now, but at one time they may have served other purposes. I only know how to get from the tree to the cemetery. What else is down here, you'd have to ask the Avedons."

They continued on for some time, eventually reaching a fork lit by an oil lamp. "From here, the lamps will lead you to the cemetery. I need to return to the manor." Ulrich bowed. "Good luck, Sir Arames..." Ulrich turned to Arrin. "Sir."

Ulrich turned back the way they had come. Arames looked down the passage straight ahead and saw the flickering glow of a light just out of view. "Well, we should continue on."

Arrin led with his torch held high. "Something tells me we'll be exploring more of these tunnels before we're done."

"I certainly hope not... and watch your volume, Arrin. I suspect voices carry well here."

Fourteen lamps later, the passage opened into a large cavern with a high ceiling well beyond Arames's range of vision. "Obviously we are under the mountain," Arrin said. The cave was eerily lit by the same rocks they had seen in the caves outside of town. "Odd that we've never heard of this mineral before."

At the center of the cavern was the cemetery. Completely unnecessary but present were an iron fence and a sign that read "Avedon Family Plot."

"Actually, you haven't heard of this mineral because these rocks lose their glow as soon as they are taken outside. No one knows why—although exposure to sunlight seems most likely. It makes them worthless, except in places such as this." Arames followed the voice until he came upon its owner: Gloria Platt, Gretta's mother. "We simply call them glow-rocks."

Arames bowed deeply and extended his hand in friendship. "Gloria Platt, I presume. I am so sorry for your—and Avedon Hill's—loss."

Gloria Platt looked to be a few years older than Arames. A customary mourning bonnet covered her graying hair, and she wore a very distinguished black funeral dress. Even after days of grieving, her face held an unmistakable grace and determination. "Thank you, sir monk. Lord Avedon sent word that you were coming. I have great respect for your Order. I'm willing to do whatever it takes to help you discover who stole my daughter from me—although I am concerned to hear that the search for justice is not your sole motive."

Arames stepped to the left and Arrin moved slightly forward. "This is Arrin, my student. We are both at your service. While our initial reason for coming to Avedon Hill was driven by our need to use the Olviaran Pass, I give you my word here and now that I will not depart this place until you personally give me your leave." Arames bowed again. "In the short time we have been here, we have already seen how your daughter touched the lives of so many. Her death, while it has certainly been in vain, will not go unanswered."

Tears streamed from Gloria Platt's eyes. "That's all I needed to hear." She turned toward a large mausoleum that was set aside from two even larger ones. She pointed to the largest tomb and said, "That is the first Avedon family mausoleum. It has forty-seven tombs inside." She moved her hand to point at the next one. "This is the second mausoleum. It has room for at least seventy tombs inside. Its last addition was our deceased Lady Avedon."

"God rest her soul, Miss Gloria." A man now came into view as they approached the third mausoleum. "Lady Avedon should have never had that last child... It certainly killed her."

"Stop it, Kell." She turned back to Arames. "She was weak, but she thought she could handle another childbirth. Something was wrong with the baby, though, and it was stillborn. Lady Avedon just seemed to waste away after that."

"Nothing could be done?"

"No. Her will seemed to die with that baby." The four stopped in front of the third mausoleum. Written in the stone above the door was the name "Platt."

"This is my family's mausoleum. A Platt has served the Avedons for nearly four hundred years... as maids, caretakers, and finally as Housemistress. Lord Bryony Avedon built this mausoleum over two hundred and fifty years ago, and members of my family have been laid to rest here ever since." She noticed Arames's attire. "Your robes are torn."

"It is nothing. I just have to be more careful where I walk." He attempted to disarm her with a smile and changed the subject. "Is it always a Housemistress? Are there never sons who come to work for the Avedons?"

"Tradition is important to us, Sir Arames. Ella Platt arrived in Avedon Hill in the year 37 A.I. to offer herself as a servant to the Avedon family at the tender age of thirteen. Ella returned home to Dallard's Glen after twenty-two years of faithful service... and immediately sent her niece Hallie to take her place. Over the next hundred years, seven different Platt women served six different Lord Avedons. Eventually we were granted the title of Housemistress. Three male Platts have served the Avedon family in the past in different ways, but tradition holds that the Housemistress has always been a woman and a Platt."

"What exactly does the title mean? What are the duties of the Housemistress?"

"We manage the household, of course. We choose and manage the manor staff... which means that the Housemistress's purview includes anything those people are responsible for. In addition, we serve as the family scribe, historian, bookkeeper... anything that falls under the control of Avedon Manor."

"It appears that Lord Avedon can barely function now. Closing the town... his demeanor... somewhat beyond what some might call mourning?"

Gloria shrugged. "While it is true that Lord Avedon relied on Gretta very much, he will be fine—especially if you do your job, Sir Arames—and I will take over Gretta's duties until my grand-niece Selene finishes her education."

Arames turned to the man standing beside Gloria Platt. "Kell, you are the groundskeeper here?"

The white-haired man seemed very uneasy. Kell was much older than anyone Arames and Arrin had met in town. He was unshaven and unkempt, his clothes dirty and worn at the knees—and his hands looked permanently stained from years of gardening. But underneath all that, a handsomeness shone through. "Yes sir... for forty-three years now."

"I assume much of your time is spent caring for the plants and flowers in the courtyard?"

Kell's eyes brightened. "Oh yes, sir monk. The courtyard is my pride... my joy."

"So you were there many times with Gretta?"

Kell nodded. "She loved the western hylantia. I just laid some out by her—" Kell's voice broke.

Arames pressed on. "Did Gretta ever meet with people in the courtyard while you were there?"

"At times..."

Arames asked, "Was there anyone in particular that either of you know of, that Gretta particularly disliked meeting with... or anyone you witnessed Gretta arguing with?"

A wild look crossed Kell's face. "Arguments?! She was killed by a demon, sir monk. You should be scouring the countryside for the vampire that did this, not asking us about meetings and arguments!"

Gloria reached out and took Kell's shaking hands into hers. "Now, Kell, calm down. Sir Arames and... Arrin, is it? They must ask these questions. They need all the information they can get. I know you believe this vampire theory—"

"Not theory, Miss Gloria... not theory. Father Jorrus, he knows. He's warned us for months now, but no one would listen..." He paused, gathering himself. "I only saw one person argue with Miss Gretta... Talik Bore."

"The innkeeper?" asked Arrin.

"Yes. He was unhappy with some decision of... Lord Avedon's, I guess. I'm sure Miss Gretta was just passing it on to him, but he took it out on her. But this was weeks ago, and he was fine after that."

"Miss Platt, is there anyone that may have disliked you while you were Housemistress, or anyone Gretta spoke of in a negative way to you?"

"Well, the day I left Avedon Hill was the last day I spoke to anyone—including Gretta—about Avedon Hill and what goes on here, and she didn't share anything with me concerning anyone not liking her. And as for me... no one that I know of held animosity toward me, and certainly not anything that would pass on to my daughter."

"One last question, Gloria, if you do not mind?"

"Of course not." Gloria said, but she was beginning to look tired. Arames had more questions, but they would keep for now.

"Was Gretta raised here?"

"Gretta was groomed to be my replacement ever since she was a child. She spent a season here each year, until she moved here permanently twelve years ago—she was fifteen—but before that, she lived most of the year in Dallard's Glen with my sister and mother. My family has access to the best educators in the region."

"And Gretta's father?"

The question seemed to take Gloria by surprise. "He—he died years ago. He was a sailor by trade." Her face paled as she spoke. "I know one question you haven't asked that you need to..." She leaned heavily against Kell. "The answer is 'No.' I don't know if she was seeing anyone. But I am sure she wouldn't have been seeing anyone here in town."

"Why is that?"

Kell swayed on his feet as more of Gloria's weight pressed against him. "That's enough, Sir Arames. You're upsetting her."

Arames moved forward and assisted Gloria, carefully leading her to a bench just outside the mausoleum. "I apologize if our questions caused you more grief."

"No, of course not, Sir Arames. I am simply an old woman. Stop fussing over me." She shooed the men away with her hands. "You have something more important you need to do. Kell will take you in to see Gretta's tomb... I... think it is best that I stay here."

Arames bowed. "We will return shortly, madam."

Kell pulled out a set of keys and opened the door to the mausoleum. The three men walked in. A series of lit torches hung on the wall.

"It is the third door on the left. You can't miss the flowers."

Arames and Arrin went forward, leaving Kell to stand guard by the exit. The door that Kell had indicated had been left open slightly. While heavy, the door was well-balanced and opened easily when Arames pushed on it. There were several stone sarcophagi in the room, but it was obvious which one was Gretta's. Kell had not been kidding about the flowers in the tomb. Hundreds of flowers of differing varieties surrounded her coffin, many covering the lid.

"Are you ready, Arrin?"

"I've seen dead bodies before, Arames."

Arames smiled. "I do not care about your stomach, Arrin. I just need your help opening the tomb."

Arrin, embarrassed, responded with a quiet, "Oh."

The two men went to what seemed to be the head of the sarcophagus and felt around the edge. In the soft glow of torchlight it wasn't easy to find handholds, but after a moment they braced themselves and pushed up on the stone lid... which did not budge.

"Wait a moment. What is this?" The winch and pulley that had been used to lower the lid onto the coffin sat in the shadows. A few moments later they had reattached the brackets to the top of the coffin. The handle for the winch was built so both of them could work it at once. They cranked the handle counterclockwise until the coffin lid was three feet off the ground.

They locked the winch in place. Arames turned to Arrin. "Go ahead, take a look."

Concern stretched across Arrin's face. "Um—I don't think a prince of Yew should be sticking his head under a hanging stone slab."

"Do not be foolish. The lid will not fall."

Arrin walked over to the small podium where the sarcophagus lay and climbed up. For a moment he watched the lid of the sarcophagus suspended in the air. The height of the coffin's top edge was such that he had to climb to the tips of his toes in order to see within. Arrin gasped and immediately pulled his head back, momentarily losing his balance. He secured himself and called Arames over.

"What is it, Arrin?"

"Well, Sir Arames... we have a slight problem." Arrin held onto the edge of the sarcophagus with one hand and ran the fingers of his other hand through his hair.

"What is it? Do they have her wrapped or covered?"

"Um ... no, that's not it." Arrin had a sheepish look on his face.

Arames grunted. "I thought you said you had seen dead bodies before." A moment later Arames stood beside Arrin. The monk was shorter than his student by two hands, and it was much more of an effort for him to see over the edge. "What have we—" Arames stopped in mid-question. "Oh. I see."

The two men walked out of the tomb and brought Kell along as they left the mausoleum, making their way to Gloria's bench. Arames sat down next to her and took one of her hands in his.

"When was Gretta's funeral? How long ago?"

Gloria was confused by the question. "She was laid to rest three days ago."

"Have you spent much time away from the cemetery?"

"I've slept at Gretta's home in town at night, but other than that I've been here."

"Has anyone stood guard or been around here at night?"

Kell spoke up. "I have a shack over there, just beyond the last mausoleum. I've slept there the last three nights."

Arames patted Gloria's hand. "Well, it seems murder is not the only crime that has been committed in Avedon Hill. We're sorry to have to be the ones to tell you... but your daughter's coffin is empty."

Kell cursed explosively, ranting about vampires rising from the dead. Gloria Platt fainted.

Arames caught Gloria before her slumped body could fall from the bench. Arrin leaned over to help him hold her up. "Arames, this is definitely turning out to be one of your 'learning experiences.'"

The Investigation Begins

Iberian will continue to push back the boundaries,
the walls that separate us from the forbidden knowledge of Az.
At the end only he and Kalin will be left standing.
But it may not be enough to save the Age of Man.

—3rd Collected Prophecies of Iberian, Book 3, Chapter 3

Arames walked toward the oldest of the mausoleums, leaving Kell and Arrin to revive Gloria Platt. Arames smiled inwardly as he scribbled more hasty notes—he could easily read his writing in the cavern's glow.

Could the tunnels under the manor have been used by the murderer?

Must take time to learn what I can about vampire masters...

Arames unfolded a small parchment from the back of his notebook, something Constable Louis had handed to him in the courtyard. In a clear, squarish script, Louis had catalogued the names of everyone he had interviewed in town about the murder, with their whereabouts that night—whether he could verify those stories or not—and his impressions.

Arames folded the parchment and replaced it inside his notebook, then walked back over to the group. Gloria Platt was now awake, and even standing. She still shook, but her face was now set with determination and anger. "Sir Arames?"

"Yes, Mrs. Platt?"

"Vampires or no..." Hearing those words, Kell walked away, muttering to himself about the living dead. Gloria ignored him. "I want my daughter laid to rest. Find me her killer. But more importantly, find her and bring her back to me... please."

"You have my word. Where will I find you, when we have further need to talk?"

"I'll be at Gretta's house... my old house. It's just west of the town circle."

Arames nodded, remembering how the road branched off at the center of town and wound its way to each side of the butcher shop. "Thank you, Mrs. Platt. Arrin, we need to go." He turned to backtrack toward the mansion.

"No, no, no," Gloria said. "Come this way." She pointed to a tunnel entrance opposite the one through which they had entered.

"Lady Platt! We shouldn't do that," Kell protested.

Gloria waved him off. "I want to go home, Kell. I can't climb the ladder alone. And I need these gentlemen to get to their work as quickly as possible. Let's go." She took Kell by the arm and started toward the tunnel. Arames held Arrin back for a moment so the two others could walk ahead.

Arrin whispered, "Interesting display back there..."

Gloria whispered something to Kell that Arames could not hear, and the groundskeeper patted her arm in response. Confident that the distance was great enough that he would not be overheard either, Arames whispered to Arrin, "Did you notice anything that would suggest Mother Platt faked her fainting spell?"

"No."

"Hmmm... keep an eye out for any branching passages. We need to gather as much information as we can. I believe you might be right about returning to these tunnels."

Arrin sighed.

They entered a wide passage. The tunnel seemed to end about ten feet ahead... until Kell touched one of the stones on the wall. Arames heard an audible *click*; Kell pushed on the rough surface until a door was revealed. He held it open, waving for them all to continue through.

The passage did not have any of the glow-rocks from the main cavern, and Arrin's torch was needed again, requiring the party to gather closer. They walked for a long time, longer than it had taken to reach the cemetery. Kell led them past several side passages, continuing down a winding path until they reached the tunnel's end, where a ladder had been built into the wall. Kell climbed up until he reached the ceiling. There was no apparent door or hatch, but again Kell touched the rocks, this time at three specific points that did not appear distinguishable from the rest of the ceiling, and when he pushed up on the rock above him, a seal appeared. Arrin, having placed his torch within a nearby sconce once light was no longer an issue, moved forward and offered Gloria Platt his help climbing the ladder.

The four of them emerged in a meadow just north of the Avedon stables. Arames could see the road they had traveled earlier that morning, and he recognized the temple of Az beyond it. The sun still shone brightly although more than half the day was gone.

After Kell closed the hatch that covered the opening and the ladder, Arames could not see the seal at all. The sod covering the secret door meshed perfectly with the rest of the meadow. Kell was good at his job.

Arrin whispered, "Well, this is certainly proof that someone might have gotten to the manor without being seen."

Arames spoke once more to Gloria Platt, assuring her that they would get back to her with information as soon as they could. He then asked Kell to tell Lord Avedon and no one else of Gretta's empty coffin. As Kell began walking Gloria to her daughter's home, Arrin asked, "Where to now, master?"

At one time, it had made Arames uncomfortable to be referred to as "master" by a member of the royal family; but the bond between Arames and Arrin had grown strong over the last half year. The term was only appropriate for a student to use with a member of the Aarronic Order, and Arames had come to accept in the spirit in which it was intended.

Arames surveyed their surroundings, noticing activity inside the large barn. "We might as well visit the stables. Maybe we will get to meet our first Avedon child."

There were three people in the barn. Arames assumed the dark haired man in his late thirties was Lonne Garret, the farrier. Of the two others, both not yet full grown men, the teenager closest to Arames had a nose that matched Lord Avedon's perfectly. Arames recognized him as the one who had waved to them as they passed earlier that day. As Arames approached Jon Avedon, Lonne moved forward to place himself between Arames and his lord's youngest son.

Jon moved forward a step and touched Lonne's arm. "It's okay, Lonne. Sir Kragen is a guest of my father." Jon bowed deeply to the monk.

"Word travels fast here."

Jon smiled. "Yes, sir. One of the constables stopped to let me know what was going on, probably before you finished meeting with Father. I see Lady Gloria finally came up for air." Jon released his horse into the care of another young man, slightly older than himself, whom he called Shane.

Once they were alone again, Arames leaned in and said, "There was little reason for her to stay at the cemetery. It seems someone has removed Gretta's body from her coffin."

Jon's eyes widened and his mouth fell open. Jon wasn't able to produce sound until his third attempt. "R-really!?" Arames saw Jon's reaction mirrored on Arrin's face—his student's surprise that Arames would provide Jon with the news so soon after telling Kell to keep it a secret. Arames hoped his next words would show Arrin his intentions.

"Or she has risen from the dead, if you believe what some will say."

"Vampires? I—I don't think so." Jon stammered. His eyes darted from side to side.

Jon was mature for his age, but he was still only fourteen. Arames had wanted to off-balance the boy, not to unnerve him completely. Lord Avedon's threat was loud in the back of his mind.

"Do not worry, young Jon. I do not believe your former Housemistress has risen from the dead. We just want to find out who sent her there in the first place. Can we ask you a couple of questions?"

"Yes, of course."

"Did you know anyone that Gretta had problems with... at all? Anyone she didn't like to meet with, argued with, disliked?"

"Everyone liked Miss Gretta. She was a great Housemistress."

"I'm sure she was. But someone in town killed her, even if it was some sort of accident. Anything you can think of will help us."

Jon thought to himself for a moment. "I do remember... one time, Blake—he's our butler—I had to help him remove Talik Bore from the foyer. He wanted to see Gretta about something, and I guess Blake had been instructed to turn him away."

"Talik wanted to see Gretta—or was it your father—about something?"

Jon smiled. "If you want to get something to my father, you had to get it past Gretta first. Talik has some new scheme every month or so. Once I came into the room, Talik left."

"Anything else? How about the town itself? From what we've heard, you spend more time outside the manor than the rest of your family. Anything that you have seen, anything strange or out of place, might help."

Jon Avedon stared at Arames, then took a moment to look into Arrin's eyes, as if searching for something. "I don't want to get anyone here in trouble. One day I might be asked to become Lord over Avedon Hill, if my brothers choose other paths..."

Arrin spoke up. "But someone here murdered Gretta. You know that..."

Jon closed his eyes. "I know. I can't believe it, or understand it... but I know. There isn't really anything specific. You've met some of the townspeople already. I could probably tell you something 'strange' about almost everyone here."

"Well, does anything come to mind that might help us?"

Jon leaned in toward both men and spoke in a whisper. "Jilly Hemming—she's the baker's daughter. She likes to go outside of town. She likes—she likes to burn things."

"Burn?"

"I once saw her burning some... they were dolls, I think." Jon paused and looked over toward the young man who had taken over the cleaning of his horse. "I'm sorry I'm whispering, but Shane really likes Jilly. I don't think she's taken to him, but he keeps trying."

"Anything else?"

"I know Jilly and Gretta were friends, but not as close lately. Maybe Gretta got too busy with her work. They're around the same age and they spent a lot of time together before Gretta took up her duties. Friends are hard to keep close in her position, I'm sure."

"Do you have any close friends here in town?"

Jon laughed. "I have six horses here, four of them Grozhian purebloods. They are my friends—and my brothers and sisters, of course. I'm friends with the new cleric, Father Livasdawn."

"What do you think of Father Jorrus?"

"I've never had a problem with him. In truth, I've spent a few evenings in the town cemetery listening to stories of his youth—he was a Protector, you know. Being a temple priest wasn't a good fit for him, and retirement suits him even less."

A member of the select group of Brothers of Arjun that sought out the undead in the Wastes of Inarra... that explains a lot.

"Thank you, Jon. We will see each other again soon."

"Good luck, Sir Kragen. Please let me know if you need anything."

Before they left, Arames spoke to the farrier while Arrin spoke with Shane, his apprentice. Arames scribbled notes as they walked back down the path toward the center of town. "What did you learn from the farrier's assistant?"

Arrin shifted his pack on his shoulder. "Olivet... Shane Olivet. He definitely likes the baker's daughter. Wouldn't stop talking about her. I think he wanted to read me a love poem he wrote her."

"You could help him out with that," Arames chided.

"Oh, yes, I've spent a lot of time writing poetry, Master Arames."

"What else?"

"He apparently does most of the work around the stables. I told him to get used to it—it's the lot of the apprentice."

"Ha, ha. What else?"

Arrin turned serious. "He saw Constable Tanner arguing with Leilah the morning after Gretta was murdered. He didn't know what it was about."

Arames scribbled furiously in his notebook. "More?"

"No, that was it. Though, Shane looks to be the type who might remember more if the right questions were asked."

"I see. Lonne Garrett mentioned something that might be worth looking into."

"What do you mean?"

"Gretta liked to ride, as Constable Louis told us. Lonne said that she used to take her horse, Firefly, out at least three days a week, for a mid-day meal—and she always took more food than one person would eat."

"So you think she was seeing someone here in town?"

"Yes, I do. But only the manor uses these stables, so he has no idea who she might have been meeting. It was no one who kept a horse here."

"Should I go back and ask Shane?"

"No. Although I do know someone to ask when we get the chance—your friend Cletus."

Arrin nodded. "Now who's telling jokes? Friend? I still need to clean his spit off my boot. So, back to the gate now?"

Arames glanced down at his notes. "Constable Louis gave me a list of everyone in town who had any real contact with Gretta Platt. If we continue in a clockwise path, we should meet everyone Louis considered possible suspects. We will start with the clothier."

"Tremaine, right?"

"Yes, very good. Sarah Tremaine."

When they walked through the door of the town's only commercial seamstress and clothier, Arames was immediately impressed. Bolts of fine fabric lined one wall of the main room. There were several dresses on manikins in different areas of the main floor. One displayed a fine suit. But the garments were so luxurious that there was no one in Avedon Hill, not even the Avedons, that Arames could imagine wearing them. He could only assume that Sarah received orders from other places, or sold garments to the travelers and merchants who used the Olviaran Pass.

"It smells nice in here."

Arames didn't have to sniff to agree. Incense burned somewhere in the shop. Arames scanned the room, attempting to discover its origin. The monk found himself staring at a manikin near the only other door in the room, amazed by its lifelike limbs. A few moments passed and Arames discovered his gaze still focused on the figure. He sniffed hard, shook his head, and moved his shoulders in an attempt to get his blood flowing.

I wonder what else Miss Tremaine has burning in that pot.

"Sirs, I bid you welcome to my shop and home."

Arames turned to find himself staring at beauty. When he had met Lane Niccols earlier in the day, Arames had felt an instant connection to the librarian, but he was unprepared to meet a woman such as Sarah Tremaine.

The seamstress stood, smiling. Arames noticed the counter between them only because it blocked his view of her lower half, which irritated him much more than it should have. Sarah wore a dress that was both elegant and revealing at the same time. Her fire-red hair flowed around her neck and tumbled over her shoulders. She was incomparable. Arames had seen a representation of one of the avatars of Iruna at a temple, and that came to mind—but it still was not Sarah Tremaine.

Sarah smiled patiently, and Arames realized belatedly that she was waiting for them to speak. Apparently, she was used to taking men's breath away. She looked from Arames to his companion, and then back. Arrin's jaw hung open at a somewhat unattractive angle. Arames considered saying something to him about it, but realized that his own was in the same embarrassing position. He closed his mouth; Arrin took the opportunity to seize control of the conversation.

"Miss Tremaine, my name is Arrin. Lord Avedon has asked us to investigate the murder of Gretta Platt. We have a few questions for you, if you don't mind?" Arrin moved forward—close enough to touch her—and completely blocked Sarah from Arames's view.

The seamstress's smile didn't waver. "Of course. Anything I can do to help."

"Thank you so much, Miss Tremaine... It is Miss Tremaine, isn't it?"

Arames was surprised that Arrin didn't follow with, "I am the grandson of King Renoir Perti of Yew... won't you come away with me?"

Arames moved to his right, far enough to see Sarah's face. She was blushing; Arames was suddenly sure she had the ability to blush at will. He found it hard to keep his jaw where it belonged when her eyelashes fluttered, as well. *The incense... Is it the incense doing this, or is it just her?*

"Yes, Arrin. Miss Tremaine is fine."

"Oh good... I mean, I'm glad I called you by your proper name... I mean—"

Sarah touched Arrin's arm, and his voice trailed off.

"What is it you need to ask me, Sir Arrin?"

Arrin held her gaze; it seemed to take him a moment to find his voice. "Miss Tremaine, where were you the night Gretta Platt was killed?"

Sarah stopped smiling but her face was still radiant. "Oh, my. Do you think I was involved somehow?"

⁂

It had been two days since Arrin's last bath, and he was suddenly quite aware of his current state. He ran his fingers through his hair, which only served to pull a good bit of it from his ponytail. "Oh, no, Miss Tremaine, we just need to ask this of everyone... to clear everyone we can, up front..."

Sarah smiled again. "Sarah..."

Arrin stared at her. "C-Come again?"

"Call me Sarah."

"Yes, of course."

Sarah took her hand away from Arrin's arm. He instantly felt lost. "I was here. Alone, I'm afraid. I live and work out of this building. I ate an early dinner at the inn, but I understand Gretta was killed later in the evening. I have no one who can vouch for my presence here."

"Thank you, Miss—Sarah. Did you know Gretta well?"

"She came here," Sarah glanced from Arrin to Arames and back, "once or twice a month, to check out fabrics. She never bought much. A plain dress, once or twice a year. She was beautiful, and I always wanted her to try new things. She wore her neckline too high for my tastes."

Arrin found it hard not to look toward Sarah's own neckline. Watching the rise and fall of her bosom, he could swear his breathing matched hers—but then Arames was beside him, speaking, and the spell seemed to break for a moment. "How does your business survive here, Miss Tremaine?"

Arames frowned at his own tone. It sounded almost harsh.

If it was, Sarah didn't seem to notice. She smiled. "Your garment needs mending, sir monk."

As Gloria Platt had noted earlier, Arames's robe was still tattered on one side. "I will return with it once I have time to change. Arames... Arames Kragen."

Sarah nodded in response to his name, and then addressed the monk's question. "I do very well here. I have—a sort of reputation. Merchants buy my fabrics and some of my dresses and resell them in other cities. The governor of Taxx uses my services, as do many in his court."

"Why do you stay here? Would you not do better in a more... prosperous location?"

Sarah smiled. "Possibly. But I love it here. I can do my job without distraction, without too many eyes watching over me—but I am still on a good trade route. And believe me, people travel out of their way for my services."

"I believe you, Miss Tremaine. I do."

"As to Gretta, I can't think of anyone who had a problem with her. She did her job well, and got along with everyone, as far as I know. I'm sorry I cannot be of more help."

Arrin spoke up. "No, thank you for your time. If you can think of anything... anything at all, please call on me—us."

"Oh, I will—and if you need anything, Sir Arrin. I'm here for you, as well."

"Good day to you, Miss Tremaine." Arames answered, before Arrin could say anything more; the monk pulled his student out of the building by the arm.

"What did you do that for?" There was fire in Arrin's eyes.

"Breathe, Arrin—breathe the air in. Then speak."

Arrin saw the worried look on Arames's face, and did as he asked. He focused on breathing in and out as Arames led him further away from the shop, heading west down the main path. "What do you feel?" asked Arames.

"I feel... light-headed. No, worse than that. I'm getting a headache now."

"But your head is clearing, is it not?"

Arrin stopped walking. "What just happened? Is she a sorceress?"

Arames smiled. "No, I think not. She is as beautiful and alluring as you perceived her to be. I believe, however, that she has filled her shop with some smells that... *heighten the mood,* so to speak."

"She is a seamstress. What is she doing?"

"I did not sense anything particularly sinister about her, but like much of Avedon Hill, Miss Tremain is not entirely what she seems. My guess is that we will have to revisit her at some point."

Arrin shook his head again, clearing the last of the scent from his senses. "Somewhere other than her shop, I hope."

"At least you held back from telling her who you were."

"I think I need a bath."

Arames laughed. "No, we should continue on! I want to visit the blacksmith next."

"What's his name?"

Arames consulted his notebook. "Herrjarr. He wasn't a favorite of the constable's, according to his notes. Let us see what he can tell us."

It looked to be a typical smithy, with a forge at the edge of the shop that Herrjarr could use either inside or outside. Arames knocked on the door, then entered. The blacksmith, unlike the smithy, was unlike any he had seen before. Herrjarr had Outworld blood in him.

"Surprised by the look of me, eh, Master Kragen?" The hulk of a man was disfigured by more than his orcish blood. His face and shoulders held the scars of multiple beatings.

Arames smiled at the blacksmith. "Well, that settles it. I am never going to pass as a simple traveler here."

Herrjarr made a guttural noise. Only the smile on the blacksmith's face told Arames it was a laugh. "I was at the butcher's shop when I heard you had been given consta... constab... what the 'ell is it?"

"Constabulary powers. To discover who murdered Gretta Platt."

Herrjarr brandished a great hammer he had been clutching tightly since Arames's arrival. "And who snatched her body."

"Common knowledge already?" Arames shook his head. "So, let us begin again. Yes, Herrjarr, I am surprised by your look. Your father was an orc?"

"Straight from the Rift, I'd expect. The monster took my mother and left her for dead. She was a tough woman, though, my mum. She fought for her life, and then fought for mine when her village tried to take me from her." He pointed to his face. "They were able to do this to me, but she kept me alive." Herrjarr laughed his grumble of a laugh again. "Broke the arm of the clan elder, too, so she told me later. So we left Inarra and made our way south. Lord Avedon accepted my mum and me, let us live here... and I trained under Lolch Svennet. I took over twelve years ago, when he died."

"Is your mother still here?"

"She died four—no, five years ago." Herrjarr set the hammer on a worktable and sat down on a bench. It strained under his huge frame. "Constable Louis send you to talk to me?"

"No. Louis just gave me a list of townspeople, and you were next on the list."

"Ah. Where's your lackey?"

Arames smiled. Arrin had remained outside to rest, his head still throbbing from the incense at the clothier's shop. "He's indisposed at the moment. You were here the night Gretta was murdered?" he asked, recalling the constable's notes.

"Yes, working on a sword for Lord Avedon. He's giving it to his son Richard at some sort of party."

"Can someone confirm that you were here?"

"Confirm? I have an apprentice, Ollus Wenk. He was here part of the night, but not all of it. I didn't do it. But I can't prove I didn't do it, other than by telling you I didn't do it." Herrjarr leaned forward for emphasis. "I didn't do it."

Arames nodded. "Did you know of anyone who had a reason to hurt Gretta Platt?"

Herrjarr shook his head. "No. I don't know anyone that would have. Do you think it really was a vampire?"

"I do not know, Herrjarr. You know where her body was found?"

"The courtyard?"

"Yes. If it was a vampire, it had to have access to the manor courtyard. And that is not likely... unless someone here in town is a vampire."

Herrjarr scrunched his nose in thought. "Vampires... They came through the Rift, just like my bastard father, didn't they?"

Arames shrugged. "Originally, maybe. Many creatures have entered Caern through the Great Rift, or through other portals from Outworld. Some think humans might have come through there, as well. We certainly know the Old Races have been in Caern much longer than we have."

"Hmmm... I had not heard that. I would like that, if my human blood came from the same place as my orc blood."

"It is not your blood that makes you who you are."

"HA! You are funny, Master Arames!"

Arames wasn't sure Herrjarr understood what he meant, but the blacksmith seemed to be in a good mood, so he didn't push the matter. After telling Herrjarr that he would return with more questions when he had them, Arames let himself out of the shop. Arrin was stretching just outside, and seemed much more clear-headed. "And how was Herrjarr?"

"Not what I expected." He explained as they headed north. A short time later, they stood in front of the general store. "Alex Dewirin, Owner. Let's go in."

The store was devoid of customers, as every other store had been. There was little need for shops to be open when travelers were not permitted to enter the town gates... but the general store served the town's few residents, and Alex Dewirin was happy to have anyone enter his doors.

"Good afternoon to you. I must assume you are Lord Avedon's investigators. I hope you'll have need of some of my goods... investigators or not." Alex flashed an inviting smile.

Arames nodded. "We will definitely need to stock up on provisions before we leave town. But for now, just some answers."

Alex rubbed his hands together. "Fire away."

"What do you make of this?" Arames pulled out the piece of curved metal from the courtyard.

The shopkeeper took the metal piece from Arames and studied it closely. He then turned and disappeared through a curtain-covered doorway. Arrin started forward to make sure he wasn't trying to run out a back door, but Arames motioned for him to stop. When Alex pushed the curtain aside and returned, he held the piece of metal in one hand and just the sort of tool Arames was expecting him to supply, in the other.

"It doesn't match exactly, but it sort of looks like this, don't you think?" He held out the tool—a three-pronged gardening fork. The broken piece of metal was shorter than the prongs of the gardening tool, but they were alike enough to suggest that the piece could have come from a similar implement. "Kell knows more about tools like this, but this is what it made me think of."

"May I see it for a moment?" Arames asked, and Alex Dewirin passed the fork over to him. The monk took out his notebook and opened it to a blank page, and then pressed the three points of the fork against the page and used his pen to mark the distance between them. Satisfied, Arames returned the tool to the shopkeeper in exchange for the broken prong.

After a few more questions, the two men were back on the main road, heading toward Avedon Manor.

Arrin asked, "Are we going to talk to Kell?"

"Not specifically. I think we have met almost everyone in town, other than Jilly Hemming. As you said earlier, the people at the manor had the most access to the courtyard, so we will need to speak to all of the manor help..."

"And the other Avedon children?"

"Jon was easy enough to talk to, and we did not seem to upset him. Hopefully we can *arrange* meetings with the other children, without offending Lord Avedon."

Arrin looked up at the sky. "The sun is beginning to set."

Arames sniffed the air around them. "Maybe Avedon Hill has more of a night life."

Arrin smirked to himself. *I doubt it.*

THE MANOR REVISITED

"Treygh turned his eyes from Caern,
and walked through the tears in the Fabric.
There he was met by the Tourim,
and they called him Father!"

—The Lay of Blame

It had been a long day, but Arames had one last stop to make before the sun crossed its threshold and day became night. He and Arrin hurried back to the northeast, again passing the town's graveyard.

Arames spied a makeshift tent in the cemetery. *Empty. Father Jorrus must still be at home preparing for tonight's graveyard vigil.*

Arrin still massaged his temples, lessening the pounding behind his eyes. His head was clear—whatever "spell" had affected him in Sarah Tremaine's shop had lost its hold on him—but the ache in his head lingered as a powerful after-effect. He glanced over at his mentor and tried not to be envious of Arames's quick recovery. *I should have begun my studies with the Aaronic Order when I was ten.*

They expected to meet a constable at the manor gate, but Lord Avedon had apparently given Louis and his men leave to resume their normal duties. Once inside the mansion, they were again greeted by Blake Weathertop, Lord Avedon's butler.

"Welcome back, sirs." His voice was tinged with only slightly veiled sarcasm.

Arames bowed his head slightly. "Blake, we have a request."

"Lord Avedon asked me to give you whatever you might need."

The monk pulled out his notebook and opened it. "We need to speak to Lord Avedon's manor help as a group—"

"Help... do you mean the staff?"

"Staff, yes. My apologies. If you would, please gather the staff in the great hall."

Blake Weathertop sniffed and turned on his heel, leaving them standing in the foyer.

Arrin leaned over Arames's shoulder. "He doesn't like us very much."

"I have concluded he does not like anyone very much."

The two men followed the path they had taken earlier that day and soon found themselves in the great hall. Lord Avedon was walking through at the same time, and approached them near the elaborate table in the center of the room. "Gentlemen... do you have news already?"

Arames smiled but shook his head. "Not much yet, Lord Avedon. You have already heard about Gretta's missing corpse."

Lord Avedon turned, pacing back and forth in front of the two men. "I could send the constables through the town, tearing down doors and searching every home."

"I'm not sure that would be wise. It is unlikely that Gretta's corpse is going to be found in someone's home. Either she has become one of the undead... or someone is taking great steps to make it look that way."

Lord Avedon stopped and faced Arames directly. "No. It wasn't a vampire killing. I'm just sure of it. But you're right... searching homes is not the answer."

"My lord, we are learning more about Gretta by the moment. I took the liberty of asking Blake to gather the manor staff here in the great hall. If you want to stay while we question them, I understand."

Avedon looked around at nothing in particular. "No... they will feel more comfortable without my presence. In any case, I am tired... very tired. I will retire for the night. Dine here after you are done with the staff. Chef Roland will take care of you."

Arames nodded. "Thank you, my lord, but Arrin and I will be eating at the inn this evening. Talik Bore has promised us an Olviaran Whitetail."

"Ah, yes... his specialty. Please come back tomorrow and report on your progress."

While Arames watched the distraught man leave, Blake entered the great hall with several servants, all dressed in white. Arrin directed the staff to sit at the table, facing him. Arames walked over and stood in front of the five expectant faces.

"Kell is not here?"

Blake answered. "No. He spent most of the day with Gloria Platt. He is probably at home, resting."

Arames addressed the group. "My name is Arames Kragen. As you certainly know by now, my student Arrin and I have been tasked with discovering who or what gained entry into Avedon Manor and murdered Gretta Platt." One of the ladies paled at his choice of words. "I am a monk of the Aarronic Order and a retired Aarronic Advisor. I care not who is high-born or low, who is rich and who is poor. Your position matters not to me. I care only for the truth... to uncover who committed this vile act. You will be helping me. You all knew Gretta. Even if you were not her friend, you knew her better than most. Together we will discover what happened that night."

Blake Weathertop had a disgusted look on his face. The four others looked at each other and then back to Arames.

Arames looked at the two women sitting beside each other, and then to his notes. "Brianna Ray... and Ally Morr?"

The older of the two servants spoke up. "I'm Ally, sir." Both women were attractive and young. Ally looked to be the more assertive of the two maids. "You were upstairs when Lord Avedon shouted that night?"

All eyes focused on the young maid. "Yes. I was dusting along the main upstairs hallway when I heard the shout. Then I heard Constable Ulrich running... saw him at the top of the stairs. It looked like he didn't know where the sound had come from. I pointed down, where I'd heard it from, and he ran off in that direction."

"What did you do then?"

"I didn't know what to do. I must have frozen for... I don't know how long. But I was near Sir Richard's bedroom, so I went to let him know."

"He's the oldest son?"

Ally nodded. "I knew all of the children were in their rooms, and that Lord Avedon had not come up for bed. I didn't know until later that it was Lord Avedon who had shouted. I woke up Sir Richard and he ran over to his brother's room."

"Which brother?"

"Edvard. He went into Edvard's room. I figured he would take care of the other children after that, so I went down the servants' stairs back to the kitchens."

Brianna broke in. "I was in the main kitchen sitting at a table, talking to one of the manor guards... Roc." Her eyes seemed to twinkle as she mentioned him. "Ally came running in, talking about a shout from somewhere in the manor. Roc, me, Ally, and Ley went together and eventually found everyone in the courtyard... poor Gretta."

"No one in the kitchens heard the shout?"

Brianna replied, "Roc heard something, but the kitchens are noisy... ovens blazing, pots being scrubbed... no one was sure until Ally came down."

Arames looked at his notes. "Ley?"

A boy of twelve or thirteen sitting beside Chef Roland stood up. "Me, sir... Ley Nallon... Chef's assistant."

Arrin asked, "You're a bit young to be a chef's assistant, aren't you?"

Chef Roland pulled Ley back down into his chair. "It helps that he's my son. He washes dishes mostly, Master Arrin."

Arames kept writing. "And you, Roland? Where were you during this time?"

"In the back kitchen, cutting vegetables and preparing for the next morning's meal. I didn't hear anything until Ley came and got me."

"And you, Blake? Where were you?"

The butler wrinkled his nose. "I was given leave to retire early. I had been here late several evenings in a row and the Housemistress was kind enough to dismiss me just before sundown. I have a house near the town gate."

"Do you live with anyone?"

A snicker escaped from Ally Morr. Blake shot a nasty glare in her direction. "I live alone. I have never been married. The prospects here are... less than appealing."

Arames cleared his throat. "The point is... no one saw you that night?" Blake shook his head no, and Arames changed the subject. "Do any of you know of anyone who had problems with Gretta, either personally or professionally?"

No one said anything, but Arames sensed a change in Chef Roland's posture. He made eye contact with the chef before moving on.

"Was there anything about her job or her personal life that I should know about... anything that might help us in our investigation?"

Again, there was no response from the staff at first. Ally spoke up after a moment. "We all want to help you, but Miss Gretta was the Housemistress. She might have been manor staff, but she wasn't one of us, if you understand my meaning. Whatever was her business wasn't any of ours, that's for sure."

Everyone but Weathertop nodded. He sat motionless, waiting for the interview to end.

"Did any of you, on that day, or on any other day, see anyone in or around the manor who didn't belong... or seemed out of place?"

After a short pause, Brianna raised her hand. "One day I saw Jilly Hemming sitting in the courtyard by herself. She was crying."

Ally pulled Brianna's hand down. "Oh, that's not so strange. Miss Gretta had Jilly over lots of times... not so much in the past couple of years, but she was always welcome here."

Arames smiled. "No, Brianna... thank you. Even if it does not mean anything, that is exactly the type of information we need."

After writing a bit more in his notebook, Arames tucked it away in a pocket of his robe. "Thank you all very much. We will most likely speak to each of you individually in the days to come." They all stood and began walking away. "Remember, we only seek justice here. We are not here to get any of you into trouble with Lord Avedon. So, if you can think of anything at all, please let us know."

Blake Weathertop snorted. "Unless you think one of us was involved—then we'll be in plenty of trouble with Lord Avedon." He walked away as quickly as he could.

Arrin whispered, "I've got my sights set on that one, master..."

Arames looked around at the others in the room. Once he was sure no one was looking, he gave a hand signal to Arrin, who immediately followed after Blake. Arames moved quickly and stopped Roland before he could leave. For the benefit of those walking away, Arames said, "Chef Roland, I would like to speak to you about tomorrow's menu, if I could."

After a few moments, the others were out of range. Arames addressed the chef again. "Roland, was there something you wanted to tell us?"

Chef Roland appeared confused. "What do you mean?"

"What did you want to say about Blake?"

The man looked down at the ground for a moment. "Nothing really, Sir Arames. I just wanted to say that he never liked Gretta much... or any of the Platts, for that matter. His family has been here with the Avedons just as long, and he has always been jealous of the Platts. Even now, he is trying to get in Lord Avedon's business... trying to do things that only the Housemistress is supposed to do. He is really the only person who might profit from Gretta's death."

"But Gloria said that her niece would eventually take over as Housemistress... if this is the case, how will Blake Weathertop profit?"

"Ah... Miss Selene. All I can say is that Miss Selene isn't here right now, is she, sir?" With that, Chef Roland walked back toward the kitchens. Arames sat at the table and waited for Arrin.

Arames waited longer than expected, but eventually Arrin returned and took a seat beside him. "Blake went down the hallway we came up before and went into one of the doors along the hall. I listened at the door but I didn't go in. It looked to be a room and not another hallway. Then I went outside and looked around the front of the manor for a time. Blake came out the main door, cloak over his shoulders, and walked down the path toward the gate. I guess he was done for the day."

"Did he see you?"

Arrin nodded. "Yes. But I was far enough away from the door and searching in some bushes... like I was looking for something in particular. I don't think he realized I had followed him out."

"It does not matter. While the chef believes that Blake might be the sort who would kill to get ahead, I simply do not see it."

Arrin nodded, but looked like he still hoped Blake was somehow involved. "Not evil enough?"

"No, not brave enough... and certainly not smart enough to get away with it."

Both men stood and returned their chairs to the table. Arames studied the empty hall, then started toward the door that had led them to the courtyard earlier in the day. "So, are you ready to do some exploring?"

"Is this a good idea?"

"Do not worry, Arrin. Just let me do the talking if we are discovered."

The guard who had been stationed outside the great hall was no longer there. Arames suspected that the two guards on duty inside the manor were making their rounds, but had no idea where they might be. They had passed by the several doors along the hallway earlier that day. Now they took the time to listen at each one.

"This is the one." Arames said, standing beside the third door. Arrin looked at him quizzically. Arames added, "There is more air flow around this door."

Arames opened the door to find that it led to another hallway, but this one widened and eventually reached a set of stairs leading up to the second floor. The hallway continued around the stairs, but the second floor was Arames's destination.

The landing at the top of the stairs opened up to a rather large room, most likely the children's main gathering place. Desks and books were along one of the walls, and there was comfortable furniture in the center of the room—there was even an area for fencing in one corner.

"It's very quiet. Where is everyone?"

"I do not know. Let us go this way."

To the left side of the great room a hallway exited to the east. As they turned the corner they ran into Brianna Ray, sweeping the floor. "S-Sir Arames... Sir Arrin..." She curtsied. "Y-You aren't supposed to be up here, are you?"

Three doors stood along the south side of the northernmost hallway, with a fourth at the end of the corridor. "Just following up on Ally's description of events. You can help us, my dear."

Brianna shook her head quickly, mouth hanging slightly open. "I—I don't think that I should be doing that."

Arames took the broom from Brianna's hands and passed it to Arrin. "Arrin will sweep for you. Come with me." He turned her and led her down the hallway.

"Oh... sir... please be very quiet... Lord Avedon and some of the children are in their rooms."

Arames looked at the doors along the corridor. He whispered, "The door at the end of the hall... Lord Avedon's room?" Brianna nodded. "And these doors?"

Brianna pointed to the door closest to Lord Avedon's room. "Julienne, the youngest..." Arames heard a short whistle from behind him, coming from Arrin's direction, while Brianna pointed to each door in turn. "Jon... Edvard... Carin..."

"And Richard," a new voice cut in. A gasp escaped from Brianna's mouth and she turned to face Lord Avedon's oldest son. Arames looked past Richard at Arrin, still holding the broom, lips still pursed to alert Arames with a second whistle.

"Brianna, you should go." There was no mistaking Richard Avedon's tone. Eighteen and his father's heir, he carried himself with confidence and spoke with command. Brianna, stuttering and stammering, started in one direction, then spun and ran in the other. She grabbed her broom, nearly knocking Arrin down, and continued on to a door that Arames assumed led to the servants' staircase.

From the portraits Arames had studied along the entry halls earlier that day,

Richard resembled his mother more than his father. Arames told him as much.

"My mother died when I was thirteen. I may look like her, but I'd rather have her here so I could try to be like her. I'll never know how much of her is really in me."

There was unmistakable pain in Richard... but strength, as well. "I did not mean to offend, Sir Richard."

He shrugged off the apology. "Why are you up here? If you had not been with Brianna... People around here seem to trust you, but do not forget who you are and who we are. Wandering the hallway outside the unprotected rooms of Lord Avedon's children... people have been put to death for less, here in Grozh... no?"

While Yew was ruled by its royal family, with different levels of dukes and counts and mayors governing under the direction of King Perti, Grozh was a different story. Each city or town's ruler—including Lord Avedon—ultimately answered to the Council of Grozh, but within that structure, each ruler operated with a high degree of independence. As a result, laws, definitions of crimes, and levels of punishment, often differed from one city or town to the next. Trespassing might be punishable by death in some areas of Grozh, but Arames doubted that was the case in Avedon Hill. Arames knew that Richard was only probing, not actually threatening him.

"Sir Richard, your father did ask us not to cause you or your siblings any more pain than you have already endured, but we are just following up on some things that Ally Morr told us earlier. Maybe you can help us fill in the gaps, since you told Brianna to leave?"

Richard sighed. "As long as we are quiet. Julienne is already asleep."

"Of course..." After introducing Arrin to Richard, Arames continued. "Ally said she was dusting along this hall when she heard your father call out."

When Richard nodded, Arames asked, "How could she hear the shout from here, when others downstairs could not hear, or at least could not tell where the shout came from?"

Richard smiled. He pointed to the northern side of the hall where the doors were. "Bedrooms behind those doors." He then pointed to the southern wall of the corridor. "Behind that wall... what do you think?"

Arrin's internal compass may have been compromised in the confusion of the labyrinth under the manor and mountain, but he was able to see the layout of the manor in his head. "The courtyard."

Richard nodded. "Yes. The walls of the courtyard reach to the top of the manor, and the northern wall of the courtyard is on the other side of this wall."

Arames noted the young man's proud tone. "You enjoy talking about the manor?"

"Avedon Manor is an architectural wonder. You have seen the courtyard, how the manor was constructed around the entrance to the Olviaran Pass. You have even seen the catacombs underneath the manor. There are many elements here that cannot be found in any other building in Caern, and it was built over three hundred years ago."

Arames again pulled out his notebook. His hand became a blur as he wrote. "Ally said she went to your room and knocked?"

Richard couldn't tear his eyes from Arames's hand. "Um... yes, that is correct. I was sleeping, and didn't hear my father shout. I heard Ally knock, and it took me a moment to get dressed and get to the door. She was knocking, but she hadn't said anything, so I didn't know what was going on. She looked a little frightened, because she was alone and didn't know what had happened. She told me she had heard a shout, and that Constable Ulrich had come up the stairs, and that she had directed him back down again."

Arames moved toward the third door along the corridor. "Ally said you went directly to your brother Edvard's room... here?"

Richard Avedon moved between Arames and the door, barring his way. "Yes. I went to Edvard's room first, and then the others."

"We met Jon earlier today. A great rider, isn't he?"

"Yes... Jon is a wonderful horseman."

"You said Julienne is asleep. Where are Edvard and Carin?"

"Carin is probably downstairs in the kitchens. She mentioned a little while ago that she was hungry. And Edvard is in his room."

"You did not say that before."

Richard smiled. "I didn't say he wasn't. I only asked you to be quiet because Julienne is asleep. Edvard has been ill, I'm afraid. He has had a fever for a couple of days now, and needs his rest."

Arames nodded. "I'm sorry to hear that. Might we meet him? We just want everyone to get used to our faces."

Richard held out his arm. "If his fever breaks tonight as we expect, then you can meet him tomorrow. He always seems to get sick for a couple of days when the weather changes."

Arames looked into Richard's eyes, searching for something. "That will be fine..."

Richard lowered his arm. "Unless you would like me to get my father. I believe he is in his room, as well."

"That won't be necessary." Arames moved back down the corridor and into the great room. He thought for a moment while studying his notes.

Richard asked, "Is that all for now? I was on my way downstairs."

The monk smiled. "Just a couple more questions, if you don't mind."

Richard was agitated, but nodded. Arames tapped his notebook with his pen. "You didn't go down to the courtyard?"

"Not until much later... only after Constable Ulrich came up and told me what had happened. I suspected the shout had come from the courtyard, based on where Ally had been when she'd heard it, but my responsibility is to my brothers and sisters first. I knew the guards were downstairs. I had to make sure everyone was safe up here."

Arames looked back down the corridor behind Richard. "That makes sense... thank you for your time, Sir Richard."

"Let me show you out." Richard led them back down the stairs and to the front door of the manor in silence. Arrin slowed once or twice to look more closely at the Avedon family portraits that Arames had mentioned. He noted that Edvard bore the most resemblance to their father.

Arames and Arrin stepped outside and Richard started to close the door behind them. Night had fallen and it was now completely dark. "I'm sure we'll speak again tomorrow, Sir Arames."

"Yes, thank you again. I'm sorry, one more question..."

Richard stopped the door. Only his head could be seen in the darkened doorway. "Yes?"

"Why Edvard?"

Richard sounded confused. "Come again?"

Arames smiled, even though Richard probably couldn't see his face in the darkness. "You skipped Carin's bedroom and went to Edvard's first. I was just wondering why you didn't check on Carin first?"

The darkness hid Richard's face, but Arames didn't need to see it to know that Richard was on the defensive. After a few moments of silence, Richard finally responded. "I... I don't really... well, to tell you the truth, it was just instinct. Edvard is the next in line after me, even though Carin is older. And even though Carin's room is closest to mine, Edvard is the first sibling I think to protect."

Richard closed the door before Arames had a chance to thank him again for his time. For the first time since their arrival, Arames felt a real chill in the air. "Winter is coming fast, young Arrin."

Arrin started walking toward the manor gates. "We're going to have trouble with him, too, aren't we?"

"We shall see... we shall see. Hungry? There is some venison cooking for us right now... my nose is tingling."

"I just want to get off my feet. Maybe Jon will let us borrow one of his horses tomorrow."

"Come, lad. This is good exercise."

"Yes, *master*."

Arames laughed as they walked back to the Avedon Hill Inn.

The End of the Day

*Artus will break the binds that hold him
and enter Kalin's Abyss.*

—3rd Collected Prophecies of Iberian, Book 2, Chapter 4

ARAMES AND ARRIN MADE their way down the manor road back into Avedon Hill, again passing the temple and Cousin Red's darkened home. Arames assumed his cousin must be at the inn. Arames noticed smoke rising from Father Jorrus's chimney. "Arrin, you go on. I must speak to Father Jorrus."

Arrin looked at his mentor, one eyebrow raised. "Are you sure? I can stay here with you."

Arames reached out and placed both hands on Arrin's shoulders, then gave him a playful push along the path. "No, I need you to get our room ready for the evening and order our dinner. I will need a hot meal waiting for me when I arrive. But first I need some advice from our retired cleric."

Arrin frowned but didn't argue, continuing down the path and into the night. There was a greater chill in the air now, and it would only get colder as the days passed. If he and Arrin were not able to solve the murder quickly, it would not matter if Lord Avedon gave them access to the Olviaran Pass. After the first real snowstorm of the winter, portions of the Pass would become inaccessible.

Arames approached Jorrus's home and rapped his knuckles on the doorframe. "Father Jorrus?! It is Arames Kragen. May we speak?"

Arames heard movement inside the home. Through a covered window, a light that had been burning low grew brighter. Soon thereafter, the door opened. Father Jorrus's eyes were blank, and he seemed not to recognize the monk. But then the priest sniffed loudly and his eyes came in to focus. He reached out and grasped Arames by the arm.

"Kragen! Where's your boy? He looked like he might be able to help me fight tonight."

"Are you expecting an attack tonight?"

"Oh yes, always."

"Father Jorrus, what is your evening routine?"

He loosened his grip slightly. "I will go to the cemetery after Last Bells. Bah, I forget that Lord Avedon has ordered our bells silent."

"Do you expect vampires?"

Father Jorrus let go of Arames's arm. "No, I don't expect an attack on consecrated ground. But it is a good, open high area—I can see a great deal of the town from there."

"Father, I have a question—but not about vampires."

The cleric shook his shoulders and arms, as if loosening up before battle. "Yes?"

"I ran into a moon-beast in one of the caves east of town, larger than any wolfling I have ever seen. I was wondering if you had ever come across them during your travels."

His eyes lit angrily. "A moon-beast? Damnable druid-spawn. Tell me about it."

Arames left out his reason for being in the caves, but described the moon-beast and its two wolf companions. He showed Jorrus his robes, tattered by claws and teeth. He described the intelligence in the beast's eyes, and how it had fled once its counterparts had been dispatched.

"Ha! So your student *is* a fighter."

Arames attempted to direct Jorrus back to their conversation. "Father, if during the course of our investigation we find ourselves in a position to help you in your fight, we will be right by your side. But, the moon-beast?"

"You said you sensed a human-like intelligence in the beast?"

"Yes, it definitely assessed the situation and fled accordingly."

"A shifter, possibly."

"What do you mean?" Arames knew the term, but wanted Jorrus to say more.

Father Jorrus pointed a crooked finger at the monk. "You know the story of Orrence Po?"

"He was the Knight of the Rose who captured a moon-beast."

Father Jorrus's eyes focused distantly for a moment. "Yes... he should have been a Hunter, not wasted his time—" He sniffed loudly, and did not elaborate further.

Arames smiled to himself. Jorrus's dislike of the Priests of Caern—the followers of Iberian, who had displaced him as temple leader in Avedon Hill—apparently carried over to the paladins who served them.

Jorrus blinked and returned to his story. "There is part of the tale you probably have never heard. Since I no longer 'work' for anyone, I don't mind sharing certain 'secrets.' What do you know of Po's story?"

"I know that, at least three hundred years ago, Orrence Po trapped a moon-beast in a cave and sent his page for reinforcements. The Knights had been trying to capture a moon-beast alive for years. It took ten days for his attendant to return with a quad of paladins. When they arrived, they removed the stone that had blocked the entrance to the cave and found only a corpse—human—and two bloody words scratched into the dirt of the cave floor: *Help me*."

Jorrus took up the tale. "Official reports blamed Orrence Po for allowing a human to get trapped in the cave with the beast. The fact that there were no other exits from the cave and that the body found in the cave had not been mauled was never explained... officially, of course."

Arames continued. "Unofficially, it was always assumed that the beast had died at some point during the ten days and had changed into human form. And in his dying moments he wrote the message found on the ground."

"Well, here's the part you never heard. Orrence Po never spoke of the events again—until his deathbed. He described what happened in that cave to his page, the same valet who had been with him then. Orrence confessed that during those ten days, he heard the most horrible things from that cave—screams both animal and human. He thought at first he had somehow missed someone in the cave, and that the beast was torturing the man. Orrence tried to free the man, but the rock he had used to block the entrance was too heavy and he couldn't move it without aid. After the first day or so, he began to realize that the sounds coming from inside the cave were from one creature."

Arames nodded. "It was changing from wolf to human and back again."

Jorrus answered, "Yes. Orrence tried to communicate with its human form. The human voice was insane, unable to speak coherently...until the ninth day. The beast was dying—from a lack of water, most likely. It leaned against the stone and talked as a child would, about a farm in Inarra, about being taken by men on horseback, about a man who could change from man to beast with a thought."

"A shifter."

"Possibly. I believe the beast in the cave was a shifter that didn't know how to control the change." He paused, collecting his thoughts. "Moon-beasts are created when humans are attacked and bitten by other moon-beasts, and survive. Most victims transform into beasts permanently after a few days. A few change forms uncontrollably; some say they follow the cycles of the moon."

Arames finished his thought. "And a very few are shape-*shifters*, who can change form at will."

Father Jorrus nodded. "And if you encountered such a shifter, our problems are not limited to the undead. Shifters retain more of their humanoid intelligence than other moon-beasts, and can control other animals as well."

Arames had heard many legends of moon-beasts, and knew several stories of the Child Ursala—she often chose to live out her lives on Caern as a shape-shifter. "Well, as far as Gretta's murder is concerned, her wounds could not have been made by a moon-beast, correct?"

Jorrus smiled. "I never saw Gretta's body, but from the description I heard, I would have to say no. They would have torn out her throat, as well as the rest of her insides. Hers was a vampire killing, to be sure."

Arames didn't return the smile. "Thank you for your time, Father Jorrus. Until tomorrow..."

"You should come to the cemetery tonight. There is something in the air..." Father Jorrus flared his nostrils.

"Tonight we sleep. There is much we must prepare, for tomorrow. I wish you luck."

"To you, as well. You'd better take shifts sleeping if you aren't with me."

Arames nodded. "I will take that under advisement, Father Jorrus. Good evening to you."

Arames bowed and excused himself. Father Jorrus grumbled something inaudible and went back inside his home.

A short time later, over a perfectly seasoned bowl of venison stew at the inn, Arames passed along some of what Father Jorrus had told him.

Arrin was excited to hear more about the moon-beast. "Do you think that the shifter could be someone in town?"

"I do not think so, but I have been wrong before. More importantly... it seems that the creature was uninvolved in the murder. It is something we can rule out. And besides, we don't know the beast was a shifter. We just know it was intelligent, and that it was traveling with other wolves. We have only the word of a former undead hunter and some old legends to confirm that shifters even exist."

Talik stopped by their table for a chat, regaling them with a story of a spice merchant he wanted to bring to town. Arames made several small gestures with his right hand, and Arrin took his cue. Feigning a headache, he asked Talik who he needed to talk to about drawing a bath, which pulled Talik from the table. The two left together.

Arames took the opportunity to open his notebook and study what he had written during the day, comparing it to what Constable Louis had provided. Several of the townspeople could explain their whereabouts the night Gretta was murdered, but some could not. Arames's first task was to whittle away at the list of possible suspects.

The question of motive had been bothering him all day. The high-walled courtyard was too difficult to access, proving to Arames that this was not some random vampire attack—either a vampire had a reason to kill Gretta, or someone had taken great pains to make it appear so.

Then there was Gretta's personal life. No one admitted to knowing anyone with whom she might have been involved, yet when she took her excursions outside of town she carried at least enough food for two.

Greed was certainly a motive to consider. The position of Housemistress held more power than he had realized. Gretta seemed to control access to Lord Avedon himself. If someone wanted something—anything—from Lord Avedon, they had to go through her.

Why were you killed, Gretta Platt? Greed, jealousy, or some unseen agenda?

Satisfied with his plan for the next morning, Arames closed his notebook and continued his meal. His cousin peeked his head out from the kitchen. Arames invited him over with a wave.

Red limped to the table and sat down. Arames asked, "Why not have Father Livasdawn or Marrissa take a look at that leg of yours?"

He threw his folded dishtowel over his shoulder. "It's not an injury. It's like I said. It's just age-pains. It doesn't hurt that much."

Arames shrugged. "If you say so." He took another bite. "Did you cook this?"

"Talik does most of the cooking, but I helped out some tonight."

"This is great stew."

Red smiled. "Talik may know little about business, but he could fill the Abyss with what he knows about cooking. That venison has been soaking in a garlic marinade for three days. Talik gives Chef Roland a run for his money, even without the manor's fine ingredients."

Arames nodded again as he chewed. It felt good to have some time with his cousin.

Red looked around and whispered, "Don't want Talik to find me sitting here. He should be busy with our young Arrin for a while though, eh?" Arames knew 'our young Arrin' was a reference to his student's lineage. "How is your investigation going, cousin?"

"Still too early to tell. We have met everyone in town who had any sort of access to Gretta Platt, other than Jilly Hemming and the blacksmith's apprentice."

"Ollus Wenk?"

Arames nodded. "Tomorrow we will speak to everyone without an alibi—try to find out if anyone had motivation to kill her."

Red stood up. "Well, good luck, Arames. Since it is slow again tonight, Talik should let me go home soon. I should be there most of tomorrow. You can stop by if you like." He actually sounded somewhat hopeful.

"If there is any way I can, I will. Thanks, Red."

"No worries—see you, cousin." Red bowed his head slightly, and walked back to the kitchen.

Arames finished his meal in peace. Leilah entered the common room and began clearing the table just as Arames folded his hand towel, as if on cue. It was the first he had seen of her since the morning.

"Good evening to you, Sir Arames."

"And to you, Leilah."

Leilah smiled. She still seemed a little uneasy, however, and Arames didn't want to scare the maid off again. "How busy do you get when the town is open to travelers, Leilah?

"Oh, never very busy... that's why Talik only has me and Red working here. I know he'd love to have a bustling inn with a full staff and twenty patrons a night, but that just isn't Avedon Hill."

Arames tested the waters. "You understand we have been asked by Lord Avedon to investigate the events that occurred at the manor last week?"

Leilah nodded. "Yes, Sir Arames."

"I am too tired to ask you anything this evening. We can talk tomorrow. I just want you to think about Gretta and the other townspeople—if anything comes to mind that might help us, please let me know."

Leilah didn't flee as she had that morning, but looked concerned nonetheless. "What do you mean?"

Arames replied, "If you remember anyone acting peculiar, or anything that seemed out of place over these last few weeks, I would like to hear about it."

"Yes, Sir Arames."

The monk smiled and patted the maid's hand. "Good. Now answer me this... how many bathtubs are in my room?"

"One, Sir Arames."

"Okay, then. Please bring me one of those ales that people keep telling me about. When Arrin is done with his bath and the water has been changed, please let me know."

"Yes, Sir Arames."

"And please just call me Arames, Leilah... please?"

"Yes, Sir... yes, Arames."

Arrin ran his fingers through his long blond hair, shaking out the excess water. He was dressed for sleep and looking forward to climbing into the soft bed. Arames lounged in the bathtub, relaxing.

"Arrin, please pull out my other robes. These will have to be mended."

Arrin smiled. "Should I take them to Sarah Tremaine's shop tomorrow?"

"We will see. I don't want you going into her establishment alone, I think."

Arames saw the mirth in Arrin's eyes. "I don't think you should go in there alone either."

Arames slid down so that the water covered his head. A few moments later he bobbed back up. "Perhaps... but I trust myself more than I trust you." He was only half-joking.

Arrin pulled out Arames's clothes and sat on the edge of his bed. Arames would enjoy his bath as long as the water remained warm. "Do you need anything else?"

Arames looked over and shook his head. "No, get some sleep. I will be up for a while, and I'll wake you when I can no longer sit watch."

"Watch? We don't really need to do that, do we?"

"I have to agree with Father Jorrus. While I am not expecting an undead attack, by now everyone in town, including Gretta's murderer, knows we are investigating her death. Three constables and a few manor guards will not keep us safe if the killer decides to get to us first."

Arrin threw his head back onto his pillow. "Wake me when you need me."

⁂

Light... enveloping me... holding me... carrying me... oh the rapture—
The light extinguishes in an instant.
AHH... darkness? why do you come? NOT again...
Images and sensations rush by, unhindered by the darkness. The feeling of movement threatens to overpower her, the colors of a kaleidoscope transformed by a windstorm.
Childhood to adulthood... life unto death.... unto life...
Open eyes... open... light... no, not light... not light...
The rapture is gone... the nothing leaves a hole as wide as the ocean ... the pain of life could never match the nothing she now felt...
How can this be? move... move... I cannot... I cannot... how does this work...?
What should be a hand cannot reach her mouth, her face.
Try again... where am I? who am I?
"Az... Iruna... save me..."
smell... blood?... who... what... water... not blood...
"Az and his Children cannot save you... You are lost to Him."
The voice... not mine, is it? isn't it?
The nothing is replaced with skin peeling from flesh— The voice that she knows is not hers speaks to her through the pain. "Now, we talk."
*No!!! ...*The pain overwhelms the nothing in an instant.
Oh, how could I have been so wrong?

To Sleep

Dreams are the passage between day and night,
between Caern and Kalin's Abyss,
between The Land and The River

—High Priest Kallan, the Sisters of Kaelee

ARAMES STOOD AT THE room's only window, fully dressed for action and looking out over the town in a northerly direction. The moon, nearly full, illuminated much of the lower half of the town, including the town circle—he could even see smoke rising from the bakery and from several nearby homes. To the east of the inn, Arames spied some small structures that appeared to be one-room homes. Weeds and grasses hid any paths that might have led to them.

Far in the distance at the top of a rise, Arames could make out the faintest outline of the town's cemetery. It was well past Last Bells and he was sure Father Jorrus was at the cemetery by now. Even now, Arames instinctively sensed when the temple bells should be rung. He attributed it to being more attuned to the Land and its cycles than most.

Temples dedicated to Az and his ten Children could be found throughout Caern, and despite their various differences all followed the same schedule of the Bells. Four sets were rung daily: the Bells of Dawn rang in the morning; Worship Bells followed two cykes later, signifying the start of organized worship rituals; Bells of Dusk rang out in the evening; and Last Bells came four cykes after the Bells of Dusk. In addition, there were special 'songs' for each Child of Az (and Az himself), for which bells were rung weekly or on special holy days throughout the ten months of the year.

The Bells of Dawn and the Bells of Dusk were not rung at sunrise and sunset. One of the great achievements of the Priests of Caern was the development of a water-driven time mechanism that allowed all temples across Caern to ring the four common Bells at exactly the same time.

Even though Lord Avedon had given the order to silence the bells at the temple, Arames heard Last Bells in his mind when they should have been rung. He hoped he would have the opportunity to actually hear them before they left Avedon Hill. As Father Jorrus had stated, the temple had a grand set of bells.

Comforted by the lack of movement on the town streets, Arames decided it would be safe to return to the inn's common room. Since the inn was the only business open after sundown, Arames wondered if anyone might be visiting, possibly sampling Talik's ale. He double-checked the lock on the window, and then performed another thorough search of the room's walls and floor. He may not have been a cutpurse like his own mentor Drona Twoblade had been, but Arames felt confident that no one could access the room without using the only door. And to get to that door, one would have to pass through the common room.

All the tables downstairs were empty, save for one. In the back corner Cletus and Talik Bore sat at a booth. Talik didn't notice Arames's approach. Only after Cletus ticked his head to the left, nodding it toward Arames, did Talik realize the monk stood by their table. Talik stood and bowed slightly.

"I'm so sorry, Sir Arames. I thought you'd gone to bed. Is there anything you need? An ale, perhaps?"

Arames thought on it. "I guess I can manage one more ale this evening." He took the seat Talik had vacated. "Bring us both a mug… and another bowl of that stew."

Cletus, eating one of the largest plates of food Arames had ever seen, shook his head and let out a large belch. Talik gathered up three empty flagons from in front of Cletus. "Thank you but no, Sir Monk. I have to get back to the gate soon."

"Who is watching it now?"

"Constable Tanner. I get a couple of hours here and there to eat or bathe."

Talik, already on his way to the kitchen, called, "He saves time by not bathing, I think."

Cletus picked his teeth with the point of a small knife. "Good one." He looked over at the monk, who was smiling back at him. "So, how was your first day in Avedon Hill?"

"Well, I was not evicted by Lord Avedon, so that was a start."

Apparently finding his second wind, Cletus started in on the rack of ribs on his plate. "So, you gonna tell me what you ran into outside of town?"

Arames knew Cletus hadn't missed his tattered robes when they had returned from the caves. Cletus never missed much, Arames suspected. Even though he had consulted Father Jorrus about the moon-beast, he was not ready to acknowledge the beast as a danger to Avedon Hill... yet. "We had some trouble with some of the indigenous fauna. We survived." Arames smiled.

Cletus raised an eyebrow, but didn't press the subject. Talik returned to the table with ale and a steaming bowl of venison stew for Arames. Along with the food,

Talik also brought a chair from another table. He joined them and began telling Arames about a man who lived in southern Inarra who could call down rain on a clear day. "You would pay good money to see that, wouldn't you, Sir Arames?"

Cletus interrupted. "For Doppin's sake, Talik. Do you actually think a Brother of Aarron would pay to see some charlatan predict the weather?"

Talik turned on Cletus. "You're just jealous. Rules or no, we could make some real money here if the Avedons just gave me a chance—"

Cletus held up a hand. "Do us a favor, Talik. Go clean the Estates and get them ready for next spring."

Arames didn't understand Cletus's reference, but it certainly elicited the desired response from the innkeeper. Talik's face turned three shades of red as he stood. Sounds escaped from Talik's mouth, but he was unable to form actual words. Whether it was because he was in the presence of a potential returning customer or because he feared Cletus's girth, Talik stormed off without saying another word.

Cletus laughed out loud. "At last... peace."

Arames allowed himself a smile. "What did you mean, 'Estates'?"

Cletus finished chewing before answering. "I hope you didn't mind. You're a new set of ears. You'll be hard-pressed to keep him quiet."

"So I have learned."

The gateman continued. "Talik has a good heart, and you can't deny his entrepreneurial spirit. But his ideas, for lack of a better phrase, could suck the life out of a *Talin* tree."

"The Estates?"

Cletus held up a bone as a pointer. "Ah, yes... the Avedon Hill Estates. Talik got it in his skull that if he only had better accommodations, the merchants and traders that use the Pass would stay in town longer. So he built some small one-room homes and named them the Avedon Hill Estates.'

"Are those the buildings to the east of the inn?"

Cletus nodded. "You saw them, then. Of course, Talik didn't understand that Avedon Hill is in no way a stopping point for traders... just a pause on a journey. The longer patrons stay here, the longer it is before they reach their destinations." Cletus had been watching Arames eating his stew. "You gonna eat those dainties?"

Arames shook his head. "No, do you want them?"

Cletus coughed out a laugh and used the sharp end of the bone in his hand to expertly spear the orbs floating in the monk's bowl. "I love me some dainties!"

Arames cleared his throat, steering Cletus back from deer testicles to the topic at hand. "What did Talik mean by 'rules'?"

Cletus shrugged. "What...? Oh, that. The Avedons have kept this town afloat because they understand the town's strengths—which aren't many. They don't waste the town's resources on foolhardy schemes to turn short-term visitors into long-term ones."

Arames wanted to explore this topic further, but it was Cletus's turn to change the subject. "So, has anyone talked to you about the other killings?"

Economics were suddenly quite far from Arames's mind. "What *other* killings?"

Arrin found himself walking down a path overgrown with weeds that moved, stretched, and receded, as if they were living creatures reaching out to touch his ankles. In the distance they thickened, extending high into the air, obscuring a building with tall, rock walls. The rocks crumbled, falling away, crushing the weeds and tree limbs. Debris rolled and bounced erratically down the path toward Arrin.

Arrin found himself standing in someone's home. He was no longer dressed as Arames's valet, but as the prince that he was... and, as in many of his dreams, he wore his grandfather's crown. He carried the Scepter of Yew, which—as the laws of his land dictated—gave him the power over life and death. Arrin looked around. He was in the great hall of Avedon Manor. "I need to hide... they can't discover who I am." Lord Avedon called from behind him, "King Arrin, how good of you to come." Arrin turned; the lord's left arm was outstretched. He raised it above his head. Ten archers looked down from balconies he had not seen, bows drawn. Lord Avedon dropped his arm, and arrows flew at Arrin from all directions.

Arrin blinked and found himself dressed in his traveling garments, and felt his sword strapped to his back. Wildfire radiated heat through the scabbard and through two layers of clothing. A pull at a leather strap on his chest and a twist of his shoulder brought his sword into reach. When he pulled it free, it gleamed as if it had just been lifted from a forge. "Why do you glow? You are not magic." Even so, Arrin swung it before him, just now noticing his surroundings. He was in a cavern not unlike the cave they had fought in that morning. The dirt and stone beneath his feet began to bubble, transforming into liquid. He jumped away to solid ground, turning to look at the gurgling mass. The light of his sword suddenly became flame. A form began to emerge from the mass—arms, torso, legs—the mud fell away, revealing a woman... a younger Gloria Platt, but with lighter hair... beautiful, yet with eyes that held no life. She opened her mouth and a hiss escaped between the pointed teeth of a vampire. Arrin held his sword between himself and—he could only assume—Gretta Platt.

Behind him, Arrin heard the growl of a beast. His sword still pointing at Gretta, Arrin turned to see a moon-beast preparing itself to leap at his exposed back. His empty hand was suddenly holding a burning torch. "Did I do that?" Arrin turned, fiery torch pointed at the vampire while he kept his sword between himself and the beast. Again behind him, he heard a new noise: laughter. He craned his head and saw a figure in the distance, floating inches above the ground. He could not make out a face, but from somewhere deep inside, Arrin knew this new figure had killed Gretta Platt.

The moon-beast howled and began its change. The killer laughed louder as the wolf changed into a giant of a man. Naked, the man reached down and pulled up some dirt. As he rubbed it on his body, it changed—first into a brown nightshirt, and then a white one.

Gretta moved forward, ignoring the torch between her and her prey. Arrin, unable to stop the undead creature, pushed the torch into her chest. Gretta's hiss turned into a scream and she burst into flames. Arrin focused on Gretta's eyes, no longer lifeless. "WHY?" The shriek almost made Arrin drop his weapons. The killer's laugh, maniacal now, resonated through the cave. Gretta fell to the ground at Arrin's feet, charred and very dead.

The walls of the cavern—walls that had certainly brightened since he had first arrived—were filled with the glow-rocks he had seen in the caves. The shifter jumped in apparent glee, also staring at the rocks, watching their greenish glow approach the brightness of day.

The blade in Arrin's hand abruptly ceased its burning, as if the sword had sucked all the flames into itself. The shifter ran from him. At the far end of the cave, it jumped with an agile twist to the side, bracing one foot against the wall and pushing off, gaining even more height… and then disappeared just before it would have landed, leaving Arrin with the killer. As Arrin turned to face Gretta's murderer, a figure appeared behind the killer and struck. The head fell to the ground, rolling toward Arrin. It came to a stop at Arrin's feet, face-up.

The face was featureless except for a mouth opened in a dying scream. A yell forced Arrin to look up at the new figure in the cave. "I knew you would be of good use, BOY!!" Father Jorrus stood above the headless corpse, delighting in his triumph.

There was a flash of light, and Arrin found himself on a horse, riding between Jon Avedon and Constable Louis. "Arrin, I hope you will return to visit. I will one day be Lord here, and you will always be welcome" … "What about your brother? Won't he become Lord of Avedon Hill before you?"… Louis laughed… "They're all dead now, Arrin… don't you remember anything? No wonder you and Sir Arames failed." Jon smiled, and Arrin could swear he saw the distinctive teeth of a vampire… With a hiss and a leap both Constable Louis and Jon Avedon landed on top of Arrin, each straining to reach his neck—

Arrin shot up in bed. The sweat streaming down his face and back mocked him and the bath he had taken just two cykes before.

Cletus held up his messy hands to calm Arames. "Not killings *in* Avedon Hill, Sir Arames, but killings nevertheless."

Arames frowned. "No one mentioned any murders outside of town."

Cletus nodded. "There have been several in the last few years, mostly along the roads to the south and west."

"How many?"

"Maybe two or three a year—including the people who've simply gone missing, more like eight or nine a year."

Cletus told Arames what he knew. Lone travelers had been found dead on or near the roads—some within a day's travel, others two or three days' journey by horse. Still others were frequent users of the Avedon Pass who just never arrived; in some cases, wagons were found alongside the road, horses gone—sometimes with their goods left untouched. "The bodies that were found... how were they killed?"

"In most cases, the heads had been removed and were never found. When the heads remained, there were bite marks on the victims' necks."

"The killer decapitated the victims?"

Cletus waved his hands as he spoke. "Killer, killers... it may just be bandits who leave bite marks or remove heads as a warning, or to make themselves seem more fearsome."

Arames pressed the gatekeeper. "Just teeth marks? No maulings, like from a wolf or a bear?"

Cletus shook his head. "Not that I've heard."

Arames clenched his fist for a moment, but then relaxed... anger served no purpose. "Why have Constable Louis or Lord Avedon not shared this with me?"

"Honestly, they may not even know. I only know the details because I hear things, in my position—from the Grozhian patrols that find the bodies, or from those who come asking about missing traders. None of these deaths occurred within a league of town."

Arames realized Cletus was correct. The Grozhian army, controlled loosely by the Council of Grozh, would not include any local leaders in their investigations. Furthermore, if the killings were being carried out by bandits, Arames wouldn't be surprised at all if the Council condoned them. If the traders weren't paying their taxes, perhaps they were being punished; or perhaps the Council wanted to secretly divert trading guild traffic away from the Avedon Pass. It was not uncommon for the three provinces of Caern to take steps to keep products from being exported—though murder was not the usual method of controlling trade routes.

But the appearance of vampire-style killings and decapitated corpses led Arames to believe that something else was at play.

"Tell me something, Cletus... who in town regularly leaves for extended periods of time?"

"What do you mean by 'extended'?"

"More than just going out for a picnic at the lake, for example."

Cletus was finally finished with his plate. He attempted to clean his hands with an already messy cloth napkin. "Let's see... well, Gretta certainly—before her death, of course... Jon Avedon, for riding competitions or when he hears about a new foal born at one of the better stables in Grozh... Hemming, at times..."

"The baker?"

"Yes, he makes supply runs and deliveries every so often, to some of the closer towns to our south."

"Who else?"

Cletus wiped his chin. "Lane Niccols, the librarian... and Constable Ulrich..."

"Why would the constable need to leave town?"

"He has only lived in Avedon Hill a few years. He visits family in southern Grozh at least two or three times a year."

Images of Lane Niccols flashed in Arames's mind. "And the librarian?"

"Books, mostly. She meets book traders at appointed times at certain crossroads—saves travel time for both parties. In any case, she sometimes leaves with packages, but mostly she just returns with them. She'll travel day or night if it means adding a new item to her collection."

Arames nodded. Cletus pointed past him. "Your boy doesn't look so good."

Arames turned to find Arrin walking toward the table. He was still dressed in his sleeping attire, and Arames could see that Cletus was right. Arrin's clothes were drenched. Arames wondered if he had left the fire in the room burning too hot.

"Arrin, are you well?"

Arrin looked past Arames at Cletus, who was already pushing himself up from the booth. The far corner booth in the tavern was the largest in the room, and was the only booth that could easily accommodate someone as large as Cletus. The gatekeeper patted Arrin on the shoulder as he walked by. "Not sleeping, pup? I'll grab Talik on the way out, if you like. Listening to him will put you right to sleep."

Arames disregarded Cletus's jest. "Thank you for your information, Cletus. I am sure we will see you tomorrow."

"I'm sure of that, as well." Cletus bowed his head slightly and then exited the inn. Hearing the door, Talik emerged from the kitchen. "Do you need anything else, Sir Arames?"

Arames waved the innkeeper off to keep him from coming to the table. "No, thank you, Talik. Arrin and I need some privacy, if you do not mind."

Talik nodded and returned to the kitchen. Arames thought he could still see the form of the innkeeper watching them through the crack of the door. He ignored Talik, pulling Arrin into the booth and pushing his nearly untouched ale into his student's hands. "What happened?"

Arrin downed half the ale. "I had a dream—at least, I hope it was just a dream."

Arames sat up a bit straighter. "Tell me about it." Arrin's own mother, Serena Perti, was the strongest dream-walker Arames had ever seen or heard tell of. Arrin had not shown any proclivity toward dream-walking, but his mention of dreams drew Arames's immediate attention.

Dream-walking wasn't about seeing the future. Earlier that day, Arames had described magic as a river, and had told Arrin that certain types of people could interact with that river—priests, sorcerers, and even monks such as Arames himself.

Dream-walkers could also interact with the river of magic. Arames imagined dream-walkers as those who could walk across a low-hanging bridge that spanned over the widest part of the River, splashed continuously by the spray from the currents below them. While sleeping, dream-walkers were inundated by images of events—of the past, and of possible futures. And as Arrin whispered about seeing vampires, moon-beasts, and townspeople transformed, Arames realized that the events of the day may have triggered the latent power within Arrin, creating something new within Arrin's dream.

It was not a certainty that Lord Avedon was going to assassinate Arrin or that all of Jon Avedon's brothers were going to die—but it was very possible that some elements of his dream might eventually open up new paths for their investigation. As Arames considered what those paths might be, the door to the inn swung open, crashing against the wall. Its return was halted by Father Jorrus's staff.

Jorrus spotted Arames and Arrin and hurried over to their table. "Tonight, you must sleep—" Jorrus repeated Arames's sentiment from earlier that night. "But not until I am done with you."

"What is it, Jorrus?" Arames tried to prevent irreverence from seeping into his words.

"I feel them. They are outside the walls, trying to get in. You must come with me, both of you."

Arames pointed a finger at Arrin. "Go upstairs. I need you rested for tomorrow."

Jorrus growled under his breath. "We need his arm."

Arames Kragen stood. "You have both of mine. That will have to do."

⌒⊸⊶⊷⊷⊷⊷⊶⊸⌒

"You see? Arjun guides me."

Arames had certainly been impressed by the cleric's hunting skills. At times a bluish halo surrounded Father Jorrus's holy symbol; at other times Jorrus hid the symbol under his robes, as if he believed the creatures they sought would not sense the symbol if it was covered by cloth.

The two men crouched silently in the woods directly southeast of town. It was a further sign of Jorrus's ability that they were downwind of the three creatures they now studied through the branches of the trees. Though his eyes had adjusted to the forest's darkness and the creatures were only a stone's throw away, Arames could barely discern any details. The three fed on the remains of several small animals, most likely rabbits and squirrels. Every so often one of the things would raise its head and look around, sniffing at the air, but it would immediately throw itself back at feeding lest the others take its share of the meal.

Vampire tales were a staple of bards and storytellers. Arames loved to listen to stories—most tales of the fantastic were usually a result of some past action of one of the Children, and he liked to listen and find the connections. But if the storyteller began describing the stench of death surrounding a vampire, Arames knew there was no educational value in listening further. While the smells of the sewers and marshes that were home to these creatures could be overwhelming, soulless, undead creatures such as the vampires before Jorrus and Arames produced no inherent odor.

Except, apparently, to undead hunters. "Come, monk. Time to send these creatures to the great abyss." A moment later Arames found himself crouching alone, the cleric bounding ahead of him toward the vampires.

Arames pulled a concealed sai from each of his arm sheaths as he ran after the cleric. While initially upset at Jorrus's apparent disregard for the element of surprise, Arames soon discovered that Jorrus truly knew what he was doing. As Jorrus ran forward, he shouted an Inarran battle-cry, holding his holy symbol high. All three vampires turned at the same time, startled into stillness by the human's wild approach. As soon as all eyes had locked on Jorrus, he called on his holy symbol's power again, filling the area with a blue-tinged white light. One of the vampires tried to turn its head away, while the other two attempted to cover their eyes with arms and hands that still dripped gore from their recent kills. But before they could shield themselves, the halo of light became a blast of radiance. The discharge of energy, the white swallowing the blue as it was released from above Jorrus's head, erupted in all directions.

Arames closed his eyes instinctively, even though he knew the light of Arjun would not harm him. As the blast dissipated, two of the vampires ripped at their blinded eyes while the third rolled across the ground away from the charging cleric, one arm draped across his face.

Arames was amazed by the older man's agility. While time had obviously slowed Father Jorrus, every step the man took was strong and sure. His white robes billowed behind him as he reached the two closest creatures. Wielding his holy symbol now as a bludgeon, Jorrus crushed the head of the closest vampire with a single blow. As the first fell upon the remains of its meal, the second relied on its sense of smell to direct its own attack upon Father Jorrus.

Arames focused on reaching the third vampire. It had now regained its footing and was shaking its head from side to side.

As he charged forward, Arames inelegantly reached out to the creature's mind. It was like driving a team of horses through the only door of a small home. Ordinarily, Arames would never have attempted to use his abilities without complete focus. But now, facing a vampire with possible intelligence, in open air, he had no choice.

The only thoughts he sensed were not thoughts at all—they were the mixed emotions of hunger and fear, and they threatened to overwhelm him. He slashed down with the sai in his left hand, a physical gesture severing the psychic connection between himself and the vampire. But Arames had successfully discovered two facts: first, that the vampire he faced was stronger and older than the two Father Jorrus faced; and second, that this vampire had not been blinded.

Still, it had been dazed by the light of Jorrus's holy symbol, and Arames attempted to take advantage of this, first thrusting the blade in his left hand, then following with a slash from high to low with the sai in his right.

The vampire raised its right arm to block the monk's first blow. The blade grazed flesh and the vampire jumped back in pain, just out of range—Arames's second blow fell short of its mark.

Arames pressed his attack; the longer this lasted, the greater the chance his age would catch up with him. The vampire had retreated twenty paces and took a moment to lick the wound on its arm. The taste of its own blood seemed to renew its strength. Arames continued forward, but just before he reached the creature, it jumped up and out of reach.

Arames directed the points of his blades above his head, half-expecting the creature to fall upon him from above, but instead found the vampire staring back down at him.

Light still emanated from Jorrus's weapon, even as he used it to pound flesh and bone. The light, broken by the many branches of the thick wood, cast strange, moving shadows across the trees. Flashes of light traversed the distance between Jorrus and the vampire above Arames, illuminating the monster's face like some demonic perversion of a children's game of hide-and-seek.

By the holy symbol's glare, Arames could see mottled, gray-tinted hide that looked more like leather than skin, stretched tightly over a lithe, muscular body. Its hairless head and sunken cheeks gave the vampire a false appearance of weakness, but its fangs—curved teeth that reached well below its bottom lip—proved to be a great equalizer in that regard.

A ragged hiss brought Arames out of his momentary reverie. The creature stared down at him upside down, impossibly gripping the trunk of the great tree like some giant lizard, feet over hands.

"Kalin calls for you, soulless one!" Arames called upon the Destroyer—the Child of Az most likely responsible for the existence of vampires. "Do you hear her voice?"

The monster seemed to strain a bit, possibly trying listening for the voice of the Child of Destruction. Arames smiled a bit. He brought his left arm down, preparing to take advantage of the monster's confusion and throw his sai.

Arames was tossed into the air by a blast that seemed to erupt from the very ground below him. The tree to which the vampire clung met a harsher fate, torn at its roots by a powerful burst of magic. While Arames landed softly on his knees, the vampire was thrown harshly against the upper branches of another nearby tree. The creature fell to the ground, arm bent at an impossible angle, and it hissed in Arames's direction as it struggled to its feet. But then the vampire ran, away from the grove and toward the town of Avedon Hill.

Arames, from his knees, hurled his sai at the vampire's back.

The sai only made it a short distance before Father Jorrus's holy symbol knocked it from its path. Jorrus stood in bloodied robes, holding his weapon and breathing heavily. He picked up the sai and walked over to Arames, helping the monk to his feet.

"Sorry I knocked you down. I couldn't let you dispatch their leader."

Arames sheathed his knives, looking over at the nearly unrecognizable remains of the two vampires Jorrus had destroyed. Blood and gore dripped from Jorrus's holy symbol. "Come, we need to hurry."

Jorrus pulled a great knife from his belt and quickly removed the heads from the vampires. He unceremoniously tossed them deeper into the woods. "The leader—the one we follow—has come to find the vampire that created it. It will lead us to the vampire that killed Gretta Platt. Come!"

They rushed after the vampire. It was not hard to follow, but it was obvious to Arames that Jorrus followed more than a physical trail—he never slowed for a moment. Though the priest had several years on Arames, he ran at a pace that threatened to exhaust the monk.

They approached the edge of the forest and Jorrus slowed, holding up a hand. Arames came to a stop at Jorrus's side.

Through the last trees before them, Arames saw the main road. Just beyond was the great wall that surrounded the town. The vampire had led them back to Avedon Hill.

Arames saw the creature then, leaning against the town wall, feeling its way along the great oak beams. It was working its way toward the gate.

"Jorrus! We have to attack it now." Arames hissed under his breath at Jorrus.

Father Jorrus grabbed Arames by his robes. "No. This vampire will find a way in and we'll be right behind it. It knows its mother or father is here."

"But Cletus—"

Father Jorrus had told Cletus they were hunting. Cletus had laughed, but seemed used to Jorrus's requests. *"Bring me back something good, Jorrus."*

"He'll be fine if he stays out of the way. Just watch!"

The vampire had found the gate. Instead of trying to force its way through the gate, however, it began climbing the wall. It slithered up a short distance, then gathered itself and jumped at least two body lengths, gripping the wall as easily as a lizard climbing up the side of a rock. Jorrus laughed. "In case you wondered if a vampire could have gotten into that courtyard, monk."

The vampire had covered a third of the barrier's height when Arames saw the orange glow of a flame pierce the darkness near the top of the wall. "What is that?" The flame flickered as it shot down the wall, accompanied by the tell-tale twang of bow string vibrations. The arrow pierced the vampire's shoulder; the flames flared briefly as the arrow struck. The creature screeched and used its opposite hand to beat at the flames, sacrificing its grip on the wall. A second arrow struck its left arm, and the vampire lost its purchase completely. It fell some thirty feet to the ground, landing hard on its back.

Jorrus clenched a fist. "No!!"

Two more flaming arrows flew from the bow and slammed into the vampire's chest. The creature thrashed upon the ground as the flames spread, nearly engulfing the upper half of its body. Arames had seen men burn alive; that was a slow searing process, painful to watch. Here, though, he watched with interest as the skin and flesh of the undead creature seemingly fueled the flames. A last arrow through the vampire's left eye brought an end to the show, impaling the creature to the ground. A few moments later the fiery body crumbled in on itself. It disintegrated, leaving only some ash, smoldering clothing and the four arrows that had caused all the damage. The fire extinguished itself soon thereafter.

"Damnable gateman!"

Arames smiled. "He was only protecting himself. You cannot be angry at him for that."

Jorrus glared for a moment but then his face softened. "Yes, of course. But now we have proof that there is a vampire in Avedon Hill."

"Proof? This vampire fled toward civilization to escape us. If it had previously lived in the sewers of a city, then instinct might have told it that there was a place of refuge beyond these walls."

"You know nothing of this, Kragen. These vampires were here because they sensed a vampire master. It fled this way, as I knew it would, because it sought the safe embrace of the one who created it. And now…"

"What?"

"Now the proof I wanted you to see is gone." Jorrus strode forward, leaving Arames to follow.

Jorrus refused to speak to Cletus when the gatekeeper let him through the town gate, and walked off into the night, sparing no parting words for his hunting companion. Arames remained at the gate with Cletus.

"I said bring me something good. I'd best be clearer about what I consider *good* the next time Father Jorrus goes a-hunting."

"You handled yourself well. Fire arrows?"

"I saw your robes earlier today, and I know the types of creatures Father Jorrus likes to hunt. I wasn't taking any chances tonight."

Arames bowed his head slightly and wished Cletus a safe night.

<hr />

Arames put away his notebook and climbed into bed. Arrin, who had remained quiet since Arames's return, finally raised his head from his own pillow and asked what had happened.

After Arames shared his account of events, Arrin asked, "What does this mean for me? Do I have to endure dreams like this for the rest of my life?"

Arames knew the question would come. "If you are to be a dream-walker, then that is the will of Az, Arrin Perti. Your mother has lived with the ability for many years, and without her, you and I would not be here."

Arrin only knew a portion of the history between Arames and Arrin's mother, and Arames would not tell him more. *That is up to your mother, not to me.*

Arames continued. "If you have the ability, you will eventually learn how to control it. There were only a few moments in your dream where you controlled your surroundings—like when you made the torch appear in your hand. In time, you will learn how to control events instead of being controlled by them."

"Yes, Arames."

<hr />

"So, the boy has the gift."

Arames blinked. Part of him wished he had nodded off, but he had no doubt that he was awake and still on his watch. "Gareth, I have not seen you in a year and now you appear twice in one day."

"Ari, you've told me before that I'm simply a manifestation of your conscience.

Are you feeling guilty about something?"

Arames pursed his lips in thought. He looked to his left and confirmed that Arrin was snoring in his bed. "Dream-walking is his family's legacy. I played no part in that."

Gareth nodded, but had a smile on his face. "Yes of course, of course. And the rest?"

Arames was not prepared to discuss the rest. "I made my choice."

"You have made many choices, old friend. One of them has kept me with you all these years. If I have not earned my place by Az's side, I should be living as a young man somewhere in the world—not here with you."

Arames waved a hand. "You probably are. And this is after Az asked you to join him in his kingdom. I see you laughing at his offer, asking only to be reincarnated as a farmer's son, working a glebe for one of the bishops of the Priests of Caern."

"Now why would I do that?"

"So you could one day lead an uprising against your master."

Gareth Beckwin laughed. "Or at least poison the bishop's food. Revenge is Treygh's calling, not mine. Maybe I was born as your prince, here. That would be much more poetic."

"Poetry is Balin's calling, not yours." Arames sighed. "If you were reincarnated, do you think our connection would allow me to find you?"

Gareth laughed once more, but it was tinged with sadness. "What would you do if you could? Tell me about my past life?"

"I do not know."

"Well, no need for that. I'm here because you're an old soul, Arames. You can believe I'm your conscience or your guilt if you like. I know I'm here because of our medallion bond, and because your powers are that strong." Gareth paused while Arames snorted. "Do what you must here. Arrin's powers have peeked from under those covers." He pointed to Arrin's bed. "I hope you both survive long enough to find a use for them."

Arames looked at Arrin's sleeping form for a moment. When he turned back to respond to Gareth, his old friend was gone.

For Love or Money

THE NEXT MORNING ARRIVED, just as they always seemed to do. Arames appeared refreshed and prepared to tackle whatever may come his way, but Arrin doubted the same could be said for him. He had spent a restless watch going over the notes Arames had transcribed about his dream.

The fact that he was showing signs of becoming a dream-walker did not disturb him. What did disturb him was how suddenly the ability seemed to have manifested. His mother, quite possibly the most powerful *dream-walker* of her generation, had experienced extra-sensory dreams seemingly from the moment she was born. As a child, her dreams were considered royal portents, and she had been given the title of dream-walker at the tender age of six. Until the night before, Arrin had shown no predilection for *walking the bridge*. In fact, he rarely remembered any of his dreams... and the dreams he could remember after a long night's sleep had more to do with ladies at royal court than with death and the battle between good and evil.

"Arrin, we are going to split up this morning. We can cover more territory working separately."

Arrin's concern showed on his face. "Are you sure that's a good idea? People aren't going to want to talk to me without you there."

Arames shrugged. "I'm sure you will find ways to win people over. This will be good practice for you. Besides, I want you to talk to some people with whom you have already established a rapport... like Cletus."

Arrin cringed. *I finally get the tobacco stains out of my boot and you want me to go talk to him again?*

"You will concentrate on finding out who Gretta might have been having a relationship with. We know she spent afternoons outside the town walls. We need to find out with whom she might have been meeting."

Arrin asked, "And you?"

"I will concentrate on her work. The only real evidence we have thus far is the page from her schedule book. I am going to examine her office. Her schedule book may be missing, but I hope there will be other clues there that haven't been found. Frankly, I do not believe we have discovered the extent of her powers as Housemistress. Besides, gold is as good a motive as any for murder."

They agreed to meet back at the inn for lunch. When they reached the path that led to the stables, Arames waved and walked on toward the manor. Arrin spotted Shane Olivet carrying buckets of water in for the horses. He didn't see Lonne Garrett, or the youth who seemed to be a semi-permanent fixture at the stables, Jon Avedon.

Shane smiled as he walked over. They had spoken for a short time the day before and the younger Shane seemed to like Arrin. Arrin believed it was because he was somebody new that Shane could talk to about the baker's daughter.

"Sir Arrin, back so soon, are ye?"

"I guess I am. How are you today?"

Shane pulled off his gloves and sat down on a bale of hay. "Great! With you here maybe things will get back ta' normal soon."

Arrin sat next to Shane. "Yesterday, Lonne told us Gretta went riding a few times a week."

"Yes."

"He also said that she took a large picnic basket with her?"

"Yeah, sometimes she would give us what she had left when she came back—but most of the time the food was gone."

"Have you thought about who might have been meeting her?"

Shane shook his head. "Whoever it was, they weren't using a horse from these stables. She could have been meeting Jon, since he spends a lot more time riding than anyone else. But not the way you're thinkin'... I think." Shane appeared to have confused himself.

"No, I don't think Jon was meeting Gretta for secret lunches outside of town."

"You know, I've invited Jilly Hemming to go on picnics."

"Has she accepted?"

"No, not yet. But she will. She'll come around soon."

Arrin tried to get Shane back on topic. "Who doesn't board their horses here?"

"Well, Hemming has two, for the wagon he uses to make deliveries and pick up his supplies. Lonne offered to let him stable them here, but he enjoys caring for them himself."

"Hemming, the baker?"

"Yeah... I'm not sure what his first name is. Everyone just calls him Hemming."

"Thank you, Shane." Arrin stood up, ready to go.

Shane stood up as well and pulled some parchment out of a pocket. "Arrin, can you read a poem I wrote for Jilly? I'm sure you can read, being an apprentice to a monk and all... You can read, can't you?"

The remnants of yesterday's headache began creeping in from the edge of Arrin's senses. He sighed. "Yes I can read. Who taught you how to read?"

Shane looked down at the ground. "Gretta Platt. When she became Housemistress, she decided all the kids needed to know their letters. Three days a week, we went to the manor. I had never been there before that."

<hr>

Arames Kragen knew there was going to be trouble as soon as Blake Weathertop let him into the manor. Blake was smiling

"Lord Avedon is waiting for you. In fact, I believe he just finished giving Constable Louis orders to drag you to his presence."

Arames smiled in return. "Good thing I am here, then. I would not want to cause unnecessary work for Constable Louis."

Blake turned on his heels and led Arames to the great hall. Lord Avedon sat at the large round table in the center of the hall, talking to Constable Louis. The butler announced Arames as if he had walked to the inn and retrieved the monk himself. Constable Louis stood up and moved away from the table so that Lord Avedon could speak directly with Arames.

"My son Richard tells me he had to usher you out of the manor last night—that you were sneaking around upstairs."

"Lord Avedon, Arrin and I were only retracing the steps of Constable Ulrich the night of Gretta's murder. We found Brianna Ray and spoke to her about that night. It had nothing to do with your children, and we did not mean to disturb Richard or any of your family."

Lord Avedon still looked like he hadn't slept in days. "Fine... what did you learn?"

"Nothing of great importance—although we did learn that sound travels strangely through your manor. Multi-floor rooms such as this great hall and the courtyard can cause tricks on the ear."

"What are your plans for today? Studying the region's weather patterns?"

Arames bowed his head slightly, ignoring the jest. "We spent the better half of yesterday meeting the townspeople. Today we will concentrate on the relationships that Gretta had with people in town. We need to learn why someone might want to kill her. My student Arrin is in town right now, talking to people.

With your permission, I will search Gretta's office for anything that might shed some light on the matter."

Lord Avedon found no complaint with Arames's plan. "Constable Louis will take you." With that, Lord Avedon stood and walked out of the hall.

Louis smiled, twisting the hairs of his moustache between his thumb and index finger. "Now, you understand. You had better watch how you approach his children; Lord Avedon could only be so angry with me. You, on the other hand—"

Arames held out his hand, inviting Louis to lead the way. They began walking.

"So, Arames, you were on your way to a conference? Will this detour impact your prior obligations?"

"Frankly, constable, I no longer care about the conference in Kith-Karn. I believe this is much more important."

They walked down the long northern corridor that had led them to the courtyard the day before. They also passed the door that led to the stairs to the second floor. Louis asked, "Anything in Iberian's prophecies warn you about walking into more trouble than you can handle?"

Arames recalled something Arrin had said the day before about the front of the manor, with its great door to the Olviaran Pass... that it resembled the face of a lion. "Iberian once said: *Into the lion an acolyte will fall, and the dead and undead will flow through its veins as ducks on a river. Secret paths will be revealed, and the dead will push through the eyes of Artus.*"

Constable Louis stopped in front of a door and pulled out a set of keys. He opened the door and let Arames walk through first. "Don't you mean Arjun?"

Arames knew Constable Louis was old enough and intelligent enough to know the history between Artus and the Priests of Caern. "Depends on how old the text you are looking at is, of course."

"Ducks on a river?"

Arames smiled. "Iberian tended to ramble when he drank." He gave Louis a wink. "But you did not hear that from me." The walls of the expansive office were lined with books and papers, all neatly organized. At the back of the office was an enormous desk. "Was this always a desk?"

"It was originally a dinner table. Gretta Platt had this room converted into an office soon after she began as Housemistress. Originally, it was where the Avedon children dined when a formal event was held in the main dining room. But since such events are rare, this room was primarily used by the staff. The original Housemistress's office is on the other side of the floor, not too far from the kitchens, but Gretta felt that her mother's office would not give her the space she needed."

Arames walked around the desk, not touching anything at first. Even the top of her desk was clean and organized, with not a book or parchment out of place.

"Nothing has been removed?"

"I shifted things around in my initial search, but everything is back where I found it. No schedule book, just lots of paperwork detailing supply orders, business dealings—" his voice trailed off.

Arames sat in the chair behind the desk. He began looking through the neat stacks page by page. "Any personal papers?"

"None—no diary, no personal notes. If there were any, they must be in that missing book."

The desk had one drawer on each side. Arames opened them both and found more papers, organized in smaller compartments and categorized by date. They appeared to list the names of people who had used the Pass, along with some sort of codes tied to what they might have been charged for access to the trade route. "All right, let us think this through. You found the torn page of what we believe to be Gretta's schedule book—"

"Not believe. The thinness of the torn page proves it. Lane Niccols gave her the book as a gift when Gretta became Housemistress. It is the only book of its kind here. Lane even confirmed it."

"You showed the librarian the page?"

"I covered the text, of course. All Lane needed to see was the thickness of the paper itself."

"So the first question is: why did she have it with her in the first place? I would not carry a large tome with me if my goal was to relax in the courtyard."

Constable Louis replied, "But I'm pretty sure you have a book with you at all times, don't you, Sir Arames?"

Arames looked at his notebook. "Point taken, my good constable."

Louis continued. "Gretta spent many an evening in the courtyard, reading books or writing notes in her schedule book. And she always took her schedule book home with her—always."

Arames still had to search Gretta's house, but knew that if Louis had not found the book in her home, it was not there. "Is there anyone in town who owes Lord Avedon gold? Anyone who may have taken it out on Gretta?"

"No one is in debt to Lord Avedon. Taxes are rarely an issue here. Our few inhabitants are happy. And no one has borrowed large sums of gold from Lord Avedon that I know of." After a bit Louis spoke again. The words almost seemed forced. "There is one person whom you might want to look at more closely: Alex Dewirin."

Arames looked up from some papers. "Owns the general store?"

"Yes. I know he had several heated discussions with Gretta about his... monetary situation."

Arames pressed further; it was a strange thing for Louis to be having trouble with. "Where was he the night Gretta was killed?"

"He had dinner with Marrissa, the herbalist. He left her home with enough time to get here and murder Gretta. But how he could have gotten into the manor, committed the murder, and left unseen is beyond me."

Arames spent nearly a cyke going through the papers in Gretta's office. Most dealt with tracking supplies and outgoing payments. Other than the logs of people who used the Pass, Arames could find nothing that detailed the monies coming into the town or the manor. "Where are her books?"

Louis was confused. "Books? There are many books along those shelves there."

Arames stood up from her desk and walked back toward the door. "There is too much that is missing here—not just Gretta's schedule book."

Constable Louis raised his voice. "I told you nothing has been moved from this room!"

Arames held his hands up in front of him. "That is not what I meant. I cannot find any accounting books here. I see invoices and receipts, but nothing about the income generated by the Pass or any other businesses that might be tied to Lord Avedon."

"Maybe Lord Avedon has those books."

Judging by what he had seen of Lord Avedon, Arames could not picture him going through ledgers of transactions. "Possibly. What about the former office?"

"No one uses it. It's still there, if you would like to see it."

Arames thought on it. "No, not right now. May I go speak to some of the staff without your supervision, Head Constable?"

Louis laughed. "Of course. Just watch yourself. I doubt you will be able to talk your way out of another run-in with the Avedon children."

Arames bowed his head slightly. "Thank you. I will be careful."

<hr/>

"Your eyes remind me of my horse Ethel. They're dark and they see really well..." *Is that even poetry?* Arrin had listened to pages of Shane's poetry in hopes that building a rapport would earn his trust and encourage the boy to provide more information. Shane promised to come find him if he remembered anything else that might help. After he extricated himself from Shane's poems—and against his better judgment—Arrin found himself heading back to the town gate for another encounter with Cletus.

Cletus appeared to be sleeping in a chair outside the gatehouse, a hat pulled down over his eyes. The sun was shining brightly and it was a nearly breezeless morning. It wasn't exactly warm, but it was good napping weather.

Arrin approached quietly. He was tempted to make Cletus pay somehow for his actions the day before, but nothing was coming to mind that didn't involve a dagger or a rope.

He stopped a few paces away. Without lifting his hat, Cletus said, "Any more night-sweats, youngling?"

Arrin kept his expression steady. "Arames asked me to follow up on something you talked about last night. If you don't mind?"

Apparently impressed that Arrin had sidestepped his barb, Cletus sat up and pushed his hat back so he could look Arrin in the eyes. "Okay, what you lookin' for?"

"You said you keep logs of when people come and go through the gate, correct?"

"Yes. What would you like to know?"

"The days that Gretta would leave on her mid-day excursions... Sir Arames wanted me to see if anyone might have been meeting her."

"Like I told your *master*, no one left or came in with Gretta."

Arrin worded his request carefully and did his best to hide his emotions. "Please, may I look at your logs from the days Gretta came and went?"

Cletus squinted for a moment in thought. "Sure, laddie—go right ahead." He stood up and walked into his gatehouse. A short time later, he returned with a ledger. He handed it to Arrin and pointed to his chair. Arrin sat down and opened the logbook, looking for days when Gretta had been outside the town walls for more than two cykes. As Cletus had said, no one left or came in with Gretta. But as he studied the pages he began to see a pattern. Arrin scanned back over several months, and the pattern was reinforced even more. *Arames will like this.*

As Arrin continued scanning further back, he began seeing another name leaving and returning with Gretta on some of those days. "Gretta used to spend a lot of time with Jilly Hemming, didn't she?"

Cletus nodded. "Yes, they were best friends, but as Gretta became more 'busy' she stopped inviting Jilly to have lunch with her."

"The time Gretta spent outside the town didn't change all that much—she just stopped spending the time with Jilly?" Arrin suspected he already knew the answer.

Cletus shrugged. "Don't ask me what happened. Maybe they had a falling out. My guess is that Gretta just outgrew Jilly, if you know what I mean."

Arrin shook his head. "Please explain?"

"Jilly's a nice enough girl, but she's what you might call simple-minded. I don't have much room to talk, so I don't make no judgments. But Gretta, she was a smart lady. As she grew into her position, I'd wager Gretta discovered she and Jilly had nothing in common."

Arrin had other ideas, but he left them unspoken. "Thank you, Cletus." He stood and handed the logbook back to the giant of a man. "I would love to stay and chat, but I have to meet back up with Arames."

Cletus nodded. Arrin could tell that Cletus had a sarcastic comment ready to fly, but he apparently swallowed it and simply bowed his head. "Good day to you, Sir Arrin."

Arrin raised an eyebrow at his "sir", but didn't respond. He turned north along the main avenue toward the inn. Arrin did not see Cletus go back into his gatehouse. And a few moments later, Arrin did not see Cletus release a bird. It flew up and out of town, heading west.

Arames left Constable Louis and made his way to the kitchens. He spoke to Chef Roland, who reaffirmed his earlier suspicion that Blake Weathertop might have had something to do with Gretta's murder. Of course, Roland had no evidence—just a feeling.

Ley Nallon, Chef Roland's son, spoke up next, saying he remembered something that had happened between Gretta and the blacksmith a few months earlier. Ley had been walking home, and had seen Herrjarr arguing with the Housemistress. He even witnessed Herrjarr raise his arms in the air and let out a howl of some sort, then turn and walk away.

The more questions Arames asked, the more Ley remembered. "She noticed me standing there and told me not to worry about it. The funny thing about it, Sir Arames, was that I was more scared than she seemed to be. I was shaking, but all she did was smile at me and say everything was going to be fine."

"What was the argument about?"

"I'm not certain. I heard something about a delivery, but I missed most of it. And when Herrjarr got angry and raised his arms, I wasn't really listening to what they were saying."

"Thanks, Ley. Keep thinking about anything like that. It all helps, even if you do not think it is very important." Arames gave the boy a wink.

Ley smiled. "Yessir."

As Arames walked through the great hall, an unfamiliar young lady was passing through from a different entrance. The dress she wore was informal, a woolen kirtle made for movement and daily activities. Arames approached her, even though he knew she had to be one of Lord Avedon's daughters. The girl had a mischievous grin on her face as he neared, and she curtsied. "Sir Arames. Are you sure you should be speaking to me?"

Arames had not worked with children since his days as Aarronic Advisor for King Renoir, so he wasn't the best judge of age; still, seventeen and ten were far enough apart that he was certain he now met Lord Avedon's older daughter.

Arames heard no malice in her voice. With his hands tucked inside the sleeves of his robe, he bowed deeply and responded. "You must be Carin Avedon. I should have nothing to fear—as long as you do not plan on running to your father with horrific tales of me."

His tone turned her grin into a large, infectious smile. "Oh, good. I was hoping you wouldn't be afraid to speak to me." Carin grabbed Arames by the sleeve and led him over to the octagonal table in the center of the great hall. He allowed himself to be pulled along and soon they were both sitting at the table, facing each other. Carin had her hands in her lap and had the eager look of a child ready to share gossip with another schoolgirl. "So, what do you want to know?"

Arames squinted in thought. "I do not have anything specific to ask you right now, Carin. Do you have something you wish to tell me?"

Carin frowned, but her eyes sparkled as if they held a secret. "Brianna says that you've been asking if anyone disliked Gretta."

"Yes."

"You don't think it was a vampire?"

"I do not know. Someone has taken her corpse, so I cannot examine—"

Carin's eyes widened. "Couldn't that mean that she's a vampire, too? That she just—" She paused, searching for the right word, "awakened and escaped her tomb?"

"That is a possibility. But let me ask you this: what are the chances that a vampire could have gotten access to the manor courtyard, killed Gretta, and escaped unnoticed?"

Carin paused, deep in thought. "Can vampires climb walls? If so, they could have made it into the courtyard without walking into the manor at all."

Arames recalled the vampires he and Father Jorus had faced. While they certainly possessed the ability to scale the walls of Avedon Manor, they could never have pulled off such a planned attack.

But a vampire master? Arames had never encountered such a creature, but he believed the claims and the lore—too many people he trusted had told him stories of vampire masters. Even so, Arames still believed that motive, not a search for a vampire that might not even exist, would lead him to the murderer.

Arames nodded. "Again, it is possible."

Carin Avedon's face lost some of its color. "I just wanted to tell you about something I saw—about Talik Bore—"

She was interrupted by the heavy footfalls of two guards who entered the great hall and moved to each side of the entry door, pikes in hand. As they stood at attention, Lord Avedon walked through after them. Avedon spotted Arames Kragen sitting at the table speaking to his daughter, and his face contorted and flushed a bright red. Carin sprung out of her chair and practically ran to him.

"Don't be angry, Father—"

Lord Avedon pushed past his daughter and stormed to the table. He slammed his fist down and yelled at the monk. "How *dare* you speak to my daughter? I expressly told you *not* to bother my children again."

Arames did not respond; his only hope rested with Carin. She did not disappoint. "Father, it was I who kidnapped Sir Arames. I wanted desperately to talk to him about Gretta. He is going to find out who did this—I know it!" She lifted a hand to caress one of her father's cheeks. "He is going to help us. Please, Father!"

Arames studied Carin out of the corner of his eye. The tone of her voice told Arames she was speaking the truth—but that there was much more behind her words. And the opportunity to probe further would not present itself any time soon.

It took a moment, but Lord Avedon let go of his anger. "Sir Arames, if you are done with Gretta's office, I suggest you continue your investigation with the townspeople."

Arames rose from his chair without removing his hands from his sleeves. "By your leave, Lord Avedon." He bowed, then turned and exited the great hall. As he did so, Arames noticed Blake Weathertop staring down at him from a balcony.

As Arames had hoped, Blake caught up to the monk before he reached the door leading out of manor. "So close—I hope to be watching the next time you incur Lord Avedon's wrath."

"Thank you for telling Lord Avedon that I was speaking with his daughter."

Blake blinked in surprise, but shrugged it off. "Glad to oblige. I will be keeping an eye on you, monk. You will not threaten this family or my relationship with Lord Avedon."

Arames refused to acknowledge the butler's threat. "I need you to answer a question for me, Blake. I am sure you will follow Lord Avedon's instructions and help me in this matter."

Blake did not respond, so Arames continued. "Prior to Gretta's murder, you had to prevent Talik Bore from entering the manor. In fact, you had to forcibly remove him."

The butler nodded, more than willing to speak ill of a townsperson. "Talik Bore is a buffoon. If I was Lord Avedon, I would have thrown him out of town years ago."

"What happened?"

"Lord Avedon finally tired of hearing of the innkeeper's outrageous propositions and assigned the Housemistress as a go-between. Eventually Talik became frustrated with the run-around. Once, he nearly became violent when

Gretta refused to take some idea to Lord Avedon for him. Following that, Gretta gave orders to deny Talik entry into the manor."

"That must have been difficult for Talik, being from one of the oldest families in Avedon Hill."

The smirk on Blake's face was unmistakable. "Family lineage... you would think some of the people here had royal blood running through their veins. The Bores, the Hemmings—Lord Avedon has more loyalty to these people than they deserve."

Arames simply stared and Blake's smirk melted away, as if he realized for the first time that he had said too much. "Anyway, the last time Talik came to the manor, I told him he was not welcome without an appointment, and that if he wished an audience, I could take a note to Gretta for him. He became enraged and demanded entry, stating he had a once-in-a-lifetime opportunity that Lord Avedon could not pass up."

"You and Jon had to remove him physically?"

"Yes—I had him nearly out the door, but Jon came along and made sure Talik left without causing any more problems."

Arames bowed his head slightly. "Thank you very much, Blake. See? That was not difficult, now was it?"

Blake's smirk returned as Arames saw himself out.

<hr />

While Arames searched Gretta's office, Arrin found himself alone at the inn. After eating a midday meal, the prince decided he could not wait any longer. The information he had gleaned from Cletus's ledger was calling to him. Arames would be pleased to hear what he had deduced on his own. *But what if I got a confession from the man himself?*

Arrin left the inn and walked to the bakery, his arrival announced by the same bell that rang the day before. Thankfully, Hemming was the only person behind the counter.

The baker rubbed his hands together. "Ah, the young student—Arrin, is it?"

Arrin nodded. "Are you running the bakery alone today?"

Hemming smiled. "Dally and my daughter are delivering orders. They make the rounds every day around this time."

Well, that makes this a little easier. Arrin walked up to the counter and took a good look at the baker. Though balding slightly, he was a sturdy looking man, slightly shorter than Arrin but wider in the shoulders by nearly four hands. "You do not have the stomach of any baker I have ever known. Don't you sample your own confections?"

Hemming smiled and patted his tight stomach. "Ah, this. It comes from never sitting down. I sample most of what I bake each day, but I work very hard and I have been lucky. And remember, generations of my family worked in the mines. I guess it's like comparing draft horses to racers. The hard work of my ancestors can still be seen in me, even though I've never lifted a pickaxe or pushed a cart of rocks."

Arrin knew his next question wouldn't elicit the same smile. "I need to ask you about Gretta."

The baker began wiping the counter. "What about her? Have you found her body yet?"

"No... no, we have not. Right now, we are piecing together what we can about her life; her work, her personal life."

Hemming's hand stopped. "What do you need to know?"

"Gretta hid it well, but she was having a relationship with someone who met with her outside of town. Picnics, that sort of thing—"

Hemming's brow wrinkled. "You don't say. Picnics are a dangerous activity now, I take it?"

"No, of course not. It's just that she hid these excursions from everyone, like she was ashamed of them or something."

A vein appeared in the center of Hemming's forehead, and his free hand had clenched into a fist. "And what does this have to do with me?"

"Well, I didn't say it had anything to do with you. But now that you ask: you know Cletus keeps a pretty good log of entry and exits through the town gate, right?"

"I don't think I ever noticed."

Arrin nodded. "It's easy to miss things with Cletus, but he keeps great records." "And?"

"At least six or seven days a month, Gretta spent cykes relaxing in the forest outside of town—and on many of these same days, you traveled outside of town, as well."

Hemming was controlled, but still defensive. "I don't recall ever leaving or entering the town gates with Gretta Platt."

"Oh no, that's true." Arrin paused in reflection. "Do you always travel to the same place for your supplies?"

Hemming thought for a moment. "Yes, I do. I have a distributor in Ellyonne. I buy supplies from him in bulk and he sells my longer-lasting confections in his bakeries."

Another piece fell into place. "On days when you and Gretta were both outside of town, it consistently took you two cykes longer to make your round trip."

There was a long, uncomfortable pause. "So? Some trips take longer than others—more supplies, longer visits with shop owners... There are many reasons my trips might be extended—other than secret lunches with the Housemistress."

"There is more, sir. For years, your daughter Jilly was Gretta's constant companion."

Hemming nodded. "Jilly and Gretta were very close."

"Then one day she stopped spending time with your daughter."

"Jilly began working more, and Gretta lost touch with all the townspeople as her work took up more and more of her time. Nobody blamed Gretta for that, least of all my Jilly."

Arrin nodded one more time. "All true, but the timing offers up a different explanation. There wasn't a gradual drop-off. Jilly's name suddenly stopped appearing with Gretta's on Cletus's ledger around five months ago. Coincidentally, it was at this time that your trips increased—"

Hemming's voice increased in intensity and volume. "I already explained that—"

"And during that same period, your three trips a month to Ellyonne turned into six or seven. One month you traveled—I assume to Ellyonne—ten times, was it?"

"Ellyonne, Ellyonne," a female voice teased. Dally and Jilly Hemming walked in from the kitchen. Hemming jumped in surprise. Arrin had not heard the ladies enter through the back door, and the baker obviously had not, either. Dally continued, "Always your trips to Ellyonne. One good thing about Lord Avedon shutting down our fair town is that you have not left me for your other lover in Ellyonne..."

"Dally?!"

"Your lover Henri, of course—" She patted Hemming on the arm and smiled at Arrin. "Henri owns a bakery in Ellyonne. I think Hemming would leave me for Henri if he would only give up his recipe for brandywine torts!" Dally laughed.

Jilly smiled at her parents, amused by the interplay between them. "Actually, Momma, Da hasn't traveled to Ellyonne much in the last month or so. Right, Da?"

Hemming nodded. "Yes, pumpkin. The season is turning. I won't have to travel to Ellyonne much until next spring."

Jilly Hemming was lithe of body and full of spirit, with her mother's hair and her father's eyes. Arrin could see immediately why Shane Olivet was smitten with the girl. She looked at Arrin once and smiled, and then turned and walked into the kitchen to resume work. Dally followed, already calling out to her daughter about their next task.

Hemming turned back to Arrin. "You have nothing. You can speak to anyone in Ellyonne. They will confirm I have spent more time there because of work. And you leave my family alone."

"Of course, sir. I will leave you to your work. Good day to you and your family." Arrin left the bakery and headed back to the inn.

A Baker's Dozen

"Shem, why do I love so many women?"
"Because humanity is Doppin's plaything?"
"Ah, and Lem said you'd never learn."

—Ballix Poe (a comic play about an avatar of Doppin)

Arames looked forward to his rendezvous with Arrin. Particularly, he looked forward to sitting down to a good lunch at the inn, even though it was only a cyke after Worship Bells.

Arames had resigned from his position as Aarronic Advisor to Prince Ren at the young age of twenty-six for several reasons, the primary being what he referred to as the *Call of the Land*. Arames spent the next four years in seclusion on a small patch of isolated swampland in southeastern Yew. During these years of ascetic study and meditation Arames became even more attuned to the needs of the Land, and his abilities, gained initially through his training as a member of the Aarronic Brotherhood, became more powerful. But Arames's connection to the Land had its drawbacks as well. Simply put, Arames became very weak if he did not eat frequently. It seemed as though he needed nourishment every cyke that he was awake.

Arames found it ironic that he could feel the ebbs and flows of the Land better than most, yet he was required to take from the Land more often simply to function. Arames was rarely seen without some piece of fruit or bread in his hand; currently, he was looking forward to examining Talik Bore's menu.

When Arames spotted Arrin in the distance, his pupil's pace and demeanor told Arames that lunch was not going to go quite as he hoped.

Arrin related his discovery that Hemming had most likely been having an affair with Gretta Platt, and described how Hemming had reacted to the suggestion that he had been involved with Gretta.

Arames, in turn, shared what he had found in Gretta's office, and related Ley Nallon's story concerning her heated argument with Herrjarr. Arrin was not surprised to hear that Talik Bore had worn out his welcome at Avedon Manor.

After further discussion, Arames asked Arrin to turn around so that he could access his backpack. Arames pulled out a pear and began cutting it into small pieces. "Well, Arrin, it looks like lunch will have to wait. I was so looking forward to seeing what Talik is doing with Olviaran Whitetail today." Arrin didn't have it in him to tell Arames that he had already eaten a hearty lunch at the inn.

Richard, oldest son of Lord Avedon, watched Arames and Arrin from the corner of the herbalist's shop. He could not make out what they were saying, but that didn't matter. Richard waited until they had moved out of view, toward the center of town. Once he was sure he wouldn't be seen, Richard entered Marrissa's shop.

It only took him four long strides to reach the top platform where Marrissa was hard at work. She nearly dropped the glass she held when Richard appeared before her.

"Are you done yet?" His voice dripped with the threat of violence.

She steadied a glass filled with bluish liquid and carefully set it on the workbench. "Boy, you'd better watch yourself. You almost ruined any chance to save—"

Richard slammed his hand on the workbench. "Don't be so theatrical. When will it be done?"

Marrissa wanted to say a great many things to the future Lord Avedon, but she controlled herself. "Tomorrow at the earliest, but most likely the day after that. I am doing my best to force the caterpillar to transform—something that shouldn't occur until next spring—but subverting the laws of nature is..."

Richard glared at her. She looked as if she hadn't slept for days. "For your sake, potion-maker—you had better deliver on your promise before sundown tomorrow." He pointed a finger at her to emphasize his threat, then turned on his heel and stormed out of the shop.

Arrin and Arames continued toward the center of town. "You know, I don't know how you do it, Arames."

"Hmmm?"

"Cletus. From the moment we arrived you seemed to like him, even though he's probably the most rude and insulting person I have ever met."

"And?"

"It's just... he ended up helping me connect the threads between Hemming and Gretta."

Arames smiled. "You were polite and he was polite in kind, right?"

"Yes."

"There is something you need to understand about Cletus. He is more than he appears—and he has been testing you since we arrived. While he is definitely rude and insulting, he is far more intelligent than most give him credit for. I think he will continue to help us as long as it remains in his best interests. I don't know whom Cletus serves, but it is most likely himself. You said that I 'like' Cletus. While I do respect him, keep in mind that I do not trust him."

They slowed their pace once the bakery came into view. Approaching the shop from the other side of the road was a young woman around Arrin's age: she had sandy-blonde hair, green eyes, and Dally Hemming's face, only younger. His hunger temporarily abated, Arames hurried to intercept the woman before she entered the bakery's door.

"Good day, young lady. Why, you must be Jilly." Arrin had never seen his friend and mentor act so cheery. It caught both him and Jilly a bit off-guard.

"Y-Yes... Yes, sir." Her eyes lit up as she recognized Arrin. "You're going to find out who killed Gretta, aren't you?"

Arames nodded. "That is the plan, yes." His broad smile nearly scared Arrin, only used to Arames's knowing smirk. From the look on Jilly's face, it might have been scaring her, too. "I was wondering if you had a little time to speak with us."

Jilly looked down at her empty basket. "I don't think I have any more deliveries today, but I should check in with my mother first."

Arames had purposely placed himself between Jilly and the bakery door. "No need for that—it will only take a moment, and I am sure your parents will understand. They have been most helpful, and I am sure they would want you to help us in any way you can."

Jilly was still unsure, but she allowed herself to be ushered toward a bench in front of the butcher shop. "Of course I want to help. Gretta was my best friend in the world."

"Very good. Now since you were so close with Gretta, do you know anyone who wanted to hurt her?"

Jilly looked to the ground. "No. I've been thinking about that since I heard—" She fell silent for a moment. "Why would anyone want to hurt Gretta? I haven't been able to think of anyone."

While Jilly didn't appear to be lying, Arames felt the anger behind her words. But whether it was over her inability to be of help, or something more... "No one? You and Gretta were close. She must have commented over the years about people she did not like—those she had trouble with as Housemistress."

Jilly raised her face to Arames. The sun, behind her, cleared the edge of a cloud, and the girl's eyes seemed to gleam in the light. "It's not that, Sir Arames. I just shouldn't say. I'm probably wrong. I don't want to get anyone in trouble."

"Please, any information you have will be helpful. We are not going to accuse anyone of anything until we have proof. What you tell us will remain with us unless the person actually did something wrong."

Jilly stared at the ground for a moment, worrying at her lower lip. She looked once more into Arames's eyes, then nodded. "Richard and Edvard were both in love with Gretta. She wouldn't have anything to do with them. Edvard is too young, and Richard will be the next Lord Avedon, and a Housemistress has never—would never—"

Arames let Jilly's words hang in the air. "Did she rebuff their advances?"

Jilly shook her head. "Edvard just had a crush on her. I think Gretta sat him down and explained things to him. But *no* is a word that Richard Avedon doesn't hear—or like—very much. I think she had to go to his father about it, and that didn't sit well with Richard."

"Interesting... What about you?" Arames asked pointedly.

Jilly seemed embarrassed by the question. "What do you mean?"

"Has Richard Avedon made any advances toward you?"

The muscles around Jilly's eyes relaxed, but the anger remained in her voice. "He wouldn't dare. He knew I hated him after how he acted toward Gretta, and that I wouldn't have anything to do with him."

"Are you interested in anyone here in town? I know at least one young man who thinks the world of you."

"Is Shane talking about me again? I don't know how many times I've told him to quit fawning over me." Jilly's voice was not angry now, but resigned.

Arrin asked, "You don't ever see yourself feeling the same way about him?"

Jilly licked her lips—not provocatively, but as a point of emphasis. "No." Her tone left no room for discussion.

"We need to ask you more about your friendship with Gretta." Jilly nodded. Arames continued, "You knew Gretta since you were both children?"

"Yes. She started spending the winters here with her mother when she was six. I'm a year younger, and we played together. We were always friends, but when she moved here, we became even closer." Jilly sighed wistfully; her eyes took on a faraway quality. "Gretta grew up in the world, Sir Arames. I have spent my whole life here. My father has taken me to Ellyonne twice—*twice*—but when I was twelve I was allowed to travel with Gretta and her mother to see Thorn's Way. I even got to see your brotherhood's Academy—at least from the outside.

"But that's it. Most of my life I have only heard about the world from the stories Gretta told me. She traveled all around Yew and even into Grozh and Inarra. It was all part of her education. And when she moved here, I got to hear even more. Have you ever seen the smoke billowing out of the Great Rift?"

The Rift was an Inarran volcano that, legend held, led directly to Kalin's Abyss in the underworld. Arames nodded. "I will tell you of it another time. From what people have told us, your relationship with Gretta changed over the last half-year or so."

Jilly's brow furrowed and a line crossed her forehead. She was not happy, but she did her best to mask it in her voice. "Gretta became so busy with her work. I knew the day would come. Her mother even warned me. But it still hurt when she told me we couldn't go on picnics together anymore—that she needed to work."

"And you were not welcomed as warmly at the manor after that?"

"No, I was always welcome. But Gretta couldn't spend time with me, and once Gretta turned Richard down, he loved trying to get to Gretta through me. Eventually I just stopped going."

Arames exchanged a pointed look with Arrin, then continued. "Jilly, we have good reason to believe that Gretta was having an affair."

Jilly Hemming looked at both Arames and Arrin, dumbfounded. "What... that's... not possible."

"We believe not only that it was possible, but that it happened."

Jilly rose to her feet. "But she had no time for something like that. She never had visitors at her home." Arames didn't ask how she knew such a thing. Jilly continued, "And no one was meeting her outside of town." She thought for a moment. "Unless it was Jon. But Jon is only fourteen. Gretta wouldn't do that."

Arames looked into Jilly's eyes, wanting to see her next reaction. "What about your father?"

Jilly's mouth fell open. Arames waited silently. "My father!? The only time he leaves town is to go to Ellyonne. There isn't—he wouldn't—" Arames didn't need to use his Aarronic abilities to read Jilly's emotions. The increasing number of trips to Ellyonne; that Hemming returned to town much later in the day once she had stopped going on picnics with Gretta... the facts were sinking in without the need for Arames to speak them aloud.

The tension in the air was palpable, like the build-up of pressure in a pot of water about to boil. Tears brimmed in Jilly's eyes and spilled down her face and she clenched her hands against her side. Pulses of her emotion reached Arames, passing through him like waves of heat. Arames stood and placed his hand on Jilly's arm. "I believe they broke it off months before Gretta—"

Jilly would not be calmed with words. She exploded. "*You* know *nothing!* It didn't happen! You've got it wrong! Gretta wouldn't—my father wouldn't—my father and mother LOVE each other!" Jilly picked up the basket she had dropped and stormed off toward the bakery. They watched as Jilly stopped under the awning, collected herself, and then walked through the door. She looked back one more time before the door closed. Her face was calm now, tears wiped away—but her eyes held a hatred and fire that Arames could feel even from where he stood. The door closed, and Arames and Arrin were alone on the empty street.

Arames took Arrin by the arm and directed him down the path to the east. Arrin commented, "That went well, don't you think?"

Arames smiled. "Actually, it did."

"Do you think she is going to talk to her parents about what just happened?"

Arames continued toward the inn. "Oh, I think not."

Arames did not say more. As with most conversations between them, this was a test for Arrin. *What did I learn from Jilly's reaction and words?* But instead of commenting on Jilly, Arrin asked, "Why didn't you ask Jilly about burning the dolls?"

Arames changed direction slightly, heading back in toward the stables. "I did not have to. It is obvious that Jilly has some issues. We will save that for another time. I did not want to push her too far."

"Oh no, you wouldn't want to do that." Arrin rolled his eyes at his mentor. "Well, at least it's obvious now why Gretta stopped having lunches with Jilly."

"Is it?"

"Gretta began having an affair with Jilly's father. The time she usually spent with Jilly was the time she could rendezvous with Hemming."

Arames nodded. "True—but like most things, there is more than one reason why Gretta might have stopped seeing Jilly. Don't assume anything, Arrin."

Jon Avedon was leading a horse down the path away from the stables. He smiled and approached Arames and Arrin, looping the reins of his horse on the low branch of a nearby tree. Even though Arames would never own a horse of his own again, he knew horses. Jon's would have remained in place even without the bridle. Jon shook Arames's hand fervently. "Good day, gents! How goes the investigation?" He leaned in conspiratorially. "Any suspects yet?"

"It is too early to say, Jon."

They exchanged pleasantries for a few moments. Jon had a good laugh at his father's reaction to Arames's actions the evening before. "*Da* loves us very much, even if he is a bit overprotective at times. I think that my interest in horses has lessened his attention to my well being. I don't mean that in a bad way. I just think he knows I'm well, and that I will have a life even though I have no desire to become the next Lord Avedon."

"We still have not met Edvard or Julienne."

Jon's face lost its smile. "Edvard has been ill, I'm afraid, and Richard says his recovery is slow. Hopefully he'll be able to have visitors soon."

Arrin asked, "You don't see him when he's sick?"

"Not this time. I'm preparing for a competition in Taxx and haven't spent much time in the manor. Richard and Carin think it best if us *youngins* keep our distance while he's sick, anyway. Julienne is having a hard time of it. Edvard is her favorite."

"What does Julienne like to do? Does she have interests, like you?"

"Yes, she actually wants to travel to Thorn's Way and join the Priests of Caern."

Arames was surprised. While some temples to the Children of Az welcomed or even encouraged female clerics, such as the sisterhoods of Iruna and Kaelee, the Priests of Caern never accepted female acolytes. "I know," Jon said. "It's a long shot. But her plan is to travel to Thorn's Way next year and offer her services. She hopes her status as the daughter of a lord of Grozh will sway the High Priests."

Arames nodded. "I would love the opportunity to talk with her about this—but I have an important matter to discuss with you."

Jon frowned. "This doesn't sound good."

Arames continued. "When we first met, you told us you had seen Gretta riding outside the town walls."

"I believe what I said was that I sometimes saw her horse, Firefly. I know there was some sort of clearing where she spent time—but I never actually saw her."

Arames nodded. "And that is how you could deny seeing who she met there."

Jon's smile returned. "I see where this is going. Let's skip the small talk. What do you have on Hemming?"

Arames's brows raised. He was going to have to reassess his opinion of the Avedon family.

"I didn't want to say anything until you had evidence yourself. I don't like speaking ill of anyone, especially without proof. But on several occasions I saw Hemming's cart off of the main road near where Gretta spent her afternoons. I never saw them together, but I can tell you one thing for sure—the road to Ellyonne is nowhere near Gretta's grove. This went on until… probably three or four months ago. After that, I never saw Hemming's wagon anywhere near the area."

Arames didn't say anything for a moment. "Still not proof of the act, but enough to take to Hemming himself. Thank you, Jon. At some point we might need you to take us to that clearing, to see if Gretta might have left anything important there."

Jon grabbed the reins of his horse and started toward the town gate. "If you ever need me, I'm at your service."

⁕

Hemming was not happy to see Arames enter the bakery.

Arames spoke before Hemming could. "We should go outside—unless you want your wife to hear what I have to say."

Hemming sighed, somewhat defeated. "Wait a moment." He walked into the back. Arames could not hear the words, but Hemming's voice spoke, then Dally's, louder and questioning. When the baker returned, he gestured to the door.

Arames led Hemming a fair distance from the bakery, and then spoke quietly, his tone even rather than accusing. "You had an affair with Gretta Platt, which ended several months ago. Which of you called it off, and why?"

Hemming was angry, but did not deny the monk's words. "I would like to be able to say I did, but it was her decision. I loved Gretta. I wouldn't hurt a hair on her head. She called it off, stating the obvious: I'm married, and too old for her. She would never marry anyone from Avedon Hill, even if I left my Dally. She was the most beautiful—" Hemming's voice broke.

"Hemming, I believe you, but you've got to be honest with me from now on."

The baker nodded emphatically. "Yes, yes, I promise. Besides, I can prove I didn't kill Gretta. My wife and I were dining with Father Livasdawn that night."

"Was your daughter with you?"

Hemming began to answer, but then stopped. "Why do you ask?"

"Was your daughter with you, at Father Livasdawn's home?"

Hemming grabbed for Arames, but the monk quickly shifted his weight to the right. Hemming missed and wavered, off-balance. Before he could regain his footing, Arames grabbed the baker's arm tightly and moved in with his left hip, trapping Hemming so that he was unable to move without falling.

Physically, Hemming may have been completely at Arames's mercy, but his anger had not abated. "My daughter was Gretta's friend! You're looking in the wrong place, *monk!* Gretta was killed by a vampire. *You know that!*"

Hemming was a large man, but Arames's leverage and balance offset most of the baker's weight. "I know nothing of the sort, Master Hemming. I know that I have been lied to for over a day now, and I am beginning to tire of it. The only thing that has become clear is that no one is as innocent as they would like me to believe. I am trying to clear everyone I can, including your daughter. If she was not with you when Gretta was murdered, she had to be somewhere. If your daughter had nothing to do with Gretta's murder, then you have nothing to worry about."

Arames pulled Hemming up until he had his feet under him again. Constable Louis had entered the town circle and had stopped, just watching them. He was far enough away that he could not have heard their conversation. Arames said very quietly, "Does your wife know of your affair?"

"No."

"Keep it that way. That is a pain she does not deserve."

With that, Arames turned and walked away. Constable Louis simply smiled and walked in the opposite direction. Arames turned toward the butcher shop; no matter what, a meal was next on his list.

THE SMELL OF GOLD

I'm richer than the King of Yew. I'm richer than Az. And nobody knows who I am. One benefit? I'm rarely the target of one of my own thieves.

—The Autobiography of Arlen Gricca

AFTER A MUCH-NEEDED MEAL of lamb and beef strips wrapped in a hollowed-out loaf of bread, Arames and his student made their way back to the northwestern part of town. They again passed the dilapidated theatre and heard the sound of hammering from inside. Arrin suggested, "Maybe they are fixing the place up." Arames took out his journal and wrote a few quick notes.

Alex Dewirin was reading a book when they arrived at the general store. He looked up and smiled. "Made your way back to the outskirts?"

Arrin spoke as they approached the counter. "Why *is* your store in this corner of town? It's off the path from the town gate and the Olviaran Pass. Surely your business suffers from your location."

"I have only lived in Avedon Hill for... six years now. Possibly by the time I'm ready to retire, Lord Avedon will allow me to set up shop in the town circle. For now, I survive here. Most of the regulars know where I am."

Arames asked, "Did your dissatisfaction about your location carry over into your relationship with Gretta Platt?"

Alex Dewirin appeared confused. "My dissatisfaction about this location has always been directed at Lord Avedon."

"That's not what we have heard from those at the manor."

Alex Dewirin looked to be around thirty-five, with short-cropped hair. His pale skin seemed to get paler by the moment. "I have no idea what you're talking about."

Arames looked at his notes. "You argued with Gretta on more than one occasion about your financial difficulties, did you not?"

Alex pursed his lips. "Argued—that's a strong word. If you consider pleading with the Housemistress to loosen Lord Avedon's rules on trade as *arguing*—then yes, I guess so."

"Rules?"

Alex shook his head at the monk. "You have your work cut out for you, Sir Arames. The Housemistress kept watch over the gold coming in and going out—always a good motive for murder."

Arames was unmoved. "You didn't answer my question."

"So I didn't. You are probably on the right track, but I am not your man. I've certainly run headlong into a wall when it comes to changing how things work here. As a merchant, I can buy, sell, and trade items within these walls, but I'm not allowed to export any of my stock outside of town. That goes for some of the other merchants here—ask Herrjarr about his frustrations."

He continued. "For example, last season I came across a case of wine from eastern Inarra that I knew would fetch a goodly sum in Haven. I knew the seller was unable to travel to Haven because of a few warrants..." he waved his hand, "harmless fellow, all things told. In any case, I decided to buy the wine myself and send it to a merchant I know in Haven. By chance, a shipping company on its way to Haven came through Avedon Hill the next week. I would have made a nice profit, but Gretta put a stop to it."

Arrin asked, "How could she even have known that the wine was yours?"

Arames supplied the answer. "The wine was on the books as cargo coming through the Pass. When your 'friend' left, Cletus marked the wine as missing."

Alex nodded. "Yes, they keep good records. Cletus gets a cargo list from the manor every day... sometimes two or three times a day, depending on how many merchants come in through the Pass. Cletus notes any differences in cargo and asks about items that are added or absent. Gretta knew I had acquired the wine the day I bought it. So when it came time to ship it, it had already been tagged as goods meant for sale here. The man transporting the wine slipped—he admitted he was taking it on my behalf. All he had to do was say he bought it from me and I would have paid the tax on it."

"So you cannot ship your own goods? You only can buy and sell from within your store?"

"Yes sir. It's the price we pay for doing business in Avedon Hill."

Arrin thought for a moment. "Are you allowed, as you suggested, to use merchants traveling through Avedon Hill as middle men? You sell to merchants, and then they sell to your customers in other cities?"

"If you can get away with it. For most of my wares, certainly. For unique items, like the wine, I can only do that two or three times a year without raising suspicion."

Arrin shook his head. "What about Hemming? He sells his goods in Ellyonne and other places, doesn't he?"

Alex snapped his fingers, finishing with his index finger pointing in the air.

"There you have it. You're following the right lead, you just have to knock on the right doors—unless you're one of those who believes in vampires."

"So, help us," Arrin pressed. "Explain it to us."

Alex smiled. "There's no chance of that, son. There's a fundamental truth you'll have to learn about Avedon Hill if you want to understand why Gretta was murdered, but you'll have to learn it for yourselves. I'm not the one to share it with you. I have a business to keep afloat. I have learned how to work the system as well as I can—I can only hope the next Housemistress will have a different view of the world than Gretta had."

He paused for emphasis. "And besides, I was with Marrissa the night Gretta was murdered."

Arames nodded. "So I have heard."

"Oh, and by the way, I certainly didn't kill Gretta Platt over some wine. She ended up buying the wine from me, herself. And she paid me nearly what I would have gotten from my contact in Haven."

"Why did she do that?"

Alex shrugged. "I don't rightly know. Maybe she felt guilty about the whole thing. Maybe Lord Avedon has a taste for the desert grapes of eastern Inarra. I don't know. But I do know that I didn't kill her."

They closed the door behind them and headed southeast. Arrin said, "We should have pressed him harder. He knows more than he is saying."

"True, but we cannot *make* him talk. Like with Hemming, once we have enough evidence, Alex will have more of a reason to talk. I understand his resistance."

Arames stopped and thought for a moment. "We need to expand our search again. I want you to go to Marrissa's shop. Confirm what Alex told us. Constable Louis still believes Alex had enough time to make it to the manor after he left Marrissa's company."

"What will you be doing?"

Arames smiled. "I think I will return to the library."

"You just want to see that librarian again."

"The prospect of visiting Lane Niccols is appealing, but this has more to do with Avedon Hill's history. Everything we have learned thus far about Gretta Platt deals with her role as Housemistress. As Alex just stated, we need to consider all possible motives. The rules Alex spoke of seem to change depending on the townsperson. A look at the history might explain why things work the way they do."

"I know why things work the way they do. These people are all *touched in the head.*"

Arames laughed and turned south toward the library. "Meet me at the town circle when you are done. I might be a while, so if you find anyone else to talk to, be friendly and learn what you can."

Lane Niccols was the first woman that Arames could remember ever feeling an instant, personal connection with. Even though he had been retired from the Aarronic order for years, he had always shied away from pursuing physical relationships—the one foray he had allowed himself into that arena had ended very badly for both involved. Arames had no intention of losing his focus, but he still found himself looking forward to a second meeting with the librarian.

The monk found Lane Niccols behind the counter that separated the reading room of the library from the stairs that led down to the bulk of the collection. Lane appeared to be stitching some leather over the spine of *The Linus Compendium*, the book they had used the day before. She was wearing her hair down; silky and black, it hung nearly to her waist.

"Good morning." Her smile touched him, and he could only smile in return. "Where is your young student today?"

"Arrin had an errand to run for me."

"I couldn't help but notice that your stay here has more of a purpose now. Have you determined who murdered Gretta Platt?"

"No. Not yet, I am afraid. We are running into many obstacles, the greatest of which seems to revolve around the relationship between the Avedons, the Housemistress, and the rest of Avedon Hill."

Lane nodded. "By 'Housemistress' you refer to the position and not to Gretta."

"Yes..." Arames felt his heart rate increase. He and Arrin had nearly lost control of themselves in the clothing shop the day before, but Arames's reactions to Lane were far more subtle. Her intelligence affected him the most... although her seemingly ageless beauty was a draw, as well. "Which is why I am here. I was hoping you might have something that details the history of Avedon Hill."

Her eyes lit up. "Of course..." But her expression shifted to disappointment almost as quickly. "You're not going to find too much in the way of details, I should warn you. Anonymity seems to be one of Avedon Hill's strengths." She turned and walked down the stairs. "Give me a moment."

She returned a few moments later, her blue dress billowing around her feet as she walked. The grace in her step was unmistakable. "Here you are, Sir Arames." Arames looked at the title: *The Journal of Aubrey Avedon, 208-240 AI*.

"May I?" Arames pointed to the reading area behind him.

"Please." She lifted a hinge underneath the counter that allowed her to cross into the room. The two walked over to the largest table and sat together.

Arrin walked reluctantly to Marrissa's house and workshop. Marrissa had secured them entry into Avedon Manor, but she had not been happy to see them. He expected that she would be even less excited to see him again.

Arrin opened the door and stepped into the shop. Marrissa rushed to the railing that separated her work area from her living space and yelled, "May Az cut you down—"

Arrin looked behind him to be sure no one else was the focus of her apparent rage. "Expecting someone?"

The herbalist closed her eyes for a moment, gathering herself. "I'm sorry... what was your name again?"

"Arrin." He bowed slightly.

"Right. I don't know why you're here, but I'm very busy. Please go."

Arrin crossed the room and climbed the stairs to the raised workshop. Marrissa threw her hands up in disgust. "Does no one respect my *wishes!*"

Arrin smiled. He doubted a friendly demeanor would diffuse the woman's anger, but he had seen it work for Arames. "I apologize, ma'am. I just need to ask you a couple of questions."

Marrissa returned to her worktable, where she began mixing colored liquids in a small bowl. It was as if she thought that ignoring Arrin would make him disappear. He took a breath and plunged on.

"Alex Dewirin had dinner with you the night Gretta was murdered?"

Without looking at Arrin, the herbalist muttered, "How many times do I have to say so? I spent the early part of the evening with Alex here in my shop. I make a salve for his leg. We get together for dinner every two weeks or so, when he needs a new batch of medicine."

"But he left your home before the murder is thought to have taken place, correct?"

Marrissa kept her head bent to her work. "Yes... and to answer your next three questions: he could have made it to the manor and murdered Gretta; I don't know of any reason he would have killed Gretta; and I don't know how he could have entered and left the manor unseen."

Marrissa fell silent, pointedly mixing her potions, and Arrin took the opportunity to look around. Below the raised platform where they both stood, a desk was set in a small recess under a window, nearly out of the line of sight from the workbench. The desk was bare, save for a small piece of parchment that Arrin didn't remember having seen the day before. "So... can you go now?"

"Yes, ma'am. I'm sorry I interrupted your work."

"No you're not. Please tell your master that I have no information that will help him."

Arrin bowed, then turned and walked down the stairs as if to take his leave. When he passed near Marrissa's desk, he shuffled as if he had tripped over his own feet, dropping his pack to the floor and making sure it bounced over against the desk. He looked back toward the herbalist as he moved to retrieve the pack—absorbed in the billow of purple smoke spilling over the edge of one of her glass containers, she had barely noticed.

Arrin took his time picking up his pack and retrieving two apples that had fallen out of one pocket, so that he could read the note on Marrissa's desk. There was no signature, but Arrin had a good idea who had written it.

You said you had what you needed to fix the potion. I don't know how long I can continue this. It had better work.

Arrin resisted the impulse to grab the parchment. Straightening, he threw his pack over his right shoulder and continued out the door and toward the town circle. He had to find Arames quickly.

⁂

Arames read *The Journal of Aubrey Avedon* with one eye fixed on the enchanting librarian sitting to his left. While the journal did not provide any shattering insights on the Avedon family, it did shed a little more light on the relationship between the Avedons, the Platts, and the town. Aubrey Avedon had lived almost two hundred years after the first Housemistress, Ella Platt, had held the station. Many times, Aubrey mentioned his own Housemistress, Nora Platt. It was plain that she was his confidant, and that she did more than just run his household... but he provided no specifics.

The second and more useful facet of the journal was Aubrey's description of Avedon Hill itself. It had been more of a mining town during his time, but Arames was amazed to discover that the town Aubrey described could easily have been the Avedon Hill of the present. Many familiar names were present in the journal: Hemming, Bore, Garrett, Ray... and at one point, Aubrey Avedon listed the number of inhabitants of Avedon Hill at forty-eight. A few more than lived there presently, but certainly not as many as Arames had expected.

"Do you have any more information on the population of Avedon Hill over its history?"

Lane smiled. "It's more of the same. As far as I can tell, at no point except when the Pass was being built, have there ever been more than fifty permanent inhabitants."

"Visitors welcomed, but never encouraged to stay."

Lane nodded. "You noticed the chapter about Rayne's Outpost?"

The gate at the other end of the Olviaran Pass was named after the member of the Praentis barony who controlled it. During Aubrey's life, efforts had been made to build more of a settlement around the other end of the Pass. It wasn't spelled out exactly, but Aubrey intimated that Praentis had been paid or otherwise convinced to disregard the idea. Lane asked, "What do you know of the Praentis family?"

Arames thought for a long moment. "I do not believe I have ever had the pleasure."

"Exactly. It seems they lost power around the same time that they began to infringe on the Avedon monopoly."

Lane Niccols stood. Arames rose as well. Unable to help himself, Arames inhaled as quietly as possible, hoping to take in the fragrance of the woman by his side, but the only scents he detected were those of books and candles. Lane touched the monk's arm. "Thank you, Sir Arames. I can't tell you the last time I've had so much fun. I have some work to do downstairs, so I will take my leave of you."

Arames bowed, unable to speak. The touch of Lane's fingers on his arm left him wanting more.

"Lane..."

"Yes, Sir Arames?"

Arames was a poor judge of age; she could have been anywhere between thirty and forty-five. "How old are you?" His own age and his growing feelings for her prompted the question, but he was not surprised when she evaded it.

The librarian smiled. "A gentleman does not ask such questions. Let's just say I am older than I look, but younger than I feel most of the time. Good day, Arames."

For the first time, Lane had not called him "sir." Arames left the library a happy man.

⚜

Shane Olivet caught up with Arrin halfway to the library.

"Arrin, wait!" The stable boy was nearly out of breath. "I need to tell you... remembered something..."

Arrin took Shane over to a nearby rock to sit and catch his breath. "You told me earlier to find you if I remembered anything out of the ordinary. Well, the morning before Gretta was murdered—or was it the day before that? I can't remember—I was walking through town and rounded the corner of the butcher shop and ran into Brianna Ray. And I mean, ran into her—knocked her right on her arse..."

"How could you run into her? It's not like the streets are narrow and busy..."

Shane waved a hand at Arrin and suppressed a chuckle. "No, I have a short cut that takes me around the back of the butcher shop. It was just bad luck. That's why I remembered it. She wasn't using the road. She was on a side trail, almost like she didn't want to be seen."

Arrin nodded. He waited patiently—there had to be more to the story than knocking the maid from her feet.

"What she was carrying was the strange thing. Packages went flying out of her hands, and when I helped her pick them up, they were packages of meat."

"How is that strange?"

"The butcher delivers orders to the manor himself. Chef Roland wouldn't send Brianna to the shop."

"Maybe she was picking up an order for herself?"

"I guess that's possible, but she was heading back to the manor. And I haven't told you the strangest thing of all..." Shane leaned in dramatically. When Arrin did not lean in as well, Shane straightened up and rolled his eyes. "Fine. When I bent down to help her, she got all upset. And when I was done refilling her bag, my hands came away all bloody."

"Bloody?"

"She wasn't just carrying raw meat, Arrin. She was carrying blood-soaked packages—a lot more blood than you would expect. My hands looked like I'd butchered the animals myself. They were wrapped, so I couldn't tell what they were. All I know is that it wasn't your run-of-the-mill order. Someone had to have wanted it that way."

"Did you ask her why there was so much blood?"

"No, she practically ran off."

Shane watched Arrin eagerly, expecting him to leap on the possible connection between blood and vampires, but Arrin refused to go down that path until he found Arames. "Thank you, Shane. If you remember anything else, please let me know."

HART'S BLOOD

The blood of the stag is the most powerful claret of the animal world.
You will never find me without a vial or two, in case of injury or malaise.

—The Linus Compendium

ARRIN DROPPED HIS PACK to the ground in front of Arames, who sat on a bench in the center of the town circle. "We've got to talk." He remained standing, nearly bouncing from one foot to the other.

Arames took notes as Arrin described the parchment he had found—and his suspicion that the potion Marrissa was creating was for Lord Avedon, and that time was becoming an issue. He also detailed Shane's encounter with Brianna Ray and the blood-soaked packages.

While Arrin caught his breath, Arames shared what he had learned. Aubrey Avedon's journal had confirmed that "housemistress" was a misnomer—a Platt family member had been tied to Avedon Hill's leaders for nearly four hundred years, and the scope of her duties, while still unclear to Arames, went well beyond managing the manor and its staff. The journal had also raised a more intriguing point: since the completion of the Pass, there had been no rise or fall in the population of Avedon Hill. The question remained: why?

"So, what's next?"

Arames closed the notebook. "There are still several people we have not met yet: the guard Roc, who was in the kitchens when Gretta was killed, and the constable, Tanner, who argued with Leilah the morning after Gretta's murder. And if we are lucky, maybe we will meet Edvard and Julienne. Once we do that, we can move on to some of these new things we have learned."

Arrin stopped his restless shifting and stared at Arames. His left eyelid twitched uncontrollably and his face slowly flushed red. Arames started to smile. *Ah, here it comes.*

"Arames, what are we *doing* here!?" Arrin implored, arms spread wide. "History!? Population? We've got a murderer, a moon-beast outside of town, I'm apparently dream-walking now, and you seem more interested in bookkeeping! Now you want to talk to more people who did not kill Gretta and seem to know nothing that can help us? Why?"

Arames spoke slowly and without emotion. 'I would have to disagree with your last point, Arrin. As your friend Shane has shown, these townspeople know more than they think they know... or they choose to remain silent until we ask the right questions."

Arrin rubbed his forehead. "But why do you *insist* on going down this path of gold and power when more and more evidence points toward a vampire? Father Jorrus feels it... the vampires you faced outside of town... Gretta's corpse disappearing... bloody packages carried around by the manor *staff*, for Az's sake!"

Arames smiled. "Yes, it is becoming clear that something is going on at the manor, and that Gretta might have been murdered by someone who is not what he or she seems. But what would you have us do? Do you have someone in mind to confront, to accuse of Gretta's murder?"

Arrin winced. "It's not that I want to accuse anyone. I just want to investigate this undead presence. But you would rather investigate how many people lived here three hundred years ago."

Arames bowed his head for a moment. "You have heard me say this many times, Arrin. *Knowledge is Power*. But more than that, knowledge is our *only* power here. We are outsiders. The more information we have, the more leverage we will have at our disposal when the time comes. Yes, Gretta Platt may have been killed by a vampire. But even if that is so, we know it was not random. She died for a very specific reason... love, hate, jealousy, greed, or something else we have yet to even consider. We need to learn all we can about Gretta and her own power in order to learn why she was killed—and once we know why, the who will follow."

Arames used an analogy Arrin's mother was fond of: "Avedon Hill is a house of cards, young prince. We are pulling the cards out... *one by one*. We have to do this slowly, or the house will fall—right on top of us. And we cannot afford to have that happen. That being said," Arames stood, picking up Arrin's pack and handing it back to the young prince. "Let's go and visit our friend Caasz. He might have some of that lamb left, and he might be able to shed more light on your bloody packages."

⟡

"Avedon Manor is my primary customer—at least fifteen deliveries a month, and Chef Roland makes special requests, too, for guests and the like." Caasz brought his large cleaver down sharply, hacking the hind quarters from a deer carcass.

"A few days ago someone saw Brianna Ray carrying bloody packages of meat back to the manor. Did she get them from you?"

"Yes."

"Chef Roland needed something special?"

Caasz shook his head. "He would come himself, not send a maid. It was Olviaran Whitetail, but it wasn't your normal cuts."

Arrin guessed, "Livers?"

Caasz nodded. "And hearts."

The heart of a hart. "This didn't strike you as strange?"

Caasz shrugged his shoulders. "You get used to strange requests. Marrissa asks for blood, as does the clothier, Sarah. And Lane Niccols requests the bloodiest livers I can give her."

"Lane?" Arames was surprised at the way his voice sounded. He hoped Arrin hadn't noticed. He understood why the herbalist and someone who worked with dyes might collect blood... *but why would Lane need bloody livers?*

Caasz smiled. "Liver stew, bloody as the Abyss. She made it for me once. I've been trying to get the recipe ever since."

After a few more questions and another quick bite to eat, Arames and Arrin left Caasz's shop. "Let us see if any of the manor staff are at their communal home," Arames said. "Maybe they will open up more to us there."

⁂

As luck would have it, Brianna Ray was exiting her home as they approached. She could barely bring herself to meet Arames's gaze. "Good day, Sir A-Arames."

"Brianna, I have a couple more questions for you. ...Brianna?" She reminded Arames of an animal that had been abused, and he didn't like to see that in anyone.

She finally looked up into his eyes. "Yes, Sir Arames?"

"Don't be scared. I am not going to get you in trouble."

"I know that, sir. I ... just..." Brianna's voice trailed off.

"May we come in? I'm an old man and need my rest. Arrin, can you get me some water?"

Arrin nodded, hiding his knowing smile. "Yes, of course."

Brianna had already led them into the common room, but now she turned, horrified. "No, Sir Arames. I should do that."

The monk took her hand. "No. You are at home, not at the manor. My student can get me some water. He's good at fetching. Please, sit here with me."

She did as he asked, and perched stiffly at the edge of a chair. Arames asked, "Did you like Gretta Platt?"

Brianna smiled; it was the first time Arames had seen her do so. "Oh yes, yes sir. She was a wonderful lady."

"You do understand that we are only trying to find out what happened to her, and no one will be punished if they have done nothing wrong."

Brianna nodded. "I know."

"Good. I need to ask you about something and you need to be honest with me."

She had relaxed a great deal, but Arames could see that she was expecting a difficult question. He didn't disappoint her. "We know you picked up some strange items from Caasz last week. What was that all about?"

Tears immediately began welling up in Brianna's eyes. "I... they weren't for me, Sir Arames."

Arames smiled. "I did not assume that they were, Brianna. I surmised that someone sent you. I just need to know who that was, and what the items were for, if you know."

Brianna's hand started shaking in Arames's, and the brimming tears spilled over, streaming down her face. "Carin Avedon told me not to talk about it. She told me she's learning how to cook, to surprise her father with a birthday meal. She's working on a special recipe—some sort of meat pudding. Oh, please don't tell her I told you, Sir Arames... *please*!"

Arames patted her hand. "No need to worry, Brianna... but didn't you find it strange?"

"Oh, Sir Arames, sure. Hearts, bloody livers—that doesn't sound like good food to me." Brianna turned pale just thinking about it. "My hands were stained by the time I was done, even though they were wrapped."

"So, if my timeline is correct, this was days before Gretta was killed, correct?"

Brianna nodded. "Yes, Sir Arames. The first time was two or three days before that."

"First?"

"Yes. The second time was the day after Gretta's death."

"Has Carin sent you to Caasz before or since?"

"No, Sir Arames. She... hasn't felt like practicing since."

Arames let go of Brianna's hand and stood as Arrin entered with a cup of water. The monk smiled. "Good timing, Arrin. Give that to Brianna. She looks like she needs it more than I do."

Arrin handed the cup to Brianna, who smiled faintly and nodded her thanks. The two men took their leave and Arames turned northeast, toward Avedon Manor. "We need to learn more about Carin Avedon's new hobby—without being thrown out of town."

THE MARK OF AZ

"And Kaelee, silent for generations,
will appear and aid us at the end of the day."

—3rd Collected Prophecies of Iberian, Book 1, Chapter 5

WHILE THE FARMS NEAR the town walls may have been busily preparing for the impending winter, Avedon Hill's main streets remained unaffected. Arames and Arrin made their way back to the gates of Avedon Manor without crossing paths with anyone.

At the manor, Arames was surprised to see Constable Louis with a young girl perched on his back, her arms wrapped tightly around the constable's neck. The girl laughed as Louis extricated her from his back and set her gently on the ground. Standing, she looked to be older than Arames would have initially guessed, her height and bearing placing her between probably eight and ten years of age. Louis mockingly adopted the voice of a stern taskmaster. "Stand up straight, Julienne. You need to meet our esteemed guests." His tone was belied by the smile on his face.

"You're the man who's going to find out who killed our Gretta. Thank you." Arames was transfixed by the child's sparkling eyes. She smiled and extended her hand in gratitude, her smile beaming like the sun. *It has been years since I have seen such a smile... such a mark.* The Priests of Caern would likely claim the light in Julienne's eyes as the touch of Iberian. To Arames, the light was a sign of something else altogether.

"You are welcome, young miss."

"Do you need anything from me? I want to help, but I don't know who would hurt Miss Gretta."

Arames certainly had questions for the young Avedon, but none of them involved his investigation. Julienne's eyes had become a conduit, pulling Arames deep inside the young girl. It was remarkably different than the power he used to *truth-read* or *mind-walk*. Now Arames felt more than saw—warmth, power, and love, converging and coursing through Julienne.

Some Priests of Caern claimed to have this power, calling it *soul-searching*. Those who possessed the ability but did not follow Iberian were vilified by the Priests of Caern as charlatans and sorcerers. In truth, Arames knew of only one Priest of Caern who had ever possessed the talent. Soul-searching seemed to manifest itself more often in Aarronic Advisors, which pained the followers of Iberian to no end.

Arames felt Arrin touch his shoulder. From the confused look on Julienne's face, he knew he had been silent for an inappropriate amount of time. "I—I am sorry, Miss Julienne. I am afraid this has been a long day already. If you think of anything out of the ordinary that you may have seen or heard over the last few months, even if it had nothing directly to do with Gretta, please tell Constable Louis. He can pass it on to us."

Julienne crinkled her nose. "Is my father scaring you, Sir Arames?"

Constable Louis laughed. "I'm sure he has *tried*, but you'll find they are not so easily scared. Come along, my dear. Your riding lesson awaits."

Julienne smiled. "My brother Jon is finally teaching me how to jump!"

Louis put his arm around Julienne's shoulders and led her away. "I'll come find you if I learn anything new, Sir Arames."

⚬⚭⚬

"What happened back there, Arames?" Arrin asked as they walked to the entrance of the manor.

Arames was silent for a moment, and Arrin knew he was weighing his response. "You know that during my time as a member of the Aarronic Order, certain powers manifested in me, perhaps by the will of Az and his Children, or simply a greater attunement to the Land itself. Some of these powers, I may call upon. My truth-reading, not as strong as some in the Order, is linked to my concentration. It is an active event. But other powers, such as what you just witnessed—those I do not control. Let me ask you, Arrin. When you looked at Julienne Avedon, what did you notice?"

Arrin thought for a moment. "She's bright, engaging—and she has a commanding relationship with Constable Louis, even though it was he who led her around."

Arames nodded. "Good. What else?"

"Well... she seems honest... and I'm sure her smile lights up whatever room she is in."

"Yes, truly." Arames stopped before the door of the manor. To their left was the entrance to the Olviaran Pass, its guard station empty. The Pass didn't need constant guarding while it was closed to traffic, and an alarm protected the complicated mechanism of the gate itself.

"Certain people have a presence about them. To most it would appear that they 'glow,' or 'light up the room.' A very small number of these people are truly special. Some would say they have a destiny so ingrained in them that others can sense it without understanding its meaning. These few possess what the Aarronic Order calls the *Mark of Az*. The Priests of Caern call it the *Mark of Iberian*, but that is another story. In any case, I have the ability to sense this mark in people."

"What does it mean?"

"It means that Julienne Avedon has an intended purpose in this world. What it is, I have no idea. All I know is that she has the potential to become someone very special." Arames looked pointedly at Arrin. "This *sense* is not an ability that one can gain through training. It is a *power* that is simply part of someone. While I have sensed the Mark of Az in several people over the years, only once have I sensed it as strongly as I did today."

"Only once?"

"Yes—the day I met your mother."

Arrin could only watch as Arames moved past him and entered Avedon Manor. *He did it again. Another piece of the puzzle that is my family, dangled before me like a carrot leading a horse.* Arrin frowned and then followed Arames through the door.

⚜

In the manor kitchen, Arames asked Chef Roland about Carin's new hobby.

"Carin Avedon, *cooking*? I don't think so, Sir Arames." Chef Roland stood with hands on hips, looking very amused. His son Ley stood in the corner with a mop, laughing.

Ley spoke. "Don't get us wrong, Sir Arames. We love Miss Carin. She's always very nice to us. But she knows as much about working in a kitchen as I do about shoeing a horse—which would be nothing."

"Maybe she's trying to keep it a secret—as a surprise?" Arrin offered.

Chef Roland shook his head. "If she's learning how to cook, it's not in this kitchen. And if she was trying to learn, she would have consulted me. I've pulled all of those kids into the kitchen over the years and none of them has shown even the slightest interest."

Arames nodded. "Thank you, Roland. Please don't mention to Lord Avedon that we spoke about this."

"Spoke about what?" Lord Avedon had walked into the kitchen and was standing behind Arames and Arrin. Arames cursed himself silently for placing his back to the main entry. He turned slowly to face Lord Avedon, who—as always—appeared unhappy.

Arrin spoke first. "We were asking Chef Roland for his best Olviaran Whitetail dish. Talik Bore claims his venison stew is the best in the region. We were giving Roland a chance to prove him wrong."

Lord Avedon blinked once, stared at Chef Roland's blank expression, and then exploded. "You waste time asking my people about *food*!?"

Arrin knew that Arames would not lie to Lord Avedon. He, however, had no qualms about doing so. "We were following up on some questions about Gretta's eating habits," he said.

Arames nodded to Arrin and they both bowed slightly to Lord Avedon and moved to leave the kitchen. Avedon stuck out his arm to prevent Arames from passing, but the monk slid effortlessly to the side, avoiding contact without making a move that could be considered aggressive.

Lord Avedon's face was red. "I'm beginning to think I made a mistake about you."

Arames did not stand down. "You have placed restrictions on our investigation, Lord Avedon. I am abiding these restrictions as well as possible, but at this point I am here to solve a murder. I no longer care about obtaining safe passage through your mountains. I will succeed at this—but how quickly and efficiently I succeed depends greatly on how much you impede my investigation."

"*Impede?!*" Lord Avedon waved a finger at the monk. "Give me something right now, or I will lead the procession of constables as they haul you and your servant out of my town. Show me something to prove that you are not simply here to add to my grief!"

"Where are the books?"

"What?"

"The *books*—the ledgers that Gretta used to track monies; to record the taxes and tariffs levied on those who travel through the Pass—where are they?"

"That is none of your business."

"You cannot tell me because you have no idea where they are."

Lord Avedon raised an eyebrow, taken aback by the monk's words. He whirled, his purple cloak spinning around him, and strode from the kitchen. Arames followed, flashing a sign to Arrin that ordered him to stay behind.

Once they reached the great hall, Arames spoke first. "Lord Avedon—I do not *care* how much gold you have, or what secrets you and Gretta Platt shared. You lost not only a Housemistress, but the one person required to keep this town running smoothly. I believe you do not even know if Gretta's books are simply hidden or if they were taken, possibly by her murderer."

Lord Avedon's anger melted away, overtaken by the same defeat Arames had seen in him the day before. "You're correct. No one, not even her mother, knows for sure if the ledgers are simply missing or have been stolen."

"So this is why you do not believe this is a vampire killing. You believe this is about your gold."

"No vampire murdered Gretta. I'm sure of that."

"What makes you so sure?" Arames pressed.

He paused and blinked twice, lost in thought. "I—just continue your investigation, Arames Kragen. You may pursue this lead, but again, do not involve my children." Lord Avedon turned and exited the great hall, leaving Arames to contemplate his next move.

THE KING'S CROWN

For riches do not endure,
and a crown is never secure.

—Tales of the Children

WHILE LORD AVEDON'S ADMISSION should have sent Arames further down the path he had already started along, it did the exact opposite. His notes did not lie. "Arrin, I believe I missed something very important."

"Arames, what in Az's name are you talking about?"

"The King's Head moth."

Arrin wanted to cry out in frustration. Arames had refused time and time again to concentrate on the possibility that a vampire had killed Gretta Platt.

"What about the moth? We were only able to get Marrissa a King's Head caterpillar."

"Yes, but we know that Marrissa is being compelled to work without rest to create a potion, most likely for Lord Avedon. And currently she is subverting the laws of nature, forcing this caterpillar to transform months before it should."

"What I saw at Marrissa's shop makes me believe that, yes."

"Well, when we researched the King's Head moth, we only examined texts pertaining to where they might live."

By the time they arrived at the library it was nearly dusk. Arames didn't mind—if he was right, their next destination would require the cover of night. Lane was surprised to see the two men. "Back again? I'm starting to think you like me, sir monk."

The playful tone of Lane's voice was as engaging as everything else about her, but Arames was able to keep his focus, even with Arrin snickering behind him. He bowed slightly. "Ma'am, sorry to bother you so near to the end of your day, but we need to see a copy of *Lappin's Codex*. Do you have it in your collection?"

For the briefest of moments Arames thought he might have seen something, a slight tightening of the muscles around Lane's eyes, but it was gone before he could be certain. The librarian grinned. "A copy? My dear brother of Aarron, I have the original."

Arames could hardly believe his ears. As Lane walked down the stairs toward where she kept the more valuable books, Arames turned to Arrin. "The actual codex—did you hear that?"

Arrin had heard, but didn't understand his mentor's delight. "Lappin? Wasn't he a heretic?"

Arames frowned. "Does your family no longer hire competent teachers?" He sighed heavily. "Yes, Lappin was branded as a heretic by the Priests of Caern. But before that, Lappin Jaynes was one of the most respected alchemists in all the Land." They walked to the table where Arames had read through Aubrey Avedon's journal. "He dedicated his life to studying the elements that make up the world: herbs, living things, minerals... everything. Combining the essences of different items can sometimes produce something new—whether it be potions, salves—even the spirits we love to imbibe. He catalogued what he and many others had learned over hundreds of years into a book called *Lappin's Codex*."

"It is a guide to potions?"

"In some ways. The codex is a list of ingredients—agents, reagents—and explanations of what they are used for, and in."

"So the Priests of Caern branded him a heretic because he used magic?"

"That was their charge. And even if you can look past the fact that equating magic use with heresy is incomprehensible to anyone with the most basic understanding of how magic is connected to Az, Lappin still was not a heretic. Alchemy does not have anything to do with magic. Lappin Jaynes could not dip from the river of magic. He only understood how the elements that make up our world could be used to create new and powerful things."

"Then why was he killed?"

"Because three generations ago, the leadership of the Priests of Caern had an agenda that relied heavily on the fears of the common people: fear of the monsters that had come through the Great Rift and that could one day come again; fear of the prophecies of Iberian; and most importantly, it relied upon building fear of any form of magic other than that granted to clerics by Az and his Children."

"They accused Lappin of sorcery," Lane added, "even though his whole life had been devoted to helping people and to the study of the nature of our world. No one stepped forward to speak on Lappin's behalf, for fear of their own lives." As she had the day before, Lane had re-entered the room without them noticing. She placed one of the largest tomes Arrin had ever seen on the table in front of Arames. "They suspended Lappin in a tree for three days. Remarkably, he was still alive on the third day. So they burned both him and the tree to the ground, calling it the will of Iberian."

"How in the world did the Priests of Caern survive as a group? From everything you have taught me, they did little more than cause terror and fear."

Lane Niccols spoke as she walked away. "History usually shows that no group is completely good or evil, young sir. Even the Aarronic Advisors had their share of problems during those years. Wouldn't you say, Sir Arames?"

"Yes, it was a dark time for most everyone." He turned to face the librarian. "Please, before you go, I am afraid there is something I need to ask you."

Lane turned and faced the table. "Where was I the night Gretta Platt was murdered?"

"Yes."

"I'm sure Constable Louis told you I wasn't here in town and could not have possibly been at the manor?"

"Yes, his notes show you were out of town on business that night. I just wanted you to tell me where you were, in your own words."

"I left that evening just past sundown to meet one of my contacts from Dolman Tear. He had sent me a message stating that he had one of the first copies of the autobiography of Arlen Gricca."

Arlen Gricca, the one-time governor of Taxx, was one of the only members of the Council of Grozh to have revealed his identity as a Councilor to the world—an act that had gotten him killed within a year. A scrivener's copy of his autobiography would be quite an addition to Lane's collection. "Do you often meet your contacts at night?"

Lane nodded. "Not necessarily at night, but I often meet book dealers at the crossroads several cykes west of town. Some of my contacts travel from Haven to the cities along the southern coast, and meeting them at the crossroads is the only way I can trade with them. Rarely do booksellers come through the Pass."

"Were you able to get the autobiography?"

"Alas, no. My contact didn't show. He had never missed an appointment with me before. I still don't know what happened. I made it back to Avedon Hill just before dawn. I'm sure Cletus can verify that for you."

"Thank you."

Lane bowed her head slightly to both men, and then left the room to give them privacy.

Arames stroked the edge of the cover of the codex as if it were some sort of religious artifact. He opened the collection of parchments and began reading.

Arrin sat back in his chair, patiently waiting; the first pangs of hunger creeped into his thoughts. *Maybe I should pull out an—*

"AH HA!" Arames pointed at a page. "I should have known. We must go." He quickly gathered the parchments, folding them neatly and replacing them. He ran his fingers across the spine of the book one last time, marveling at the workmanship, then pulled away to focus on the task at hand. They did not wait to pay their respects; they instead exited the library and started down the path leading east.

"The King's Head moth—it is the main component of the King's Crown potion. Have you ever heard of it?"

Arrin increased his pace to keep up with Arames. "No, sir. I haven't."

"I did not make the connection when Marrissa—I am obviously getting too old for this." The monk shook his head and continued, "The King's Crown potion has to do with vampirism—specifically, with saving someone from it."

"What? How?"

"While most see vampirism as the result of demonic forces at work, some feel that it is a disease. The King's Crown potion is no more than a legend, really. Lappin recorded it in his codex because it was a possible use for the King's Head moth."

"What does this potion do?"

"As you know, when a vampire kills a victim, the corpse rises from the dead in three days, undead."

"Which is what might have happened to Gretta Platt, since her corpse has disappeared."

Arames could not deny that point. "Well, most believe that once a corpse has risen, it is already a vampire. But a few believe that there is a second part to the transformation—they believe that until a risen corpse has tasted human blood, they can be saved."

"Saved?"

"Yes. The King's Crown potion is rumored to be able to reverse the transformation of a vampire."

"What if the vampire has tasted human blood?"

"Ah, there is the rub. If a vampire that has taken a human victim drinks the potion, that vampire will become even more powerful, inheriting the strength of ten vampires."

"And you think that's what Marrissa is making for Lord Avedon?"

"I do." They had left the path to the manor gate and now approached the stables. The sun had set, and the moon had yet to rise, yet Arames was studying something in his journal very closely in the darkness.

"Where are we going? The manor is over there."

"We are going to the manor... just not through the front door. Do you think Lord Avedon would be excited to hear about our discovery?"

"No, of course not."

"So we must enter from a different direction."

THE MANOR CALLS

There will be a shelter to provide shade from the sun,
and protection from the storm and the rain.

—Tales of the Children

" ... A DIFFERENT DIRECTION."

They were going to try to enter undetected through the catacombs. Arrin had initially been excited at the prospect of action, but now he felt only the near certainty of Lord Avedon's wrath. Arrin instinctively flexed his shoulders until he felt the sword strapped against his back.

From Arrin's vantage point, slightly behind Arames and to his right, he could watch Arames begin his mental preparation for what they were about to attempt. Arames's connection to the Land was palpable. He once described it to Arrin as feeling a sea-breeze while walking along the beach, but all of the time. As they walked toward the stables and the entrance to the catacombs, Arrin imagined Arames sensing the energy of the world around him... the wind, the light, the life-force flowing through the air. To Arrin, it looked like Arames was withdrawing into himself.

⁂

To Arames, however, the experience was the exact opposite—he was reaching out into the world around him.

The heightened consciousness inherent to his connection to the Land served him well. It gave him powers. In this state, for example, he could see auras around people, see how they were connected to the river of magic all around them. It helped him to detect if someone was using magic or hiding something, or even to predict someone's actions.

The connection was all but severed when a tall figure approached them, one arm held high and ready to strike. For a moment, all Arames could see before him was an aura of blue tinged with green. Then the aura disappeared, and Father Jorrus remained.

Arrin was as surprised as Arames when Father Jorrus jumped out from behind the corner of his house, his holy symbol high above his head. Arames did not move to defend himself, but Arrin leaped forward, placing himself between Arames and the priest. The symbol of Arjun again glowed with the unnatural light of the Child of Protection's power. For a moment it appeared that Father Jorrus was going to strike, but after a tightening of his facial muscles and a blink of his eyes, he finally recognized the two men before him. Almost immediately, the light of his holy symbol began to fade into the darkening night.

"Devils! What are you doing, skulking around after dark?!"

Arames had recovered and moved beside Arrin. "We have an appointment. We will not keep you, Father."

Jorrus's hair was no longer the tangled mess of the day before, but was now tied in a long braid that lay over his shoulder. Jorrus pulled on the braid with his free hand. "You promised you would join me in the cemetery this evening, monk."

Arames opened his mouth, but Arrin spoke first. "This is the second time you've nearly attacked us with your symbol of Arjun, Father. You should be more careful." All Arrin could see was the Father Jorrus from his dream the night before, standing over a beheaded corpse and laughing at his triumph over evil.

Jorrus raised an eyebrow; he extended his arm until the end of his weapon stopped just short of Arrin's chest. "And if you had been a vampire, boy, the power of Arjun would have changed that blue light into the yellow of the sun." As Arrin stared at the symbol, it pulsed weakly—light... dark... light... dark—like a candle searching for last bit of air in a collapsed mine. "And the heat of that sun would have burned the flesh from your bones."

Arames countered, "Jorrus, as I said, we have a prior commitment. If we complete it in time, we will try to meet you."

Jorrus snorted. He moved forward and gripped the edge of Arames's robe, just below his neck. He whispered, even though Arrin stood right next to him and could clearly hear his words. "There are demons here, Arames Kragen. You've seen this for yourself. Only fools would think the gates are shut for good. You're not a fool, are you, Kragen?"

Arrin did not understand, but it was obvious that Arames was not happy. "Enough, Jorrus. There are many forms of evil in the world. Do not confuse what is happening here with the events of the past. We will meet you later if we can." He twisted to pull his robes free. "Come Arrin. We have work to do."

They left Father Jorrus and continued east until they reached the stables. Several horses were still inside the large building, Lonne Garrett and Shane Olivet had almost surely gone home for the night. Arames pulled out his notebook and held it at eye level, trying to use the light from a nearby house to look over his notes. "This is going to be harder than I thought." Soon he gave up on the handwritten pages and searched for the secret entrance to the catacombs by memory alone.

They walked thirty paces north from the northwest edge of the stable proper. Once there, Arames dropped to his knees, running his hands over the grass, looking for the trap door. Arames's memory was good—he found the sod-covered panel after only a few moments.

Once the trap door closed above them, Arames felt along the walls in the darkness. A short time later, he had lit the torch and lifted it above their heads. "Keep your voice to a whisper, Arrin. Sound travels farther than light in tunnels like this."

Arrin touched Arames's arm before the monk could start down the passage. "Gloria Platt *wanted* us to know about this tunnel, didn't she?"

Torchlight illuminated the smile on Arames's face. "I believe so. While she is undoubtedly loyal to the Avedons, her love for her daughter is even more powerful—and she knows Lord Avedon is hiding something. She wanted us to be able to get back to the mausoleum without having to go through the manor. Whether or not she planned for us to enter the manor undetected..." Arames left the sentiment unsaid.

They moved carefully through the tunnels. Arames consulted his notes often to make sure they were on course. There were several branching paths, and Arames paused at each. He started a few paces down each side passage, but would immediately turn and come back. Arrin soon realized that he was checking them for signs of use. "Do you think the killer could have come in this way to murder Gretta?"

"Yes, I do. We have already established that only a member of the Avedon family or the manor staff could have gotten into and out of the courtyard undetected. It is a simple process of elimination. If Gretta was not killed by one of those people, then her killer did not use the main entrance. All we have left is a simple truth—there has to be another way into the courtyard."

"But the gate we used to get to the underground cemetery was behind the manor, not inside."

"True. But there were several side passages near that entrance. Some might turn back toward the manor, and one may even lead under the courtyard."

Arrin was struck by the simplicity of it—and then he remembered. "The *grate!*"

Arames turned. "Hmmm?"

"I found a metal grate behind some shrubs in the courtyard. It looked rusted, like it hadn't been opened in years. Constable Louis said the courtyard was located directly above the Olviaran Pass, and that workers had accessed the Pass through the grate. He said that the grate had been locked down for at least a hundred years."

"How closely did you examine the grate?"

"I looked down through the bars, but I didn't examine the grate itself. It just looked like it hadn't been used in a long time."

"Well, maybe the grate leads somewhere other than the Pass—and as for Constable Louis, it is definitely possible that he only knows what Lord Avedon wants him to know."

———

The two men grew even more cautious once they reached the cemetery. The large open cavern was empty; still, Arames held Arrin back with an arm, hidden in the darkness beyond the last concentration of glow-rocks still active in the side tunnel, just to be sure. Arames quickly led Arrin across the large cave and through its eerie green glow, until they reached the cart-wide passage on the other side.

They followed the main tunnel, suppressing the desire to investigate side passages. Eventually they reached the heavy iron gate they had used to enter the catacombs the day before. Arrin looked through the gate and across the open grass toward the door to the manor. He saw no sign of constables or guards. Arames touched Arrin's arm, then motioned for him to follow.

Arames reversed his steps until they reached the first side passage and continued only a few paces down it before returning to the main branch. "Nothing has disturbed that passage in a very long time." He checked the next passage and the next... until they were about a third of the way back to the underground cemetery. Finally they reached a passage in which Arames lowered himself to one knee. He indicated the places where the layers of dust were not as thick. "This tunnel has been used."

Arrin pointed to the bottom edge of the wall. "Look there, Arames. Like bristle marks. Someone used a broom here."

Arames nodded. "Good eyes, pup."

Arrin bowed his head slightly and smirked. "Yes, master."

Arames led the way down the passage. They encountered several more branching intersections, and as they proceeded they checked the side tunnels for signs of recent use. Eventually they reached an apparent dead end. Arrin passed his hands over the wall in search of any sign of hidden doors. Arames held his torch high, examining the low rock ceiling. "There, Arrin. Can you reach that?"

A metal rod protruded from the ceiling, not unlike the many other pieces of metal bracing that the miners had used to reinforce the tunnel walls and ceilings, preventing the passages from collapsing in on them as they worked. Arrin was forced to jump, but he reached the metal rod easily when he did so. It supported Arrin's weight, but the first jerk of his body pulled the bar away from the ceiling.

At first, Arrin thought the tunnel was caving in on them, but his fears were unwarranted. While dirt and dust exploded from the ceiling and instantly filled the tunnel, no rocks or metal bracing fell from above. Still holding onto the handle, his feet now touching the tunnel floor, Arrin stared up at the imposing section of ceiling that had folded down toward them. Arames studied the hinge mechanism enthusiastically, but Arrin could only gaze at the hole that had opened above. It took a moment for his eyes to adjust, but at the other end of the hole, Arrin could make out a small circle of light.

The bottom rung of a ladder was just within Arrin's reach. Using the handle for leverage, he pulled himself up and then reached below to help Arames. They climbed until they reached the top—as Arames had suspected, the grate from the courtyard did not connect to the Pass. It led to the catacombs. The grate was locked from the inside, but the bolt slid easily. Arrin pushed the grate open and emerged, hidden behind the line of box-shaped shrubs, staring toward the bench on which Gretta had been known to sit. Once the grate was closed behind them, it looked the same as it had the day before—as if it had not been opened in a hundred years or more.

Arames whispered, "One mystery solved. Now we need to get upstairs without being seen."

"Upstairs?"

"There is one Avedon we have not met. I wish to discover why."

A search through the manor in the middle of the night was a risky proposition. "Edvard? You're not buying that Edvard has been ill?"

"I am not *buying* anything anymore."

Before Arrin could ask how they were going to get to Edvard's quarters without being discovered, Arames grabbed his arm and pulled him to the ground. The double doors on the western wall of the courtyard creaked open a moment later and Constable Louis entered. Luckily the tall shrubs hid them from view. Louis approached the bench where Gretta's body had been found and began searching around and under it. Arrin shifted his weight slightly to get a better view of Louis through the branches. The head constable walked in circles, searching for any evidence that might have been missed. On three separate occasions Louis crouched and pawed at the ground with his gloved hands. Each time he eventually stopped, pounded the ground once with a fist, and then smoothed the dirt with the palm of his hand.

Constable Louis made his way back to the stone bench. He sat, staring blankly for a time, then turned his gaze upward to the stars filling the night sky. Arrin didn't dare to ease the growing ache in his knees. Arames hadn't moved at all since Louis had entered the courtyard, and showed no signs of discomfort.

As he watched, Constable Louis's face fell into his hands and he sobbed silently. But as quickly as it happened, it was over. Heavy footsteps strode through the hallway near the west entrance, and Louis's head shot up. The head constable regained his composure and was standing at near attention by the time Constable Tanner entered the courtyard. "Sir, Lord Avedon is calling for you. He is in the great hall." Louis nodded and started toward Constable Tanner. Before exiting, however, Louis scanned the courtyard one last time. Arrin worried that the constable's eyes might meet his, no matter how well he was hidden, but instead Louis focused on the upper half of the north wall—and then he was gone.

Once the two of them were alone again, Arames stared thoughtfully at the same spot of wall. Arrin whispered, "What was he looking at?"

"Beyond that wall lies the hallway where we met Richard Avedon, and the family's bedrooms." Arames kept low but moved away from their hiding place and toward the eastern wall.

"How are we going to get upstairs without being seen?"

"You tell me. How many homes of royals have you visited during your life?"

"Too many to count."

"And how many of them did not have secret passages?"

"I asked Constable Louis about that. He would only say that the manor has its secrets." Arrin smiled, and turned to start searching for signs of a secret door.

⁂

It wasn't long before they found a stone along the courtyard's eastern wall that jutted out slightly farther than its neighbors. A push sent it and several other stones mechanically recessing into the wall, while other stones eased forward at the same time. It took a few tries to find the right combination of stones to press. A final push triggered a small section of wall—it slid back, revealing a small, dark entrance. They slipped inside, finding themselves in a passage too narrow for Arrin to enter without turning his shoulders to the side.

It took only a single push on the hidden door to seal it seamlessly behind them. Arrin expected Arames to light another torch, but instead the monk opened one of the pouches at his belt and pulled out two of the glow-rocks he had collected. The light was minimal, but it allowed them to proceed safely in the only direction available to them: north.

And, as if the manor understood exactly where they needed to go, the passage began an ascent, angling upward as much as possible without the benefit of stairs. After twenty paces or so, Arrin realized they had probably reached the upper level of the manor. The passage leveled out, ending at a wall that forced them to turn west.

A few moments later they reached the end of the passage. Arames pressed his ear to the wooden wall, listening. Satisfied, he returned the glow-rocks to their pouch, and then felt around the paneling until he found what he was looking for. Slowly he pushed on a square block of wood near the right edge of the panel. With an audible *pop*, the door slid slightly to the left, leaving a crack just wide enough for fingers to slip through. Arames used his right hand to slide the door open and peered into the darkened room beyond.

Even without direct light, the room was slightly brighter than the secret passage. While not empty, it was unfinished and minimally furnished, as if it were an afterthought. Outlines of a few pieces of furniture stood out in the darkness: a table in one corner, and some sort of mound in the center of the floor. Arrin's eyes had not adjusted well enough to identify the knee-high mass.

They had still not reached the bedrooms. Instead, they had found what was commonly called a *watch-room*—a room in which occupants could hide in the event of an attack.

Arrin realized the grate hadn't been built as a way for someone to enter the courtyard. It provided a means of escape for the Avecons if the manor came under threat. *How ironic...*

But it wasn't the sight of the room that made Arrin hesitate. It was the smell—the stench of death.

Direction was unnecessary. The corridor had widened enough for Arames and Arrin to draw their weapons. Arames held a sai in each hand; Arrin extended Wildfire before him. His sword did not shine or burst into flame as it had in his dream the night before, but Arrin knew the blade could cut flesh from bone as well as any weapon ever made.

Though he was relatively sure the alcove was empty, Arames used a hand signal to direct Arrin to move cautiously to the left as he moved right. Arrin reached the table at the far wall of the room and found the source of the stench—and he also identified the mound in the center of the room: three Olviaran Whitetail carcasses.

The watch-room had three other doors, one on each wall. Arrin checked the western door as Arames listened at the opposite exit. They detected nothing from beyond their doors, but from where both men stood they could hear at least one voice from behind the door on the northern wall. Arrin, eyes now fully adjusted to the light, saw Arames's hand signal—*Stay*—and nodded. Arames approached the northern wall, placed a hand on the door, and leaned in to lay his ear against the wood.

But before his ear reached its intended post, the door exploded in on them, sending shards of wood in all directions. Arames was thrown back; Arrin barely kept his feet as Arames slid along the floor past him. Dazed for a moment, all Arrin could hear was a horrible sound somewhere between a growl and a hiss, and all he could see was a hunched shape crouching in the splintered doorway.

Arrin allowed his instincts to take over—and charged.

Lord Avedon's Gambit

The River is Az's very breath.
Every creature and beast rose from the River
to take its place and be named.
As for the Tourim?
They were never touched by the River.
Something other than Az named them.

—Tales of the Children

ARRIN LAUNCHED HIMSELF AT the creature that had just separated one of the watch-room doors from its hinges. As he propelled himself forward, he only had time to determine that the creature was small—the light spilling into the watch-room from behind the creature outlined its form but hid its features—and that it was not alone. Arrin heard a voice from behind the creature, crying out in a tone of fear and supplication. Just before Arrin collided into the creature, realization struck him: *I'm about to kill something in Lord Avedon's home.*

Whether it was that thought, or his sudden awareness of the creature's size, Arrin chose to lead not with his blade, but with his body. He kept his sword high and threw himself shoulder-first into the shorter creature.

Arrin and the growling thing went down in a flailing heap, sliding across the floor of the bedroom beyond the door. The creature was fast, wrestling Arrin face-down on the wood floor; Arrin re-oriented himself and found the thing on his back, beating at his backpack with its fists. The pack was saving his life: instead of reaching around it to get to Arrin's flesh, the creature was tearing its way through the leather, clawing and pulling at it. Arrin, sword still in his right hand, used the opportunity to pull his left knee up under him to regain his balance.

A voice yelled from the distance. The creature had ripped most of Arrin's pack from his shoulders and Arrin felt claws tearing through the wool and linen covering his flesh. Arrin still could not see his attacker, but its screeches and shrieks could not be human. Arrin felt something clamp down on his shoulder. The creature drew first blood, just as Arrin was finally balanced enough to take action.

Arrin pushed up with his left leg and arm, rolling back and to the right. As he did so, he brought the pommel of his sword around and connected with the creature's face. The glancing, off-balance blow was just solid enough to displace the creature's hold.

Arrin growled in anger. The shallow wound on his back and shoulder shot searing pain through his upper body with an intensity that shocked him. A rage exploded within him, and Arrin found himself on his feet standing over the creature. It was human—or at least had been at one time—and it was hunched down on its legs like some sort of frog. The thing had its face turned away from him, but Arrin could see blood dripping from the creature's hand.

Arrin barely saw Richard Avedon rushing toward them. The pain pulsating from the wound in his back prevented him from thinking about the consequences. The creature had to be destroyed. Arrin raised his sword—

⁂

Arames opened his eyes and found himself against the far wall of the watch-room. He shook his head, clearing it, and took a few moments to process what had happened. Arames put his hands behind his head and pushed hard, flipping his legs underneath him and landing deftly on his feet. Just as quickly, he was forced to one knee, nearly crying out in pain—the pain from the shard of wood protruding from his left arm.

Arames instinctively opened himself up to the pain, accepting it as part of his being. *Give me strength, Caern.* The pain did not leave him, but after a single breath he was able to gather himself and focus. Arrin was in the next room—a bedroom, by the looks of it—and he was under attack. A creature had latched onto Arrin's back, but it appeared confused by his pack. Instead of attacking the prince's exposed areas, it was tearing at the backpack itself.

It is a vampire—Edvard Avedon!

Arames retrieved the sai that rested against his foot. The simple action made his heart throb; each pulse forced him to focus on the blood seeping around the edges of his wound. He considered pulling out the dagger-sized shard of wood, but he did not know how much more damage that would cause. Besides, the sight before Arames left him no time to make a choice.

Arrin was now up on his feet, having extricated himself from Edvard's grasp. His pack was hanging from his shoulder by one strap, and Arames could see a red stain spreading across Arrin's shirt—the fingernails of a vampire, even one so newly turned, hardened and grew to great lengths, eventually resembling bone-sharpened knives. And these had apparently found flesh. Even a scratch from one of those nails caused searing pain—Arames had heard it compared to vinegar in an open wound. Arrin blinked and shook his head, blade still fixed on Edward Avedon's crouched form. Arames knew what would happen next.

The monk rushed forward, but Arrin was already raising his sword above his head. He would not reach his student in time to stop the prince from striking. Arames entered the room and left his feet—hoping his change in direction might save them all.

⁂

Before Arrin's sword could connect, his intended target was struck full-force by some sort of human missile. The impact threw the creature into the side of the nearby bed, leaving another in its place. Arrin could not have halted the descent of his sword under any circumstances, but the pain of his wound had affected his mind and intensified the power behind his swing. Arrin recognized that it was Arames who now lay on the ground beneath him, and that there was nothing he could do to halt the fatal blow.

But his sword stopped short of flesh and bone, impact jarring painfully up his arm. Arames, lying on his back, blocked the prince's blade with the guard of his left sai. Once Arrin saw the monk's all-knowing smirk beneath their crossed weapons, he felt the battle rage drain out of him, replaced by a wave of pure relief. Arrin exhaled a heavy sigh and fell to the ground.

⁂

Arames twisted his sai as Arrin slumped to the ground, pulling the blade from the prince's hand. A quick glance confirmed that the vampire had been knocked out by the blow—but that simple fact troubled him, too. Undead creatures were usually either conscious, or destroyed. *There is more to this than I understand.*

Richard stood at the foot of Edvard's bed, fists clenched at his sides, surveying the damage to the room. As Arames expected, once Richard saw the unmoving form of his brother, he looked no further.

"Good evening, Richard." Arames rolled Arrin onto his stomach to ease the weight on his wounded back.

"Arames! What? I—"

He was dealing with it about as well as Arames would have expected. "Help us, Richard."

The future Lord Avedon turned instead toward his brother, stepping over Arames and easily pulling Edvard up onto the bed. In moments he had his brother's arms and feet shackled. Richard moved to the other side of the bed and picked up a bottle that had been knocked onto its side. He pulled the cork from it and poured an unmeasured amount of liquid into his brother's open mouth.

Only then did Richard turn his attention to the two men on the floor. He collected some of the bandages that had fallen from Arrin's pack and began inspecting the wound on the monk's arm, but Arames directed him to help Arrin first. Richard pulled off the remnants of the shredded pack and raised what was left of Arrin's ruined shirt and outer garments. After studying Arrin's back for a moment, Richard wetted a bandage in a basin of soapy water on a stand near Edvard's bed, then moved to a chest at the foot of the bed and retrieved some sort of cloth wrap. When he unfolded the material, Arames could see some sort of salve on the cloth. Richard cleaned the wound and then rubbed some of the salve directly onto Arrin's skin, then began wrapping the bandage around the wounded man's upper torso.

The effects of the salve were instantaneous, restoring both Arrin's consciousness and his composure. He winced as Richard pulled the bandages tight, and sought out his mentor's gaze. The fear in Arrin's eyes showed not only concern regarding their presence in Edvard's room, but awareness of the intricate leather straps that held his scabbard tight to his back—and the sword that would never belong to a monk's apprentice. Arames signaled back with small hand gestures that Richard, still concentrating on the bandaging, would not see. *He is nearly in as much shock as you are... he probably won't notice a thing.*

Richard spoke only after he was satisfied with his work. "It wasn't deep, thank the Children." His shaky voice possessed none of the bravado they had heard the day before, confirming Arames's silent assertion.

"By Az!" Arrin moved gingerly over to Arames and touched his sleeve, staring at the jagged wooden shard. "Let me find my kit."

Arrin and Richard worked together to remove the wood from Arames's arm. Arrin inspected the empty wound and, to his relief, found that it had bypassed the major blood vessels and nerves. "The wood missed nearly everything. You should have had at least one broken bone."

"As it was missing everything else, it could have done the courtesy of missing my arm completely."

Arrin smiled, even under the circumstances. After ensuring the wound was clean, he pulled a large needle and a length of slender, sturdy thread from the kit.

Arames turned away, addressing Richard. "Tell me about Edvard."

Richard sat down at the foot of the bed. "A vampire... took him."

Arames wanted to move closer to Edvard, to study him, but Arrin was far from done. "How long ago?"

"Eleven days ago, he disappeared. Three days later I found him wandering through the secret passages of the manor. Edvard always loved the secret passages. He attacked me, but he was weak. I can only figure that he had been killed and left somewhere, and after he—changed—he came back home. I was able to hold him down, and Carin helped me get him to his room."

"Who else knows about this?"

Before Richard could answer, the outer door crashed open against the wall. Lord Avedon bellowed, "*What are you doing, monk?!*"

Arrin, his back to the doorway, jumped at the slam of the door, his jerking motion pushing the needle farther into Arames's arm than he had intended. Arames did his best to remain calm. In mid-grunt, he replied from the floor, "At the moment, Lord Avedon, I am being sewed upon."

Lord Avedon's eyes shot from one side of the room to the other. "How did you get in here? Through the secret passage!?"

Arames nodded. "Yes. We were determining how someone might have entered to kill Gretta."

Lord Avedon reached down and retrieved Arrin's longsword. "This *intention* led you to attack my son?!"

Arrin heard his sword blade slide against the wooden floor as it was lifted, and raised his head in alarm. Arames locked eyes with his student, demanding his silence. "We did not attack Edvard," the monk answered. "He attacked us."

Before Lord Avedon could respond, Arames continued, "You have been less than honest with us, so we decided to return to the manor courtyard for another look. While searching the garden, we found a secret door and it led us here. We did not know what we would find, but hindsight being what it is, I should not have been surprised."

"Edvard did *not* kill Gretta Platt!" Lord Avedon pointed the sword at Arames. It shook in his hand.

"I never said he did."

The sword wavered. Arames continued. "Lord Avedon, you can kill us now, or you can let us help you. Either way, please do me the courtesy of answering my questions. When I am finished, if you still feel the need to raise that sword against us, you may do what you must."

Arrin finished stitching Arames's arm and cut the thread. Richard rubbed a good bit of the salve on the wound and then started to wrap it. As the two older men spoke, Arrin and Richard continued tending to Arames.

Lord Avedon looked around as if he wanted a chair. "Did Edvard do that to you?"

Richard answered. "Yes. Edvard had just awakened and I was about to feed him, but he seemed to sense them through the wall. He was more alert this time—he broke free and crashed through his watch-room door before I could stop him."

"Feed?" Arames asked. "You've been feeding him meat from the butcher shop? Bloody livers and hearts?"

Richard nodded. "Yes. And a buck I killed three days ago."

"And Marrissa gave you something to keep Edvard sedated?"

"Yes."

That explains how easily I knocked him out. Arames looked at Lord Avedon. "Do you really believe the King's Crown potion will bring your son back?"

Richard stood up. "How did you know about that?"

It seemed that Lord Avedon could no longer be surprised. He ignored his son's interruption. "It's all I've got left, Sir Arames."

"And what about the second half of the legend—if the King's Crown potion is given to a vampire that has tasted human blood?"

Lord Avedon slid the point of Arrin's blade slowly across the wood floor, oblivious to the damage he was causing to the floorboards. "That's why you were allowed to stay, brother of Aarron. If we can prove that the vampire that took Edvard also killed Gretta, or that it wasn't a vampire at all, then we can try the King's Crown potion."

"You mean to tell me that Edvard has not attacked you since you captured him... not scratched you once, drawn blood and tasted it? Not even a drop?"

Richard jumped to his feet. "Arjun's light!" He retrieved a bowl of soapy water from its stand so quickly that some of the contents sloshed over the basin's edge. He scrubbed at Edvard's hand and nails, scouring away the remnants of Arrin's blood. "No human blood—only the blood of the stag—as the legend states."

Arames stood and pulled Arrin to his feet. "Fine. Richard, I know you have been pressuring Marrissa to complete the potion. Stop now. Let her do the work and do it well, or the potion will surely be worthless. Lord Avedon, you must promise me that you will not use the potion until we can prove that Edvard did not kill Gretta."

Lord Avedon nodded and spoke barely above a whisper. "You have my word."

Arames crossed toward the bed. "Good. Now, who else knows about Edvard?"

"Only Marrissa, Carin, Richard, and myself."

"Constable Louis does not know?"

"Louis? Absolutely not. My— my head constable has a particular view of the world. He would not approve of my plan to save Edvard."

"And that is why you took him off of the investigation?"

"Yes. He had similar thoughts about the secret passage from the courtyard to the second floor. He's still angry that I won't let him see Edvard or talk to any of my children but Jon and Julienne. He and Edvard were .. are close."

"And Jon and Julienne do not know? Nor any of the staff?"

"Absolutely not. They haven't been allowed inside this room. And since Edvard has always been prone to illness, especially since his mother's death, it hasn't been difficult to keep people from him."

Arames leaned in close, unable to resist the opportunity to study an incapacitated vampire. Edvard was only sixteen years old, but his face had the sickly pallor of a dying man. His skin was cold to the touch. Arames lifted Edvard's top lip and confirmed that the incisors were only slightly longer than normal. It was a common misconception that all vampires had extremely long incisors—a new vampire's canines would be barely longer than normal teeth, and would grow slowly throughout the undead's continued existence. It was rumored that an ancient vampire's canines would be long enough to cut through its lower lip and extend below its chin. Arames took out his notebook and opened it to a blank page. He pressed the paper against Edvard's upper teeth until they made two holes.

"What are you doing?" Richard had regained some of his bravado.

Arames answered as if Richard's tone has not changed. "If I ever get to see Gretta's body, I will be able to rule out Edvard as her murderer." Richard grunted once, and Arames added, "...if the bite marks on her neck do not match his teeth."

Arames turned Edvard's head to the side and looked at his neck. The wounds that had taken his life were nearly faded. Arames measured the distance between the two primary punctures. There were several smaller bite marks, with a faint gash between them where blood had been drained from his body. *Whatever did this bit down hard. Interesting... the space between the primary marks on Edvard's neck are nearly the same as the distance between Edvard's fangs.*

Arames turned his attention to Edvard's left hand. As he had suspected, the fingernails had already hardened and grown to nearly twice their normal length.

"Has Edvard spoken since his capture? Has he displayed any signs of intelligence or memory? Does he recognize you at all?"

Richard said, "No. He does scream in his sleep. He may be dead, but he still dreams. He only grunts and shrieks like an animal when he's awake."

Lord Avedon countered, "But there have been times, especially after he feeds, when we see the intelligence in his eyes."

Arames thought for a moment. "Do not be fooled by that, Lord Avedon. What you know as Edvard is gone. All that remains is a vampire that wants to be freed. If Edvard did kill Gretta, then the sedative you are giving him does not dampen his intelligence, it only serves to prevent him from killing again. If Edvard was killed by a vampire master, and that vampire master offered his own blood to Edvard in return, then—if the rumors are true—the intelligence you see in his eyes could be his own. But it will only return completely if he drinks human blood."

Richard's face brightened with hope. "So that means he couldn't have killed Gretta. He would be able to talk to us if he had consumed her blood!"

"No, I did not say that. If Edvard was killed by a common vampire that found its way through the tunnels into Avedon Hill, his memories and intelligence are forever gone, whether he killed Gretta or not." Arames paused, still working through the possibilities. "And if Edvard had been killed by a vampire master, your drug might be all that is keeping him from speaking to you." He stared into Richard's eyes. "But if he does speak to you, Richard—before you even realize it, you will have unlocked his chains and he will be drinking from your throat."

Lord Avedon raised an empty hand. "That's enough, Kragen."

Arames bowed his head. "Of course, Lord Avedon, I do have one bit of good news for you, if you can call it that. The reason we were in the courtyard to begin with—we were able to reach it directly from the catacombs."

Richard's jaw dropped; Lord Avedon only shook his head. The elder man found his voice first. "The grate in the courtyard? But it's been locked for generations."

"From this side, yes. But it opened easily from below. We also found evidence that someone had been in those passages recently and had attempted to cover their tracks."

"That all but proves it wasn't Edvard."

Arames shook his head. "I am sorry, Lord Avedon, but not necessarily. It just means that someone knows how to get into and out of the manor without being seen. As Richard told us, Edvard knew those secret passages better than most."

Lord Avedon's smile faded as quickly as it had appeared. "Very well. It is late. Richard will show you out." He leaned Arrin's sword hilt against the edge of the bed and sat down beside his unconscious son. Richard extended his hand toward the door, inviting them to leave.

"If you do not mind, Lord Avedon, I would like to take another look at Gretta's office on our way out. I promise not to disturb you or any other members of your family—that way Richard can stay here with you if you like."

Lord Avedon shook his hand dismissively. "Fine. Just go, monk."

"One last question... do any of the tunnels under the town lead outside the walls?"

Lord Avedon answered, "None that I know of. We never wanted to provide the means to bypass the town gates."

Arames nodded. Arrin had done his best to collect all the items that had fallen out of his backpack. The shredded pack was now quite the sight, held together by more of the same bandages that were wrapped around Arames's arm. Arames took Arrin's sword and the two men started toward the bedroom door. Arames paused after a few steps and turned back to Lord Avedon. The dots of the timeline had connected within his head. "You neglected to mention the one other person who knew about Edvard."

A frown of confusion crossed Lord Avedon's face, but only for a moment. "Yes, of course—Gretta knew."

Arames nodded once more, bowed, and then followed Arrin out of Edvard's bedroom.

THE PLATT FAMILY SECRET

"I know myself, even as I am pulled from my birth mother." – Doppin
"Ah, but can you speak?" – Lem
"What?" – Doppin
"Can you talk? I'd like to see the look on your momma's
face if you said 'Put me back in!'" –Lem

—Ballix Poe (a play)

Aᴙᴀᴍᴇꜱ ᴀɴᴅ Aʀʀɪɴ ᴍᴇᴛ no guards along the way to Gretta's office. Arames walked around the desk, motioning for Arrin to light a lamp on the ledge by the door. Arrin did so silently, then carried the oil lamp over. Arames's slumped shoulders and heavy eyes made him appear weakened as he sat heavily at the desk, but it wasn't from the injury he had sustained a short while before.

"Arrin, do you think you can find the kitchens from here?"

"Do you need food?"

"Yes, whatever you can find. I will stay here."

Arames wanted to lay his head down on Gretta's desk, but he refused to allow himself the luxury. At one time, Arames had performed many fasts, going days without food and water; now the monk could barely go a cyke without sustenance and the exertions of the evening had left him spent. Taking his mind off his hunger, Arames again considered the mystery surrounding the Avedon family.

It would be logical to assume that Edvard Avedon killed Gretta Platt. He had the motivation—hunger; the opportunity—knowledge of the secret passages; and the method—the ability to drain Gretta while leaving little blood at the scene.

We know Gretta wasn't killed by a moon-beast, since her corpse was relatively undamaged by her attacker, aside from the marks on her neck.

Almost as important is how Lord Avedon continues to act. He fears for more than just his son... unless I am mistaken, he fears for his family's way of life. Why was Gretta so important to him? Obviously she was his confidant, his advisor, and his business partner in many respects. But there is something more... there has to be. What is the true nature of the relationship between the Avedons and Flatts? He looked at the office around him. *The secret has to be here somewhere.*

✦

It was some time before Arrin returned with bread and dried meats in hand. He found Arames surrounded by stacks of books and papers that he had removed from their shelves and piled neatly on the floor. Arames stared at the walls as if willing them to reveal some hidden secret.

"Redecorating?" Arrin quipped as he handed Arames a piece of bread.

The monk ignored the jest. "No hidden doors, no secret compartments... this room does not connect to anything except the hall. I—" he paused to take a bite. "I even moved the desk and searched the floor. Help me return the books to the shelves. I hope for better luck in Gloria Platt's old office down the hall."

Once the room was tidied and the food consumed, Arames led Arrin toward the Housemistress's former office, located near the kitchens. They passed two guards along the way, both of whom nodded but otherwise ignored their presence.

"Lord Avedon must have passed along word that we were here. They didn't stop me when I went to the kitchens, either."

Arames tried the door and found it locked. He knew he could unlock it easily, but decided to test Arrin. "Ah, something for you to do. Please open this door, while I make sure the guards we just passed do not find the need to investigate what we are doing."

Arrin unsuccessfully concealed his smirk. "Aye, master."

Arames smiled and walked back to the end of the short hallway. He peered around the corner at the hall guard, who was leaning against a wall and doing his best to stay awake. The monk quietly shuffled back to Arrin, who was still working on the lock with slender metal picks.

Arames sighed. "Your mother gave you that lockpick set, did she not?"

"Yes, you know she did."

"And you know it saved your mother's life on more than one occasion?"

Arrin didn't pause from his work. "So I've heard. No one bothers to share the details, but I've been told it was her favorite toy."

Arames, chewing on the last of the bread, shook his head. "Toy? Those pieces of metal were so important to your mother, such a part of who she was, that she used to carry them tied to her waist underneath her dress." He paused, watching Arrin's slow progress. "By the age of eight, your mother could unlock every door and chest at Castle Pen in the time it took me to walk to the corner of this hall and back. Drona Twoblade is shuddering in his crypt as we speak. Your current instructors at Castle Pen wouldn't be qualified to teach students how to muck horse stalls at Thorn's Way."

The lock clicked and Arrin let out a satisfied sigh. "I hope not. The Priests of Caern did not send stable hands to school us." Disregarding his mentor's snort, Arrin stood and entered the room.

The office was much larger than Gretta's, but it was immediately clear why Gretta had moved her daily activities to the smaller room down the hall. If appearances were truth, nothing that had ever been written in this room or carried here had ever been discarded.

At a glance, the walls appeared to have been made of paper and not of stone and wood. Stacks of parchments, scrolls, and bound texts encircled the room. Bookcases lined most of the walls, and even the spaces in between were filled with piles of papers and texts that climbed to the ceiling. Only after his eyes adjusted to the darkness did Arrin see the strings and ribbons that acted as a sort of net against some of the weight that threatened to bring the towering stacks down on top of them.

Arames spotted a small lamp hanging from the ceiling above the main desk. He motioned to Arrin; within moments, a yellow glow illuminated the room. Arames crossed to one of the shelves.

"What exactly are we looking for, Arames?"

"I believe these shelves hold much of the same information that we found in Gretta's office, only extending back for centuries. While we would learn much from the information in this room, we do not have the time to spend in that endeavor. But there is something else—something important that we are missing. There is a reason Lord Avedon is so lost without Gretta. While the secrets of the Avedon Manor might be sitting here in the open just waiting for us to find them ..." Arames left the statement unfinished.

Arrin didn't wait for Arames to continue his thought, and instead started his search at the wall opposite the office door, scanning the shelves for any books that appeared out of place. He looked for hinges, levers—anything that could be pushed or moved in such a way that it might uncover a door. Arames had emptied the bookcases in Gretta's smaller office, but that was not an option here; Arrin didn't know how to even attempt it without chancing a collapse of the walls around them. If the room did have a secret door, it would have to be easy to access. It was just a matter of finding the trigger.

After his initial scan of the room, Arrin turned his attention upward, to the edges where the walls and ceiling met. All of the bookcases on the far wall were capped with long, thin strips of oak molding that ran across the entire length of the room. The molding was unbroken, with no discernable cracks that might indicate a door. While it would make sense architecturally to build a secret room behind the wall opposite the office's entrance, Arrin turned his attention to the north wall—and to another bookcase to the left of the door. He looked for any seams or lines, starting at the ceiling and working his way down. There was a crack in the wood along the ceiling where the bookcases on the northern and eastern walls met, but no evidence of a door.

Arrin turned next to the books and parchments on the northern wall's single bookcase. These shelves primarily held boxes and crates filled with documents. He pulled and pushed on the boxes, moving them from side to side, looking for anything that might act as a lever or trigger. Next, he tried shifting books one at a time, in case one of them might be the key; when he met no success yet again, he then moved to the scrolls. They were each held in place by ribbons attached to the shelves. He found nothing.

Unswayed, Arrin stepped back and studied the wall as a whole. A section of the northwest corner, just wider than Arrin's shoulders, held a few boxes, but mostly it was a pile of papers stacked on top of each other from floor to ceiling. The same series of ribbons and strings seemed to be holding the tower of papers and loosely bound texts in place... but in this case, the strings—beginning at hooks that protruded from the ceiling—were not as taut as their counterparts elsewhere in the room. From all appearances, there was little keeping the flying buttress of paper upright. The imposing stack of documents should have fallen in an unruly avalanche long ago.

"There."

⁂

Arames had been looking in and around the large desk in the center of the room, searching for levers or secret drawers. Hearing Arrin, the monk raised his head and saw his young friend poking and prodding what appeared to be the most perilous area of the entire room.

But nothing fell. And a few moments later when Arrin pushed on the spine of a large book with strange symbols on it, there was a mechanical "click" and a six-hands-wide section of wall rolled back from floor to ceiling, leaving a small opening for them to enter.

Arames looked at the papers and books that should have fallen on them. "Ingenious... all of these papers and books and boxes... they are all glued together against the wall. How did you know?"

Arrin smiled and pointed out the strings. They were still in their place, extending from ceiling to floor, holding nothing. "The strings were not taut like the others. I knew the stacks here were being held up by some other means."

Arames poked at Arrin's head with a finger. "There is intelligence in there. I am so proud."

Arrin smirked. He pointed to the book that had triggered the secret door. "What do those symbols mean? I don't recognize them."

Arames studied the book's spine. He recognized the symbols as early Inarran icons. They were sometimes found on the walls of caves where the earliest barbarians of the north had lived. "That is the symbol of Doppin."

"The Trickster?"

"Yes... and this one means 'path' or 'way'. It makes sense." *Doppin's Way...* Arames smiled. "Let us see what a secret door that invokes the name of the 'one who extends across all boundaries' has hidden behind it."

Arrin had not heard that phrase before. "What do you mean by that?"

Arames paused at the entrance to the passage. "We have talked of the Children of Az, and how they have walked the Land from time to time—sometimes to help their Father's creation, and other times to perform their sacred duties, no matter how destructive they may be to our world."

Arrin nodded and Arames continued. "And how Az was forced to take steps to prevent his Children from inadvertently destroying his Land with their uncontrollable powers and desires."

The Constraints of the Children... "For eons Az's Children could leave the immortal plane and enter our world. They could pose as one of any humanoid race, or—in the case of Ursala or Treygh—as any intelligent creature. Or they could simply walk Caern in their immortal forms, causing all manner of death and destruction at their whim. But after Az set the Constraints, they could only enter this world under certain conditions."

Arrin continued Arames's thought. "They would live in this world as mortals, with no knowledge of their true identity. They would be born as we are, live as we do, die as we do..."

"Unless they receive their epiphany."

Arrin nodded his head. "If one of the other Children—or Az himself—wills it, an avatar will most likely come to understand his true nature... this is their 'epiphany'. Once this occurs, the avatar is still mortal, but with all the knowledge— and, legend says, some of the powers—of their immortal self." Arrin thought for a moment. "*The one who extends across all boundaries*—I still don't understand why Doppin is called that."

"Doppin is most often the one that causes another avatar to learn his true nature; and mostly for Doppin's own reasons. Legend states that Doppin is unaffected by some of the constraints—namely the restriction that keeps the knowledge of his true nature hidden from him. Doppin is said to have full knowledge of himself, even at birth."

Arrin concluded, "As a result, the boundary that is crossed with epiphany does not apply to Doppin— 'The one who extends across all boundaries.'"

Arames nodded once and proceeded through the secret door, lamp in hand. They followed a short passage and found themselves in a small alcove, smaller even than the watch-room upstairs. The room was completely empty, save for a small desk against the opposite wall. Five large ledgers rested on the desk, stacked on top of each other. Arames approached, looked around to make sure they hadn't missed anything else in the room, and then opened the top book.

"A ledger... large numbers listed in columns... income? Could these columns represent receipts and payments?" Arames rubbed his forehead. "This makes no sense. The numbers listed here are far more than the town collects yearly in tolls for the Olviaran Pass, or for any tariffs on goods."

Arrin worked his away around to look at the page for himself. "What are those?"

"TB, H, ST, LA, C..." *Talik Bore; Hemming, the baker; Sarah Tremaine; Caasz... LA?* "Initials of some of the townspeople. If I understand the columns correctly, these might represent payments made to them."

"Are you serious? Look at the numbers next to—who would that be, Talik and Hemming? They could live off of one of these payments for a year. And there are multiple entries for each of them. If this is accurate, there are some very rich people here."

There were codes on what appeared to be the income side of the ledger as well, possibly for accumulated amounts of the tolls and tariffs detailed in some of Gretta's documents. But there were other abbreviations that Arames did not understand at all. And these were tied to the ledger entries with the largest payments—undocumented in any of the paperwork Arames had seen in Gretta's office.

"Oh my..." All the pieces shifted slightly, falling into place—the unchanging population of the town; the families that remained in Avedon Hill for generations; the quietness of a town that by all accounts should have been thriving—*it was all by design.*

Arames slammed the ledger shut. He knew after looking at just a few pages that the five tomes on the table represented at least the last three hundred years.

"Come, Arrin. We have a grieving mother to visit."

❦

"You certainly realize how late it is?" Gloria Platt barred the doorway to her daughter's home. Her eyes glared, but she still used that calm, soothing voice.

"I gave you a promise that I would find out what happened to your daughter and bring her back to you for a proper burial. I plan to keep that promise. Please let us in so that we can talk." Arames had his hand on the door, preventing her from closing it on them.

Gloria had abandoned her black dress for one of dark blue, but she still wore the black mourning bonnet from the day before. Arames looked past her to a recently stoked fire, and a chair with a blanket next to the fireplace. That and the steaming cup next to the chair made it easy for Arames to say, "Besides, it does not appear that you were sleeping."

Gloria looked at both men for a moment. "You may come in, Sir Arames. Your companion will wait for you outside."

Arames, ignoring the ire he sensed from the prince, entered and closed the door behind him.

Gloria motioned Arames toward a chair and seated herself in the other, facing him. "You made it into the manor through the catacombs?"

Arames nodded. "Yes, thanks to your help."

"And have you discovered much tonight?"

"Yes, as you knew I would."

Gloria covered her arms with a light blanket. The flames from the fireplace reflected in her eyes. "Lord Avedon has done his best to keep me in the dark. I knew you were the one person who could help me learn what he is hiding."

Arames considered her statements. "We have made certain promises to Lord Avedon. You can rest assured that your suspicions were well-warranted and that we are much further down the path of discovery due to your help. I cannot tell you what we have learned, but that there is a good chance of further attacks on the townspeople. I would suggest taking every precaution you can."

"You cannot tell me? I'm not one accustomed to being kept in the dark." Gloria's face changed—for only a moment, more than the light of the fire flashed across her eyes.

Arames bowed his head slightly. "Of that, I am sure." *Now to make matters worse.* "How long have the Platt family been the true rulers of Avedon Hill?"

Gloria Platt smiled slightly. "Rulers? We have no desire for power, Sir Arames. The Avedon family has played their part as well as any family could—maybe not on the level of the Perti royals, but well enough for a town such as this."

Arames hoped that Gloria only invoked the Perti name because she knew he had been Aarronic Advisor to the royal family of Yew. "I have some experience advising those in power, my lady. I believe the Platt influence over the Avedon family has been far greater."

Gloria smiled but did not respond.

"I found some ledgers in your former office. They made for interesting reading."

"Really?"

Arames leaned forward. "I do not care why or how so much gold flows into the Avedon coffers. I do not care that you and your family have managed to keep the wealth of this town a secret for, what... four hundred years? All I care about is discovering who or what killed your daughter, and then returning her to her sacred home." Arames let the statement hang in the air for a moment. "Talk to me. I think you know you can trust me."

Gloria could no longer meet the monk's eyes. "Trust isn't something I possess at this point in my life, Sir Arames. I am not so unlike you and your kind. You Advisors may serve the Land, but primarily you do your best to control the actions of the powerful and wealthy. My family has only sought to do the same, just on a much smaller stage."

Gloria's eyes gave no indication of the motive behind her words. *She plays this game well.* "I am not sure that the control that you have over this town—the personal wealth your family has attained through the generations—merits comparison to the work of the Aarronic Advisors."

Gloria raised a hand from underneath her blanket and waved him off. "I will tell you this: while what you have uncovered may help you in your investigation, if you dig too deeply and try to discover *all* the secrets of Avedon Hill, you may find yourself in a hole you cannot escape."

Arames did his best not to react to Gloria's words. *Which is the exact response she was looking for... that was definitely the most polite threat I have ever received.*

"I think you should go now, Sir Arames. I need my rest."

Arames stood to take his leave. At the door he turned back to face her. "I must ask you one last question."

Gloria guessed the question before Arames had the chance to ask it. "Lord Avedon is so worried because Gretta's schedule book is missing."

"What is so important about her schedule book?"

"I believe it has something written in it, nothing to do with her daily schedule."

Not to be outdone, Arames said, "The journal is the key... to the ledgers. The letters, the numbers in the accounting books—they are not initials and payment amounts. They are a code. Without her book, the next Housemistress will have no idea who owes and who is owed—"

"And how much—and when—as well, sir monk."

BACK AT THE INN

"They will tire. It is then we will strike."
"They are Tourim, Theuroik. What if they never tire?"
"We will nip at their heels. We will cut off a finger here, a toe there.
Even a horde will tire of losing appendages, eventually."

—Theuroik Ironblade

THE TWO MEN WALKED back to the inn in exhausted silence. Arrin favored his back, still tender from the claws of the vampire that had once been Edvard Avedon. While they walked, Arames checked the bandage on his own arm. The healing salve Richard had applied was doing its work; the pain had lessened and the throbbing in his muscles had subsided.

Marrissa does have talent.

The now-full moon was high on its journey through the night. The Avedon Hill cemetery was behind them and out of sight, but Arames sensed that Father Jorrus was there, watching over the town as its two visitors made their way back to their room for a short night's sleep.

⁂

Arrin yawned and dropped his shredded pack to the floor. Though it was late, Arames had asked Leilah to bring them dinner and to draw a bath. Both men were exhausted, but still too wound up from the night's events to sleep. "So, how do we root out a vampire?"

Arames shut the door, then crossed the room to check that the window was secure. "That, young Arrin, is a good question. If the creature that murdered Edvard Avedon is a vampire master, as seems likely, it can pass itself off as human. And since we have met everyone of note here in town, either someone is very good at hiding their secret, or our vampire has the ability to enter and leave town without being noticed."

"There is a third option."

Arames raised an eyebrow. "Yes... Edvard could have met the vampire outside of town."

"But only if Edvard had his own ways of getting in and out, and Lord Avedon said that none of the tunnels bypass the town gates. When Cletus let me look at his log books, I was looking more at Gretta's comings and goings, but I did my best to memorize who used the town gate over the last few weeks. Edvard Avedon never left town through the front gate, unless Cletus neglected to record it."

"And I do not think that would be the case."

Arrin scowled a little. "Me either."

"So, we have two paths to follow: one to find the vampire who turned Edvard, and the other to find *who* killed Gretta."

"After this evening, you still believe that Gretta wasn't killed by a vampire? It was either Edvard Avedon or the vampire that turned him."

"Or, there is a third option."

Arrin collapsed on his bed, careful not to land on his injury. "That Gretta's murder had nothing to do with vampires, even though her blood-drained body tells us otherwise."

The monk paused in the process of removing his robes to shake a finger in Arrin's direction. "We never saw Gretta's body."

Arrin rubbed his face with his hands. "Even so, we know there was very little blood where her body was found. We believe her murderer entered the courtyard—most likely from the tunnels—attacked her, drained her blood through the wounds on her neck, and then escaped. And you think a vampire wasn't involved?"

Arames stood by the bathtub in the middle of the room, now wearing a long shirt that nearly reached the floor. "You are absolutely right. As far as I know, so much blood could only have been removed from her body if it had been sucked out. It is what I *do not know* that bothers me so much."

"What is that?"

"The lack of blood troubles me—even a vampire feasting slowly is going to leave a bloody corpse, and this killer did not linger. Next, why would a vampire master choose to kill Gretta Platt? And why kill her in the middle of the courtyard? It still comes down to *why*."

"Maybe Gretta discovered who the vampire was, so the vampire was forced to kill—"

The creak of the room's only door silenced Arrin mid-thought. Leilah entered, carrying a platter of food. The smile on her face suggested she had not overheard their conversation. Arrin stood and walked over to take the platter from her. He half-tripped over the remains of the backpack in the middle of the floor, and the maid giggled to herself. Arrin failed to keep a flush from blooming across his face.

"I'll be right back with your hot water, gentlemen."

Arrin opened his eyes and looked around, still groggy from sleep. He wasn't in his room any longer. He stood outside the library. The stars and the full moon were bright on this cloudless night, and he could feel grass beneath his bare feet. He found he was completely naked, but thankfully oblivious to the cold. He knew he had to be dreaming... his back felt completely healed. He thought of Arames and how he had described dream-walking.

"I must be walking the bridge again." He heard his voice clearly when he spoke, but the only response was the sound of the wind through the scattered trees surrounding the library.

Arrin didn't appreciate his nakedness, even without the freezing temperatures of an Avedon Hill evening, and it triggered him to try to control more of his dream. He concentrated on summoning clothes for his lower body—but the thought of someone seeing him hunched over at the shoulders and staring at his torso, straining to make clothing appear, did little to help his concentration. After a few moments, he stopped. "Naked it is, then. Maybe Sarah Tremaine will show up; that would certainly be better than the dream I had last night."

The library's windows were well tinted, like the stained glass in many of the temples he had visited. If there were candles lit within the library, Arrin couldn't tell. He took two steps toward the door, but his progress was halted by a pulse of energy. It struck him in the chest like a gust of heavy wind; he staggered, understanding instinctively that the pulse had originated from inside. But even as Arrin started forward again, a second blast erupted. This time, the concussion knocked Arrin from his feet and shattered every window in sight. Seemingly out of order, they exploded outward, sending shards and slivers of glass raining down onto Arrin as he lay on the ground.

Arrin rolled over, doing his best to protect his bare skin. He realized that he had only heard the glass break. Whatever had caused the explosion had made no noise at all.

Arrin got to his feet and found himself unmarked and uninjured, and not before the library but in front of the blacksmith's shop. Again, determined to control more of his dream, Arrin entered the smithy. Inside were two men, or at least one small man and one giant that had to be Herrjarr. Arrin assumed the smaller man was Herrjarr's apprentice, Ollus Wenk. They stood at the edge of a large table, speaking to each other, but Arrin could hear only the fire from the forge.

On the table was some sort of garment or loose material. The two men were oblivious to Arrin's presence, so he approached and studied the fabric. As he stared, it changed shape before his eyes. Arrin could not tell what it was supposed to be—a dress, an apron, a cloak?

Whatever it was, it was stained with blood.

Arrin reached out to touch the piece of clothing—

Arrin found himself lying on his back, arms extended above him. Unlike in his two earlier dreams, Arrin now could not hear anything at all. Although he knew his eyes to be open, he could not see. *Am I deaf and blind?* Arrin tried to climb to his feet and found that he was lying on a bed and not on the floor. He also realized that he was wearing the night clothes he had worn to bed. "What in Az's name—?"

Even though he spoke aloud, no sound reached his ears; more troubling, he knew he was not dreaming.

The prince blinked, staring in the direction he believed the window to be. Something had to be covering it—he could not even discern its outline through the blackness. He stretched his arms out in front of him and tried to make his way to the window, to uncover it, to let the moonlight in.

Wait, Arames had started a fire… Arrin turned to find the fireplace; he was met with a darkness that left him no other conclusion. *Magic?*

Arrin was turned around now uncertain which direction he faced. "Arames!?" he shouted, but his voice did not penetrate the silence.

Something solid struck Arrin's right thigh, dropping him to one knee. Before he could react, something struck the back of his neck—and then he was forced to the ground.

Arrin struggled, but a strong weight pushed down on his chest. He gasped for air. He tried to raise his arms but could not. Blood rushed to his throbbing head, and Arrin knew something was against his neck... something sharp... something draining...

No! I won't go like this. This isn't right! But Arrin found he could no longer move a muscle. Even in the black of the room, Arrin felt a different darkness creep in from the corners of his eyes. He was dying.

A faint light pierced the darkness above him. *So this is how it ends...* First a flicker, growing brighter until it was more brilliant than the lamp at Kaelin's Perch. He did not know whether he should reach out for it or not, but he had no choice. His arms were stone.

The light pulsed brightly, then began to fade. Try as he might, he could not move toward it. Arrin gradually realized that it wasn't the light that was fading—it was his ability to see the light. One last time, he tried to strike whatever was attacking him, or at least to see what it was. But it was too late.

Arames checked that the door and window were locked, and settled in to keep watch while Arrin slept. He had nearly fallen asleep in his chair when the light from the fire began to grow dim. The monk, assuming it was a trick of his tired mind, shook his head and rubbed at his eyes. When the light continued to fade, Arames stood and stretched his legs, intending to check the fire.

Moments later the entire room was black as pitch. *By Doppin?!*

Arames leaped forward, knowing he had at least five paces' leeway between his chair and the tub in the center of the room—and realized that in so doing he had made no sound at all.

Silence and darkness. Arames reached out with his mind, to contact Arrin or to touch the mind of whatever else was in the room, but the unnatural dark was somehow affecting his connection to the River.

Arames Kragen was no sorcerer, but he was not without other links to the magic that flowed through the Land. He reached into the folds of his robes, closing his fingers around a gold medallion, and held it out in front of him. He concentrated on the disc he could not see, instinctively calling forth a power that he himself had imbued into the round metal when he had forged it thirty years before.

Arames wasn't sure what would happen. The gold grew warm in his hand, and a sphere of light he could only sense pulsed outward from it, growing larger as he continued to focus his energies on the metallic disc. In moments the growing orb of light reached his head, and then he could see the bright light emanating from his hand. He edged forward with the growing sphere and the darkness receded in its path. Once the orb was large enough to reach the floor, the light spread further, pulsating tendrils out in different directions. The black flowed backwards, like smoke billowing in reverse.

When the sphere of light reached the fireplace, the light from the medallion met the flames of the fire and the resulting flash flared up the chimney. The sound of the blaze finally reached the monk's ears. The darkness had to be flowing back toward its creator; watching its path, he determined that whatever it was, it had to be based in the corner beyond Arrin's bed.

Arames turned and tensed his muscles, ready to charge into the middle of the receding black. Before he could spring into action, an explosion of sound filled the room. The monk released the medallion, hands flying to his ears. A memory from his youth rushed into his mind: he had once hidden in a bell tower, not knowing that the Song of Artus was about to be rung. Just as on that occasion, Arames now fell to his knees, hoping his eardrums had not burst.

The light of the medallion sucked back into itself, as if someone had thrown it into a chest and closed the lid. But the magical darkness had left the room, as well. Arames shook off the ringing in his ears and blinked to adjust his eyes to the light.

Arames soon had a sai in his good hand. No one was in the room—no intruder, but most importantly, not his student. "Arrin!" Arames ran to the window, even though it was closed. He did not see anyone outside on the streets. He turned back and finally saw Arrin on the floor and unmoving—his view of the prince had been blocked by the bed.

Arames rushed to Arrin's side and placed his hand on his chest. Two small, jagged wounds pierced his neck. Arames used the edge of his robes to cover Arrin's neck and staunch the healthy flow of blood.

A scream interrupted him. It was Leilah, standing at the open door. "Iberian's Light!" Talik Bore yelled, pushing past Leilah and rushing inside. "What happened? We heard noises and then you yelled—" Talik stopped short, cut off by the sight before him and Arames's steely glare. "By the Children!"

"Go now, Talik. Get Red and bring him here. Do not say anything to anyone else." Talik craned his neck to see if Arrin was breathing, but didn't move.

"Talik, GO!"

Talik ran from the room, pulling the trembling maid behind him.

Arames knew he had to calm himself. He couldn't help anyone in his current state, Arrin least of all. He concentrated on his heartbeat, forcing it to slow, then looked around the room, trying to determine how Arrin's attacker had entered and exited. Arames growled. *Hide… whoever or whatever you are. Darkness will protect you no longer. Now, I come for you.*

Part II

DOPPIN'S PLAY

ONE MAN'S QUEST

Arjun will drive his brother's chariot.
Both he and Artus will enter Kalin's Abyss.

—3rd Collected Prophecies of Iberian, Book 2, Chapter 1

Prince Arrin Perti, fifth in line to the royal throne of Yew, lived. Arrin knew he lived because he was in pain—at least, he hoped the road between this life and the next wasn't as painful as this. For what his mind translated as an eternity, the prince could not open his eyes, try as he might. He heard his breath rattle and felt the blood rush to his head—not coincidentally, the location of his most concentrated pain. Arrin tried to clench his fists but could only move his fingers enough to feel the woolen blanket covering his body, confirming that he was on his bed in the inn.

Relax... Arrin counted his breaths to take his mind off the pain. With each inhale and exhale he felt a little stronger. At thirty, he gathered himself and gave opening his eyes another try.

Arrin found Cousin Red standing over him, cup in hand. "Wh—" Arrin's voice cracked, and then failed him.

"Arames is outside talking to Father Jorrus. Sounds like you had quite an evening, young sir."

For a moment Arrin had no idea what Red was talking about. But then the night began to return to him. The manor... Edvard... and Arrin's dream—and what he had believed was the end of the dream. Apparently, it had been more than that. He lifted his hand to his neck, finding a bandage there.

Red helped Arrin sit up, then leaned him back against the wall behind his bed. "You were attacked—a vampire, by the looks of it." He brought the cup of water to Arrin's lips and helped him drink. "Arames must have scared it off, although he said he didn't get a good look at it. Jorrus tended to your neck. You didn't lose much blood."

The water did its work, soothing Arrin's throat. He wasn't sure if he should be speaking to Red about the incident, but he had found his voice and required answers. "I— I woke up and it was pitch black. I thought I was dreaming."

Red leaned in like he was sharing a big secret. "Arames hinted there was some sort of magic involved. I don't know much about demons, but apparently this one can steal away the light."

Arrin tried to pull his head away from the wall, hoping he was strong enough to move on his own. He wasn't, and dizziness joined the pounding behind his eyes. Red gently held him down. "Prince, you need to rest. Father Jorrus says you'll be fine soon—a couple of cykes at most."

Worried at first by the use of his title, Arrin looked about the room one more time to make sure no one else was there. But Red had been whispering, and the sincerity in his eyes finally made Arrin relax. "I just hate not knowing what's going on."

Red smiled. "Well, so does Arames—which means you'll both have answers soon, I'm sure."

⁂

Father Jorrus and Arames stood in a grassy area out of view of the main road, to the east of the inn. Jorrus was animated, rubbing his right hand with his left, but he kept his voice low. "Now you know, Advisor. Now you know." Jorrus's teeth gleamed between lips parted in a mix of a smile and a sneer. To Arames, Jorrus looked something close to pleased.

"I do not *know* anything, Father, other than we are dealing with something that possesses magical powers, something that can snuff light and sound from a room, something that can enter and leave a room that I had sealed—"

The white-robed cleric raised his arms at the sky, and then pointed at the monk. "All things this vampire can obviously do! Damn you, monk. You can sit back and let this thing kill you and your friend, but I won't."

Arames sighed. "What would you have me do, Jorrus? If this is a vampire master, you have as little idea who it might be as I do—even whether it is a townsperson or an outsider."

"Bah. Someone here? I would know if it was someone here. It comes and goes without warning. The town walls are no barrier to this monster. We need to seek it out—tonight, when the night is new."

"Why not now?"

Jorrus shook his head. "We would never find it. It most likely hides underground during the day. Given the leagues of mining tunnels in these mountains, I doubt we could find it if we had weeks to search. But it comes into town more often now. I can sense its presence when it's here, as I did when it attacked you and your friend. Tonight, after dusk, you will meet me at the cemetery. It will reveal itself to us and we will strike it down. And you will see how deep this goes."

Arames nodded. "I will meet you."

"Your friend must come, too."

"We'll see. He needs rest."

"He will be fine by then. In fact, he should be up and around by Second Bells." Jorrus snorted; Arames knew he was annoyed that Lord Avedon had silenced the temple bells.

"What about Father Livasdawn? Should we ask him to join us?"

"That pup? He wouldn't sense a *gate* opening at the center of the town circle, monk." Jorrus turned and started toward the path that led to his home. "You, me and your boy... that's all. I'll get you your murderer, Kragen."

"And what will you get, Jorrus?"

Jorrus stopped and turned back, pointing a finger at Arames. "You will see, and you will take my words from this place. No one believes an old man who cries warnings from the wilderness. You will be my voice and carry the word to those who would not listen." Father Jorrus started again toward his home. "The undead are rising—and they are coming for us."

⚜

Arrin opened his eyes to find that the sun had risen. Arames sat in a chair at the window, looking out to the north toward Avedon Manor. An empty plate rested in his lap. "So you saved me last night, did you?"

Arames stood up and crossed the room. He picked up a full plate of food from the bedside table and placed it on the bed next to Arrin. The prince, still propped up in a seated position, now had more use of his extremities. "No, it is more likely I almost got you killed last night."

While Arrin ate, Arames explained what had happened. Arrin stopped him when he spoke of calling light from his medallion. "That was you? I saw the light—I thought I was dying. How did you...?"

Arames smiled. He reached into his robe and pulled out the round piece of gold. "Do you recognize it?"

"It's your Advisor's medallion. Advisor Rennick wears both of his on the front of his cloak."

"Yes. Like everything else, it is tied to my connection to the river of magic." Arames turned the small disk in his hand. "I am not a wizard. I cannot shape or otherwise change the energies that make up the River. But as an Aarronic Advisor I can dip from the River, deeper than most... and that energy manifests itself within me as truth-reading, mind-walks, and the like. When I forged this medallion and its twin, I poured my heart into the act. Even though I did not understand it at the time, I imbued this piece of gold with power that I have only now discovered I can call forth. It is not unlike Father Jorrus and his holy symbol of Arjun. When the need arises, the magic answers his call. He feels his power comes directly from Az and his Children, while I visualize magic as an invisible river that flows throughout Caern. But in the end it amounts to the same thing."

Arrin wanted to ask if this magic applied to smiths and the weapons they craft, but his immediate concern was the previous night's events. "So you called forth light from your medallion and it drove the vampire away?"

Arames thought for a moment. "I do not know about that. I know the light from my medallion combatted the magical darkness and silence in the room. I do not know if your attacker fled because it feared the light, or—as I suspect—out of fear of being recognized." He patted Arrin on the knee. "What is important is that it did flee."

Arrin touched his bandage again. "What happened to me?"

"There are two puncture wounds on the left side of your neck."

Arrin described the attack, and being forced to the ground. "Whatever it was, it was stronger than me by far. I couldn't stop it." He stretched his arms. "Talik and Leilah, did they see me?"

"Yes. But what happened here will remain a secret." Arames smiled. "Talik does not want the town talking about an attack on his only guests, and Leilah is too scared to talk to anyone. I spent a good cyke calming her."

"And Father Jorrus tended to me?"

Arames's smile faded. "Yes. He said he was in the cemetery and sensed an undead presence in the town. He was drawn toward the inn. I sent Talik to get my cousin and before they returned, Father Jorrus burst through the door, holy symbol raised ready to strike. He sniffed the air a couple of times and cursed himself for arriving too late. Then he went to the window, opened it, and sniffed some more."

"Do undead hunters normally track their prey through smell?"

"I have never seen a hunter use his sense of smell to search for an enemy, but he relied on his nose the other night as well. Only after he stood at the window for a time would he acknowledge me and help you."

Arrin pushed himself into more of an upright position. "What about my back... and your arm? Did he tend to those as well?"

"No, I made sure he did not see them. I did not want to answer the questions that would follow. Besides, the salve that Richard gave us is doing good work."

Arrin stretched his back and arms, and found that the pain was nearly gone. "Oh, I almost forgot. I dreamed again last night, before the attack."

Arames crossed his arms. "Was it a dream-walk?"

"I believe so." He described the two main events from his dream: the explosion, and the bloody garment. "When I was being attacked I thought I was still in my dream—I couldn't hear anything after the explosion. What do you think it all meant?"

"Just like your other dreams, we will have to wait and see. I wonder, though. Your attacker silenced this entire room during his attack. Could that have prevented you from hearing in your dream, as well?"

Arrin didn't believe that to be the case, since there had been light in his dream, but he didn't share his thoughts; he wished to move on. "So, can I get up now?

Arames's smile returned. "I hope so. We have work to do."

ON THE TRAIL

He is filled with the Spirit of Az:
in wisdom, in understanding, and in knowledge.

—Iberian, Prophet to All, The Priests of Caern

THE MORNING AIR SMELLED of the possibility of snow. Usually this pleased Arrin, but now the growing threat of winter made him shiver. He nearly had to force his way past Leilah, who chided him for being out of bed. But he convinced both her and Talik that he was fine, and that the crisp air would do him good.

"We have a lot of ground to cover today," Arames said as they walked. "I would like you to go back to the stables. Hopefully Jon Avedon will be there."

"And you?"

Arames folded his arms within his sleeves. "My morning will begin at the smithy, to see if your dream meant something."

"You're not going to start at the library, to make sure your librarian is okay?"

"I'm sure she is fine. While the exploding windows in your dream may be important, I already have reason to visit Herrjarr." Arames took the western path. "Meet me back at the inn once you are done. Rest if you need to—use Red's house as a stopping point if you must."

<hr />

Arames could hear voices from inside the blacksmith's workshop, but could not make out what was being said. Instead of interrupting, he decided to make use of his constabulary powers, taking the opportunity to walk around Herrjarr's property.

Water was an important resource for a blacksmith, and several water barrels lined the western wall of the smithy. Arames looked in each barrel; what he found in the last confirmed his belief in Arrin's awakening powers.

<hr />

Jon's favorite horse was missing from its stall when Arrin arrived at the stables. Lonne Garrett was busy changing another horse's shoes. Arrin found a nearby bench to rest and wait. Lonne saw him and waved, but remained engrossed in his work.

Jon returned a short time later, walking in front of his unbridled horse. Arrin stood and approached, offering to help unsaddle the horse. Jon bowed his head slightly, acknowledging his aid.

"I'm glad you're still here. Things are worse at the manor today."

"How so?"

Jon handed him a brush and they soon stood on opposite sides of the stallion, brushing the large steed's thick winter coat. "It was already quiet and depressed there, but this morning I was told to move downstairs and sleep on a makeshift bed Father set up in the great hall. When I went to check on Edvard I was told to leave. I can understand Father being concerned about my health, but Carin and Richard are in Edvard's room all the time and no one's worried about them."

"Maybe they don't want you to get sick before your competition?"

"Mmmm…" Jon didn't appear satisfied, but he let the conversation drop. A moment later, though, recognition crossed his face. "I passed the cemetery yesterday, and it made me remember something."

"What was it?"

"A few months ago I walked by the cemetery late at night, and I saw Sarah Tremaine there."

"Why was she at the cemetery late at night?"

"I don't know. She was with someone—some man I didn't recognize. She seemed pretty happy. She was giggling and pulling him along between the rows of gravestones."

"What happened after that?"

"I don't know. I wasn't about to stop walking, and she led the man behind one of the mausoleums and out of view."

※※◎※※

"So, do you mind explaining this to me, Herrjarr?"

Arames dropped a wet apron on the table in front of Herrjarr and his apprentice, Ollus Wenk. Arames had found it floating in a barrel of water outside of the smithy. In addition to being soaked, the apron was stained with blood.

"Where'd you get that?" Herrjarr's voice shook, every syllable a threat.

Arames pointed to the door behind him. "Outside, in one of your water barrels."

Herrjarr was a good five hands taller than Arames. The huge hammer he held in his left hand would have made most men nervous, but Arames was still in a dark mood after Arrin's attack the night before. He didn't care that the burly

201 | P.G. Holyfield

blacksmith was angry.

"I know you are looking for Miss Gretta's killer, but that don't give you rights to search around my property." The scarred man shook his hammer to emphasize his words.

Arames folded his hands within the arms of his robes. "Lord Avedon gave me constabulary power, which means I have the right to search anywhere this investigation leads me. Now answer the question, Herrjarr."

It was Ollus Wenk who spoke. "I—It's mine, Sir Arames."

Herrjarr's towering frame completely blocked Arames's view of the apprentice. Arames had to bend to his right just to see the man. "What?"

Ollus Wenk was about as different from Herrjarr as one could be. He was of mixed race himself, but most likely a cross of human and one of the Inarran dwarf clans. Ollus was at least four hands shorter than Arames and barely reached Herrjarr's waist. Based on Herrjarr's stance and demeanor, Ollus seemed more his protected ward than his apprentice.

Herrjarr turned to Ollus as well. "Hmmm?"

"It's my apron. I cut my hand on the sword you made for Richard. Remember, Herrjarr?" Ollus held up his hand, showing a three-inch gash along the palm. "I used the apron to stop the bleeding."

Herrjarr laid his hammer down on a nearby table and spoke to Arames out of the side of his mouth. "Hmm... which was why he went home early the night Gretta was killed, just like I told you yesterday." Herrjarr continued to Ollus. "But why did you put it in the water barrel?"

"I didn't want to waste the apron. I figured the blood would soak out of it over time and I thought you wouldn't mind."

Something had to have prevented Gretta's blood from staining the ground. But of course it's not the apron. That would have been too easy.

Herrjarr obviously wasn't pleased with Ollus's conversion of his water barrel into a wash-tub. "Is that all, Sir Arames?"

"Can you tell me about the argument you had with Gretta Platt before she died?"

"Argument?"

"In the middle of town... something about a delivery?"

Arames watched his eyes widen as he recalled the incident. His first reaction was one of fear. "Oh, no, Sir Arames. I know how that might have looked—I didn't mean to get angry." His fear quickly turned to anger, as if he assumed Arames would not believe him. "I didn't hurt Miss Gretta."

Arames did not raise his voice to match the blacksmith's, and he kept his hands within his robes. "Just tell me what the argument was about, Herrjarr."

"She wouldn't let me ship my swords... my swords!" Herrjarr growled, and his face flushed a reddish green. "Hrrrr..." Rather than say anything more, he turned and stomped out of the room.

Ollus moved to the doorway, blocking Aramess's attempt to follow the blacksmith. "Herrjarr got an order from this merchant from Yew for three bastard swords. They were meant for a castellan and his two sons, both coming of age." He led Arames over to a cabinet and opened it. Three swords nearly as tall as Ollus hung there, points down. "The detail on the pommels alone was going to make Herrjarr more than he probably made all of last year."

Arames was genuinely impressed at the workmanship. It must have taken Herrjarr months of work to craft such swords, between the double-edged blades and the details of the grip and pommel.

"All we had to do was ship the blades to the merchant in the city of Pendar. The merchant didn't have anyone traveling through here in time, so I was going to take them to Haven myself. Lord Avedon refused—or at least that's what Miss Gretta told us."

"Why?"

Ollus Wenk's eyes darted toward the back room, where Herrjarr had gone. "It's just the rules."

On the way back to the inn, Arrin happened upon Carin Avedon on her way from the town circle. She seemed embarrassed to see him, most likely over her brother's actions the evening before, but he approached her.

"Are you okay?" she asked. Arrin worried that she had learned about the incident at the inn, but only for a moment. "I can't believe Edvard attacked you."

"My pride is a bit damaged, but I'll survive. I'm just glad Richard was there."

Carin's concern vanished at the assurance in Arrin's voice, and mirth washed across her face. "I wish I had been there to see you and Sir Arames stand up to my father. What a sight that must have been!"

The prince recognized a bit of himself in Carin for a moment. "Your father is trying to survive right now, Miss Avedon. He may be hard on you, but he probably needs you more than he ever has."

Carin squinted at him as if she didn't believe what he was saying.

"Can I ask you some questions about Edvard?" he asked. Carin didn't say anything, but she didn't make a move to leave, so he continued. "What did Edvard like to do? Who did he spend the most time with?"

"Edvard has always been sort of... well... his own best friend. He liked the library, reading books... and he loved maps."

"He spent a lot of time at the town library?"

"Mostly he just got books and went to read by himself somewhere. He used to spend a lot of time at the town theatre."

"We passed it yesterday and heard hammering from inside. It's being fixed up?"

"Yes. Father has Ollus Wenk and one of the constables cleaning it up. He had wanted Sarah Tremaine and Gretta to sing a concert this winter. They both have—well, Miss Tremaine has a beautiful voice."

"And Edvard spent most of his days there?"

"Yes, he loved it there. It was away from the manor, quiet, and relatively clean, other than the dust. He was… happy there."

"He wasn't happy most of the time?"

Carin licked her lips and then exhaled. She watched her breath hang in the air for a moment. "Other than my father, Edvard was affected most by my mother's death. I believe he would have… I believe he will leave Avedon Hill, as soon as he's old enough to have a say in the matter."

Arrin remembered something Arames had said the day before. "Miss Carin, when you spoke to Sir Arames last, you were going to tell him something about Talik Bore, but your father interrupted. What was it?"

She thought for a moment. "I was going to tell him that I saw Talik outside the manor the day Gretta was killed. He was talking to himself like he was rehearsing what he wanted to say. When I walked up to him and asked him what he was doing," she put her hand on Arrin's arm and smiled, "since that is what I do… Talik asked me if I knew whether Gretta was going to be leaving the manor any time soon."

"Did you tell Constable Louis?"

"I would have—but father asked us not to talk to him, after… He doesn't want Louis to find out about Edvard. He's afraid how Louis might react."

She excused herself, leaving Arrin to wonder why Lord Avedon would worry at all about Constable Louis.

※◎◎※

Arames and Arrin met back at the inn for an early lunch. The monk took notes on Arrin's discoveries, and he shared what Ollus had told him about the trade policies. Talik was nowhere to be found, but it did not matter; Leilah had prepared a fine meal.

"So, some townspeople have permission to sell their wares in other towns, like Hemming and Sarah Tremaine, but others like Herrjarr and Alex Dewirin don't."

"Yes."

Leilah had been idly sweeping closer and closer to their table, listening in. Now Arames called her over. "Do you have something you want to tell us."

Her face was red as the tomato Arrin had left uneaten on his plate. Arames only smiled.

The raven-haired waitress leaned in. "You mentioned Sarah Tremaine just now, in the graveyard. It reminded me. I saw her one time when I was cleaning the cottages. She was outside one of the 'Estates'—with a man. They were..." she averted her eyes, "having relations."

"How long ago was this?"

"Several months, now. Ms. Tremaine didn't see me, and then I saw something I'm still not sure I saw rightly."

"What?" Arames smiled his calm smile. Arrin shifted on his chair, doing his best to stay patient as Leilah grew increasingly edgy.

"She... bit him. She pushed his head to one side and looked like she bit his neck."

Arames reached for Leilah's hand. "Dear, why didn't you tell us this before?"

Leilah's eyes filled with tears. "Because... I saw the man later that night. He was staying at the inn. He was smiling ear to ear and wasn't hurt at all, although his neck looked red. I'm so... so sorry, Sir Arames."

Arames patted Leilah's hand and tried to calm her. She continued. "I saw him again the next day, before he left for the Pass. He looked fine. I didn't want to make trouble, since no one looked hurt."

Arames nodded. "That's fine, Leilah. Now one last question: What did you argue with Constable Tanner about, the day after Gretta was killed?

Leilah's eyes grew wider than Arrin would have thought possible. "How... how did you know?"

"Someone saw you arguing with him."

She shook her head. "No, I mean how did you know I told him about Ms. Tremaine?"

Arames shrugged. "I didn't. Why did it turn into an argument?"

Leilah's eyes narrowed, glaring past Arames at the memory of the fight. "He told me it was nothing. He said I probably hadn't even seen anything, that I might have even just dreamed it one night and that I remembered my dream once the word got out how Miss Gretta had been killed."

The monk patted Leilah's hand one more time. "Thank you, my dear."

The statement was clearly a dismissal; Leilah gladly took it as such, carrying her broom with her into the kitchen. Arrin was smiling. "How do you do that?"

"Do what?"

Arrin snorted. "Never mind. So we're paying the seamstress another visit?"

"No, we are not. I am. You need to sleep, at least a cyke or two. Red is upstairs in our room. He'll stay there while you sleep. Go."

Arrin was in no position to argue, although the prospect of seeing Sarah Tremaine again threatened to overcome his need for rest. "Yes, *master.*"

The Avedon Clothier

Nicollet laughed;
it was a song that shook the walls of the mountain.
Instantly Nicollet knew herself, and walked free.

—Tales of the Children

ARAMES DETOURED TO PAY a visit to Cletus at the town gate on the way to Sarah Tremaine's shop. He found the man chatting with Shane Olivet outside the guard station. Cletus struck the farrier's apprentice on the shoulder with the palm of his hand, laughing heartily. "So, Sir Arames," Cletus said, still chuckling, "how's your investigation going?"

"It's progressing. What's all the excitement about?"

Shane lowered his head, but not before Arames saw the blush on his cheeks. Cletus didn't give him a chance to speak. "Shane here is finally making *progress* too, aren't you, pup?"

Arames smiled. "Is the young Miss Hemming warming to your advances, Shane?"

Arames wouldn't have believed it possible, but Shane's face grew even redder. "I gave her another poem and she said she'd let me take her on a picnic." Just as quickly, his smile disappeared. "Oh, no. I can't cook. What am I going to do?"

Cletus slapped the wiry young man's back once more. "You just talk to Talik and have him fix up something nice. Tell him I said it was his *moral* obligation to help you win the heart of that young lass."

Shane bowed his head to Arames and wandered off in the direction of the inn. He massaged his shoulder as he walked. "A bit rough on the young man, aren't you, Cletus?"

"Ah, he needs some toughening up, Sir Arames." Arames didn't need to truth-read to *see* that Cletus cared for Shane. "So what brings you here this cold morning?"

"I'm on my way to Miss Tremaine's shop, and I wanted to ask you about her."

"And why would ye be asking me?"

"Because you seem to know a lot about the townspeople, and you have been honest with me, so far. Besides—" Arames pointed, "you can see her shop from here."

Cletus nodded. "True enough. Go ahead, then."

"It seems that Miss Tremaine provides quite an array of services—many more than you would expect from a simple seamstress."

Cletus chuckled, a rumble that seemed to originate from deep within his gut. "Like I've said before, I'm not in a position to judge anyone, sir monk. But... as you pointed out, I do spend most of my time within spitting distance of her shop. Let's just say that the men who leave Miss Tremaine's shop with smiles on their faces far outnumber the garments traded or sold."

⁂

Arames paused outside Sarah Tremaine's shop and opened himself up to the power of the Land. As always, his perception of magic was that of a flowing river; he could *see* tendrils of it flowing around his legs as he walked, as if he were wading through knee-deep water. Arames hoped it would be enough to counteract any chemical-induced advantage that Sarah Tremaine employed.

As he stepped into the shop, the muscles around his left eye began to twitch. Before closing the door behind him, he inhaled a cautious breath. He was relieved to find that Sarah Tremaine was not burning incense. Even so, the lingering smell of it hung in the air.

"Did you bring your robes for mending, Sir Arames?" Incense or not, Sarah Tremaine could only be described as one of the great beauties of the world. She wore a simple dress of the darkest blue, with only the slightest peek of cleavage on display, but her hair was what made her appearance striking today: long and red, she wore it up in a style quite common at court, emphasizing the long lines of her neck and shoulders magnificently.

"As a matter of fact, I did." Arames had to consider the possibility that Sarah possessed such a radiant charm because she was a vampire master. As he handed her the bundle of robes, he reached out and grasped her arm.

A small gasp escaped Sarah's mouth but she did not attempt to pull away. She only smiled and allowed the monk's touch. "Is there something else you need, Sir Arames?"

Sarah's skin was warm, unlike Edvard Avedon's. Arames stared deeply into her green eyes. He pushed gently with his mind, touching her consciousness—careful not to probe too deeply—and immediately sensed the barriers only one with training would have. But more importantly, he felt the spark of life he doubted any vampire could possess. Sarah placed her free hand over Arames's own, caressing it. Her lips were full, moist, pink, and growing redder by the moment, inviting Arames forward. Arames sensed the river of magic rising up around him, like waves crashing against the side of a boat during a storm. He soon realized he had stopped breathing.

With a sharp intake of breath, Arames released Sarah's arm. He believed he saw disappointment in the woman's face. It was nothing compared to the disappointment he felt himself—frustration that had nothing to do with his search for a vampire master. "I—I apologize, Miss Tremaine. Your powers of persuasion are more than I can fathom."

Sarah still smiled, but she also sighed longingly. Turning, she carried Arames's robes over to a worktable. "Did you learn what you came to learn, Brother of Aarron?"

Arames followed her. "Seamstress, clothier... these titles do not seem to capture the scope of your services... and abilities."

Sarah spread the robes out on the table in front of her, and looked up. "I'll not insult your intelligence, Sir Arames. I'm sure you've learned enough from the townspeople to understand what I do: I provide certain services to those who can afford them. I pray this doesn't offend your sensibilities."

Arames shook his head. "No, not at all. Only the Priests of Caern condemn your line of work, Miss Tremaine."

She snorted. "And considering some of my clients, that's as humorous as it is hypocritical."

Arames smiled. "And your work as a seamstress—is it simply a front?"

"Oh, no, Sir Arames. You see my work around you. I'm one of the finest dress-makers in Grozh. It just so happens that I'm even better at my other line of work."

"I have heard stories from separate individuals that would indicate a darker side to your other line of work—one that on the surface marks you as a suspect in Gretta Platt's murder."

Sarah laughed, but the expression on her face was the first Arames had seen that he would consider less than flattering. "Please, come. I'd like to show you something."

She led him through a door that led back to the rest of her shop. A set of stairs let them out into a large underground room whose construction looked to have been a considerable task. Some of the walls were lined with stone, while other areas had been covered with wood and plaster. The walls held even more proof of Sarah Tremaine's ability as a seamstress; they were lined with a wide array of garments for both men and women of various sizes. "The first thing you need to understand, Sir Arames, is that I choose my customers, and they travel here only at my invitation." Tables along one wall displayed a variety of items, from feathers and whips to implements whose uses Arames could only guess at. The center of the room was dominated by a large bed.

Sarah approached a table and retrieved something that fit in her hand before returning to Arames. "I fulfill the fantasies of men—and women, on occasion. There's a merchant who works directly for one of your royals in Southern Yew. He has visited me on several occasions over the last… four years. He brought me this on his last trip."

Arames looked down. Sarah held a curved piece of metal smaller than the palm of her hand. "On a previous visit, he had me bite down on a piece of clay to get an impression of my teeth. He took that mold and had a jeweler create this." Sarah inserted the metal form into her mouth. Arames heard a snap as it fit into place over her upper teeth. "How do day wook?"

As Sarah modeled her new teeth, Arames understood what Leilah must have seen that night. Two metallic incisors protruded from her mouth, extending nearly to the curve marking the start of her chin. "So this merchant had you act the part of a vampire?"

Sarah giggled and held up a hand while she pulled the appliance out of her mouth. The teeth snapped free, but her devilish grin remained. "To the point of drawing blood from his shoulder. I refused to bite his neck as hard as he wanted, though. An accidental death wouldn't be good for business."

Arames offered his hand and Sarah Tremaine placed the set of teeth in it. He used his index finger to measure the distance between the two vampire fangs. *Shorter than the distance between the tines of the metal gardening fork from the courtyard. If we ever find Gretta's corpse, we can examine the wounds on her neck.*

A short time later they returned upstairs. "While it is obvious, Miss Tremaine, that you are not a vampire, it does not change the fact that you were here alone most of the night Gretta Platt was murdered."

Sarah Tremaine's smile faded. She stood perfectly still and breathed slow, drawn out breaths. Arames embraced his truth-reading sensibilities; Sarah was lowering the barriers that Arames had sensed before. "I don't know what gives me my *powers of persuasion*, as you so eloquently put it, Sir Arames. Ever since I was a child I've been able to get my way with a smile or a look, and even more so with a song. I was on my way to becoming famous as a child prodigy. By the age of eight I had performed in several Grozhian cities. But when I was twelve, I sang at the court of Governor Racine at Mishkiel. My performance that day was *The Loss of Iruna*. Do you know it?"

Something about Sarah's story was familiar to Arames. He nodded. *Iruna, the first Child of Az to give up immortality and enter Caern. It was a tale of love, and of woe.*

"I sang of Iruna, of how Az decided it was time for her to cease living a normal mortal life and remember her own deific nature, and of how her epiphany destroyed the unborn child growing within her… and how that loss led her elf-husband Elias to give up hope and die of a broken heart. There was something in the words of the song that touched me. Perhaps because I was finally old enough to understand what love and loss truly meant. As a result, I sang with more emotion than I ever had before."

Arames's eyes widened in recognition. "That was you?"

Later that night, three people from the audience killed themselves, including Governor Racine's son, who threw himself from the parapets of his father's castle.

Sarah didn't need to respond. Arames's truth-sense told him all he needed to know.

"I've never sung that way again. I guess I should feel lucky that I wasn't accused of being a witch." A tear flowed down Sarah's right cheek. "The rest of my story isn't important, Sir Arames, other than to say that I still use my voice and my smile to make people happy—and to make my life safe here."

"So what *were* you doing the night Gretta was murdered?"

"I was here, but not alone."

"A client?"

Sarah smiled, but it was not her smile of persuasion; this time, it emanated from her heart. "Since you know what I am, I no longer feel the need to lie to protect myself or others. I was with Louis that night. And no, he is not a client."

So this is why Louis was indisposed the night of Gretta's murder. "Why not tell me this the last time I was here?"

Sarah took Arames's hand and led him to the door. "Because Lord Avedon *is* my client, and he would not be pleased to learn that... that Louis and I are lovers. Please respect that."

Arames bowed slightly. "Until we meet again, Miss Tremaine."

"I'll deliver your garments to the inn once they are mended and cleaned. Just find out who killed Gretta, Sir Arames. Gretta was my friend—one of the only true friends I've ever had."

The Out of Towner

The road that leads to your own reality is a warrior's path.
Life and Death lie on either side of you.
Choose neither, and you follow in Treygh's footsteps.

—Tales of the Children

Arames was so engrossed in his small journal that he barely noticed Constable Louis's approach. He had made it back to the inn and was eating another meal in the common area. "Sir Arames, I have some news."

"Please, join me."

Louis sat opposite Arames in the booth but appeared uneasy. "I was just speaking with Cletus. He told me a trader found a horse tied to a tree, and its owner dead, a few leagues west of here. The merchant said it looked like a vampire killing."

Arames pushed his nearly full plate over to Constable Louis and rose to his feet. "Here, eat. I need to get a few things, including Arrin. Can you lead us to the body?"

"Yes, I believe so. But we need to hurry. There are Grozhian patrols out. If they find it or if the merchant notifies them, we'll find nothing when we get there."

"Horses?"

"They'll be waiting at the gate."

✥

A cyke later, Arames, Arrin, and Constable Louis approached the area where the tradesman claimed to have found the body.

They had ridden in silence most of the way. A question Arrin asked about Sarah Tremaine early on had piqued Constable Louis's interest, but Arames only said, "Miss Tremaine is no longer a suspect." The look in his eyes had managed to silence Arrin's follow-up question, and Constable Louis, relieved, had urged his horse ahead at a slightly quicker pace.

They reached a crossroads and continued west, eventually reaching a tight road nearly hidden by disuse. They turned their horses down this path, proceeding southwest into a thick wooded area. Soon thereafter the men were forced to navigate past stretches of mud and large pools of standing water. Arrin was the first to spot the pair of wheel ruts in the road.

Louis checked his map. "Yes, this is where the merchant found the body; he investigated down this path after hearing a horse struggling against its restraints."

Arames heard nothing but the breeze through the trees. "The trader took the horse with him?"

Louis nodded. "Yes. He said it looked like it had been tied to the tree for days."

They continued down the narrow path until they reached a point where the wagon trail ended. Arames dismounted. "It appears the trader proceeded from here on foot. We should do the same."

After securing their horses, they slowly moved forward until they reached an open meadow. Arrin commented, "This would be a nice place to rest, if it wasn't for that dead body over there."

The corpse was seated against a tree, arms crossed over his chest. Once they moved in close, Arames discerned that it had been there only a few days at most. There were plenty of bugs and worms crawling around the body, but the face was still relatively recognizable. "Fortunate for us, it is not summer." Arames moved to his right to look at the left side of the man's neck. A jagged chunk of skin and flesh was missing. Blood had run down into his clothes, but far less blood than one would expect from such a wound. Arames took a stick from the ground and used it to carefully move some hair that had matted against the corpse's neck. "Louis, does this resemble Gretta's wound at all?"

"No, only the location of the wound is the same. Gretta had two very distinct puncture wounds. This looks like something gnawed at him. And there's more blood here than there was in the courtyard."

Arrin asked, "Could it be the moon-beast?" Constable Louis raised an eyebrow.

"I do not believe so. According to Father Jorrus, a single bite is not the mark of a moon-beast, unless it is an attempt to only injure." Arames waved his hand dismissively.

Arames's gesture had been understood by Arrin, but his simple acknowledgment of the possibility made Louis frown. "What moon-beast?"

Arames was the one to respond. "Not to worry, Louis. We are only discussing what might have happened here—and an animal attack is certainly something to consider."

Constable Louis did not appear satisfied with Arames's answer, but he didn't press the issue. "The merchant said that he took nothing but the horse. I guess we'll never know if that's true."

"Arrin, go look over by that tree, the one with the rope around the trunk. I assume that is where the horse was tied." Arames pointed to the ground. "He was not killed right here—" His finger moved to indicate the ground to the left of the body. "Not enough footprints here." The ground was soft underfoot. Arames looked at the impressions near Louis's feet, and then back at the footprints near the corpse. "These footprints were not made by a heavy man."

Arames found deeper impressions on the other side of the corpse—this set of footprints backed away from the tree where the horse had been tied. "He was attacked over by that tree and then carried to this one... and propped up like so."

"Why do that?" Louis asked.

"I do not know." Arames crouched before the body and pulled the hem of the cloak away to get to the clothing underneath. "Judging by the lack of footprints, I do not believe the merchant disturbed the body." The corpse's tunic was relatively dry. Underneath, Arames found a scroll tube connected to the tunic by a leather strap. He opened the tube and pulled out a single piece of parchment.

Louis had been searching the ground between Arames and Arrin. "What is it?" Arames ignored his query for the moment and pressed on the man's surcoat. There was something underneath it, on the man's chest. He reached behind the man's neck; finding a chain, Arames pulled up until a pendant came into view. *Interesting...* Arames continued searching the corpse until he was satisfied he had not missed anything. Then he stood and faced Louis.

Louis spoke first. "Is something wrong? You don't look well."

Arames handed the parchment to the constable. Louis read the name at the top of the page. "Carlotta's Rare Books."

"It appears I need to speak to Lane Niccols."

"This was the man she was supposed to meet the night Gretta was killed, isn't it?" Arames nodded.

Arrin walked back over with a satchel. "I found this on the other side of the tree. The trader must have missed it."

Arames took the bag and opened it. Within were several bound manuscripts, a few of which appeared to be very old. Exposure to the elements had already damaged them. As delicately as possible, Arames reached inside and looked at each of the tomes.

"What are you looking for?"

Arames handed the satchel to Arrin and started back toward the horses. "Something that should have been in that bag."

Constable Louis called to Arames, "Shouldn't we do something with the body?"

Arames looked back, but did not pause. "As you said before, Grozhian patrols could be nearby. It would be best if we are not discovered burying a corpse."

Constable Louis and Arrin looked at each other for a moment, and then followed Arames out of the grove.

The Song of Artus

The battle drums never played as loud
as they did at Ohme the next morning.
Elisia Llewellyn's song had given them hope—
a powerful magic indeed

—Tales of the Children

Arames was silent for most of the return trip, letting his horse follow Constable Louis without too much direction. Arrin rode by his mentor's side, carefully watching his actions.

Arames spent most of his time studying the pendant he had taken from the merchant's neck. Arrin couldn't quite make out what it was, but it appeared to be some sort of religious symbol.

Finally, Arames broke his concentration. He dangled the pendant so that Arrin could see it better. The symbol was three swords set in a circle of silver. The middle sword was surrounded by flames. "Do you know what this is?"

"It's a symbol I've seen before, but I can't recall from where." Arrin thought back to Arames's lectures about the Children of Az. "Is that a symbol of Artus?"

Arames smiled. "Very good."

"For an immortal that most people have forgotten, we sure have seen a lot of references to him lately."

"Yes. There are those who still worship Artus, at least in secret. But they are usually men of war, not booksellers."

Arrin rode forward, pulling Arames's mount along until the three men rode side by side with Arrin in the middle. "So, Head Constable, Arames has been teaching me lately about the Children of Az. Do you believe there is a god named Artus?"

Louis didn't appear comfortable with the conversation, and seemed less comfortable still about being drawn into it, but the look in Arames's eyes prompted him to answer. "Arrin, I'm no scholar. I was raised in a town similar to Avedon Hill, where most citizens once held great regard for Artus and his works. By the time

I became an adult, our temple to Artus had been rededicated to Iberian. When I came to Avedon Hill, the temple to Artus was no longer being used, and it was years before Father Jorrus was able to get a new temple built for the worship of Az. Now we live in a generation that barely knows who Artus was, or is."

⁂

Arames contemplated Louis's words; he smiled, once again forced to reevaluate his opinion of the man. "But what do you *believe*, constable?"

Louis still directed his words toward the student. "Arrin, have you ever heard the story of the Song of Artus?"

Arames's smile broadened. *The Song of Artus... good.*

Arrin shook his head, and Louis began telling the story. "Theuroik Ironblade was the human general who destroyed the demon army at the city of Ohme during the War of Man."

Arrin interrupted. "With the help of Queen Elisia and Iberian, correct?"

"Yes. But it was Theuroik's army that had delayed the demons for nearly five years; thousands of men had died just to make that final battle at Ohme possible. Theuroik understood from the beginning that the demons weren't just slipping into this world... they were organized and bent on the destruction of Caern. It was Theuroik's actions—his honor, his perseverance against all odds—that made Elisia Llewellyn recognize Theuroik's true nature."

Arrin remained skeptical. "That Theuroik was an incarnation of Artus?"

Louis nodded. "It's said that her presence on the battlefield outside the walls of Ohme caused Theuroik to realize his deific nature, and with that understanding came power... which ultimately allowed them to win the battle that day."

Arrin turned to Arames. "His epiphany? Why would the elf-queen's presence unlock Theuroik's memories and power?"

Arames responded, "Because some say that Queen Elisia Llewellyn was an incarnation of Iruna, the first daughter of Az."

Arrin sighed. "Oh. Well, that makes all the sense in the world. But what does this have to do with the Song of Artus?"

Louis asked Arames, "Where did you find this young man?"

Arames smiled. "Alas, he had a sheltered upbringing. I'm doing my best."

Arrin looked about to protest, but he kept his composure and Louis continued.

"On the battlefield that night, as corpses were being buried and demon carcasses burned, Queen Elisia started to sing a most inspirational song. At first she walked amongst the people while they did their work, her voice barely above a whisper; but by the time she had finished, everyone—every man, elf, and dwarf within the sound of her raised voice—surrounded her, enthralled. Her song praised Theuroik's god-like effort to preserve man against the demon threat, and his victory over the demons on the battlefield that day."

Arames broke in, continuing the story. "Theuroik and Iberian were called to the field, and stood side by side as Elisia sang her song a second time. But Queen Elisia changed the words as she went through it again. While it still raised the actions of Theuroik to mythological proportions, the elf-queen now sang of Artus, god-child of War." He turned to the constable. "Do you know some of the song, Louis?"

"Oh yes, Sir Arames. It's one of the only poems I ever learned. I can sing a little from the second telling, if you like." Arames nodded, and Louis sang in a light yet powerful voice:

> *Surrounding Artus, a living shield of man*
> *Tourim legions strove to break in vain*
> *"Shed no tears for Artus," Iberian shouted with pride!*
> *"The wall still holds! He yet lives by our side!"*
> *With weapons consecrated and with aid arrived before,*
> *On the vile Tourim did his fatal sword-thrusts pour!*
> *Then on Vir-nik, and on Vur-lik did Artus cast his gaze*
> *as he charged down his enemies like a cloud burst by the sun's rays.*
> *These and other mighty Caerim on the earthly battle slain,*
> *By their valor and their virtue walk the bright ethereal plane,*
> *They have cast their mortal bodies, crossed the radiant portal of heaven,*
> *For to win celestial kingdoms unto mortals it is given,*
> *Let them strive by steadfast action, rousing speech, endurance long,*
> *Brighter life and holier future into sons of men belong!*

Arames remained silent while Louis's singing voice flowed around them. Louis's belief in Artus and his song was apparent—the power of it brought tears to Arames's eyes. Arrin was moved as well, turning on his horse to face Arames with a look of awe. "I don't know what to say."

Arames composed himself. "Thank you, Louis. That was exactly what I needed." Louis seemed to understand. He nodded and pulled his horse back a few paces, allowing Arames and Arrin to ride ahead of him.

Arames continued, and kept his voice loud enough for Louis to hear. "Theuroik was a great general… possibly the greatest general in our race's history. Iberian's followers had their reasons for discrediting Theuroik's legacy, but raising Iberian to immortal status at the expense of Artus was wrong. I'm not saying Iberian wasn't a Child of Az. There are various legends of prophets during Caern's history that lead me to believe that there is merit to the idea that some of these prophets were incarnations of the same immortal being. But to deny the existence of the embodiment of action and war is problematic at best."

Louis responded, "Az be praised. I heard that your opinions have brought you some trouble, Sir Arames."

Arames smiled. "Yes. One problem that the Priests of Caern have with the Aarronic Brotherhood is that, though we are not a religious entity, we refuse to acknowledge the change in Az's family tree. I admit I have been one of the louder voices against the followers of Iberian."

Arames moved his horse forward and left the two men behind; the conversation, for Arames, was over.

LANE NICCOLS

But are vampires Tourim?
Some say the first vampire was the progeny of a union
between incarnations of Kalin and Treygh.
Strange that vampires are not welcome
in either Treygh's or Kalin's home.

—Tales of the Children

ARRIN WATCHED AS ARAMES rushed off towards the library and Louis galloped off toward the stables with Arames's horse in tow. To his displeasure, he was once again left behind to speak to the gatekeeper.

Cletus absently stroked the nose of the horse Arrin sat astride. "What is everyone's hurry?"

Arrin only shrugged, which elicited a grunt from the gatekeeper. "So what is you need, Sir Arrin … or did you just want to visit with me?"

Arrin rolled his eyes. "Lane Niccols—she left town the evening Gretta was—?"

Cletus interrupted the prince. "What, you don't believe me now?"

Arrin spoke with a level voice, as Arames had instructed. "Arames just wants to confirm what you said the other day. Lane Niccols exited and reentered this gate the night Gretta Platt was killed?"

"Yes!"

"Did she have any sort of package when she came back in?"

"No… but she always has a backpack with her. She showed it to me once. She had it specially made—waterproof, it is. I didn't check it when she came back. She told me the dealer she was supposed to meet never showed up."

"You keep a ledger detailing everything coming and going through the gate. Why give her special treatment?"

"The Housemistress told me not to bother. Besides, she never sells anything; I watched the woman come and go for over a year without doing anything other than add to her collection."

Adding to her collection… she's done more than that lately, I'm afraid. "Thank you, Cletus."

Arrin clicked his cheek and directed his horse onward, to handle the second half of Arames's instruction: to retrieve Father Jorrus, and then meet Arames at the library.

Louis had his assignment, too. Arames had instructed the constable to explain their findings to Lord Avedon and then to bring him to the library as well. "I do not want him to arrive too early," Arames had said. "It could be dangerous for him."

Louis agreed, and said he would retrieve the other two constables while he was at it. He also agreed to leave the horses at the stable and approach the library on foot.

⁂

Though Arrin and his own better judgment had argued against it, Arames entered the library without waiting for the others to join him. While he believed Lane had not attacked Arrin, Arames still wanted to keep the prince away from the library for as long as possible.

The last conversation he had had with Arrin's mother entered Arames's mind, but he shook it off—*I have no time for this.* Besides, Arames needed to speak to the creature alone.

⁂

Perfect… Lane retreated two steps and took a moment to admire the gold-hinged glass case that now hung against one of the stone walls in the basement of the town library.

And now for the finishing touch.

She pulled a weathered, leather-bound manuscript out of a small pack. What she held in her hands was part of history—a fact that was very important to her.

A voice traveled down the stairs from the main floor. "I have tried to figure out why you would murder a book dealer of all people, Ms. Niccols. Did he not bring the copy of Arlen Gricca's autobiography with him, or did he try to alter the terms of your arrangement?"

Arames's presence took Lane by surprise; it was a feeling she had not experienced in many years and she savored the novelty of it. *You walk quietly for one of the living, monk.* She held up the book for him to see. "I'm afraid I wasn't completely honest with you, Arames. This isn't a copy of Arlen Gricca's autobiography… it's the original." She smiled a devilish smile, deliberately allowing two short fangs to appear from underneath her upper lip.

"So why kill him?" Arames asked. He had not moved at all, and his hands were folded placidly inside the sleeves of his robe.

"Pitr was a nasty sort of man. He thought he could take advantage of me in that secluded grove." Lane walked over to the glass case. "'You pull a tiger's tail'... as the old saying goes." She gently placed the manuscript inside, propping it up so that it was on display. Then she closed the lid. "By the way, I never gave you permission to come down here."

"I have constabulary powers, Ms. Niccols."

"And I've just admitted to taking the life of a man far from Avedon Hill on the night of Miss Platt's murder. Your powers only extend to the matter of Gretta Platt's unfortunate death."

Arames's expression did not change. "You may not have killed the Housemistress, but you took the life of Lord Avedon's son."

Even from across the room, Lane's heightened senses could pick out Arames's scent. The disgust emanating from his pores tainted everything, but his odor remained laced with another emotion more important to Lane: *desire*. Even though the monk had positioned himself with a long table between them and had kept his back to the basement's only obvious exit, Lane knew it would take little effort to reach his side. *You will ask for me before we are through, sir monk.*

"No, Sir Arames. I only gave the boy what he asked for, nothing more." Lane swung her arm out and pulled on a handle against the wall. Before Arames could move, the lamps in the room went dark.

⚜

"What Edvard wanted? He was a fifteen year old boy. Anything he *wanted*, you planted in his mind." Arames listened for movement, but heard nothing. He backed up slowly until the frame of the doorway was solid against his back.

He was a special one. As are you, Arames. Lane's voice echoed inside his head. Arames threw up walls to protect his mind against the vampire master's powers—but his shields did not prevent him from hearing her again. *He discovered what I was, and wasn't afraid. He begged me to take him... to give him what I have... to take him away from his pain.*

Arames stretched out with his mind to touch Lane, or at least determine where she was, but he could not locate her. Since he could hear her in his mind, Arames was relatively sure he could communicate with her the same way. *Do not speak as if you gave him some sort of gift. He is little more than an animal now.*

He sensed movement across the room, but it was not toward him. His right hand, within the sleeve of his robe, tightened on his sai.

He made it back to his family, did he? They have him? Arames refused to acknowledge the question, but he frowned inwardly. He should not have even given Lane an idea of what he knew. *He refused the gift, Arames. He drank of me, mixing my blood with his. After three days of sharing, he was ready. I took him then. He awakened the next day, his consciousness intact.*

Arames interrupted, *It was your blood that allowed his consciousness to remain?*

Arames sensed her amusement at his thirst for knowledge. *I led him down the path. All he had to do was drink the blood of the gift I presented him... He would have been the next Lord Avedon, once I removed his insolent brother from the picture. My place here in Avedon Hill—safe, with my books—would have been assured for years to come. But he couldn't do it. He fled...*

Arames kept Lane talking, giving his eyes a chance to adjust to the darkened basement. He thought he could make out the outline of the handle Lane had pulled, extending from the wall to his left. There were several large bookcases to his right, both along the walls and in the center of the room. *What gift? Who else did you kill?*

She's fine, don't you worry... although she has her own set of problems still to deal with. I let her go after Edvard ran away. She doesn't remember a thing.

Arames concentrated, feeling the flow of the River strengthen around him. *So he ran because he had some humanity left within him? You curse him for that, or only envy him?*

The sound of something brushing against wood came from behind one of the bookcases. Lane's voice spilled into Arames's mind again. *Humanity... this library holds the best and worst of humanity's history... you above all should know that humanity has nothing to do with taking life, and neither do good and evil. Edvard simply didn't have the courage to join me. I believe that trait has been bred out of the Avedon line.*

I followed, her voice continued, *but could not find him. Without the gift, his consciousness would have been driven from his mind in a day's time. But if he somehow made it to the manor...*

Arames tried to finish her thought. *How soon after that was Gretta killed?*

The next night... with his "humanity", as you put it, gone, Edvard would have killed Gretta without thinking.

Arrin was attacked last night at the inn. Was it you?

Hmmm... royal blood, from lineage that certainly includes an immortal or two. That would be a treat. But, contrary to what you may think of me, I would never attack either of you. I have too much respect for his family and too much respect for what you have done for Caern, Brother of Aarron.

It did not surprise Arames that Lane had recognized Arrin, considering the wealth of knowledge available to her. He did not have time to dwell on it now.

Lane's next few thoughts were scattered, as she pieced together the events of the last few days. *Edvard made it back to the manor... Lappin's Codex... the King's*

Head moth... No... they can't be considering a King's Crown potion?! Fools! Arames heard a hiss from far to his right.

Upstairs, the door of the library opened. It was too late to save Lane Niccols.

Arames was in complete control of the energies flowing around him. He released the grip of his sai and pulled his empty hand out of his sleeve, casting his arm out before him like he was throwing a knife. A burst of air hit the handle on the wall, knocking it upward. Flames rose from the enclosed sconces on the walls, flooding the room with brightness.

Arames sprang over the table, landing where he had last seen Lane. He looked down the rows of bookshelves, searching for her, but she was nowhere to be seen.

From farther away, he heard one last thought from Lane Niccols: *Arames, don't let them give Edvard the potion—please.*

Flight

*Theuroik drove the Tourim
to the far-flung corners of Caern;
the only exit from Caern
was straight into Kalin's Abyss.*

—Tales of the Children

Arrin found Arames in the library basement, frantically searching one of the walls. "What happened?"

Father Jorrus pushed past Arrin, nearly knocking him down. He held his holy symbol of Arjun high above his head; a powerful light flooded the room, far brighter than the light from the sconces. "You faced a vampire master alone?! Brave—and foolish, monk!"

Arrin caught up to them. "Jorrus, how could you not realize she was a vampire?"

Jorrus ignored the question. "She went this way, did she?" Jorrus had attached the holy symbol to the end of his staff. He held it before him, sweeping it across the floor. "There you are."

Arrin couldn't make out any markings on the floor, but Jorrus clearly saw something. The cleric approached the wall Arames had been searching and extended his staff until it nearly touched the stonework. "You'll not escape me so easily, bitch." He pressed several stones with his hands.

A grating sound accompanied movement along the wall, and soon an uneven door of stones and mortar slid back, just wide enough to fit through. Arames moved forward, but Jorrus moved faster, pushing his way past the monk into a narrow passage that wound its way north. Arames and Arrin followed.

Arames repeated Arrin's query to the back of Jorrus's head. "Why were your senses blind to Lane Niccols?"

Father Jorrus, staff before him, was nearly running through the roughly hewn passage. "I rarely spoke to the creature. She and her books never interested me. And she obviously never visited my temple."

Arrin was surprised to hear his excuses. After a moment, Jorrus slowed his pace, visibly upset. When the priest looked back at them, his eyes had lost their fire. "I don't know. She... fooled me." Admitting his limitations rekindled the spark of his anger; Jorrus growled. "She must have some sort of magics working for her. I can track an undead creature within a league of me." Jorrus reached a fork where the tunnel continued north and angled west. He lowered his staff to the ground. The holy symbol was even brighter now, allowing them all to see in all directions.

"What is he doing?" Arrin had stuck his head over Arames's shoulder.

"The power of his holy symbol and his connection to Arjun allow him to see what we cannot... where she touched the wall earlier—" Father Jorrus growled and turned swiftly down the passage to the west, "—and apparently the direction she takes now."

Soon the three men found themselves at the end of the western passage. Jorrus again used his holy symbol to *see* where Lane had touched the wall that blocked their advance. Moments later he had opened another doorway, and he led the way into a basement—a much smaller version of the library's lower level.

Father Jorrus bounded up the basement stairs. Arrin could feel waves of power emanating from the cleric; he thought that Jorrus seemed much younger and more coherent than he had during their previous encounters. He paused while Arames spared a moment for a quick scan of the room, then followed his master up the steps. *Father Jorrus is in his element, chasing an undead creature. He always claimed there was an undead presence here, and even in his failure to detect one, he has been vindicated.*

The two men found themselves on the main floor of a small home. The décor was elegant, yet sparse. There was a small kitchen in one corner and a sitting area made up most of the rest of the room. There was no bed in sight.

"Lane's home?" Arrin asked, and Arames nodded once. Cold drafts of air gusted in from the open front door—Father Jorrus had thrown it wide in his haste to run off in pursuit of the vampire—but nothing seemed out of place.

They moved quickly to the door, and once Arames determined which direction Father Jorrus had taken, he turned to Arrin. "Cletus. We'd better hurry."

⚜

The small door in the town gate hung at an awkward angle, partially torn from its hinges. Cletus lay on the ground beside it. Constable Ulrich knelt over the gatekeeper, fumbling at his neck for a sign of a pulse.

Arames ran over and pushed Constable Ulrich out of the way, quickly confirming that Cletus was still alive. He stood and offered Ulrich a hand up. "What did you see?"

Ulrich rose slowly, looking at Arames as if he had spoken in Old Inarran. He pulled at his moustache. "I... I don't remember. I was talking to Cletus, and then you pushed me away—" He blinked, then saw Cletus laying on the ground. "Hey, what happened?!"

Arames slapped Ulrich hard across the face. Ulrich blinked again and then shook his head. "What in Doppin's name was that for?" He raised an arm; Arrin thought he might take a swing at Arames.

The monk raised both hands in front of him, palms forward. "Ulrich, I need you to focus." Ulrich lowered his fist and waited. "I need you to go to the library and bring Constable Louis and Lord Avedon here... straight away."

Ulrich looked down and saw Cletus again, seemingly for the first time. "Is that Cletus? Is he—?"

Arames grabbed Ulrich's arm and dragged him away from the gate. "Cletus will be fine. Do you remember what I need you to do?"

"Louis and Lord Avedon..."

"Yes. From the library. Thank you."

The constable again looked over at Cletus, hesitating.

"Go!"

Finally, Ulrich ran off in the direction of the library.

"What is this, Sir Arames?" Lord Avedon stared at the monk with a look of contempt tinged with hope.

Arames sat with Cletus, who was now conscious and somewhat cognizant of his surroundings. The monk had been so focused on Cletus's injuries—a stiff neck and a twisted knee—that he had barely noticed the approach of Lord Avedon and the three constables. Arrin stood off to the left, ready with a chair once Cletus needed it.

Arames rose to his feet and went to them. "How does your head feel, Constable Ulrich?"

Ulrich initially pulled back from Arames's outstretched hands, but he relented once he realized that the monk was only checking for injury. "I... It's fuzzy."

"Ulrich, have you been into Talik's ale again?" Lord Avedon barked. He did not appreciate being ignored.

Arames nodded to the constable. "I had hoped the walk to the library and back would have been enough to clear your head." He pointed to the chair by Arrin. "Sit. It will be some time before Cletus will be able to use it."

Arames turned to face Lord Avedon and Louis. "Head Constable—you updated Lord Avedon on what we found outside of town?"

"Yes, and then I brought him and Tanner to the lib—"

"Kragen!"

Lord Avedon's face was red and livid. "Talk to me, not to Louis!"

Arames dipped his head. "I do not wish to repeat what you already know, sir. I meant no disrespect."

The ruler of Avedon Hill opened his mouth and then closed it without speaking. Arames continued. "Lane Niccols is a vampire. I confronted her in the library and she confirmed my suspicions, and admitted to the murder of the book dealer. Before I could capture her, she escaped through a secret tunnel in the basement.

"Father Jorrus was able to follow the vampire through the tunnel. It ended at Lane Niccols's home. Jorrus rushed ahead of us, after the vampire. We followed his trail and arrived here. We found Cletus on the ground and Ulrich incoherent."

Arames stopped. Lord Avedon rolled one hand in a circular motion. "And?"

"Those are the facts. Do you wish me to speculate further?"

"Yes, of course!"

Arames continued. "I believe that Lane Niccols used her powers to disorient Ulrich and Cletus. Possibly, Cletus resisted her charms and was attacked as a result. Father Jorrus must have arrived then, or shortly thereafter; in either case, I believe Lane escaped through the gate."

"And Father Jorrus?"

"I am sure he followed, and is tracking her as we speak. Father Jorrus was an undead hunter long before he became temple cleric. He will most likely continue his chase until either he is dead or she is destroyed."

Lord Avedon mulled over Arames's words. "Sunlight harms vampires, does it not?"

"Lane Niccols is a vampire master—or mistress, if you will. Sunlight may weaken her, but it will not destroy her as it might destroy a lesser vampire. However, the sun is most likely why Cletus and Ulrich are still with us."

Lord Avedon smiled. "Then the mystery is solved."

Louis shook his head. "No, my lord. Lane Niccols could not have killed Gretta Platt."

"But she is a vampire. She could have doubled back, entered the manor, and killed Gretta!"

Arames shook his head. "Louis is correct. Even a vampire could not have covered the distance required, bypassed the town gate twice, entered and exited Avedon Manor without being seen, and murdered Gretta."

"Twice?"

Louis responded. "Cletus's records show her exiting through the town gate two cykes before Gretta was killed, and returning after her death."

Lord Avedon growled, "Maybe Cletus's records are wrong!"

"My records are never wrong, Lord." Arames turned to see Cletus, standing. "Vampire or not, she used this gate that night and the log is correct." Cletus closed his eyes and groaned a bit, but remained on his feet.

"Maybe she lied. Someone else killed the book dealer and she never really left town. She found another way into town and killed Gretta, and then returned to enter through the gate, covering her tracks." Lord Avedon snapped. Arames knew he was growing desperate to exonerate his son.

"No... I am afraid the proof is in the basement of the library, and on this." Arames handed over the inventory list he had taken from Pitr's corpse. "Do you see the top item on the page?"

"Arlen Gricca – AG – (O). So?"

"It is Arlen Gricca's autobiography. And the 'O' indicates that it was the original, written by Arlen's own hand."

Lord Avedon handed the paper back to Arames. His anger had seeped from him, leaving only the defeated posture Arames had become accustomed to seeing. Arames pointed to his left, away from the others. "If you please, Lord Avedon."

The two men moved off until Arames was certain they would not be overheard. "As you have already guessed, we may not know who killed Gretta Platt, but we know who attacked Edvard."

The fire returned to Lord Avedon's eyes for a moment. "And you allowed her to escape!"

"Allowed is not the word I would choose. We had to assume that by the time we returned to town, Lane would have learned of our discovery of the book dealer's corpse. I took a chance confronting her alone, because I could not allow Father Jorrus to join me. If he had been there, he would have learned of Edvard's... condition. You know how he would have reacted. I also wanted a chance to capture her without destroying her—that would have been impossible with Father Jorrus at my side."

"Then why get him at all?"

"Excluding Father Jorrus from a hunt for a vampire would have aroused too much suspicion."

"How could she have fooled Jorrus all this time?"

"I believe something hid her undead nature from Father Jorrus's senses. At least a portion of this ability passed on to your son—ever since we arrived, Jorrus has insisted that he could sense a vampire in Avedon Hill, but he could not pinpoint its location. If Edvard did not possess at least some of Lane's masking ability, Father Jorrus would already have beaten down the manor door by now."

Lord Avedon's ire drained from him as Arames spoke, leaving only the despondent father.. "I do have some good news."

"Yes?"

"Louis confirmed that Gretta's wounds were much cleaner than the wound on the book dealer's neck, which was definitely from a vampire. They did not match."

"So Edvard did not kill Gretta."

"It does not prove it. But in my opinion, if Gretta had been Edvard's first kill, you would have found a much different corpse that night."

Lord Avedon placed a hand on Arames's shoulder. "Thank you, Arames. Thank you."

Arames remembered Lane's last words to him. He squeezed Lord Avedon's arm once in a gesture of solace. "You still cannot give Edvard the King's Crown potion. Not until we are sure. Even if Edvard never touched Gretta, it does not mean he did not attack someone else."

Tears filled Lord Avedon's eyes. It had only taken a moment for Arames to strip away the glimmer of hope he had just provided. "When Marrissa finishes the potion, keep it safe. We are close now. I will have answers for you soon, Lord Avedon. I promise."

If knowledge causes problems for you,
do not turn to applied ignorance.

—Tales of the Children

THE LATE AFTERNOON SUN did little to warm Avedon Hill, but two bowls of stew at the inn had done the trick for Arames Kragen.

Cletus had recovered quickly. Once up, he was grumpier than ever. He refused to leave his post, even though he could not remember what had happened at the gate. Louis insisted that Cletus sleep in his own bed that night instead of in the guardhouse, and warned that he would check in on the gatekeeper throughout the evening. Cletus argued at first, but had finally agreed.

Arames left both men with instructions to come and find him at the inn if Father Jorrus returned to town.

Arrin had barely spoken a word since they had left the town gate. Once Talik left them alone at their table, Arames shared more of what had happened at the library, but afterward they continued eating in silence.

Arrin finally slammed his spoon down on the table. "What are we doing? Dead ends all around!"

Arames glanced over at the inn's other patron, Alex Dewirin. The general store owner looked over and met Arames's eyes for a moment, but immediately turned away, focusing on his meal. Arames finished his mouthful and swallowed, then spoke in a low voice. "You are not thinking clearly, Arrin. We know so much more now than we did this morning." He pointed his own spoon at Arrin. "We solved one murder, and in so doing we proved that Lane Niccols could not have killed Gretta."

Arrin frowned. "And how is this not a dead end?"

"Well, since we know Lane did not kill Gretta, and we are for the time being ruling out Edvard as the murderer… and since we believe that there are no other vampires in Avedon Hill, we can now concentrate on other theories."

Arrin pointed at his neck. A high collar hid his bandages. "Did you forget about this?"

"Of course not, Arrin. Something or someone attacked you last night. But it was not Lane Niccols, and I do not believe it could have been Edvard. So again, this leads us back to other hypotheses."

Arrin slapped himself on the forehead. "Not your *greed* theory again."

Arames smiled. "Not necessarily—but greed is a great motivator. We know there has been some sort of money distribution system in place for hundreds of years, even though we have not learned how this money was made. One thing I do know—when money is dispersed to individuals in a group, there will always be those who feel they are not receiving their fair share. We also know that Gretta was scheduled to meet with someone the night she was killed, someone that she did not want to meet with ... and it possibly had to do with this very topic."

"The missing book—"

Arames nodded. "Yes. If Gretta's journal still exists, then it may provide us even more answers."

"What about the tunnels? You still believe the murderer used the tunnels to get into the courtyard?"

Arames nodded. "If not to get into the courtyard, then definitely to escape."

"Then I'll search the tunnels while you explore your 'greed' theory."

"Tomorrow, Arrin—and we will explore the tunnels together. We should not chance wandering those tunnels at night, especially alone."

Arrin's frustration was clear, and Arames understood how difficult waiting was for the young prince. The Perti family were men of action, and patience was a hard lesson to teach. "Go upstairs and get some rest. I suspect that sleep will not be our companion tonight. And whether you feel it or not, you still need time to recover from last night."

Arrin almost said something, but his mouth closed as soon as it had opened. After a moment of thought, he stood up. "All right. I'll be in our room."

<hr />

Arames flexed his arm, glad to find that his own wound from the night before had nearly healed. Arames's monastic training and his link to the river of magic allowed his body to recover from illness and injury faster than most. He finished a piece of honey bread and reached for another. His recent dependence on food still bothered him greatly. The same connection to the River that healed his body and had once allowed him to go for a week without sustenance, now forced him to consume as much as a man twice his size—as the prophecy stated, *As with everything in Caern, what the Land gives, the Land also takes away.* By the time he had finished his meal, Alex Dewirin had left the inn. Arames called Talik over to his booth.

"Please, Talik. Sit with me for a moment."

Talik was surprised at the request, but lowered himself into the booth across from Arames. "Thank you for moving us to another room."

Talik smiled without a glint of happiness. "Stone floor, no windows—not exactly the hospitality I usually provide."

But it is safer for us, thought Arames.

"Was your meal satisfactory, Sir Arames?"

Arames flashed a smile. "Oh yes, it hit the spot. In fact, I think I might have another of your famous ales."

Talik began to rise from the booth, but Arames stopped him. "Not right now, Talik. I want to talk with you about something else."

Talik frowned. "What is it, Sir Arames?"

"The other day, you mentioned bringing a carnival to town. How long have you been promoting this idea?"

Talik's face brightened immediately. "Oh, for several months now, Sir Arames. You should see the animals they work with—bears, wolves, even a tiger. And the acrobats! My, oh my."

Arames raised a hand to dam the river of Talik's enthusiasm. "That sounds exciting. How did Gretta take to your idea?"

The innkeeper's face lost its energy. "She… she didn't like it."

"Bringing visitors to town for purposes other than the Pass would not fit with Avedon Hill's *way of life*, would it?"

Talik coughed once. "I – I'm not sure what you mean, Sir Arames."

"Oh, I believe you do. More visitors would mean more potential residents. More residents would jeopardize everything the Avedons and Platts have created here."

Talik paled, but Arames continued. "Your family has lived in Avedon Hill since its founding, have they not?"

"Yes. The Bores are the third oldest family, after the Avedons and the Platts."

"Then you should have enough gold for ten lifetimes, if I am not mistaken."

Talik, still white, nevertheless had a little fire in his voice. "Gold?" He seemed to weigh his words very carefully. "Do you think I have seen— We are only allowed to travel once a year outside of Avedon Hill to *enjoy* what little gold we—" Talik stopped and sighed, blowing air out of his mouth. "Gretta refused to see that we could bring people to town and earn extra gold without exposing our *economic structure.*"

A distribution system, but little in the way of actual distributing, it seems. "When was your last actual meeting with Gretta?"

The uneasy look reappeared in Talik's eyes. "Two weeks before her death—she agreed to see me at the manor. It was my first time there in nearly a year."

"You spoke to her about the carnival?"

"Yes, but she had already learned of it from others. She barely listened to a word I said."

"Was that the day you were forcibly removed from the manor?"

Arames was surprised to see Talik turn an even paler shade of pale. "I— No. That was later. She wouldn't even let me tell her about the dancers and the two bards—storytellers unlike any we've ever seen here. She asked me to try and think of what is best for the town, not just for me. Can you believe that? I'm always thinking about what's best for the town, not like—" He stopped himself and stared down at Arames's empty plate.

"You went back though, the next week. Why?"

"I couldn't give up that easily, Sir Arames. You just don't know. They have this woman who walks across a rope extended across two poles. She's so high in the air, higher than the manor is tall, and she even dances up there on the rope, without a net." He paused. "But Miss Platt didn't even listen. She had instructed that fop of a butler to turn me away." Talik twisted his cloth towel in his hands. "Even so, I held no ill will toward Miss Gretta. You've got to believe me."

Arames raised his hand to silence the innkeeper. "So you still wish to see this carnival come to Avedon Hill?"

Talik nodded. "I'll wait until the next Housemistress arrives, and then I'll reopen discussions. Rondellus Marx and his Carnival of Stars would be just what the town needs, especially now. Rondellus is a powerful... a charismatic man, let's just say. And I promised him personally that I could make this happen."

"But if Lord Avedon refuses—"

"They cannot refuse—" The wild look had returned to Talik's eyes. "Excuse me, Sir Arames; I am taking up too much of your time."

"One last thing—please."

Arames's request caught Talik in the act of standing. His knees locked against the edge of the table. "I have it on good authority that even after you were escorted from the manor, you showed up a few days later and waited outside for cykes, just on the off-chance that you would run into Gretta."

"I did, around midday. I thought I might catch her on her way to the stables. But she never came out, and she was killed later that night." Talik finally slid his heavy legs to the side, extricating himself from the booth. "You said you needed an ale." Muttering under his breath about all the cleaning that needed to be done, Talik nearly ran from the table back to the kitchen.

The underground cave was not unlike the great cavern that housed the Avedon

Family Cemetery. Arrin couldn't remember how he got there, and as he tried to piece together his winding path, he realized he must be dream-walking again.

The pale green light of glow-rocks filled the great chamber. It pulsed, first bright, then dim, as if the rocks had a life of their own. 'How could we have never heard of this mineral? Just because it loses its glow when brought to the surface?' The pulses became stronger, taking on a definite rhythmic pattern.

Arrin stood in the center of the cavern. There were several openings in the walls and yellow eyes peered at him from three of the passages; life hiding in the darkness.

'Burn me; I have to learn how to control things while dream-walking.'

He was not sure if his thought had caused it, but Arrin found himself dressed for battle. Wildfire was in his right hand; his favorite shield was in his left. He looked at the shield and the falcon of his family's crest stared back at him. Arrin had complained vehemently to Arames when the monk told him he could not bring the shield. He struck it with the pommel of his sword. 'Now, this is more like it.'

Talik Bore stood almost twenty paces from him. The innkeeper wore the livery of a lord, with a white-washed leather shirt and a vest of ring mail. Talik held his hands out before him, palms extended upward, as if pleading with Arrin to stay back. Talik's mouth was moving, but no sound reached Arrin's ears. Instead, the beating pulse of the glow-rocks filled Arrin's ears with a 'whooshing' sound, in and out, in and out, drowning out everything else. The light in the chamber and the pulsing in his ears matched the beating of his own heart.

The eyes moved forward into the cavern. Wolves, at least a dozen, stared at him from behind Talik. Some growled, while others simply watched.

Arrin stood without moving, waiting to see which of them the wolves were going to attack. Talik seemed only interested in him. 'This is only a dream. Let's see what I can do.' Arrin scraped the point of his sword along the ground before him, leaving a line in the dust and dirt. He raised the sword, pointing it at several of the more aggressive wolves. 'Come for me.'

Talik's pleading immediately morphed into anger. He held his hands above his head, fists shaking, yelling at Arrin. Still only hearing the song of his own heartbeat, Arrin took his eyes off the wolves and watched the innkeeper mouth the word 'ruin.'

Two wolves charged from behind Talik and to his left. As they passed the innkeeper, three more leaped forward from Talik's right, all bounding for Arrin. Arrin had just enough time to dodge the first charging beast; he just had to choose a direction.

He jumped to his left.

<hr />

"So, what did you say to Talik?" Cousin Red smirked as he delivered a mug of ale. "He is even more upset than usual."

Arames picked up the mug and smelled its contents. "I do not have any idea."

Red made a guttural noise. "Of course. Talik told me to leave for the night, as long as you don't need anything else. He never closes the inn this early."

"Has Talik been acting strangely? I mean, before Gretta's death?"

Red shrugged. "Talik always acts strangely." Arames returned Red's smirk, the family resemblance shining through. "Okay, yes, for the last month or so it has been... worse I guess. Leilah told me that winter always makes him short-tempered."

Arames stood up, going over Constable Louis's notes in his head. "I believe I will pass on the ale. Tell me about the night Gretta was killed. You were here, along with Talik and Leilah, correct?" Red nodded. "How late did the inn close for dinner that night?"

"We had three guests that night, traders of some sort. I was here very late, and Leilah stayed the night in her room here. "

"Was Talik here the entire time?"

"He was in his basement office for two or three cykes, but he never left the inn."

"Basement office?"

"Under the kitchen. We keep supplies there, and it's where he works on his paperwork for Lord Avedon. He even sleeps down there sometimes." Red smiled. "It's also where he does his brewing."

"Where does he normally sleep?"

"Upstairs. He has a bedroom down the hall from where you are now. He just uses his cot in the basement office if there are things going on, since it is easier for us to wake him without disturbing the guests by knocking on the door at the top of the basement stairs."

Arames squeezed Red's shoulder. "Very good. Be careful walking home tonight. We will talk again tomorrow, cousin."

RONDELLUS MARX AND HIS CARNIVAL OF STARS

Iberian, do moon-beasts belong to Ursala?
'They may be called Ursala's Children,
but I believe they belong to Treygh.'

—In Iberian's Own Words

Arames entered his room to find Arrin thrashing in his bed. He suspected the young prince was dream-walking, and by all indications it did not appear to be a pleasurable experience. Arrin's arms were extended before him toward the ceiling and his body flailed from side to side; at the same time, his legs kicked at the blankets. Pure fury was etched on the prince's taut face.

Arames lifted the pitcher of water and moved to Arrin's bedside. It was not wise to physically wake a dream-walker from a *walk*, but he was afraid he was going to have to chance it. Arrin growled in pain and a streak of blood appeared on the left arm of his nightshirt, cementing Arames's decision.

Arames leaned in and splashed the water at Arrin's face—but at the same time, Arrin kicked his legs so hard that he threw himself off the opposite side of the bed. The water drenched the pillow, missing the prince entirely.

Arrin woke, shaking the dreams from his head. He stared up at Arames for a moment, confused at his presence. Then he croaked out, "Talik—I think he has something to do with the wolves."

Arames raised an eyebrow as he leaned down to help Arrin up to his bed. He pulled up the sleeve of Arrin's shirt and found a finger-length shallow gash across his forearm.

Arrin pulled his arm away from Arames, staring at the cut. "By Az! Arames, what is this? I thought it was only a dream!"

⚶☙☙⚶

While Arames bandaged the cut, Arrin shared his dream. Arames listened, then apologized for sending him away from the common room and described his conversations with Talik and Red.

"You believe we'll find another tunnel in the basement?"

"What do you think?" Arames asked in response.

Arrin thought again about his dream. "Yes, I'm sure we will."

"Well, you said you wanted to explore the tunnels tonight, didn't you?"

Arrin laughed, flexing his bandaged arm. "You're serious?"

Arames ignored the question. "We will wait a cyke or so. Talik sent Red home, but I believe our innkeeper is still cleaning up the kitchen."

***

A cyke later, both men stood at the kitchen door. Arames had listened at Leilah's door and was relatively sure she was asleep in her room. Talik's bedroom was quiet, but Arames had no way to know if the innkeeper was inside.

After a quick listen at the door, Arames and Arrin entered the kitchen and crept through it to the basement stairs.

Beyond the shelves filled with food and kitchen supplies, and beyond the casks of Talik's prized ale, Arames found what he was looking for. The wall, the only one not containing shelves or casks, had some sort of tarp nailed to it. Several papers had been attached to the tarp, mostly advertisements for the carnival Talik was so fond of mentioning.

"Rondellus Marx... ever hear of him?"

Arames shook his head. "No. From what Talik has described, this carnival of stars is made up of acrobats from eastern Inarra." Arames studied the floor; a large box sat a pace from the wall, obviously moved from its normal resting place. He leaned in and found that the lower left corner of the tarp behind the box was not attached to the wall. Arames extended his hand and felt the flow of air.

"I believe Talik is not in his room after all." Arames slid his hand up the edge of the tarp until he reached a second nail. It slid out easily and he and Arrin were able to slip underneath the tarp into a tunnel about twenty hands wide. A door, obviously meant to seal the opening covered by the tarp, stood open. "Talik must have left in a hurry." He waved for Arrin to follow.

Arrin was prepared for tunnel exploration. He had a torch lit in moments and his sword belt was around his waist instead of strapped to his back. Arames easily tracked Talik's progress through the underground passages.

After half a cyke, Arames knew they were no longer beneath Avedon Hill. *If I am right, we are east of town.* When the two men reached a fork in the tunnel, Arames stopped and lowered the torch to the ground. Both paths showed signs of recent use. "I cannot tell which direction Talik went."

"I believe I can."

Arames looked up; Arrin pointed to two deep scratches on the wall of right tunnel just past the fork. "Does that look like an arrow to you?"

Arames held up the torch, studying the wall. "This was not made today, but it is recent. Maybe Talik doesn't know the tunnels that well and needed a little help." They started down the marked trail at a quickened pace.

The passage turned upward, ascending at a slight incline, and eventually glow-rocks became more prevalent along the walls, providing their soft light. The small mine shafts opened periodically into small and then larger caverns. At the opening of the first large cavern, Arames asked Arrin to extinguish his torch.

"Look familiar?"

Arrin nodded. "We're in the caves east of Avedon Hill."

"Our innkeeper is becoming more interesting by the moment."

Arames picked up Talik's trail in one of the passages on the opposite side of the cavern. The cave floor was stone, worn smooth by a long forgotten and ancient stream. Animal signs were clearly visible in the dirt covering the stone floor, including wolf tracks, but they had yet to encounter any life.

The monk stopped some twenty paces from the end of the passage and held his index finger to his lips while using his other hand to signal Arrin to a halt. Torchlight emanated from the cavern before them.

Their tunnel opened into a large cavern, but not at ground level. The monk crawled forward on all fours and found himself peering over a ledge some three stories above the cavern floor. At some point in the past, stairs had been built into the cavern wall, allowing someone to safely reach its floor.

"Your promises mean nothing, Bore."

"But there are *reasons* why your tests have failed. Let me explain!"

"I'm done with your explanations, human. You promised us access to Avedon Hill, and you have failed us. You promised us the Hunter, and you have failed us. You promised us a power beyond our understanding, and again you have failed us."

Arames peered over the edge of the landing and saw exactly what he had feared most. Talik was being held immobile by two creatures that were at most only partly human. The creatures' backs bowed at an extreme angle. From above, Arames thought their skulls were more canine than anything else. The hair that covered most of their bodies did not supplant the need for clothing, but the creatures didn't seem to care. The only completely human features about them were their hands, forelimbs that held Talik with his feet dangling above the ground. The creatures faced away from Arames, focused on the words of possibly the largest man Arames had ever seen.

This had to be Rondellus Marx. He stood at least seven feet tall and was dressed in a white shirt that billowed to his knees—and nothing else—but seemed unaffected by the cold. He held a knife in his right hand that would have been a machete for most people. He had a short beard and long flowing black hair, and even from a distance Arames could see that his eyes glowed yellow.

The giant held an open bag in his other hand. From his vantage point Arames could not tell what it held. *Coins, perhaps?*

Talik, always the salesman, tried to talk his way out of the situation. "Rondellus, I beg you. You know Lord Avedon has closed the town completely. Once he re-opens the town, I will be able to get you in. And once you are in, we will have access to Marrissa—"

Rondellus pressed the knife to Talik's neck, silencing him. "I made a mistake, Talik. This is completely my fault."

⚜

Arrin had crawled to Arames's left. He witnessed the same conversation, but through a very different lens. *This is the cavern from my dream. But what are those creatures? They are not the moon-beast we faced two days ago, and they are certainly not wolves.*

But once Arrin saw Rondellus Marx, he could not take his eyes off the man holding the knife at Talik's throat. *His eyes. He must be the moon-beast. What is Talik doing here?*

Rondellus continued. "I believed your promises. I had heard the rumors from one of my former masters in Inarra. I have seen the ruins of the 'Old Walls' at Taxx. And you told me exactly what I wanted to hear. I should have seen that you are a child playing at a man's game."

"But I know how to make it work now, Rondellus. Please—"

"I'm sure you do."

Arrin gripped Wildfire tightly. *We have to do something. Talik doesn't deserve this, no matter what he's done.*

⚜

Arames looked over at Arrin; the prince's eyes were fixed on Rondellus Marx. Gazing past Arrin, Arames surveyed the cavern and noted that several other tunnels opened into it. He couldn't see anyone else within his field of vision, but nearly a third of the cavern below them was hidden from view.

The monk weighed their options. *We could split up. I could stay here and have Arrin back out and make his way to another opening. Or we could pull back a little and call out to Rondellus—try to negotiate Talik's release.*

There would be no time for negotiation.

Rondellus threw down his open bag and several rocks—spent glow-rocks, by the looks of them—spilled out onto the cave floor. With his hand now free,

Rondellus patted Talik on the cheek. "Don't blame yourself, Talik. Like I said, this was my fault, not yours." The giant's face remained calm as he pulled the knife across Talik's throat.

The two creatures holding Talik burst out with hyena-like laughter, heads thrown back in delight. They dropped Talik's dying body to the ground, but not before a stream of his blood splattered across Rondellus's face and shirt. Rondellus glared at the creatures as he wiped at his face. "Now look at this mess."

Before Arames could contemplate their next move, Arrin made it for them. The prince moved back and up into a crouch, with obvious plans to jump down to the cavern below.

Arames reached out with a hand, hoping to stop Arrin. But before Arames could take any real action, he sensed something was amiss. As Arrin rose into his crouch, his shoulder brushed against an invisibly thin wire strung across the opening of the cavern. Arames heard the slight sound of the wire pulling taut. Instinctively, as the wire released the latch on a spring loaded trap, Arames slammed into Arrin's legs with his left shoulder, knocking the younger man from his feet.

⁂

A tree limb whirled past, swinging just above Arrin's body as he fell. It was longer than the width of the cave opening, and Arrin could see the knives attached to it at various points. It crashed into the cave wall with a loud crack and a rain of splinters. Some of the blades were dislodged by the impact and sailed through the air, clattering to the ground at the entrance to the passage.

Crawling onto the ledge had saved their lives.

Arrin's awkward landing on the stone carved steps forced the breath from his lungs. He lay on his back, feet above his head. The only saving grace was that Rondellus and the two beasts could not see him. Arrin looked up. The broken tree branch bounced back and forth against the cavern opening.

Oh, I see.

What he could not see, but did hear, was Arames's leap to the cavern floor.

⁂

Arames knew that his opportunity for surprise was fading fast. He leapt off the ledge overlooking the cavern, pulling a sai from his sleeve and a hidden dagger from his belt as he fell through the air. He knew he could not reach Rondellus, so he concentrated on the two beasts closer to the landing.

⁂

The two creatures that had been holding Talik stopped howling when they heard the twang of wire above their heads. They turned to see what had been impaled by their invention and instead were met with a growing darkness that blocked out the light of the glow-rocks lining the ceiling of the cave.

⚜

Rondellus Marx was cleaning his face with his blood-stained shirt when he heard the *whoosh* and *crash* of one of his leashlings' knife-traps. For a moment he assumed that the trap had fired on its own, as had occurred twice during the previous week. Instead, Rondellus was surprised to see the billowing robes of a monk falling into his *trey-hyenas*. He dropped instinctively into a more defensive stance. Moments later he faced the monk he had fought in the cave two days before—the man Talik had later identified as Arames Kragen. *Talik's failure is complete.*

Rondellus silently called out to his pack. *Come to me.* Only silence answered him.

Rondellus leaned to his right, peering around Arames without moving his feet. Both of his trey-hyenas were dead: one was nearly decapitated by the sai that the monk was now wiping on his robe; the monk's dagger still protruded from the other's skull.

"Where is your friend—the warrior?" Rondellus sniffed the air. He sensed the youngling's presence still in the cavern. "It's too bad I cannot kill Talik again. He certainly deserves it."

Arames held his sai ready but did not attack. He had an inquisitive look on his face. "Trey-hyenas—I realized you could create other moon-beasts by feeding on humans. I had no idea it worked both ways. Fascinating..." A creature that had been deformed or changed from its intended state was sometimes given the prefix trey—it was a reference to Treygh, the Child of Pain. The monk poked at the spilled bag with one foot. "And this is becoming more interesting by the moment."

"Useless promises, monk. That's all Talik was."

With his wolf-sight, Rondellus made out the raised corners of the monk's mouth. He was smiling. "Maybe—but then again, maybe not."

Anger welled up in Rondellus. The innkeeper—and now the monk—had ruined his plans. He had made Talik pay, and he would now make the monk and his warrior friend pay. And then he would find the Hunter, and make him pay most of all.

⚜

Arrin rolled to his right until his back was against the cavern wall. He heard Arames's collision onto the creatures that had held Talik. He rose to his knees and crawled along the stairs, still attempting to keep his presence somewhat of a surprise. Then he heard Rondellus: "Where is your friend—the warrior?"

Arrin stopped at a point where he could safely jump from the stairs to the cavern floor and dropped into a crouch. He realized now that Arames had again saved his life, and he decided he not to enter the fray until he was called—or until he was truly needed.

⚜

Arames mirrored Rondellus as the giant moved slowly to his left. *He is placing me between himself and the stairs behind me. Rondellus may not have seen Arrin, but he knows he is there.* Arames again weighed his options. *I should attack him while he is in human form.* Rondellus could surely shape-shift into a moon-beast at will, but Arames had no idea how long the transformation would take. But more importantly, Rondellus had plans, and Arames wanted to understand exactly what they were.

"Where is the rest of your Carnival of Stars, Rondellus? Are they shifters like you?"

Rondellus flexed his free hand as if he wanted another weapon. "No need to fear my *employees*, human. They understand what I am, and accept me as their leader. Besides, my kind are not so rare in Inarra. And they know well enough to stay out of my business."

The giant sniffed the air. "I can smell the years weighing on you, monk. The Land does not sustain you as it once did. I could help you with that. You could share your wisdom with my pack and strengthen yourself in the process. You wouldn't have to watch your body weaken as the day of your death approaches."

Arames attempted to reach out to touch Rondellus's mind. Invading another's mind was an attack on that person, and it was a decision that Arames did not make lightly.

The resistance that Arames expected was absent; on the contrary, the beast's consciousness received him openly, like tobac being inhaled by a pipist. Arames found himself pulled into Rondellus's mind, and they were not alone.

Arames had heard tell that the followers of Ursala, Child of Nature, had the ability to communicate with animals. It was said that Ursala felt the pain of the animal world. There were even those who claimed that the most powerful of her druids could take the form of animals, as well. While Arames did not believe the moon-beast was a byproduct of devotion to Ursala, it was clear that the communal nature of Rondellus's power was stronger and more vast than anything Arames had experienced before.

Arames found it difficult to keep his feet under him. Images from the minds of animals rushed through his mind. The mental walls Arames had expected to find were replaced by tendrils, webs that extended from Rondellus into the cavern and out into the world. The thoughts bombarding Arames were more images than sounds, more emotions than language. Arames *felt* colors... the grays and browns of the forests, the blacks and silvers of the night sky, the blues and greens of the stream—and the reds and yellows of fire—and blood. The desire for blood struck Arames like a hammer. *Blood lust.*

Come to me!

Time was short. Arames pulled away from Rondellus, but it took much more effort than he expected. Arames felt himself lose his balance, his mental retreat becoming much more of a physical one. He managed to remain upright. "There is too much death down your path, Rondellus. I am more than content with my life. I'll leave the envy of the living to you and your kind."

With that, Arames charged the mountain of a man.

Arrin watched Arames from his hidden ledge. The monk charged at Rondellus full bore, attempting to catch him off-guard. *It's not like Arames to attack...* But Arrin soon understood why he had. *Oh no, not like this.*

Arrin jumped to the cavern floor, some thirty paces from where Rondellus and Arames were locked in battle. From this here, Arrin could finally see the entire cavern. It was roughly circular, with six different entry points: the one from which they had come, another above ground level to his right, and four more scattered around the cave at ground level. At least one set of eyes peered from each of the ground-level openings, all concentrating on the fight between Rondellus and Arames. Arrin realized he had to change that.

"Wolves—yaah!" Arrin scraped his sword along the floor, casting sparks into the air. "You want a fight!? Come for me!" Arrin readied himself for the charge. *I wish I had my shield.*

An Aarronic Advisor could use any weapon that felt natural to him. There were no restrictions set by the Order. Drona Twoblade, the Aarronic Advisor to King Desthra while Arames had served at Castle Pen, had been deadly with a longsword. Gareth Beckwin had fought only with daggers. Many Aarronic Advisors eschewed the use of weapons altogether, using only their hands and their connection to the power of the Land to survive in battle.

The length of Arames's sais were catered to the sheaths he had strapped to each arm within the sleeves of his robes. A typical sai was half a hand longer than the forearm of the wielder, but Arames required his blades to be an inch shorter than his forearms. It allowed him to carry the weapons without raising suspicion.

The sai he wielded now may have been shorter and with a thinner fork than most, but the monk was still able to use the outer tines of his pommel to catch the blade of the giant's knife. It was obvious that Rondellus had never fought against someone using a sai, and Arames tried to use this to his advantage. Twice Arames nearly disarmed Rondellus, twisting his sai while the larger man's knife was trapped between blade and pommel.

But the third time never came. While his initial charge had placed Rondellus on his heels, Arames soon found himself falling back in a balanced attempt to avoid the man's blade and bulk. He sensed Arrin had joined them on the cavern floor. Part of him wanted to call out to the prince, to yell for him to escape while he could; at the same time, he realized there was no escape from the room.

Arames had felt the wolves coming before he had pulled away from Rondellus's *pack-mind*. While it confirmed Arrin's dream-walking ability even further, he wished it weren't so.

Arames used his robes as a shield, attempting to trap Rondellus's blade within the thick folds. The robe tore; the knife barely missed Arames's still-bandaged wound from Edvard Avedon. But the giant was too strong for the twists of fabric to be able to pull his knife from his grasp.

Rondellus snarled and lunged with his knife arm, but it was only a feint—in less than a beat he flowed into a punch with his left fist that caught Arames across the top of the head. Arames staggered back, flipping his sai in his hand; he feigned disorientation and turned to the side, giving Rondellus an opening he should not have been able to resist. But the lunge that Arames expected did not come. Rondellus instead took a step back and hurled his blade at Arames's head.

※◎※

Two wolves, one large and light gray and the other a smaller gray with mottled patches on its face, charged from the cave opening closest to Arrin. Recalling his dream-walk, Arrin believed that two more would soon join them from the passage further away and to his right. He realized what he had to do.

Arrin leaned to his right and then leaped directly to his left. The first wolf directed his charge in the wrong direction and the mottled wolf slid into the back legs of the lead gray. The two wolves flailed by Arrin harmlessly. Even while diving in the opposite direction, Arrin found the sight humorous—the back legs of the lead wolf up off the ground, the dark face of the second wolf wedged underneath.

The leap he had re-enacted from his dream had given him the opportunity to get his back against the cave wall. Now he would at least be able to face the animals that would rip him apart.

※◎※

Arames's fight training and his connection to the Land allowed him to sense things occurring outside of his direct line of vision, making combat second nature to him. He had been surprised by Rondellus's swing, but his prescience had allowed him to rotate his head along with the giant's fist, changing what should have been a solid punch into more of a glancing blow. His stagger away from Rondellus should have drawn the man in for a planned counter with Arames's sai. Instead, Arames sensed the long blade—one that was not designed to be a thrown weapon—hurtling at his right ear.

Arames reacted instinctively, throwing up his right arm to protect his head, at the same time attempting to deflect the blade with the sai in his right hand. But Arames had flipped his sai in anticipation of a lunge. Arames managed to divert the blade's path away from his ear, only to be struck in the right shoulder instead. The layers of his robes cushioned the blow, but the knife still drew blood and dropped Arames to one knee.

Arames turned toward Rondellus, fully expecting to be struck in the face by the giant's foot. Instead, the monk found Rondellus retreating to the opposite end of the cavern, smiling. His wolves filed in, more than willing to do his work for him.

***

Three more wolves had entered the cave, all moving in on Arrin. The first two had regained their balance and had paused, sizing up their worthy prey.

In order to reach Arrin, Arames had to get past the two grays that had led the wolf charge. The grays were focused on finding an opening to attack the prince, and did not hear Arames coming.

Arames used his robe to temporarily blind the large gray, while stabbing the lighter gray from above; the thin-bladed sai found a path through the wolf's ribcage and met the animal's heart.

***

Arrin's sword was already bloodied by the time Arames reached his side. A female from the second wave of wolves had already fallen to his blade; he frantically waved his sword before him to keep the other two wolves at bay. He could feel Arames's left heel resting against the edge of his right boot. Arrin's left boot was wedged against the cave wall. With Arames at his side and the cavern wall at his back, Arrin felt empowered for a moment. He flicked his sword at the smaller of the two wolves facing him—the animal had come too close, and now it backed away with a gash across its nose.

Two against four. I like these—oh no.

***

Even as Arames permanently blinded the large gray wolf with two strikes of his sai, he saw what Arrin had just seen: five more wolves had emerged from the tunnels. Arames, using his fading connection to Rondellus's communal mindlink, sensed several more on the way.

Moments later, to make matters worse, Rondellus *howled*. In the short time it had taken Arames to work his way to Arrin's side, Rondellus had made the change from man to beast. A small part of Arames was upset that he had not been able to witness the change firsthand. But the disappointment passed quickly, because the wolves before them responded immediately. Their growling ceased and the two wolves closest to Arrin moved away—the wolves were giving their brothers time to join them for an even more coordinated attack.

"Arrin." Arames spoke in an even tone, "we must rush Rondellus. Wait for my signal."

The five wolves that had just entered the cave moved forward and joined the other two, creating a pack of seven. Four stood before three, creating two lines of impending death.

Arames knew that none of his abilities could prevent the wolves and Rondellus from mauling them. All he could do was to try to open a path for Arrin ... and hope.

Praise Az... The first line of wolves inched forward, growling and barking anew. Two of the four wolves shook their heads as they moved, as if they were shaking water from their ears after a swim. *Rondellus is telling them to attack, to ignore the long-toothed Fangs we hold in our hands.*

Arames concentrated on his connection to the river of magic, feeling its mists wash over him. The wolves fell back on their haunches, ready to lunge. Arames extended his left arm before him as if hurling a knife, just as he had earlier that day with Lane Niccols. But instead of the small push he had used to move the lever in the library basement, the monk released his power as a tight ball of compressed air. As the invisible orb passed over the first line of wolves the monk snapped his fingers. The ball of air expanded outward as concussive blast, beating at the wolves around it.

Arames fell to both knees, strength spent.

⁂

The four wolves directly in front of Arrin were tossed aside as if they had been lifted by the tails and flipped end over end. One was battered against the nearby wall of the cave. Two others were catapulted off to Arrin's right, squealing as they crashed against each other and the hard stone floor of the cavern. Arrin had to dodge the fourth wolf as the blast hurled it past him.

The three wolves in the back row were only slightly more fortunate than their brothers. The ball of air that discharged directly in front of them threw two of them back, head over tail. The neck of the closer of the two was snapped by the blast. The third, black and gray with a squarer muzzle than his brothers, had been furthest from the concussion; the gust of air raised him off the ground, but he rotated his body in mid-air and landed deftly on his four paws.

Arrin was buffeted by the blast, but kept his feet. Gritting his teeth, he charged through the opening that Arames had created and made his way across the cavern floor. As he rushed forward, he nearly decapitated the disoriented black wolf that had landed upright.

Assuming Arames would follow behind him, Arrin threw himself at the *moonbeast* with reckless abandon, hoping to distract the beast while Arames moved in to score a lethal blow. As Arrin landed against the wall of the cavern, knocked aside by a toss of the great beast's head and neck, he realized that he was alone.

Without time to look over to his mentor, Arrin bounced to his feet. Rondellus did not attack Arrin, instead allowing the prince to dictate the action. Arrin knew he should be afraid of the beast—it was nearly three times as large as any wolf in the cave—but the rush of the battle overwhelmed any fear inside him.

As Arames had described to him two days before, Rondellus's intelligence was evident in the moon-beast's facial expressions and actions. Arrin danced with the great monster, using Wildfire to keep Rondellus at a distance. The beast seemed content to wait for Arrin to tire, and soon Arrin understood why. Even on all fours, the moon-beast's eyes were level with Arrin's chest; just above the animal's head, Arrin saw several more wolves enter the cave.

He was out of time.

Ursala's Lament

"Ursala, you will never learn."
"Doppin, one day I will tear your throat out."
"I love you too, sister."

—The Return of the Children

Arrin attempted to ignore the growls, but soon he felt a tentative nip at his heels. At least one of the wolves had circled behind him. Arrin figured the next snap of jaws would be an attempt to take him down to the ground. Now surrounded, Arrin felt panic rise in his throat.

In the time it would take a falling leaf to make a single revolution on its travels from branch to earth, Rondellus's eyes shot to his left, toward where Arrin had left Arames. A flash of light Arrin refused to acknowledge had all too briefly distracted the moon-beast.

A thought fired through Arrin's mind—an image from his first *dream-walk*. It had belonged to another actor, but... *I have to chance it.*

Arrin reversed his sword, stabbing blindly behind him. The point of his blade entered flesh and brought forth a howl from one of the wolves closest to him. Arrin turned his back on the *moon-beast* to see three more wolves between him and the nearest egress.

Rondellus, believing Arrin was attempting an escape, lunged forward.

But instead of retreating, Arrin dodged to his right, using his momentum to climb the cavern wall—the same wall Rondellus had tossed him against a short time before. The rough wall had deep ridges that had once housed glow-rocks, but now they acted as a natural springboard, allowing Arrin to plant his feet and gather himself. Arrin flipped once more to his right, pushing himself up and away from the wall—directly into the path of the confused *moon-beast*. Rondellus braced his paws, but he had misread Arrin's intentions and it was too late to slow his charge. The great beast skidded, just as the wolves on the opposite side of the cavern had.

Arrin fell upon Rondellus. Wildfire entered the top of the moon-beast's shoulder and Arrin's weight forced the sword through the giant, stopping only as the hilt struck flesh and bone. The point of the blade burst through the monster's belly, and both man and beast fell to the ground. The moon-beast's momentum pushed them both along the floor of the cave; they slid forward until they reached the three wolves that waited to tear Arrin apart.

⁂

Arames knew without looking that Rondellus had been killed. *This had better work.*

Arames held his Advisor's medallion high above his head, flooding his immediate area with light. It had distracted Rondellus just enough, but the monk knew full well that the medallion offered him no protection from the wolves. Rondellus had prevented the wolves from attacking, and now Rondellus was dead.

But Arames still felt the vestiges of the communal mind-link that Rondellus had shared with him—the same link that Rondellus had used to call his pack. It was a link that Arames could not have established himself, but he hoped he could still use the fading connection. He couldn't speak to the wolves in words—he had to use the same language that had nearly overwhelmed him only a short time before.

The blue-gray night sky... the feeling of rushing over a forest floor at a speed few horses could match... but low to the ground... darting around trees as if they were grass... freedom!

For a moment Arames lost his focus—he had no idea how to communicate the idea of freedom. The growling of the wolves filled his ears. The largest wolf moved forward and snapped its jaws at the monk's wrist. Arames pulled his medallion down to his chest.

But he did not stop. He raised his eyes until they met the yellowed gaze of the wolf before him and opened his mind as much as possible, trying to draw the wolf in. Staring into the wolf's eyes triggered something in the monk's mind—a memory—*no, a story.*

Arames smiled.

A moment later, Arames dropped the medallion to the ground and spread his arms apart. He closed his eyes, still smiling, accepting the will of the wolf before him.

⁂

Arrin stood over Rondellus Marx. The moon-beast had reverted back to his human form while Arrin had pushed himself to his feet. Rather than focus on the metamorphosis, however, Arrin was too busy staring at the three wolves that for some unknown reason had still not attacked him. Even though he should have pulled Wildfire from Rondellus's corpse, he found he could only stand and watch them, and wait.

The growls of the wolf pack had slowly tapered off. All of them, including the three nearest to Arrin, stared at the dark wolf next to Arames. This large wolf barked once, then tilted its head to the side, as some of the wolves had done during the battle. After what seemed an eternity, every wolf in the cave, and several that had remained just outside the entrances to the cavern, moved toward the large wolf. In moments, they formed a large circle around the monk.

The large wolf shook its head twice more, bowed until its nose touched the ground, and then rose to lead the pack to the edge of the cavern. Arrin's mouth fell open. Most of the wolves focused on Rondellus's corpse. The new pack leader, however, went down on all fours and simply stared at Arames.

When the wolves parted, Arrin moved to Arames's side. The monk held himself up with one hand. He looked up at Arrin and attempted a smile, then slumped to the ground, unconscious.

⁂

After Arrin tended to the wound on Arames's shoulder, the monk had led the way back through the tunnels to Avedon Hill. Arrin had carried the corpse of Talik Bore over his shoulder, the body wrapped in a blanket from Arrin's pack.

They had made it back to the cellar of the inn in the middle of the night. Arames woke Leilah and sent her to the nearby garrison to get Constable Louis. Arames did not share the news of Talik's death until she returned with Louis and Tanner. Leilah fled the inn in tears; Louis sent Constable Tanner to ensure that she reached her home safely.

Arames detailed the events as they had occurred, leaving out the role that the glow-rocks had played in Talik's last moments. Arames also glossed over Arrin's hand in the killing of Rondellus Marx. Louis listened and shook his head from time to time, amazed. It was obvious that the constable had questions, but Arames quickly ended his statement with a request for Louis to take the information to Lord Avedon on his behalf, and a promise to meet with him in the morning to discuss matters further.

Before leaving, Louis confirmed that Father Jorrus had not returned to town. Arames left Louis with one final message: "These events confirm that someone other than a resident of Avedon Hill could have murdered Gretta Platt. Make sure Lord Avedon understands that his town is not as secure as he has led us to believe."

Finally back in their room and alone, Arrin asked Arames, "How did you do it?"

Arames turned to look at Arrin. "How did I do what?"

Arrin climbed into bed. "How did you make the wolves... let us go?"

Arames sat up in his bed with his eyes closed. "Before Rondellus and I fought, he practically invited me to enter his... his pack mind. I understood how he and the wolves communicated. It is a language made up of emotions and mental images. Rondellus used this link to control the wolves."

"So, this language prevented the wolves from attacking you while I fought Rondellus?"

"No. Rondellus kept the wolves from attacking me." Arames opened one eye. "By the way, excellent work dispatching him. Your father would be very proud."

"Actually, Mother might be even more proud. I used something I saw in my first dream-walk."

Arames opened both eyes. "Hmmm—remind me to ask you about that—later."

"Why did Rondellus do that—keep the wolves from attacking you?"

"I believe he either wanted the pleasure of killing me himself, or he wanted to force me to join his pack as another moon-beast." Realization washed over Arrin's face as Arames spoke. "After you dispatched Rondellus, there was no reason for the wolves to hold back. I communicated with them as best I could... tried to explain that they were now free, and that they had no quarrel with you and me." Arames stretched his shoulder. "It did not work, at first. But then I remembered *Ursala's Lament*."

"Ursala—the Child of Nature?"

Arames nodded. "Yes. You know the story?" he asked, but he knew the answer before he finished the question. *Ursala's Lament* was one of the more ancient legends, and would not have been part of Arrin's formal education. "Ursala is often born as an animal, or at least discovers early on the ability to change from human to animal form at will. One such avatar lived many generations ago in what is now Inarra. Ursala's avatar was a wolf; a female. The legend states that Ursala, living as this wolf and not understanding her true nature as a Child of Az, came under the spell of a magnificent beast, a great wolf with powers that she did not understand.

"Ursala followed her mate without question, creating a wolf pack called the *Rah-garl-im*. Rah-garl, Ursala's lover, drove his pack until it controlled the Dannmar Wood, one of the great forests of the north. The pack grew larger and more powerful over the years, eventually becoming a nation of wolves, but depleting their food sources in the forest.

"Without food, Rah-garl ordered his pack to attack the great Dwarven city of Corinhold. Unknown to Ursala and the rest of the wolves, Rah-garl was a moon-beast; against Ursala's wishes, he led an attack of over a thousand wolves on Corinhold. The dwarves were surprised by the attack, but after a terrible night of battle the wolves were repelled. Broken and bloodied, Ursala and the remaining members of the pack made their way back to their forest home. But none realized that the dwarves had no intention of allowing the wolf nation to rebuild. Every able dwarf from Corinhold entered the Dannmar Wood, fully prepared to slaughter every wolf they found.

"Back in the forest, the moon-beast pulled Ursala aside and changed before her eyes, becoming a dwarf with green glowing eyes. The dwarf laughed and called her by her true name. 'Ursala,' he said, 'you care too much for these creatures. They are our playthings, and they always will be.'"

"It was Doppin, wasn't it?" Arrin interjected.

"Yes—the Child of Trickery often takes great pleasure in bringing about another Child's epiphany. All Ursala wanted was to live her life helping animals and supporting the cycle of nature.

"As Ursala began to comprehend her divine nature, the dwarves of Corinhold began their attack. And though Ursala understood it had been her brother Doppin that had orchestrated events, she could not allow her wolf brothers and sisters to be destroyed. She fought back with the innate powers unleashed by her epiphany, killing thousands before the dwarves were forced to retreat to Corinhold.

"Ursala wept over the destruction she had caused. She used her powerful emotions to explain to the wolves that Rah-garl was a moon-beast that had tricked them all, had controlled them with powers that went against nature."

Arames's voice was quiet, almost as if he spoke from just beyond the veil of sleep. "*Ursala's Lament* is what I tried to convey to those wolves in the mountain tonight. Certainly Rondellus was no Doppin, but still—he controlled them like no pack leader should. I shared the images and emotions of what might have occurred that night, showed them the destruction of the only true wolf nation because of the evil nature of one moon-beast. The alpha was moved, and he convinced the rest of the pack to let us go."

Arrin snorted. "It looked like they were exacting their revenge on behalf of Ursala as we left the cavern. I don't think there's much left of Rondellus."

Arames was already snoring. Arrin moved to a chair and began his watch. He sighed, and whispered, "I guess the carnival isn't coming to town."

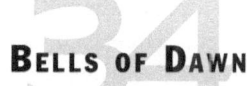

BELLS OF DAWN

Iberian awoke at dawn, hearing bells.
It was the call to battle that Iberian had embraced.

—Astika Tailir, *Reminders of Iberian*

ARAMES SLEEPILY SCRATCHED THE stubble on his cheek and pulled at his right ear, peeking his eyes open. When he whipped his head from side to side searching for Arrin, he could feel his neck crack.

"*He's fine. Don't worry yourself about Arrin.*"

Arames sat up, not in his bed but in a quiet meadow. It was just midday. A few paces away, Gareth Beckwin sat cross-legged, wearing a blue doublet and a light woolen coat lined with fur. The world seemed to shift around them. A river replaced the meadow, and Arames found himself sitting on the deck of an unmanned ship.

"*Now you appear in my dreams?*"

Gareth shrugged, but smiled at his Aarronic Brother. "You're a tired man, Arames. You should be awake right now, but you required rest even more than your Prince Arrin. It seems Arrin is protecting you more than the other way around."

Arames closed his eyes for a moment, and when he reopened them, he and Gareth were back at the inn. "If you are part of my conscience, you understand what I am doing."

"*If I am your conscience, I'm here to tell you that you don't serve Arrin by going down this path." Gareth pushed himself to his feet.*

"*You know better than anyone, Gareth—Aarronic Advisors do not serve any one person; we serve the Land."*

Gareth snorted without losing his smile. "You could have fooled me, Arames Kragen. It appears that you serve this boy's mother, just as you did during the last war."

Gareth disappeared before Arames could respond. Fog rolled over the rails onto the deck toward Arames, as if he were a channeler calling the river of magic to him. As the fog engulfed him, Arames found he could not breathe. He struggled against the mists as light became darkness…

Arames awoke with a start. Arrin, barely awake himself, looked down at him from his nearby chair. Arames gathered himself and told Arrin to lay down and sleep for the two cykes that would lead them to dawn.

Arames checked the door to their room and was surprised to find Constable Ulrich standing outside. "The Head Constable asked me to stand watch. There is a warm meal for you in the kitchen if you'd like it now."

The monk gave thanks to Ulrich for being such a great man. Ulrich left with a worried look, but returned a short time later with a platter of food.

The meal sustained Arames through the rest of the night. While he trusted the town constable to remain alert, Arames retrieved his notebook and pen. He would keep watch, as well.

⚜

Arrin sat on the dais in Lord Avedon's great hall. Lord Avedon sat beside him, angry as ever. He leaned over and growled, "Well, have you figured it out yet? Valet, warrior, whatever you are, I need answers. I need to save my son."

Arrin looked at the round table in the center of the hall. Several people sat in the large oak chairs, including Lane Niccols, Blake Weathertop, Sarah Tremaine, Herrjarr, Father Jorrus, Jilly Hemming, and others Arames had already cleared. Gretta Platt's mother Gloria stood between the table and the dais, staring at Arrin expectantly.

The town's constables and several manor guards, including Roc, surrounded the table. They held weapons at the ready, preventing anyone from leaving their chairs. Head Constable Louis stood next to Gloria Platt, watching Arrin hopefully.

"So, Arrin? Who killed Gretta!?"

"I... I don't know. We're closer, but—"

"I know it wasn't me!" Arrin looked up to see Talik Bore, previously blocked from view by one of the guards. "I'm dead, you know. Look at my throat!" The cut along Talik's throat oozed blood. His white shirt was stained red from neck to waist.

"You still had motive and opportunity, Talik."

Talik threw up his hands in disgust. "Didn't you see me in that cave? I couldn't have killed anyone. It wasn't in my nature."

Louis spoke up. "How many more people are going to die before this ends, Arrin?"

Before Arrin could respond, a scream filled the room. Arrin stood. Gloria Platt staggered forward. She was holding the side of her neck with both hands, but she could not contain the blood that escaped through her fingers. Constable Louis jumped to help her, placing his hands over hers. Gloria slipped on her own blood and fell into Louis's arms. "Damn you and your master, Arrin. You have failed us again!"

Arrin heard bells ringing somewhere in the distance; the bells from the Temple of Az.

⚜

Even without windows, Arames knew that dawn had recently arrived. He could hear Constables Tanner and Ulrich outside the room. Tanner was doing most of the talking, speaking in low, upset tones. Arames wasn't surprised when the knock sounded at the door.

As he moved to answer, Arrin sat up in his bed, fully awake. "It's Gloria Platt."

Arames smiled. "Dreaming again? I believe it is Constable Ulrich."

Arrin started to respond, but stopped himself as Arames opened the door. Constable Ulrich poked his head inside. "Sir Arames, you're needed at the playhouse. There's been another murder."

Arames frowned. "Gloria Platt?"

Constable Ulrich's eyes widened. "How did you know?"

Arames turned to Arrin. He was already out of bed, collecting what he needed for the day. "Arrin, put on your sword belt. There is no need to hide it now."

Death at the Theatre

"Death strikes the mother as swiftly as the father;
Balin strives to save them, but once the Children return
the loss of the Mother will mark the end of the age."

—3rd Collected Prophecies of Iberian, Book 2, Chapter 2

Aʀᴀᴍᴇꜱ ꜱᴛᴏᴏᴅ ᴛᴏ ᴛʜᴇ left of Gloria Platt's body; she still wore her blue dress from the night before. From the temperature of her skin, Arames surmised that she had been murdered at least three cykes before she had been found.

Father Livasdawn now prayed over the body of Gretta's mother.

"Father Livasdawn, please be careful as you stand. We cannot afford to disturb the area around her body."

For the first time, the young cleric had a fire in his voice. "Don't bother me now, Sir Arames."

Arames nodded and moved over to the other men in the theatre – constables Louis and Tanner, and Herrjarr. "Who found her?"

The large half-Tourim stepped forward. "I did, Sir Arames. I was collecting some tools."

"Tools?"

"Yes. Lord Avedon had asked Ollus to do some repair work on the theatre. He wanted to start having concerts here again."

The Head Constable corroborated his statement. "That was before Gretta was killed. Gretta and Sarah Tremaine used to sing here every season until two years ago. Lord Avedon asked the two of them to perform this winter. Their first concert was going to be next month."

Arames nodded. "Yes, Carin Avedon told Arrin as much the other day."

Herrjarr continued. "Ollus left one of my hammers here. I needed it, so I came over to pick it up."

"Do you make a habit of walking through town at dawn?"

Herrjarr looked confused, then pointed to a very thin hammer hanging from his belt. "No. I stopped my work last night because I needed this for some detail work. I woke up early and came here to retrieve it. I didn't feel like waiting for Ollus to arrive this morning—didn't want to waste half a day waiting on a tool that I could get myself."

"Did you move the body at all, or see anything else?"

"I only touched her face to see if she was still alive." Tears welled up in the blacksmith's eyes.

"Okay, Herrjarr. Unless Constable Louis has need of you, please go back to your smithy. We will come by later if we need to talk."

"She's got the marks, doesn't she? She was killed by the vampire."

Arames did not answer, instead allowing Louis to lead Herrjarr out the door of the theatre.

⚬⚬⚬

While Father Livasdawn guided Gloria's soul to Kalin's Abyss, Arames asked Arrin to search the perimeter of the theatre, both inside and out. When Louis returned, Arames pulled him aside. "You spoke to Lord Avedon last night?"

"Yes. He was unhappy, of course, but glad that you had dispatched the moon-beast. He wants to know why Rondellus could not have been Gretta's murderer."

"From what we overheard, it was clear that Rondellus Marx had not entered town at any point. He expected Talik to get him and his carnival in legally. What he planned on doing once the carnival gained entry will always remain a mystery, I fear."

Louis removed his hat and ran his fingers through his hair. He then moved over to Constable Tanner. "Please help Arrin. Look for signs of a struggle or anything out of place." Tanner nodded curtly and left their side.

Even though they were now alone, Louis leaned in close to the monk so no one else could overhear. "Sir Arames, I have faith in you and your abilities. I know that I wouldn't have survived encounters with vampires and moon-beasts. But I also know when Lord Avedon keeps things from me. Will you tell me what's going on? I'm worried about the children, especially Edvard."

Arames would not lie, so he could not answer. "Why are you worried about the children?"

"As head constable, they have always been under my care. Since Gretta's murder, Lord Avedon has kept all but Julienne and Jon away from me, and I'm sure none of the children—even Richard—will be allowed to leave the manor now that there have been more murders. Edvard has always been prone to illness, but he's been sick far too long... and no one will tell me what's wrong with him. It's just not like them."

Arames felt for the man. He himself had at one time been the primary custodian over the grandchildren of the King of Yew, and understood what it was like to be kept in the dark about events that directly affected those under his care. The monk sighed. "I am sorry, Louis. All I can say is that Lord Avedon feels he has the safety of his children under control. You need to speak to him if you want to know exactly what is going on."

Louis closed his eyes for a moment. Arames could see Louis's eyeballs moving restlessly beneath his eyelids as he contemplated what to do next. Finally he leaned back and opened his eyes, apparently resigning himself to the task at hand. "So, what do you make of this?"

Father Livasdawn had completed his ritual. Arames looked over toward the corpse. "Let us take a closer look."

⚜

After a hasty apology to Arames, Father Livasdawn took his leave. Before the cleric left, Louis promised that his men would bring Gloria's body to the temple once Arames was done.

Arames squatted down close to Gloria's corpse, careful not to disturb the wooden floor around her body. "These wounds—they are the same marks you saw on Gretta's neck?"

Louis did not need to look again. "Yes, they are the same."

"Doesn't look like Lane's work, now does it?" The book dealer Lane Niccols had killed on the night of Gretta's murder had suffered considerably more damage.

Louis shuddered, as if he had still not fully accepted that the quiet and kind librarian was a creature capable of murder. "No, it doesn't. Too *clean* to be a vampire bite—isn't that your theory?"

"It is not the bite of one we have both met, in any case." Arames pulled out his notebook and opened it to the page that had the three impressions made by the gardening fork from at the general store. One possibility Arames had to consider was that the broken piece of metal found in the manor courtyard had come from a tool of some sort, which might have been the instrument of Gretta's death. It did not explain the lack of blood, but it was a theory. The marks on Gloria's neck, however, did not match the drawing well enough to have been made by the tool.

Arames flipped the pages of his notebook until he reached the impressions of Edvard's teeth. Hiding the page from Louis's view, Arames compared the distance between Edvard's incisors and the marks on Gloria's neck. *This could be a match, but again these wounds are so clean—if Gretta was his first kill as a vampire, her wounds could be explained as a first tentative kill. But if Gloria Platt was Edvard's second kill, there should be more damage...*

"The small pool of blood here—" Arames pointed to the ground to the left of Gloria's head. "This is more than was found in the courtyard?"

"Yes. But less than we found with the body we examined in the woods yesterday."

Arames nodded. "A vampire can drain a lot of blood, but in most of the cases I have studied there is still a lot of blood found on or near the body, similar to how we found the book dealer."

Arrin approached the two men. "Sir Arames, I found a few drops of blood leading from that side door of the theatre to—near to another entrance to the underground tunnel system."

Arames snorted. "This is becoming absurd. Exactly how large is this network of tunnels underneath the town?"

Louis responded. "The tunnels are the same age as the town. The Avedon Mining Company had competitors. It is said that several went so far as to hire mercenaries to attack the settlement that was growing here. Before the outer wall was constructed, several underground shelters were built, connected by tunnels to the workers' homes, so that the miners' wives and children could hide if mercenaries or bandits attacked. Eventually the miners connected the shelters to other shafts, providing the townspeople the ability to escape an attack by making their way to the grounds behind the manor."

"Who in town knows these tunnels well enough to use them to get around?"

"My constables, Lord Avedon, Richard and Edvard, and Kell. Some of the other townspeople know about certain tunnels—like Lane, who knows only the tunnel between the library and her home. Hemming has an entrance near his home."

"Talik had one, as well."

"Yes, but those tunnels from town were only supposed to connect to the main tunnel that leads to the underground gate behind the manor. Neither I nor Lord Avedon realized any of these tunnels led outside of town. It doesn't make any sense. The tunnels were built so townspeople could escape an attack on the town from the south. No one would have built a passage that would give outsiders unfettered access to the town."

"What about Father Jorrus?"

"Jorrus? He certainly knows about them, but he was never given access to them."

Arames remembered how the old cleric had acted in the tunnel that connected the library to Lane Niccols' home. While he did not immediately know which way to go, he was not surprised by the tunnel. "And the Platts?"

Louis looked down at Gloria Platt's corpse. "Yes—yes of course. The Housemistresses knew the tunnel system inside and out—Gretta most of all. Once the weather turned cold, or on rainy days, she would use the underground passages instead of walking outside."

Arames carefully opened one of the pockets on the front of Gloria's dress. He pulled out a key. "To her home, Louis?"

"That is the right sort of key, yes."

Two of the manor guards, including Roc, had arrived at the theatre. "Louis, please post these two guards here and tell them to not disturb anything. We need to go."

⚜

"Open the tunnel door, would you, Constable Tanner?" Arrin had led Arames outside the theatre and had shown him the blood droplets on the grass and in the dirt. Tanner looked over to Louis, waiting for a signal. Louis nodded, and immediately Tanner felt around a well-groomed circle of grass until he found a hidden handle. "Does Kell tend this area's landscaping as well?" Arames remembered the secret door he and Arrin had used to enter the tunnels north of the stables, and how well concealed the entrance had been.

Louis nodded again. "Yes, he's responsible for keeping these doors hidden."

"Louis, if you are willing, I would like you to take Constable Tanner and Arrin through that passage directly to Gloria Platt's house. Look for proof that Gloria's murderer used the tunnel to transport her body to the theatre. I will proceed to the house above ground and see if this key fits her door."

⚜

The key opened the door of the Platt home, and as Arames had hoped, it allowed him access to the small dwelling before the others arrived.

The main living area that Arames had seen the night before was in complete disarray. Furniture had been moved, a bookcase had been overturned, and the chair in which Gloria had sat was on its side with one of its legs broken. Arames spotted a bloodstain on the center rug by the overturned chair, and he spied a second and larger pool of blood nearby on the wood floor.

Arames approached the bloodstains. Gloria Platt's murder had taken place here. *Still not enough blood.* "I am sorry, Gloria. I misjudged how dangerous this was for you. I will keep my promise and bring your daughter back to you." *So that you can lie by her side, if nothing else.*

Something caught Arames's eye as he focused on the bloodstained rug. Before he could study it further, he was interrupted by a muffled moan from the next room.

Arames rushed toward the sound and discovered Kell lying on the floor near Gloria's bed, a fire-poker at his side. He was dressed for sleep, and there was a great deal of blood in his hair and dried to his face. A trap door on the other side of the bedroom floor swung open. Constable Louis's head popped through the hole and his body followed. Spotting Arames, he said, "We found more blood droplets in the tunnel, but it—" but he stopped short when he saw Kell.

The groundskeeper's low moan continued as Arames studied his wounds. A deep gash on his forehead had made a bloody mess of his face, but though the wound would need sewing, it looked far worse than it actually was. "Kell, can you hear me?" Arrin passed over a clean, water-soaked cloth; Arames used it to wipe the blood from Kell's face. From the corner of his eye, Arames saw Tanner start into the next room. "Constable, there are at least two bloodstains on the floor in there. Stand clear of them, but look for anything else that might help us."

Those words seemed to snap Kell out of his stupor. He yelled and clawed at Arames's arms. Arames pulled Kell to his feet and sat him on the edge of Gloria's bed. "Kell, please! It is over."

Kell finally recognized Arames and stopped struggling. "It attacked us! The thing—it was a vampire, just like Father Jorrus warned us about!"

Kell had previously made it clear that he believed Father Jorrus's theories. Arames needed details. "What exactly did you see?"

Kell looked slowly around the room, still somewhat dazed. Eventually, he said in a very low voice, "I was in here, asleep." Arames could see that the old man blushed.

Louis patted Kell's shoulder. "Kell, we all knew that you and Miss Gloria... had a relationship. We half-expected you to retire and leave Avedon Hill with her once Gretta took over as Housemistress."

Kell's chest wracked with a sob. "I—I wanted to. Gloria wouldn't let me. Told me my life was here and not with her." Tears fell from his eyes. "She's dead, isn't she?"

Arames nodded, confirming the man's worst fears. "I need you to focus, Kell. We need your help."

Kell closed his eyes for a moment. "Gloria was sitting by the fire when I went to bed. She still refused to sleep, hadn't slept at all since she had come back to town. I was awakened sometime during the night by a ruckus in the next room. I found her on the floor, on her stomach, holding her neck. She was still alive."

"You went to her side?"

Kell nodded.

"Did you bend down to her? Did you touch her?"

"No, I couldn't move. I just stood there, staring at her. But then I heard something behind me, some sort of animal hiss. I turned and it ran into the bedroom. It was—it was surrounded by darkness."

Louis interrupted. "What do you mean by that, Kell?"

Arames remembered the darkness that had filled their room at the inn when Arrin had been attacked in his sleep. "The darkness moved with the creature, like a cloud of smoke?"

"Yes, yes… that's it. I grabbed the poker from the fireplace and ran after it. When I got into the bedroom the darkness was all around me. I couldn't see anything, even though I had left candles lit. I swung the poker, but I didn't hit anything but the wall. Then I ran into something, probably the edge of the bed, and lost my balance. Then the creature hit me—it felt like a mace… or a hammer. That's the last thing I remember."

"Are you okay to walk?"

A few moments later they joined Tanner in the living room. The constable reported that he had found nothing in particular. "It looked like the vampire was searching for something." Kell gasped. He stared at the floor; at the pool of blood and the bloodstained carpet. *And, of course,* Arames thought, *at the fact that Gloria's body is gone.*

Arames cleared his throat to draw Kell's attention. "It appears the murderer attacked Gloria first, and then ransacked this room. After knocking you out, he picked Gloria up and used the tunnel to escape."

"Kell, where did you step when you came into the room?" He held up a hand as Kell took a step forward. "No, please just tell me." Arames moved over, opposite the bloodstain. "Here? You never moved to this side, where the blood is on the floor?" A nod from Kell. "Good. You are in your bare feet. Show me their bottoms."

Kell, with Louis's assistance for balance, lifted his feet one a time and showed them to Arames. They were dirty, but nearly blood free. "Where are your boots, Kell?"

Kell pointed toward the front door.

Arrin, closer to the entrance, anticipated Arames's next question. He walked over and lifted the boots, examining their soles. "No blood here."

Kell's hand dropped from his forehead. "What is this? What are you doing?" Louis grabbed Kell's hand and guided it back up to press the cloth to his head wound.

"He's doing what must be done. Look." Louis pointed to the carpet where Gloria's head might have lain. On the carpet was a large bloody boot print.

Arames moved a step to his right and pointed to another spot on the carpet. "This is even more interesting. Come here, Louis."

Louis left Kell with Constable Tanner and walked over. He dropped to one knee, studying the carpet. "What is it?"

Arames pulled out his notebook and began drawing. "I believe *that* was Gloria Platt's last act."

"By the Children! She drew that with her own blood, didn't she?"

Arames had finished recording his interpretation of the bloodstained carpet and held it out for Louis to see. "This look right to you?"

Louis nodded. Arames said, "If my theory is correct, she did this while her attacker dealt with Kell in the next room."

Kell was visibly shaking. "Why didn't the vampire just kill me as well? And why did it take Gloria?"

"I am sorry, Kell, but I do not think Gloria was killed by a vampire. As for—"

"*Not* a vampire!? I saw the marks on her neck. The creature was here! I saw it!"

Arames approached the groundskeeper. "Kell, you told us yourself that the creature was surrounded by darkness. Did you actually see the monster?" *Or her...* He held the man by the shoulders until his shaking subsided.

"I saw—it was—large. It had to be a vampire." Kell broke down, tears streaming down his bloodstained face. "I didn't see it. It was all shadows—like a cloak made of the darkest smoke. But just because I didn't see it, it doesn't mean it wasn't a vampire. Father Jorrus has told me stories of vampires. A vampire master could do this, couldn't it?"

"In theory, Kell. And though I am only working on theories as well, I do not believe Gloria Platt and her daughter were attacked by a vampire, master or not." Arames turned to Louis. "Head Constable, an event occurred the other night. At the time I decided it was best not to share it with you. I was wrong. Arrin and I were attacked in our room two nights ago, by something that possessed the ability to engulf the room in darkness. Arrin, please... ?"

Arrin approached and pulled back his hood, exposing his nearly healed neck. "Whatever or whoever it was," Arames continued, "it attacked Arrin and gave him this wound. I countered the darkness, and the attacker fled. Father Jorrus was consulted and he called it a vampire attack. But Arrin's wounds matched the wounds on both of the Platts; and at this time I do not believe this to be the bite of a vampire." He nodded to his student. "Thank you, Arrin."

Arrin pulled his hood forward again, covering his blond hair.

Louis frowned. "Why did you not tell me this?"

Arames shook his head. "I should have told you, and I regret that I did not. But it would not have made a difference tonight. I warned Gloria myself of the danger—asked her to seek the protection of Avedon Manor. She refused."

Louis turned to his constable. "Tanner, find Ulrich and begin rounding up some of the reserve militia—Bakkis, Randall, Graves. Tell them to dress for tunnel work."

Tanner turned on his heel, grim determination on his face. Arames realized that Tanner would follow any order delivered by his superior.

Arames did not agree with Louis's course of action, but did not contradict him. The constable had gone too long without being in control of the events around him.

"Do you have a cobbler here?"

"No, not specifically. Alex does some repair work and sells boots. Sarah Tremaine stocks some higher quality footwear."

Arames pulled out his paring knife and began working at the carpet. Moments later he stood and handed Louis a stiff square about the size of the constable's chest. At its center was the best boot print left by Gloria Platt's attacker. "See if this matches some specific boot sold by either of them. You'll at least have a good idea of the foot size we're dealing with."

"Too large for most women, at least," Louis commented, and he nodded. "I'll do that as soon as I get two parties into the tunnels. Now, what about the drawing?"

Arames looked at his notebook. "I do not know what it is. It is not a letter from any alphabet I know. Maybe it is part of something larger. This center area might have been smudged. Gloria might have died before she finished, or it could have been damaged when the killer moved her."

Kell's tears began to flow again; it was time to get him out of the house. "Arrin, please wait for Kell to get dressed and take him over to the temple. Father Livasdawn can tend to his wound." Louis nodded his approval. Arames tore the drawing out of his notebook and gave it to Arrin. "Once Father Livasdawn has seen to Kell, show him this and ask him if he knows what it is. Make sure Kell is otherwise occupied when you do this."

"Why?"

Arames smiled. "All in good time. Wait for me at the inn once you are done." Arames turned back to the head constable. "Louis, do what you must with regards to the tunnels. Start your parties on opposite sides of town and search for signs of use."

"So they won't be confused by the other party's tracks... good. And you?"

Arames looked down at his notebook. "I want to see if Father Jorrus has returned from his search for Lane Niccols."

THE SCHEDULE BOOK

*The dawn of the Third Age marked
the end of the great Dwarven and Elven influence
over Caern. Iberian and Kalin were tasked with the counting.
The balance made it clear that many had escaped death.
Whether most hid on Caern or ventured through the portals
they had protected for generations, remains unclear.*

—The Return of the Children

It took several raps upon Father Jorrus's door to elicit a response. Once Arames heard a grunt, he called, "Father, it is Arames Kragen. Please open the door."

"Hold your skirts, monk." Jorrus was dressed in a relatively clean nightshirt, but his hair was even more disheveled and eyes were even more bloodshot than usual. The cleric took his time getting to the door and greeted Arames with a surly grumble. "What do you want? Can't a man rest?"

"Apologies, Father. I wanted first to make sure you had returned uninjured. Were you successful tracking Lane Niccols?"

Father Jorrus snorted. "Don't give that creature the benefit of a living name, Kragen. I tracked the thing west for several leagues, but it is as fast and as cunning as they come. Once it passed the crossroads I knew I couldn't catch it on foot. I'll rest up for a day or so, then ask Lord Avedon for a couple of horses. I'm sure he'll give them to me, since the librarian killed his girl. I'll catch it yet." Jorrus stepped out into the cold morning air, obviously not about to invite Arames into his home.

"Lane Niccols did not kill Gretta Platt."

Jorrus's chest rumbled with a low growl. Arames wasn't sure whether it was provoked by his use of Lane's name, or his statement.

"We discovered Lane was a vampire was because she committed a murder outside of town—she killed a book dealer the same night that Gretta was killed. She may be fast, but she could not have been in both places at the same time."

Jorrus's eyes moved from side to side; he appeared to be mulling over this new information. "That is… disappointing."

"There is more." Arames described the murder of Gloria Platt, providing only the details that had been found at the theatre.

"The marks were like those on your boy's neck, you say?" Arames nodded. "Which were the same as the younger Platt's? So, there is a second vampire."

"I am still not sure of that. The marks are so clean—"

"Bah, I've seen far more vampire bites than you have, Kragen. You've got a *snakebite bleeder* is all."

Arames lifted an eyebrow. Jorrus explained, "You know how to clean a snake bite, right?" He exposed his forearm and simulated cutting it with a knife. "Small incisions around the bite marks and then you suck out the poison. Well, some vampires don't like messes, and don't like thinking of themselves as animals. That's why I figured the librarian had killed Gretta Platt. A neat and fussy woman would want to leave a tiny wound." Father Jorrus paused for a moment. "Of course, there is one other possibility." He flashed a devilish grin.

"What is that?"

"Gretta Platt."

"What?"

"Gretta has risen from the dead and is a vampire herself. You'd best check her coffin. If she's missing…" Jorrus let the statement hang in the air.

"Her corpse has been missing for at least three days." Considering how quickly news seemed to travel, Arames found it hard to believe that the priest had not heard about the disappearance of Gretta's body.

Jorrus huffed. "I'd have taken care of her when she rose from the grave, only she wasn't buried in the town cemetery. The Platts are all in some underground mausoleum, but I've never had the pleasure." He laughed, pointing a finger at the monk's chest. "Secrets. Keep them close, Kragen. I need to sleep. I guess I shouldn't leave Avedon Hill quite yet. The librarian can wait."

"There is one more thing, Father Jorrus."

Jorrus had started to turn his back on Arames, but now he paused. "What?"

"Talik Bore was killed late last night, by the moon-beast I told you about the other day. It was in a cave outside of town. Arrin and I arrived too late to save Talik, but the moon-beast is dead."

"Good. It was a shifter?"

"Yes. And before it turned, Rondellus stated that one of the reasons he was here, was to kill you."

"Me? What did it say?"

"I can only assume it was you. It said it was here for the *Hunter*."

"Hmm… Rondellus you say?"

"Yes, Rondellus Marx. He ran a carnival based out of western Inarra."

"Inarra. I've killed moon-beasts, as a Hunter of Arjun. Perhaps I killed the beast's creator. Good work there, monk." Father Jerrus flashed a grin, turned, and re-entered his home, closing the door solidly behind him.

Arames shook his head. "Nice talking to you as well, Father."

∞◎∞

With Louis and Arrin performing separate tasks on his behalf, Arames hurried to the manor to see Lord Avedon. He was met at the entrance by Blake Weathertop. "Failing in your duties again, Brother of Aarron?"

Arames refused to take the bait. "Good morning, Blake. Please escort me to the great hall and let Lord Avedon know I am here to see him."

The butler opened his mouth for a retort, but cut himself short. Instead he turned on his heel and crossed the foyer toward the great hall. Arames followed.

Arames took a seat at the circular table in the center of the hall. He noted that no guard was stationed in the room, but Arames did see one guard on the second floor balcony. The butler turned to take his leave. "Blake?"

"Yes?"

"Before informing Lord Avedon, please stop by the kitchens and let them know I would like some breakfast. Thank you."

Arames smiled at the short *hmpf* that escaped from the butler before he turned and walked away.

∞◎∞

As Arames was finishing the breakfast Chef Roland had brought out to him, Richard and Carin Avedon—separately defining sternness and mischief—entered the hall. Richard spoke before Arames could rise to greet them. "I understand Miss Gloria was killed during the night. Clearly, uncovering our family secrets has not helped you find Gretta's killer."

Carin playfully smacked her brother on the arm. "Stop it, Richard. Sir Arames has already discovered who *attacked our dear brother.*" She kept her voice low to ensure the balcony guard could not hear her. "*It's only a matter of time before he finds out who has committed these murders, and then we can bring Edvard back.*"

Richard looked to the guard, who did not appear to be listening. "Hush, Carin." He faced Arames, who now stood before him. "Father is distraught over Miss Gloria's death, as you might imagine. He knew her all of his life. He does not want to see you. He is watching over Edvard now."

"I have to ask the question, Richard. You are sure *your guest* did not escape his restraints last night?"

Both Avedons shook their head in unison, and Carin answered. "I slept in the room for the first half of the night, and then Richard took over. Edvard never stirred during my watch."

"And I can assure you that the only feeding he did last night was just before dawn. He came out of his stupor long enough to eat some venison. After that, I gave him another draught. He's been out since."

Arames kept his voice low as well. "Has Marrissa delivered the potion?"

Richard rolled his eyes. "Later this morning, if she keeps her promise."

Arames moved in close, grasped Richard's right arm, and shifted his eyes from one Avedon to the other. "Speaking of promises, I need one from you. Do not let your father use the potion on Edvard until I have returned. We are close now, and once the killer is found we will know for sure if Edvard has tasted human blood. Please."

Richard stated, "He hasn't. I know it."

"You also know what will happen if you are wrong. If you want to protect the rest of your family—especially Jon and Julienne—do not use the potion until I return."

Richard didn't say a word. Carin stepped between the two men. "I promise, Sir Arames."

Arames smiled. "Thank you, my lady." He stepped back, bowed, and then turned to walk out of the room. He called out behind him in a louder voice: "We are close. I will be back soon."

⁂

Arames was more than halfway back to the inn when he heard Louis shouting behind him. "Sir Arames! Wait!"

The head constable wore a wide smile on his face. *That is the look of a man pleased to finally be contributing to the investigation.* "You found something in the tunnels."

Louis breathed heavily, nearly exhausted from running. "Yes—yes. You're going to want to see this."

Arames followed as Louis retraced his steps, and soon the two men were standing in an alcove off one of the main tunnels. "Where are we?" Louis gave him a puzzled look, so Arames added, "What is above us?"

"Ah. We are near the bakery. This tunnel leads to one of the original shelters I told you about. The Hemming family has direct access to it from their home." Louis moved to a corner of the alcove. "I didn't move it, but I recognized it right away."

In the corner beyond Louis's pointing hand were two crates, so old that they had crumbled in upon themselves. But in doing so, they had created a small gap at ground level—a gap filled with a tall, bound tome.

Gretta's journal!

Louis said, "This particular tunnel has seen some recent use, obviously. I already took the liberty of speaking to Hemming. I surprised Dally when I knocked on the door to their shelter from this side. She ran and got Hemming from the bakery—he confirmed that he has been down here several times over the last month. He uses the space for storage, and each year he sweeps the tunnels connecting his shelter to this alcove, which is consistent with the condition of the tunnels in this immediate area."

"What about his daughter?"

Louis raised an eyebrow. "What do you mean?"

"You said you surprised Dally. Was Jilly there?"

"No. I assume she's at the bakery at this hour."

"Yes, of course." Arames opened his notebook and looked at his notes on Jilly Hemming. *Jilly, who has shown signs of emotional distress in the past, including when I first spoke to her about her father; Jilly, who has been discovered burning dolls in the woods outside of town; Jilly, who was found crying in the courtyard just a few days before Gretta's murder; Jilly, who might have considered Gretta more than a friend...*

Arames retrieved a thin piece of paper from between two pages of his notebook—the partial page that had been ripped from Gretta's journal. He squatted, studying the crates and the book lodged between them. Nothing seemed out of sorts. Arames carefully extracted the book from its resting place.

Louis held his torch above the monk's shoulder, giving Arames enough light to read. It was a large journal, at least three hands high and two across. Yet the book was light, due mainly to its thin paper. Arames searched for the page to match the puzzle piece in his other hand.

It turned out to be an impossible task. "Look here, Louis." The first half of the book had pages filled with text. The last half of the journal was blank. But after the last written page, several pages were missing. "A good number of pages were ripped out. Our killer must have thought something within the journal incriminated him or her, but the book itself was too large and recognizable to carry into town."

"So we still have no idea who 'HA' is?"

Arames nodded. *HA* was written on the page fragment in Arames's hand—letters tied to a person Gretta might have been meeting with the night of her murder.

"Where are the rest of your people?"

"Still searching the tunnels on the eastern side of town."

Arames scanned the rest of the journal for any references to *HA*. There were none, but there were other sets of initials—references to several townspeople that Gretta had difficulties with at one time or another. The monk took mental notes, not wishing to write his thoughts down in front of Louis.

Though the journal provided Arames no direct link to Gretta's killer, it answered a question almost as important. Cross-referencing initials and abbreviations he had found in the Platt accounting books, Arames started to see patterns appear as he turned the pages. His experience interpreting prophecy served him well: letters and numbers that were meant to be code transformed themselves into a language that Arames could comprehend. Once those building blocks fell into place, the cryptic journal became a historical record of Gretta's work.

Most important to Arames were several references to work being performed by Marrissa on Gretta's behalf. This work was tied to deliveries made to certain visitors, again using initials for which Arames had no reference point. But in conjunction with these deliveries came the largest payments to the Avedons. As he read to himself, Louis spoke from behind him. "I have to hand it to you, Sir Arames. In only a few days you've discovered most of Avedon Hill's secrets."

From another man, the words might have been a veiled threat; though Arames did not sense danger, he was at a definite disadvantage with Louis hovering over him with a lit torch. "I have learned much, Louis. But I still do not understand what the Avedons and Platts have that is able to generate all the income listed in the ledgers."

Louis walked around and pulled Arames to his feet. "I'm part of this. I've been paid handsomely to keep the peace, but even more to keep visitors from wanting to linger. As you say, there's something here that the Avedons and Platts have used for generations to fill their coffers with gold. I don't know what it is, but I've seen enough to know that it isn't good. Some of the people that I've had to attend to, that Talik had to serve at his inn—these are not the sort of folks that you would invite over for an evening meal, if you get my meaning."

Arames had many questions, but now his mind went back to Talik and Rondellus Marx. "Talik was part of this?"

"I believe so. And I think that's why he was always so frustrated. You've seen the ledgers. I believe this is the real reason I was asked to stop investigating Gretta's murder."

"But why would Lord Avedon allow me access—" He remembered Lord Avedon's words. "*You are outsiders... you could do this.*"

"I don't believe that Lord Avedon will ever allow you to leave. I sent the rest of the men to the eastern tunnels because I wanted you to know that you need to escape while you can. The tunnels from the inn can get you outside of town. It appears Lord Avedon doesn't even know the extent of his family's network of mines. Escape with Arrin and don't come back. I have enough information here to discover who committed these murders. And I promise I won't stop with that. I'll discover what it is that the Avedons have sold to the agents and mercenaries I have seen here year after year."

Arames's mind was leaping from one thought to the next, barely hearing

Louis's words. *Talik's plea to Rondellus: "But there are REASONS why your tests have failed."* And the glow-rocks that Rondellus had in the bag, lightless.

"...why your tests failed"—when glow-rocks are exposed to sunlight they lose their glow.

Taxx... Rondellus had said it: *"I had heard the rumors from one of my former masters in Inarra. I have seen the ruins of the 'Old Walls' at Taxx."* The city walls of Taxx, breached nearly thirty years ago by an unexplained explosion, damage ten times as powerful as the largest rock ever hurled by a trebuchet—an explosion that had marked the beginning of an attack that had left over a thousand dead. An attack that had initially been linked to Yew.

Gareth... Several weeks before the attack on the city of Taxx, Gareth Beckwin had been murdered. It had been one of the only assassinations of an Aarronic Advisor. Several explosions outside of a heavily populated public building had caused chaos within; in the confusion, an assassin ended the Gareth's life with a poisoned blade—an attack that had been initially linked to Grozh.

A third voice called out from the corner of the room. "So, now you know why I'm here."

Arames blinked. Louis was still watching him. Arames looked past the constable to Gareth Beckwin, who sat on one of the crates—the wood would have collapsed under his weight, if Gareth had been real.

Gareth held a finger to his lips. "Don't speak. We wouldn't want the good constable to question your sanity. How many mysterious incidents does this explain? How many claims of magic are now disproved?" He shook his head. "You'd better listen to the good constable, and escape while you can."

"Arames?" Louis's voice brought Arames's focus back. He looked over once more to the crates, but Gareth was gone.

Arames placed his hands squarely on Louis's shoulders. "Thank you, Louis. I appreciate everything you are saying. But I made a promise to Gloria Platt: that I would return Gretta's body to its proper resting place, and discover who murdered her. I cannot fail her, especially now." The monk smiled. "Besides, I think I just figured it all out."

Louis brightened. "What?"

"It is the glow-rocks. It—" Arames stopped himself. Louis deserved to hear everything. "Listen. That is not important. There is something I need to tell you about Edvard—"

Louis raised his head, looking past Arames's shoulder. A moment later, Arames heard the echo of footsteps behind him, followed by Richard Avedon's voice. "Head Constable, Ulrich told my father that you found Gretta's journal. Lord Avedon requests your presence immediately, along with the book." Arames turned. Richard and Constable Ulrich had rounded the corner, with several guards behind them.

Louis ignored Richard for the moment, his eyes locked on Arames. "What is it?"

Arames did not know how much Richard had overheard, but his expression told Arames that his conversation with Louis was over. Richard pushed past Louis to stand between the constable and the monk. "Now, Head Constable. Sir Arames, is there anything else you need here?"

Arames shook his head. "I am fine. I can make my way back to the inn, thank you."

"Once Lord Avedon finishes with the journal, I am sure that you will be permitted to examine it as long as you like."

Arames did not allow his expression to change. "Thank you, Richard."

Louis kept his eyes locked on Arames, hoping for something. It was painfully obvious that Louis loved the Avedon children and was worried about their well-being, especially Edvard's. Arames mouthed the word *later* and walked through the alcove toward the Hemmings' basement. He hoped someone would grant him egress from the tunnels.

I must get to the inn to meet Arrin… but I have one more stop to make.

THE HUNTER OF ARTUS

The assassin stood behind Theuroik, ready to strike.
"Is your work complete, General?"
Theuroik glanced at his one remaining Hunter, bound and gagged.
"Our work will never be done. My life, however, is yours."

—Astika Tailir, *Reminders of Iberian*

ARAMES ARRIVED AT THE inn less than a cyke later, finding Arrin sitting in what had become their accustomed booth. Leilah sat across from him, her red, puffy eyes telling him all he needed to know.

Both got to their feet as Arames approached. "Please, sit," he said, but they both remained standing. Arames took Leilah's right hand in his. "Everything is going to be fine."

"Sir Arames, I realize Talik might not have been the most honorable man, especially if he got himself killed dealing with bandits." Arames looked over to Arrin, who confirmed with a nod that this was the story being circulated. "But he was like a da' to me."

Arrin interjected. "There's good news, though. Lord Avedon sent word that Leilah is to take over the inn."

Arames smiled. He brushed strands of Leilah's brown hair away from her face with a finger. "Well, now. That is good news."

"Talik didn't have a family. He kept saying that he was going to find a wife on his trips to the coast, but he never did. He only came back with ideas in his head. I've got two cousins that are tired of working on the farms. I thought maybe I could bring them here. Let Red do more of the cooking, if he likes."

Arames nodded. "I am sure he would like that very much." He cast a glance over to Arrin. "Leilah, I stopped by Red's home. He will not be coming in tonight. I hope you do not mind. In any case, Arrin and I will not require much in the way of service later today."

⚜

A short time later, the two men sat in their room, updating each other on the events since they had parted. "Yes, after speaking with Louis I felt we needed some leverage."

"I hope he can handle it." Doubt tinged Arrin's voice.

"He must. Now tell me about the rest of your morning."

Arrin handed Arames's drawing of Gloria's blood-stained carpet back to his mentor. "Father Livasdawn said it was familiar, but he couldn't place it. He suggested it might be part of something larger, because it means nothing on its own. He said he was sorry, and he'll continue to mull over it."

Arames studied the drawing. "Disappointing. I feel the same way about it. It is right there, just beyond my grasp."

Arames had already shared what he had seen in Gretta's journal. "Marrissa is involved, according to Gretta's schedule book, correct?" Arrin asked. "What if the doctor didn't feel compensated for her work?"

"But she and Alex were together the night Gretta was murdered."

"What if they killed Gretta together? We know there is magic involved here, but we also know that it took someone stronger than Marrissa to carry out these murders. We already know that Alex is unhappy with his place here."

Arames smiled at Arrin's logic. "That is a good theory—and one worthy of pursuit, my young prince." He stared at the drawing, mentally running through all the various symbology he had studied—magic, religion, alchemy, prophecy, herbology—but it was as if the knowledge hid behind a door in his mind, laughing at him. *You can tear down walls in others' minds, but you cannot access information that should be at your beck and call. Hmmm… old man.*

"What if the murderer wasn't a townsperson at all?" Arrin asked suddenly.

Arames looked up from his notebook. "How so?"

"We've been concentrating on everyone in town, but now we know that someone could have gotten in and out using the tunnels. Maybe this is more about someone that doesn't live in Avedon Hill, but has a grudge against the Platts."

"And the attack on you?"

"We were getting close, and the killer wanted to scare us off?"

Arames thought it over. "Possibly—but only the townspeople knew about us and our investigation."

Arrin stood and began pacing. "What if Father Jorrus has been right all along? What if Edvard killed Gretta? What if Gretta rose from her grave and has been wandering through the tunnels? What if it was Gretta who attacked me, out of some sort of need to keep us quiet about Edvard—or better yet, to silence us before we discovered what the Platts and the Avedons have been doing?"

"But why would she kill her own mother?"

Arrin sat on the edge of the bathtub and sighed. "I don't know."

It was Arames's turn to stand and pace. "Nor do I. And even though I do not believe that Gretta walks as a vampire, the fact remains that her corpse is missing. It is time for me to ignore my intuition and consider this possibility."

"And what about Father Jorrus?"

Arames smiled, but didn't say a word.

"I saw Father Jorrus in my first dream-walk," Arrin said. "He cut off the head of Gretta Platt's murderer. Since that time I haven't even considered the possibility that Jorrus is Gretta's killer."

"Just remember that your dream-walks can show you threads from the past and the future, but that you cannot tell what is truth and what is dream."

"So, what do you believe?"

"I believe that Father Jorrus believes he is right… to a fault. But that he might kill innocent women over his belief that the dead are rising around him, does not make sense."

Killing the innocent. Arames's eyes moved to the drawing once more. Could it be that easy?

The monk smacked the parchment with the back of his hand; the resulting thwack made Arrin jump. "Come, Arrin."

"Where are we going?"

"To the smithy."

***

"Herrjarr, we need to speak to you!" The heavy oak door barred their way into the smithy, but Arames called through it. "This is important. Please open the door."

From behind the door, Arames and Arrin heard Ollus Wenk, Herrjarr's apprentice. "Herrjarr doesn't want to speak to you, Sir Arames. He thinks you don't like him."

Arames sighed. "Tell Herrjarr I know he had nothing to do with any of the murders. Ollus, tell him I really need him."

A few moments later Arames heard the scrape of wood against wood beyond the smithy's main door. After another scrape and the thump of wood against a metal restraint, Herrjarr opened the door and stepped out, repeating his mantra from the first time Arames had met the half-orc. "I didn't do it." He clenched a fist at his side, but his eyes were sad.

"I know."

"Then what do you want?"

Arames held his version of Gloria's drawing in his left hand. He did not show it to Herrjarr just yet. "You said you were originally from Inarra. Which clan are you from?"

"Clan Msien."

Arames thought for a moment. "Western Inarra. Clan Msien belongs to Tribe Connach, does it not?"

"Yes. What does this have to with anything, Sir Arames?"

"Tell me if you recognize this."

Arames handed the page to Herrjarr. The blacksmith studied the drawing for a moment before raising his eyes to the monk. "No. What is it?"

"Look at it again. Imagine that it is part of a larger picture?"

Herrjarr studied the drawing once more. At first there was nothing, but then, slowly, the blacksmith's eyes widened. "Let me get my inkwell."

Arames handed his pen to Herrjarr, who gazed at it in amazement. "Please, Herrjarr."

Herrjarr shook his head and began to draw. "Looking for this, Sir Arames?"

Arames took the parchment and pen back from Herrjarr, and nearly laughed. "Yes, that is it!"

Herrjarr nodded, smiling back. "You had it turned wrong."

Arrin leaned in. "What is that?"

Herrjarr spoke first. "Old Inarran symbol for Arjun—" The blacksmith paused for a moment, confused. "No, not Arjun—"

Arames finished his thought. "Artus!"

Herrjarr nodded. "I bet you'd see it in some of the etchings at the old temple, if they haven't all worn away."

Arrin turned to Arames. "Did you know that already?"

"Inarra," Arames explained, "aside from its major cities, is still made up of tribes that are made up of even smaller clans. All of these tribes trace their lineage back to an apical ancestor—some warrior or mother or shaman. In many cases, the tribes believed their founders were avatars of Children of Az."

Herrjarr nodded his head as Arames spoke. "Clan Msien was directly descended from Elai. My mother always regretted having to leave her stead. She always felt less connected to Elai, living here in Grozh."

Arames continued. "Dozens of clans claim Artus as their apical ancestor. But two thousand years ago when these tribes began appearing, there was no Principle of Inclusion. Artus was known as Rhaeth, or Teiwyr—"

"Clan Msien's founder was Onomar."

Arames looked up at Herrjarr. "Onomar, who drove the dragon from Mount Iraki and found the Horn of the Eye, giving Clan Msien power over all their enemies."

Herrjarr smiled. "Yes."

Arrin had tired of the history lesson. He tapped the parchment with his index finger. "So what does this mean?"

Arames held up his left hand. "In a moment, young Arrin." He turned back to the blacksmith. "Herrjarr, have you ever done any work for Father Jorrus?"

"Once. He has an old ring mail shirt. I repaired a few links and shined it up for him."

"And that rod." It was Ollus, standing inside the smithy, peering around the door.

"Yes. Jorrus brought in a rod once. It was ivory—had symbols, carved end to end, that I did not recognize."

"Why did he bring the rod to you?"

"It had silver bands, one on each end and another not quite halfway up. He wanted to use my silver cleaner, but he wouldn't leave the rod with me."

Arames held up the drawing once more. "Did any of the carvings on the rod look like this?"

"No. Most were just decorative. But a few near the middle of the rod looked … more important. Religious, maybe."

Ollus called out, "Arcane, more like."

Herrjarr nodded. "But nothing either of us knew. Unless—did you recognize them, Ollus?" Ollus shook his head from side to side, eyes wide, and then disappeared behind the door.

A guttural noise escaped Herrjarr, his version of a laugh. "You need anything else, Sir Arames? Ollus may need some tending to. That's the most he's said since I've known him."

⚜

"So, are you going to tell me what in Az's name is going on?"

Arames and Arrin headed northwest from the smithy. "I accepted Father Jorrus's word that he had been an undead hunter for the Brotherhood of Arjun. That was … foolish of me. Gloria obviously could not write out her murderer's name in blood. It would have been noticed and wiped clean. But drawing a symbol, or at least part of one—that, she succeeded in doing. So I began thinking about all the symbols associated with herbology, the arcane arts, even symbols used in the mercantile arena—in case, as you suggested, it was Alex Dewirin who had killed her. Nothing fit."

"But then I remembered the book you found in Gloria's office, with the Inarran symbol of Doppin on the cover. The last time I spoke with Gloria, she realized that we had discovered the secret room connected to her office. She knew I understood something about Inarran symbology. While I do know many of the Inarran symbols for Doppin, there are many more symbols for Artus, since the Child of War is a very popular figure with the Inarran tribes."

Arames pointed to the drawing. "I knew I had seen this before, and when I remembered the icon for Doppin I came to suspect that this was Inarran as well, but there are so many symbols for Artus; I could not be sure. But then I remembered Herrjarr was from Inarra, and that the blacksmith who had apprenticed him was Lolch Svennet—another Inarran name. Considering that most Inarran metalwork includes the etching of symbols and icons, I thought Herrjarr might be able to confirm my suspicions."

"We're going to Father Jorrus?" Arrin asked.

Arames nodded. "I said it would not make sense for Father Jorrus to murder innocent women, but I based that on the assumption that he was an undead hunter for the Brotherhood of Arjun. The Brotherhood of Arjun—even one of their undead hunters—would never intentionally harm someone."

Arrin thought to himself: *Arjun, the Child of Protection.*

Arames sighed. "But a Hunter of Artus—I should have seen it." They continued on, the monk collecting his thoughts. "The Hunters of Artus go back to the time of Theuroik—" Arames began.

"The possible avatar of Artus, the Child of War."

"Right. Following the War of Man, Theuroik—in an attempt, some say, to flee from guilt over his part in the assassination of Iberian—personally led a small army north into what is now Inarra to eradicate any remaining Tourim presence in Caern. Theuroik drove this army, not caring about himself or anyone around him. After three years of searching through the worst environments of Caern—the mountains of Inarra, the deserts of eastern Grozh—only a small loyal band of men remained at Theuroik's side.

"Some say it was at this point that warrior-priests of Iberian, the Knights of the Rose, confronted Theuroik and executed him for his part in Iberian's death. The men that were left—the ones that followed Theuroik until the end, driven to destroy any undead presence they found, no matter the cost—became the Hunters of Artus. They believed in one single vision—Theuroik's vision—a Caern that was undead-free."

The two men were nearing Father Jorrus's home. The door stood open, swaying in the breeze.

Arames paused, compelled to finish his explanation. "After the Priests of Caern successfully removed Artus as a recognized Child of Az, the Hunters of Artus were officially disbanded. But some still live, and for these men, the war against the undead never ends."

Arames recalled one of the first things Father Jorrus had said to them—*Regrettable loss, Gretta. She was a casualty of war that did not need to be. But there will be more losses here.* Arames growled at his own failure to recognize the truth—he had assumed the rant of an aging undead hunter was only that, and nothing more.

Arrin followed with an insight of his own. "HA—the torn page from Gretta's journal—that stood for Hunter of Artus, didn't it?"

Arames nodded, too angry with himself to enjoy Arrin's realization. He shook the drawing that was now rolled up like a scroll in his hand. "Gloria Platt knew what Jorrus was when he came to Avedon Hill, and referred to him as HA. Gretta used these initials for him as well."

"And when Gloria died, she made sure that we knew it, too."

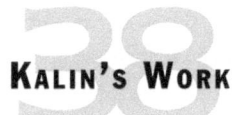

KALIN'S WORK

Reynaud Fortas, now named Kalin by his brother Doppin,
fell to his knees, surrounded by his burning fields.
"Why do you deny yourself, Kalin!?
Look, even the grasses bow down to you!"

—The Return of the Children

Aʀᴀᴍᴇs ᴀɴᴅ Aʀʀɪɴ ᴀᴘᴘʀᴏᴀᴄʜᴇᴅ quietly from the right edge of Father Jorrus's home, with an oblique advance meant to prevent Jorrus from seeing them through the open doorway. Both men had drawn their weapons, but their blades were unneeded: the home was empty. Arames quickly searched the small dwelling but found nothing that linked the cleric to Artus, or to the murders. *Where are you, Jorrus?*

Arames straightened and his breath caught in his throat. *Oh no.* "We need to find Louis, now." He nearly ran from the house, heading toward the cemetery.

As they neared the fork where the road branched to the west and toward Avedon Manor, they were met by Richard and Constables Tanner and Ulrich. Richard now had a sword belt at his side and wore leather armor. Richard looked past Arames, scanning the road to the west.

"What is it, Richard?"

"I'm looking for Louis. He's—*disappeared.*" The tone of his voice suggested that it had something to do with Edvard.

"So are we. Father Jorrus killed Gloria Platt, and most likely Gretta as well. We need to find him—and hopefully capture him."

"Jorrus?" Richard had a shocked look on his face, as did Constable Tanner, but the normally unflappable Ulrich looked angry. "Why would Jorrus do that?"

"There's no time for that now. Where was Louis headed?"

When Richard didn't answer, Ulrich supplied, "The library, most likely."

"Fine. We will find him." Arames took Richard by the shoulders, forcing the young man to meet his gaze. "Richard, I need you to go back to the manor and tell your father about Jorrus—that Gloria left us proof that Jorrus killed her, even as she died—and that he was probably behind Gretta's death as well. He needs to know."

"Arames, look!" Arrin cried.

Richard had already turned to leave, but he stopped in his tracks. Arrin rushed forward to intercept Lonne Garrett. The stablemaster approached from the west, battered and beaten, and fell into Arrin's arms, coughing up blood. Much of his face had been shredded, as if he had been clawed by a bear. One of his hands was pressed to his neck, barely holding in his lifeblood. Arrin shouted, "Lonne… Lonne!" But the farrier slumped against him, passing out from the effort of his escape.

Arames did not stop to help. Instead, he yelled back toward Arrin as he ran toward the town cemetery. "Try to stop his bleeding. We will be back soon!"

Richard, his father forgotten, followed Arames. Constables Ulrich and Tanner were on their heels. It took only moments for the four men to reach the edge of the cemetery—and to discover the worst had occurred.

Head Constable Louis lay on the ground, throat torn and bloodied. His legs lay askew; one of his arms was bent at an impossible angle, nearly ripped from its socket. Remarkably, he used his other hand to cover the gaping wound on his neck. Even more remarkably, Louis still breathed. The sword at his side was bloodied, as well.

There was a second man on the ground near Louis, lying face down. Arames recognized Shane Olivet's short cropped hair. He could not tell how the damage had been done, but it was clear that Shane was dead.

Richard ran forward and fell to his knees at Louis's side. He seemed overwhelmed, frustrated at the sudden realization that he didn't know what to do, and he let out a wail that shook Arames to his core. "No! Uncle Louis!"

Surprise was an emotion Arames Kragen had managed to avoid much of his life, but now he found himself caught completely off-guard. Driving back his own tears, Arames reached Louis's side moments later. He forced the barely conscious constable to focus on his face. "Who did this to you? Jorrus?"

A wild look of denial stared back at Arames. The wound Louis was failing to cover with his one good hand prevented any sound from escaping his mouth. He managed to mouth the word, "Lane."

Lane Niccols! She has returned? Why?

As Richard shouted to the sky in anger, Arames watched Ulrich look off toward the library; his sword was drawn.

"Cletus came to the manor and told Louis that Lane Niccols was back—that she had broken through the town gate and run off toward the library," Ulrich explained.

"And you did not go with Louis?"

Tanner answered, "We weren't there. Cletus stopped by the garrison on his way back and told us we'd better get to the manor. We didn't see Louis on the way, but we met Richard as he was coming out of the manor—he told us that Louis had run off after he spoke with Cletus."

As Tanner spoke, Louis's stony stare never strayed from Richard's face. Louis's life-stealing wounds may have prevented sound from reaching his mouth, but he mouthed the words, "Edvard… Richard… How could you?" and the power of his anger forced Richard to avert his gaze.

Louis coughed. Blood spurted from his mouth and struck Richard's cheek. Louis's defiant eyes lost their focus and his head fell back onto Richard's left hand. Arames reached down and touched the uninjured side of Louis's neck. He could not feel a pulse. Knowing Louis's love of Az and Artus, Arames prayed silently. *Artus… if you live with your Father and not on Caern, receive your fallen soldier. He earned his entry into your kingdom this day.*

Leaning over Louis, Arames was eye level with Richard. "You need to go to your father—now. Tell him what has happened. We will deal with Lane first, and then with Father Jorrus." Richard opened his mouth in protest, but the look on Arames's face silenced him. His tears mixed with his uncle's blood on his cheeks. Richard took a deep breath and his face hardened—not in anger, but with the strength and resolve of a heartfelt decision firmly made. Slowly, Richard stood and faced his two remaining constables.

"Do whatever Sir Arames orders you to do—without question."

⚜

As Arames and the two constables turned to leave, Arrin and Lonne Garrett approached from the east. Much of Lonne's head was wrapped in bandages and Arrin supported him every step of the way, but the look in the farrier's eyes told Arames that nothing was going to keep him from returning to his apprentice's side. Arrin helped Lonne to his knees beside Shane. The farrier pointed past Arrin. "Get that Tourim. She must pay Kalin's toll for what she's done." Arrin paused, reluctant to leave the wounded man. "Go on," Lonne insisted. "I'll be fine. I've got worse than this from a stallion's hoof. Go!"

Arames gave Richard one last look. Tears streaming, Richard sheathed his sword and ran off toward Avedon Manor.

Arames called out his orders. "Come. To the library."

⚜

It was only a short distance to the library, but the changing elevation and the trees that lined the path hid the structure until they were less than an arrow's flight away. As a result, when they rounded the edge of a copse of trees Arames was surprised once again. The library was burning.

Smoke already billowed from two gaping holes in the roof. The walls were just starting to smoke in several places, removing any doubt that the fire had originated on the inside. Arames turned to the two constables. "We need people to help with the fire."

Ulrich looked at Arames as if he were speaking another language. "What about the vampire? You need us!"

Even drawn up to his full height, Arames didn't reach Ulrich's chin. "We do not have time for this. Arrin and I can take care of Lane, but the contents of that library are more valuable than you realize." Ulrich did not back down; apparently Richard's orders didn't carry as much weight as Arames had hoped. "Tanner, where are the men who searched the tunnels?"

"Most are at the inn. Louis had asked Leilah to set them up with dinner and ale for their efforts."

Arames broke out into a run toward the library. As the others followed, Arames yelled, "Tanner, go get those men to help with the fire!" Tanner nodded and broke off, running east.

"There is a well between the library and Lane's house," Ulrich said as they ran. "They keep buckets at the inn for just such an event. We'll stop the—fire…?" Ulrich's voice trailed off and his mouth fell open.

Arames had come to a stop; he threw his arms outward to bar the two other men from passing him, but he needn't have bothered. The sight had stopped Arrin and Ulrich in their tracks. Ulrich was the first to regain his voice. "What in Az's name?!"

⁂

Jilly Hemming stood before the library, half-naked, flailing her arms about her as she danced. She hummed a tune in time with her movements, as if gyrating in front of a burning building was the most natural thing in the world.

The sight of Jilly transfixed the three men; she whirled and twirled in some sort of private ritual. It took a moment for Jilly's lack of clothing to register for Arames, or at least for him to realize the cause of it. To the rest, it may have appeared that Jilly had ripped her clothes off, but Arames could now see that the clothing had all but burned away.

And Jilly's next actions confirmed Arames's suspicions: the enigmatic dance came to an end, and the girl lowered her arms to her side. She turned to face the library door and lifted her hands up before her nearly bare chest, palms toward each other, as if holding a ball the size of a grapefruit. Arames couldn't see the girl's eyes, but he could feel the fire in them—the fire he had seen but not fully recognized two days before.

"No!" Arames ran forward, but Jilly's concentration was unbroken by his shout. She raised her right hand above her head, and now in place of the imaginary globe, she wielded a grapefruit-sized sphere of liquid fire. Strands of blistering heat dripped down from the ball and onto her shoulder. Clothing that was unfortunate enough to touch the molten liquor immediately burned away, but Jilly herself appeared unharmed. The girl screamed in the direction of the library's open entrance—the door had already fallen inward, a victim of her attack. "You bitch!! You killed my Gretta! You killed my Shane!!"

Arames pushed to the limits of his speed and abiligy, but he saw with a sinking heart that he was not going to make it to Jilly before she hurled the sphere of fire. At the same time, he realized that he would be exposed and defenseless if Jilly decided to loose her missile in his direction.

But Jilly was as oblivious to Arames's approach as she had been to his shout. The ball of flame arced from her hand, landing just inside the building and breaking into several smaller orbs. Moments too late, Arames crashed headlong into Jilly Hemming, tackling her to the ground.

⁂

"Damn you, girl, what have you done!?" Ulrich stood over Jilly's unconscious body. Arames stood between them and the library's entrance, watching the quick spread of the fire. "She cannot hear you, Constable."

Ulrich started to retort that he knew as much, but Arames did not allow him the opportunity. "Do what you must to keep her unconscious, lest she harm more than a building." The monk turned to Arrin. "Stay here, no matter what."

Before Arrin could respond, Arames charged into the burning library.

⁂

The heat was nearly unbearable. Flames had engulfed several walls and most of the ceiling. Streaks of burnt carpet and scorched wood crisscrossed the floor, the trails left by Jilly's orbs as they fractured and bounced in all directions. The drop from the main landing near the library entrance had provided even more acceleration, allowing the spheres to travel to every corner of the room.

A wall of fire stretched across the floor, separating Arames from the reading area. He held an arm across his forehead to stave off some of the heat, but it would soon become intolerable.

Arames made out the form of Lane Niccols through the flames. Lane's dress smoldered; her arms were filled with books and she carried cloth sacks overflowing with scrolls and papers.

Arames understood what drove Lane better than anyone, and—against his better judgment—he was touched by her actions. Arames knew it would end badly, but he still ran forward and jumped through the flames without a second thought.

Fire licked at Arames. The wood floor, already compromised, cracked and groaned under his feet as he landed. Before he could start a roll to disperse his weight across the weakened floor, a strong hand had him by the neck, lifting him off the ground.

Lane's grasp crushed his throat; Arames could not speak, but he could still look into her eyes. He hoped she was not too far gone to hear his thoughts. *Lane, let me help you!*

The flames had spread underneath Arames's dangling feet and licked at the books Lane had dropped. "I had to come back!" she cried.

I know. The vice around Arames's neck loosened slightly, but not enough for him to escape Lane's grasp. It was not sentimentality that weakened her grip; Arames could now see a wound just below Lane's heart, along her ribcage, that would have rendered any mortal being immobile.

Lane followed the monk's gaze toward her chest. *Like what you see, Arames?* She laughed, but the effort quickly morphed into a cough. *Damned gatekeeper. I should have killed him. I could have been in and out of here before anyone ever knew.*

But Louis found out, and he came to find you. Why did you kill him?

I came back for more books—the ceiling was now completely ablaze. A small burning beam fell, landing on a bookshelf. Lane cursed and dropped Arames to the floor, rushing over to gather up several items that she must have considered the most valuable. *Louis and two others met me at the fork. I didn't see them at first. I was unfocused. The stableman came at me with a scythe. He was not a threat, but then Louis ran me through with his sword. I'm not proud of my actions, but they attacked me. I had to defend myself. And as if that were not enough, I was attacked by a wilder when I got here—my library and possibly my life in danger because some little girl can't control her powers.*

Arames picked up several of the items Lane had dropped to the floor. *Lane, I am sorry. In another life...*

And what exactly do you plan on doing, Sir Arames?

Arames leaped back through the flames, arms full. The bottom edge of his robes caught fire, but the flames trailed behind him as he ran toward the exit. Without pausing, Arames cast a final thought at Lane: *Follow me and you will be destroyed.*

⁂

Lane Niccols had been wounded several times during her second life, but never like this. Her creator, a vampire master and officer in the army of Yew, had nearly disemboweled her in a fit of anger. She and her two sisters had been prepared for his attack, and Lucien Talfair had met his end. It had taken several days to recover from the cut that had opened her torso, but her sisters had helped her through that pain as well.

But now, a century later and with her sisters long ago taken to Kalin's Abyss, no one would come to help her. *As soon as that bastard Jorrus hears of this, he'll hunt me across all of Caern.* She had expended too much energy on Arames. Lane's blood, the life-force that maintained her hold in this world, was draining out of her. The wound itself would not end her existence—the fire would do the rest.

Lane spun around, gasping in pain. The whole room was now ablaze, her own special funeral pyre. *Not to worry, Arames Kragen. I have no intentions of exiting through that door.* Not as graceful now as in days past, Lane limped toward the stairs that led to the stone-walled library basement.

⚜

Arrin extinguished the flames that smoldered along the edges of Arames's robes. During Arames's short time in the library, Hemming, Caasz, Herrjarr, and Ollus Wenk had all arrived at the scene. In the distance, Arames spotted Constable Tanner returning with several men, all carrying buckets. Other than Hemming, who sat on the ground holding his unconscious daughter, the rest of the men appeared ready to tackle the fire.

Arames addressed the closer of the two constables. "Ulrich, take some men over to Lane's house. If she makes it to the tunnel under—"

Before Arames could finish his thought, a small concussion shattered every remaining window of the library, sending glass in all directions. Arrin, his back to the library, flinched and turned to face the building.

My dream...

"Arames—" Arrin began, but his voice was low and Arames interrupted him.

"Lane will try to escape the same way she did before, through her—"

A great rumbling explosion—several blasts, one after the other, much more powerful than the first—blew out the northern and western walls of the library. Stone, plaster and flaming wood flew outward, and everyone near the building was knocked from their feet. The blasts dismantled the library, but a great section of land to the east of the building was also affected. It collapsed and exploded upward at the same instant, like some great whale erupting through the surface of the ocean. The blast uprooted a tree and sent it flying through the air. It landed harmlessly in some bushes near the well.

Arrin shook his head, ears ringing from the explosions. He looked over to see that Arames had already reached his feet. Ulrich lay on the ground on the other side of Arames, pulling on his left earlobe and shaking his head.

Arames moved away from them, over to a large rock. He sat down on it, ignoring the chaos going on around him, and stared at the shattered remains of the library in disgust.

⁂

So, the circle is complete, eh, Ari?

This time it was only Gareth's voice in his head, and not the visage Arames usually found smiling back at him. Arames responded, *Explosives. In some tunnel near the library, most likely. set off by the fire. Going off one after another.*

I'll see you again someday, my friend. I must go now. Gareth laughed one final time. *Don't hurt anyone you're not supposed to.*

Arames lowered his gaze from the remains of the library, unable to look any longer. *I cannot promise that, old friend.*

⁂

The explosion had served one purpose. By leveling the building and scattering the flaming wood in all directions, it deprived the raging fire of its source of fuel. Smoldering material lay strewn everywhere. The men continued to bring water from the nearby well, splashing it on the smaller fires all around them. On the other side of the ruined library, Herrjarr found Ollus Wenk pinned under the remains of a bookcase. The smith lifted the shelving by himself and Ollus crawled out, amazingly uninjured.

Arames turned back to Ulrich. "I doubt Lane survived, but take three experienced men over to her home and search for her."

Ulrich frowned. "You're not coming?"

"No, Arrin and I have somewhere to go. Even if Lane somehow made it to safety before that blast, she is gravely injured. Louis ran her through before she killed him. As long as you work together, you should be fine." Arames walked away from Ulrich, leading Arrin by the arm.

"What is it, Arames?"

Arames picked up the pace, directing Arrin down a path toward the entrance to the town. "Marrissa."

THE TEMPLE OF ARTUS

While Artus resides in heaven's arena, the dead will play.
The gates are sealed, but the tears have not healed.
A generation after the Tourim threat turned,
The last great war of man will be revealed.

—3rd Collected Prophecies of Iberian, Book 4

How DOES IT WORK, Marrissa? Sulfur? Phosphorite?" Arames stood in Marrissa's workshop, just barely holding his voice below a shout. He and Arrin faced an exhausted woman. Marrissa stood on the opposite side of her work table, as if she could use it to keep the two men at bay. She looked as if the explosions at the library had awakened her. That, combined with Arames's tone, had quickly changed the woman's expression from fatigued to frightened.

Even so, Marrissa didn't answer Arames immediately. She seemed to be going over her words in her mind, as if she had been practicing her answer all her life.

Arames did not have time to wait for Marrissa to formulate her thoughts. He probed into her mind with such speed and strength that there was no hiding what he was doing. Marrissa gasped and beat her fists against her head. "Stop that!"

Arames relented; his initial probe showed him that Marrissa knew how to raise mental barriers against someone with powers such as his. The monk knew he could tear them down, but only at a great cost to both of them, and he couldn't afford to damage the doctor's mind.

Arames turned his attention to the shelves directly behind Marrissa and pointed past her shoulder. He did not need to perform the gesture, but he wanted Marrissa to understand exactly what he was doing. The bottles on the top shelf of the case began to shake. Marrissa gasped; turning toward the wall, she raised her hands, reaching out to steady her supplies. But Arames had chosen the top-most shelf for that exact reason. He focused his energies, violently rattling the largest bottle on the shelf. It spun for a moment, hung on the edge like a salmon fighting the current at the top of a waterfall, and then fell.

Marrissa moved forward and caught the bottle before it hit the ground, but the other bottles continued to shake. One in particular must have held a particularly active ingredient—the cork stopper popped out of the rocking bottle and brown foam began pouring out. Marrissa yelled over her shoulder, tears welling up in her eyes. "It's a fulminate! Please… stop." The last two words were barely audible.

Arames lowered his hand and the bottles stopped moving. One of the smaller containers toppled onto its side, but did not fall.

A fulminate… a salt gathered from acids under proper conditions. Arames suddenly wished he had made more time to study alchemy; he also wished he had saved *Lappin's Codex* from the fire.

With trembling hands, Marrissa pulled out two small vials and a glass tube. "Mixed with mercury and placed in one of these tubes… and then set within the core of a glow-rock."

"What triggers the explosion?"

"It is pretty unstable as it is. It could detonate if the glow-rock is thrown, or even dropped. But most of the time they're detonated with a burn-wire, to control the timing."

Arrin, standing at the bottom of the landing below Marrissa's work area, spoke for the first time since he and Arames had entered the shop. "But what do the glow-rocks have to do with it?"

Marrissa startled at the sound of his voice. "The glow-rocks add fuel to the fire, so to speak. The explosion breaks the ore into a great number of shards with little to no loss of energy, and the blast itself transforms even the smallest slivers of rock into missiles that fracture even further upon impact."

Arames interrupted. "And the explosions that just destroyed the library? How much of this did it take to cause such destruction?"

Marrissa shook her head. "I have no idea. The *cretches* are stored in several caves—"

"Cretches?"

"That's what they're called. I never see where they're taken after I make them."

"These explosives… are how the Avedons were able to carve their way through the Lantis mountains in the first place?"

Marrissa nodded. "Gaelen Avedon had his own munitions, and when his mining company came upon the first glow-rocks, the resulting explosion nearly brought down the entire mountain. The surviving miners eventually learned their power through trial and error, and also after great loss of life."

"Who knows this?"

Marrissa hesitated. Arames slammed his fist on the workbench. "Who!?"

"The Avedons—and two or three of the oldest families of Avedon Hill."

Arrin asked the question Arames didn't want to ask. "What about Louis?!"

"No. He would not have approved."

Arames recalled Richard's grieved outcry. "Louis was Lord Avedon's brother-in-law?"

"Was? He is dead?"

Arames nodded and Marrissa answered, "Yes, he was."

The remaining pieces fall into place—another reason why Lord Avedon did not want Louis investigating Gretta's murder or learning about Edvard, why Louis was so worried about the safety of the Avedon children… and why he was compelled to go after Lane Niccols.

After a few more questions, the two men left Marrissa. Arames led them back to Lane's home, where they found Constables Tanner and Ulrich.

From their expressions, Arames knew the two men had not found Lane Niccols. "Enough of Lane. If she was not destroyed in the explosion, she has certainly left town. We must now concentrate on Father Jorrus."

Tanner held up a hand. "You said that earlier. What makes you think Father Jorrus has anything to do with this?"

Arames looked from one constable to the other and sighed. "We have evidence that links Father Jorrus to the murder of Gloria Platt."

A pained expression crossed the taller constable's face. Ulrich asked, "What do you mean? Tanner was there with you at Gloria's house. From what he told me, there wasn't anything there that implicated Father Jorrus. A vampire killed Gretta's mother."

Tanner interjected, "The boot print? Did you match that to Father Jorrus?"

Arames shook his head. "No, not yet."

Tanner thought for a moment. "The drawing—in the blood on the floor."

Ulrich whipped his head around and faced his fellow constable. "Drawing? What drawing?"

Arames raised his hands. "We must move past this, gentlemen. Rest assured that Gloria Platt left us information that implicates Father Jorrus. At the least, we need to speak to him."

Ulrich snorted. "If he was involved, I'm sure he's left town by now, just like the vampire."

"No, I think not. I realize now that Father Jorrus has extensive knowledge of the labyrinth underneath Avedon Hill. Have either of you showed Jorrus how to traverse the tunnel system?"

Both men claimed they had not, and Arames continued. "From Kell's reactions to all things vampiric, I believe he is the one who provided Father Jorrus his knowledge of the tunnels. Tanner, the tunnels need to be searched once more. Please gather the men from this morning and go through again. If you run into Father Jorrus, only tell him I have information on the vampire that killed Gretta Platt. That should get him to the surface."

Arames gave Tanner a few more instructions and then sent him on his way. Ulrich now stood beside Arrin, his anger seemingly abated. "I apologize for snapping at you, Sir Arames. I just can't believe that Father Jorrus murdered the Platts." He sighed. "So, what are your orders?"

The monk focused on Arrin. "Have you determined our next destination, my young student?"

Arrin blinked and opened his mouth. It was clear he was thinking through all they had learned over the last cyke. After a few moments his eyes widened. Arrin raised his arm and pointed over Arames's right shoulder. "There."

The long-abandoned Temple of Artus, half-hidden by nearly thirty years of unimpeded plant growth, still managed to loom above them in the distance.

⚜

The approach to the temple from the southeast was marked by a slope that increased as the three men advanced. By the time they were within shouting distance of the temple, the path to its formerly grand entrance was obscured to the point of uselessness. If Father Jorrus was using the temple, he had found another way inside.

The narrowing trail forced them to walk single file. Arames slowed his pace, allowing Ulrich to lead the way. Arames was tired; ten steps later, he realized how ravenous he had suddenly become. But then, when Arames stubbed his toe on a root and nearly fell, he was truly unnerved. He caught himself—Arrin and Ulrich never noticed the misstep—but the monk knew that something was amiss; he immediately began exploring his connection to the Land, extending his energies all around him.

Arames had been through a lot over the last cyke, but the hunger and weakness that had become a constant presence in his life had never before affected his balance. He felt his breathing become heavier and more labored, and a new realization hit him like a slap across the face.

Arames whispered, "Stop." The others halted and turned toward him expectantly. "Arrin, do you sense anything... different?"

Arrin looked around, not fully understanding Arames's question. "It's quiet—maybe too quiet."

Arames bent down and touched the cold ground. "My connection to the

Land, to the river of magic—it is gone."

Ulrich unsuccessfully held back a snort. "Come on, old man." The constable tightened his grip on his sword as if in confirmation that steel was all he required.

Arames focused on Arrin. "The River is how I have described the means by which the power of Az flows through Caern. Others portray this power as mists that hover over the ground, or as a fog. The metaphors do not matter—they all describe magic as an ever-changing entity. The River may run strong along a certain path, but the next day that same path may only hold a trickling stream. A raging current may be found here one day," he pointed to his left, "but the same current may flow here the next." He pointed to his right. "Yet, no geographic entity, no mountain, no forest, no city, not even the great oceans themselves affect the currents of the river of magic."

Ulrich had less patience than Arrin, but managed to keep his voice at a low volume. "What does this have to do with us? I thought you were hell-bent on finding Father Jorrus."

Arames stood up. "No matter the strength of the River at any particular place, it can always be sensed by those with the gift. Yet, right here, right now... I cannot feel the River."

Arames walked forward, moving past the two men. Ulrich shook his head as if the monk had lost his mind. Arrin cast an angry glare at the constable and then turned to follow his mentor toward the temple entrance.

⚶☙⚶

Arames knew he had to concentrate on the task at hand, but his mind kept turning back to Louis's death. *He asked me to leave town, to save myself and Arrin from harm.* As they neared the temple, Arames was reminded of the Song of Artus that Louis had sung the day before.

The Song of Artus has a power matched only by some of the great rituals of the various priesthoods dedicated to the Children. If only...

Wait. The bells at the Temple of Az.

"That is it!" Arames raised a finger, and all three men stopped. They were some thirty paces short of the temple entrance.

Arrin whispered, "What is it?"

The night Arrin was attacked at the inn... I could not touch the River, except through my medallion. Kell also saw the darkness that surrounded Gloria's attacker. The loss of his connection to the Land made more sense now. "Jorrus is here. I know it." He looked out toward what he could see of the horizon, and noted the position of the sun. "Ulrich, I need you to go to the Temple of Az. Have Father Livasdawn ring the Bells of Dusk. Tell him he has to play the Song of Artus!"

"But Lord Avedon ordered that no bells—"

Arames raised a hand. "No time... I need you to run to the temple—now." Whatever Jorrus was doing to keep Arames from touching the River had not affected his internal clock. Arames knew that less than a quarter of a cyke remained before the Bells.

"The Song of Artus?" Ulrich's brow furrowed in confusion.

Arrin asked, "If Father Jorrus is a disciple of Artus—?"

Arames ignored both men, physically turning Ulrich and pushing him back down the path. "No time, Ulrich. Do as you promised Richard and follow this order!"

Ulrich sheathed his sword and ran back down the path, still shaking his head.

Arrin waited until Arames had turned back to the temple. "Are you sure about this? Ulrich looks like he can handle a sword."

The monk moved past Arrin toward the temple entrance. "If this works, we may not need our weapons."

⁂

The main floor of the abandoned temple had been devoid of human presence for many years. Walls had crumbled in on themselves in several areas, with vines coming through the holes as if they had been solely responsible for the damage. The two men carefully navigated past both plant life and rubble—to ensure they would not fall through weakened sections of the temple floor, but also to keep their presence quiet.

It was dark within the main sanctum and growing darker by the moment. Arames knew they had to quicken their pace. Even in the gloom and with his connection to the Land severed, Arames knew exactly how much time they had until the bells would ring. *That is, if Ulrich convinces Father Livasdawn.*

They moved forward, staying close to the less damaged western wall and avoiding the center of the floor. Rats scurried off in different directions, unaccustomed to invaders in their home.

At the rear of the sanctum, they found a set of circular stairs leading down to the lower floor of the temple. Most temples had at least one sub-level, for offices and private sanctuaries. Arames felt confident that they would find the temple connected to the tunnels underneath Avedon Hill. He motioned to Arrin to be as silent as possible as they began their descent.

⁂

Arrin removed his pack from his shoulders and placed it gently on the stairs. After only a few steps downward, Arrin knew that entering the temple from above had been a wise choice. Light flickered from multiple torches below them, just out of their direct line of sight. Faint sounds reached Arrin's ears. *Voices?*

Arames, three steps below, flashed Arrin a hand signal and then moved forward. Arames had not drawn his weapons, but Arrin held his longsword tightly. Arames reached the lower level and stepped silently into the corridor before him.

The prince entered the corridor four paces behind Arames. Multiple doorways lined both sides of the hallway, and light emanated from a room at the far end. The voice they had heard from the stairs became more distinct as they neared the lighted room.

"A name—that is all I want. One name. I know we've been through this so many times, but I know it is in there. I can end this all for you—just tell me who it is."

Father Jorrus! Arrin increased his pace, but Arames held up a finger, gesturing him to a halt.

The silence allowed a new sound to reach Arrin's ears—the low moan of a creature in pain. *It has to be an animal—please be an animal.*

Arrin watched Arames purse his lips; tears filled the monk's eyes. *He cannot 'see' anything if he cannot sense the River. What has he figured out?*

Arames silently unsheathed both of his blades and crept forward.

⚜

Time was not on Arames's side, if Ulrich succeeded in convincing Father Livasdawn to ring the Bells of Dusk. But more importantly, Arames had finally realized what Jorrus's game had been all along, and he had to take action.

Still, the sight stopped him in his tracks. At one time, the room below the temple had been a large office. Father Jorrus, clad as always in the white robes of a priest of Arjun, stood a short distance away. Jorrus faced a side wall, and the profile view afforded to Arames displayed the edges of the tell-tale armor Jorrus wore underneath his robes—namely, the tanned and stretched hides of the kills he had made as a Hunter of Artus.

But Father Jorrus's attire wasn't what had halted Arames Kragen—rather, it was what Father Jorrus was focused so intently upon.

"By the Children!"

Arames cringed at the volume of Arrin's voice.

⚜

Arrin didn't want to believe his eyes. Chained to the wall before Father Jorrus, was a woman—or at least what had at one time been a woman. Her face and her nearly-naked body were so thoroughly cut and maimed that Arrin thought she had more wounds than actual skin left. Long strips of flesh hung loosely from her body—flayed, yet grotesquely still attached. A low, continuous moan escaped the woman's mouth, but she was far from conscious.

Father Jorrus either had not heard Arrin's outburst, cr was ignoring it. "I'm tired, girl—so tired." The priest held his holy symbol of Arjun, but instead of topping Jorrus's wooden walking staff, it was now attached to a rod—the white ivory rod that Herrjarr had described earlier that day.

Arrin studied the face of the woman chained to the wall. In her current state, Arrin could not determine her age. Her hair was matted with so much dirt and blood that it was impossible to even guess its color from this distance. Even so, Arrin had no doubt as to who lay painfully limp against Father Jorrus's shackles.

Gretta's alive!

EPIPHANY

"Do you doubt Elisia Llewellyn?"
"She never said the words. She never said 'Theuroik is Artus!'"
"For Az's sake! Artus wasn't Artus until Iberian named him so!"

—Council of Names, 57 AI (After Iberian)

Arames didn't have the time nor the heart to explain to Arrin that the woman chained to the wall was no longer human. Living, yes, but little more than an animal in the throes of slaughter.

Jorrus still ignored the two men, giving Arames a moment to study the priest's ivory staff from a distance. *Just as Herrjarr described: a rod of power. It must be what keeps me from touching the River, and what gives Jorrus the ability to call forth that cloud of darkness.*

But it is more than that.

Just as Arames's medallion had been infused with magic at its creation, so too was the rod Father Jorrus held. While icons such as holy symbols allowed clerics to harness the power of the river of magic within their bodies, a rod of power was a vessel that could contain great amounts of unfiltered magic. While humans were not as adept at magic in general as the Old Races were, they excelled at creating magical objects; rods of power were perhaps the most powerful examples of human magic.

With this rod, Jorrus had the power to bring Gretta back from what should have been her final release.

Arames entered the office, stepping to his right to approach the old Hunter from behind. Father Jorrus raised his voice to the heavens, as if the ceiling was not there. "*Artus!* She continues to hide the truth from us!"

The silver bands at each end of the ivory rod began to glow. Jorrus raised his hand; he may have been using the rod as a method of communication, but it seemed equally likely to Arames that he was about to use it as a weapon.

"Stop, Jorrus!" Arrin's shout ended Arames's opportunity to use the element of surprise. "Don't hurt her!"

Jorrus whirled to face the two men. Arames was still more than five strides away, while Arrin stood just inside the only entrance to the room. The power pulsing through the rod lifted most of Jorrus's hair off his shoulders. The cleric's eyes darted between the two men, and he cackled. "Friends! You've finally come to help me see this to the end!"

⁂

Arames was disappointed that Arrin had cried out, but he knew it was because the youth believed that Jorrus was about to strike his captive. Arames hoped that Arrin would remain silent now, but to his dismay Arrin asked Jorus, "Gretta—is she a vampire?"

Arames, moved into a defensive position, holding both sais between himself and Jorrus. "No, Gretta is not a vampire and never was. Jorrus killed her."

Arrin pointed his sword at the moaning woman. "But she's there—breathing. She's alive, then?" He took two steps toward her.

Jorrus lowered his arm, aiming the symbol of Arjun at Arrin. Arames also shifted his left arm out toward Arrin, twirling the sai until its blade pointed at the prince—both warning him to stay where he was.

Arrin halted, and Arames relaxed. "Her heart may beat, but her soul has been shattered—Gretta no longer exists."

Jorrus shook his head, smiling an unnerving grin. "You are mistaken, Brother of Aarron. Her soul is here. And she's just about to tell me everything she knows."

"What could she possibly know that would give you cause you to kill her in the first place, Hunter? She was an innocent!"

Jorrus waved his rod and scowled. "Innocent! No one is innocent, Arames. For three years I attempted to *educate* Gretta Platt—I showed her missives I received from my brothers, detailing the growing threat of the undead throughout Caern. I personally took her to the corpses I discovered in the forests outside of town, all the obvious work of a vampire."

Arrin yelled, "...that was Lane Niccols!"

Jorrus waved his free arm dismissively. "Yes, I know that now—right under my nose! But that was not the vampire I began to sense a little over a week ago. That *er-ralght*," he snarled the old Inarran word for *demonspawn*, "is an old and powerful vampire, with the ability to block my senses." Jorrus tapped the side of his nose. "But the bitch made a mistake—she turned someone."

Arames slid two steps to his left, angling himself between Jorrus and Arrin. He did not trust Arrin to resist the urge to charge the cleric.

Don't let me down, Ulrich. Arames spoke again, to keep Jorrus focused on him.

"You started to sense a vampire?"

"Yes, but again, it was *different*. While the bitch was invisible to me, this new vampire was... unusual. It was like... a *hole*. I'm sure over time the thing would have become invisible to me, just like Niccols, but a hole... it took some time, but a hole can be tracked just as easily as something you *can* sense."

"If you could track it, why couldn't you find it?"

Father Jorrus snorted. "For a day or two I could sense the beast, mostly in the tunnels outside of town. But it evaded me. It knew the tunnels much better than I did."

Edvard...

"But then it made its way under the town, probably trying to get back to its dark mother. I chased it for hours but I eventually lost its track. It ended in a passage underneath Avedon Manor."

Arames continued Jorrus's line of thought. "But you eventually found the hidden door to the manor courtyard. Is that when you killed Gretta?"

Jorrus grunted, casting a glance at the slumped form of Gretta Platt. "No, monk. For the next two days I tried to meet with Gretta, but she avoided me. At the same time, my senses lost that new vampire. Since that night, I've sensed the creature for short periods of time, but erratically, as if it's here one moment and gone the next, slipping through tears in the fabric. But one thing remained consistent. Every time I sensed it, it came from the direction of the manor."

Arames carefully kept his expression even. *Edvard is invisible to Jorrus while sedated.*

"I'd trusted Gretta for years, and she betrayed me. She was the one who got that dolt Livasdawn sent here, and then she protected an undead beast—hid it from me!"

"Still, Jorrus, why did you kill her?"

"I already explained why, Arames. There's a war coming, and it's closer than you think. I prayed, and Artus answered my call. He told me Gretta had to be destroyed—her and all of her *secrets*."

Arames smiled to himself. *I have you Jorrus.*

"Artus? The Child of War has no say in this, Jorrus."

"I tire of you, Brother of Aarron." Jorrus flipped the rod in his hands until he held it vertically, like an altar attendant at morning bells. There was an almost imperceptible click, and two spikes—each around three inches in length—extended from the base of the rod, stopping with an audible *snap*. "But at least you still recognize Artus."

"Yes, I recognize Artus as a Child of Az. I also recognize that you are not acting on his behalf."

Anger twisted Jorrus's wrinkled face. Waves of energy flowed from the rod, washing over Arames. "You know the prophecies better than anyone, Kragen."

While Artus resides in heaven's arena, the dead will play.
The gates are sealed, but the tears have not healed.
A generation after the Tourim threat turned,
The last great war of man will be revealed.

From Iberian's last prophecy—Arames shook his head. "So you believe that *now* is the time for the Great Battle, and that it will not be with the Tourim, but with the Children of Kalin?"

Jorrus smiled. "Artus himself has counseled me. I know it to be true."

Arames smiled back. "Artus did not counsel you. He has better things to do." Before Jorrus could retort, Arames called out:

The Riders will join together and they will meet the dead and the undead.
The Riders are the best of men – palms free of the blood of innocent

Jorrus raged. "You doubt me? You quote the Priests of Caern? You have battled the followers of Iberian even more stridently than I, even though they brought about the dismantling of Artus."

"You can find the best and the worst of humanity in any sect, Jorrus. But just as I know that Iberian would be disappointed in the current state of the Priests of Caern, I know that Artus had nothing to do with the death of Gretta Platt."

"Enough, monk! You will see! The Power of Artus will strike you down!"

Jorrus brandished the rod—it was as long as a short sword with the holy symbol attached to it. The pulses of power quickened.

Arames felt a sensation move from his head to his stomach, like swallowing a hot drink.

It is time.

Arames shouted, hoping his raised voice would delay Jorrus's attack: "No, Jorrus! That rod has nothing to do with Artus! If you want to see the power of Artus, you only need to hear his Song." Jorrus faltered. Arames knew he had broken the cleric's concentration, if only for the moment. "You know the power of the Song of Artus, Jorrus. Artus has no place for your failures and indiscretions. The Bells of Artus will ring once more, and the whole of Artus's will shall rain down upon you, *apostae*! The bells will RING!"

<hr />

The timing should have been perfect. Even disconnected from the river of magic, Arames was as sure that Dusk Bells had arrived as if he stood before the temple's water-clock. The air crackled with the power of Jorrus's staff, and as Arames had hoped, his threat had made Father Jorrus pause in spite of himself, listening for the Bells of Artus.

"Ding, Dong—"

Arames whirled and found himself staring at Constable Ulrich. He stood in the doorway directly behind Arrin, sword in hand. "It was a nice plan, monk." Ulrich smiled a toothy grin.

Arrin turned, his sword between himself and Ulrich. Through the doorway, Arames saw two more men. The first he did not recognize, but the second was the manor guard, Roc. "Too bad you chose the wrong constable. Tanner would have convinced Livasdawn to play your silly song."

Attempt to trick me, will you? Father Jorrus pointed his staff at Arames. *Enough talking, monk,* he thought. Jorrus shuddered; the power of the many souls he had captured over the years coursed through him. Green lightning exploded from the end opposite the holy symbol of Arjun, directed through the two metal fangs that protruded from the base of the weapon.

But Arames had turned toward Ulrich, and the bolt meant for the monk's chest struck his right arm instead. Still, its force drove Arames to his left knee; the sai flew from the monk's right hand, skidding across the stone floor to halt a few feet away. Jorrus cackled with glee.

Pain shot through Arames's arm, lessening only slightly as it spread throughout his body. The bolt of green energy confirmed one thing for the monk. *No cleric of Artus created that rod of power.* His robes, already singed from the library, disintegrated where he had been struck. Arames had no wish to see his arm. He knew the blast had burnt him; at least the heat of battle allowed him to close himself off from the pain, for the moment.

Arames had no idea how long it would take Jorrus to summon a second strike. He reacted instinctively, attempting to push a blast of air toward Father Jorrus's staff. *Nothing.* Jorrus's power still separated Arames from the river of magic.

Arrin's body sang with adrenaline. He was well aware how lucky he was that Ulrich had chosen to make a joke instead of plunging a sword into Arrin's back. Facing the new arrivals, Arrin angled himself against the doorframe to make sure he faced no more than one attacker at a time. Roc pushed past Ulrich to reach Arrin, disturbing Ulrich's balance just enough to leave an opening for Arrin's blade. Ulrich was quicker than Arrin expected, however; he easily blocked the lunge with the buckler strapped to his arm.

As Arrin prepared to meet Ulrich's counter-attack, he heard a voice rising in song. Arrin saw in Ulrich's eyes that he heard it as well. The voice rose in volume, filling their ears as if the singer stood directly between them.

⚜

The voice reached Arames just as it reached Arrin and Ulrich. He smiled despite his pain.

Ah, even better.

"Jorrus, Artus does not need me to show you the error of your ways. The Song of Artus is more powerful than any temple bells!"

The voice, mellifluous and beautiful, filled the room:

Here stands Artus, his essence filling the vessel named Theuroik
He is worshipped, along with the Children,
By righteous men and the host of kings
who are all denizens of Caern.
Fear not for those that have fallen.
By pouring themselves as a libation on the fire of battle,
They have obtained the prize, the end,
the attainment of a hero's welcome in heaven.

A shout in the distance told Arames that the song, and more importantly, the *voice* behind the song, was doing its work. The guard behind Roc fell to the ground, calling out to Iruna for forgiveness. Iruna—who, five hundred years before, in the form of Queen Elisia Llewellyn, sang about the deific nature of Theuroik Ironblade as an avatar of Artus. Roc, a man with little regard for the history and mysticism of the song, stood over the fallen guard, yelling at the man to rise.

Even so, Roc covered his ears as best he could with his free arm while he shouted.

⚜

Ulrich stood, unable to move, tears in his eyes. The constable's gruff attitude toward magic and Artus had been an act meant to mislead Arames. In truth, the song that now filled his senses nearly dropped him to the ground, right along with Paris, the impressionable young guard he had enlisted to help Jorrus two years before. *Iruna's voice? What magic is this?* The constable's hair stood on end. *Artus's Song? Was the monk right all along?*

Confusion turned to bewilderment as the point of Arrin's sword plunged deep through Ulrich's abdomen. Ulrich fell to the ground; the last thing he felt was the sword sliding back through his body.

DOPPIN'S JEST

Movement begets growth; growth begets change;
Without change, nothing happens.

—Ballix Poe

ARAMES LEANED ON HIS left foot, still expending most of his immediate energy maintaining his balance. But the Song of Artus had changed matters. Fear seemed to have taken hold of Father Jorrus. The cleric still held tightly to his pulsing weapon, its metallic fangs still aimed directly at Arames, but Jorrus himself swayed and stared about him, lost. Even if Jorrus openly feared the retribution of Artus, Arames had no desire to charge toward the cleric and those metal spikes.

And the Song continued. But now the voice changed; it rose and fell like a breeze, flowing through the room like a spirit moving around and through them.

Then Arames felt its touch, and he gasped involuntarily. It was just a wisp—a tendril of invisible mist—but he could touch it with the edges of his senses. In moments the mist became a rolling fog, surrounding him and filling his heart. It was the river of magic. The voice was pulling the River along as it made its way through the temple. Jorrus's powers were no match for the song and its singer. *She is a Channeler, able to change the course of the River through her song.*

⚜

Roc stood silent now, his back to Arrin. Covering his ears did nothing to prevent the song from filling his head, so the guard lowered his arm to his side. He knew that it was only a woman's voice, *only a damned song*, but it was not simply lyrics that filled his mind. Impossibly, he heard instruments, the trumpets and drums of war. Roc shook his head in wonder—he was no longer in the Temple of Artus, but on a field of battle.

Roc scanned the field. The dead surrounded him, and for every armored humanoid corpse at least ten misshapen creatures littered the landscape. Most of the demons —*they must be demons, right?*—lay in piles, and most of the piles burned. The smells of burnt flesh, scorched fur and blistered abomination filled his nose as completely as the Song filled his ears.

Roc finally found the strength to focus on the only other person moving on the battlefield. A woman: lithe, tall, gray-eyed, with blonde hair that reached far below her waist, stood among the wounded, singing the song that resounded in his head. Roc instinctively knew the woman wore a white dress—but then realized there was no way he could possibly *know* that; it was completely stained red with the blood of countless creatures.

These and other mighty Caerim on the earthly battle slain,

Roc moved forward, toward the woman; no, it wasn't a woman... it was the elf-queen. Even Roc recognized Elisia Llewellyn. Everyone around the elf, some wounded and bloodied, others simply weary from battle, sat or kneeled with heads bowed, listening to her song. *How am I at Ohme, five hundred years ago—did Jorrus and Artus send me? No, this has to be a dream.*

By their valor and their virtue walk the bright ethereal plane,

Roc approached Elisia, close enough to reach out and touch the noblewoman. She sang on, staring into his eyes. *She's singing to me.* Roc raised his arms, opening himself to Elisia's embrace. But as he gazed into Queen Elisia's eyes, they changed. The almond-shaped gray eyes shifted orb-shaped and green. The golden hair shortened and deepened to a fiery red.

They have cast their mortal bodies, crossed the radiant portal of heaven,

The voice behind the Song strained for a moment—just a moment. There were tears on the woman's cheeks, anger in her eyes, and just as Roc began to recognize Sarah Tremaine, her dagger entered his left side, just below his outstretched arm.

꧁◦◦◦꧂

Arrin stood over Ulrich, the Song filling his head as well. Arrin's sword point nearly touched the ground; he had been rendered immobile by the Song of Artus. Arrin saw the battlefield just as Roc did, and he saw Sarah Tremaine walk into view, just beyond Roc and the prostrate guard, Paris.

Arames had described Sarah Tremaine's abilities as a singer, but Arrin had been unprepared for the true power of her voice. She held a long dagger; it shook in her trembling hands and tears fell down her face. The huge guard blocked Arrin's view of Sarah; Arrin could only watch as Roc reached out to touch the seamstress. But instead of knocking her down, he staggered, lost his grip on the woman, and then slumped to the floor.

꧁◦◦◦꧂

Father Jorrus stared at the events transpiring at the door, unsure of himself for the first time in years. *The Song of Artus, called from the heavens by a Brother of Aarron?* He licked his lips and let his chin fall nearly to his chest. For less than a breath, Jorrus doubted. But the power coursing through his body was all the truth he needed. And when Sarah Tremaine entered his field of vision, Jorrus realized the Song of Artus was simply another of the Advisor's tricks.

Ulrich and Paris's failure did not matter. Kragen's ploys meant nothing. *I will scorch your very souls from this plane. But first I must take care of the seamstress. I can't allow her charms to—*

Roc fell to the floor, and Jorrus screamed.

All of you... NOW!

Father Jorrus was accustomed to the sensations of shifting power as his collection of trapped souls slipped back and forth between his own body and his holy weapon. But now the souls became focused, more intent. The souls—the beautiful spirits that had raised him up, that had empowered him beyond his years—all of them streamed from his body and entered his instrument of war. With the rod's fangs extended toward the opposite side of the room, Jorrus unleashed the rage of his holy war upon his enemies.

⁂

Arames had little time to savor the discovery of Sarah Tremaine's talent. The return of his connection to the River provided the monk immediate command over the pain in his right arm. He sensed Roc's fall at the edge of his perception, but he still focused on Father Jorrus.

The monk felt the power within Jorrus and heard the cleric scream. He reached into his robes for his medallion. He had no idea what Jorrus was doing, but he knew it was up to him to counter it.

When the attack came this time, it was not a lightning strike but a liquid abomination, a wild and uncontrollable flow of dark power that spewed from the end of the staff like water through a crack in a dam. Again the release of malevolent energy was tinged with the green glow that meant everything to Arames.

Light burst from Arames's medallion. The strength of the River coursed through him and intensified the force of the radiance before him; it expanded much faster and more powerfully than it had in the inn two nights before. Less than ten paces separated Arames and Jorrus, and the two emanations of power—light and dark—converged directly between them. Like water poured onto hot oil, the resulting liquefied conflagration sent tendrils of rage in all directions. Green-tinged blackness struck the large wooden desk in the corner of the office, nearly cutting it in half. Liquid splattered against walls to either side of Arames, melting wood and plaster away like acid on wet parchment.

A rivulet of the unholy liquid flew over Arames's head and landed near the doorway. Droplets splashed across Ulrich's back. The resulting disintegration of clothing and corrosion of flesh finally brought Paris out of his reverie. As Ulrich's body rotted away like a discarded vegetable in the summer heat, Paris struggled to his feet and fled. He did not notice that he ran directly toward Sarah Tremaine, and barely felt her blade plunge into him. The impact knocked Sarah from her feet and into the wall behind her. The Song of Artus came to an abrupt end, the singer losing both voice and consciousness.

Droplets of the dark liquid landed on Arrin's hood and cloak. He ripped at his shoulders, spinning, fighting to shed the cloak before any of the vitriol could burn through and touch his skin.

Jorrus let out an angry scream. The dark torrent pressed harder to engulf Arames, but the monk's cone of light had expanded, stretching across the width of the room, becoming a barrier against the darkness and the corrosive fluid. The priest snarled, and the torrent ceased as quickly as it had begun.

Instead of attacking again, Father Jorrus lunged to his right, impaling his weapon into his prisoner's chest. The impact slammed Gretta into the wall behind her. An unnatural scream erupted from her throat, and she thrashed involuntarily against the chains that held her upright. It mattered little—Gretta was pinned against the stone wall, and Jorrus's weapon kept the priest safe from her flailing limbs.

Arames lowered his medallion and its light extinguished. *This cannot continue, Jorrus.* The monk took a breath and, as he had only attempted twice before, he reached out with his power to destroy another's mind.

It should have worked. Jorrus possessed no formal defenses against a mental attack and Arames met little resistance. But as he reached the deep place where he would unleash his blast, Arames found himself surrounded by flashes of light. They took shape, becoming shimmering images; wisps of light floated around Arames's presence as he moved through Jorrus's mind. The wisps took on more solid forms, becoming ghost-like visages floating around him, and finally calling to him—

Free us!

The forms faded away as quickly as they had appeared. They were still there, but they had become too focused on Jorrus's attack on Gretta to pay Arames further heed.

Arames closed his eyes, focusing his physical self and the projection of himself within Jorrus's mind. The monk no longer heard Gretta's screaming, and did not see Arrin charging toward his side.

Arames had taken a deep breath; now he blew the air out of his mouth—a physical release that mirrored the psychic attack the monk unleashed in the cleric's mind.

"You didn't think I would actually allow that, did you?"

Arames's mental form still *stood* in Jorrus's mind, but he now faced a dark-haired man flashing a wry smile. The man was dressed in formal attire, a buckled surcoat of green trimmed with leather and cone-shaped metal studs. His leather-gloved hand was balled into a fist, as if he had just caught a fly. He shook his hand and whipped it down in front of him. The mental attack that Arames had hoped would take down Father Jorrus dissipated into nothing.

"Doppin." It was not a question.

The Child of Trickery bowed. He leaned in and held a hand up to his cheek, as if he were sharing a secret. "The one who calls himself Arames Kragen."

Arames ignored Doppin's choice of words. "Jorrus is not you. You are not Jorrus."

Arames always translated being within another's mind as walking through a maze of rooms with shifting walls and doorways, real-world images and imagery he could understand. Being so grounded, Arames was openly surprised when Doppin pulled up his legs to sit cross-legged, hovering above the ground, still eye-level with Arames.

"The green gave me away, didn't it?" It was color traditionally associated with his energy; his magic. "I so wish dear old Dad didn't hold on to so many 'absolutes.'" Arames was reminded of the blues associated with Kaelee, the browns of Ursala.

Arames closed his eyes to slip away, but realized he could not withdraw from Father Jorrus's mind. He also could sense no movement in the physical world—it had all ceased. "Nice trick."

Doppin focused on the latter. "I cannot stop time. Even Father Az cannot do that now. Kalin possibly—" Doppin's smile widened at the thought. "In here, however—" he pointed around them both, "time is not as... codified."

"Jorrus is not yours. He belongs to Artus."

Doppin shook a finger. "Belonged—your Priests of Caern removed Artus from the discussion. What is it you've said about me? 'He who extends across all boundaries.' Just because I'm here, it doesn't mean I'm not also living my life as a jester at some court in Yew, or as a member of the Council of Grozh."

Arames ignored Doppin's references to some of his previous avatars. He also ignored the tone of the statement '*your* Priests of Caern.' "Just because the followers of Iberian have allowed their hatred of Theuroik Ironblade to discredit Artus, it does not give you the right to bend the will of one of his own!"

The Child of Az dropped his legs back to the ground and took a step toward Arames. The smile never left his face, yet his eyes hardened. "He still belongs to Artus. I have only—" he looked around him, his eyes softening, "given him the opportunity to realize his potential."

Arames opened his mouth to speak, but Doppin held up a hand and Arames found he had no voice. "Brother of Aarron—look how you have aged. You have wasted so much of your life in darkness." Arames tried again to shout, but could not. Doppin continued. "Yes, you have accomplished much as a *mortai*, Arames. You have seen the tears in the fabric. You helped drive back the Tourim—so well, in fact, that only a handful remember how close this age came to ending.

"That's the problem with mortality. Your memories are worthless. By the time you *mortai* are old enough to make a difference, you care only for the next generation, completely discounting your own. It is as if Az forbade you to learn from the mistakes of the generations before you. Your mortality makes you forget too fast, too soon."

Arames found his voice. "Our memories are not so faulty, Doppin. We still remember that the tears in the fabric were the fault of the Children."

Doppin turned his back on Arames, now watching the spirits fly around them. He reached out to touch one, but it swerved its path out of his reach. "Jorrus is right, you know. The undead are rising. And they are not simply slipping through the gates of Kalin's Abyss."

Arames scowled, but he suspected the goading was simply an attempt to distract him from what was happening around them. "That may very well be. But that does not excuse Jorrus. These spirits need their release."

Doppin turned his head just enough for Arames to see his profile. "Yes, but it will not be you who ends this. I think ... yes. Your precious prince needs another lesson today." Doppin took a step forward and a small diamond-shaped opening appeared before him. It folded back upon itself, like a curtain pulled back in four different directions. Through the opening Arames saw a dark forest, and a tall tower he did not recognize. *If that is Caern, it must be somewhere east of here—it looks to be well past sundown.* Doppin stepped through the opening. A bright light filled the aperture for a moment, blotting out the landscape. As the light extinguished itself, the doorway closed, leaving Arames alone with Jorrus's tortured souls.

Doppin must have been shielding Arames from the emotions that flowed between Jorrus and the souls he had imprisoned. Anger, loss, fear, and pain pulsated around and through Arames's psychic self. The monk screamed, drawing the attention of the souls that had given Jorrus such great power, while stripping away his sanity. Arames lost his balance and felt himself fall, but before the spirits could destroy him, he broke free from the priest's mind.

❧

Jorrus slammed his rod teeth-first into Gretta's chest and felt it pulling at her soul. The rod drained the blood from its victims, and the soul came along for the ride. Blood fed the weapon, somehow, and the souls gave Jorrus a power that had allowed him to wage his war on the undead for years past his prime.

The *voice* had shown him how to use the rod in the first place. *Praise Artus.* And the voice Jorrus knew belonged to Artus had also explained how to reverse the process, to send life back into a lifeless body and return its soul.

The souls had always seemed to move unhindered between himself and the rod; but the first time Jorrus raised Gretta, he had been amazed—they had fled his instrument then, and attempted to hide in the recesses of his mind. As Jorrus had plunged the teeth of the relic into the chest of Gretta's corpse, the mystical energies pulled at the ethereal form that was Gretta's soul, driving it back into the remains of the Avedon Housemistress. A wave of energy followed, sending seizures through both Jorrus and Gretta. The Housemistress got the worst of it, tearing skin from muscle, tendon from bone. When it was over, Gretta Platt, after three full days of death, had shuddered and sputtered to life.

And then had come the screams.

Less than a cyke later, Jorrus resurrected Gretta a second time. He hadn't anticipated how weak her hold on life would be, and his first violent outburst at her had resulted in the woman's death. Jorrus was more careful the next time around, and by this point Gretta had grasped the extent of what was going on... for, as Jorrus had stated to Arames, her soul had truly returned to her.

Jorrus had questioned Gretta, had used the tools at his disposal to loosen her tongue, but she refused to give him what he wanted. He knew there was one vampire at Avedon Hill, if not two, but Gretta remained steadfast in her silence. Jorrus tortured her with the relic, using one of the blades to peel the skin from her flesh. Still she gave away nothing—nothing but her screams. And then, once again, she was gone.

Over the next two nights, Gretta Platt died three more times. Each time Jorrus pulled her back, she had less of a hold on her sanity. The atrocities committed against her—against the very cycle of life and death—had irrevocably driven away Gretta's humanity. By the time Arames and Arrin arrived on the scene, Gretta may have possessed her life and her soul, but she no longer possessed the information Father Jorrus longed for.

Free us!!!

Jorrus felt the souls to him, a disjointed mass of voices converging from all corners of his mind into a single maelstrom. At first, Jorrus thought Arames had found a way past the protections of his holy relic, but it only took a moment for him to realize that something was very wrong. *Artus! Hast thou forsaken me?*

Jorrus turned to find the monk's young warrior charging toward him. Even with the emotions running rampant through him, Jorrus found his center and called on the power of the rod once more.

Arrin led with the point of his sword, intent on running Father Jorrus through. Though Jorrus watched Arrin charge him, he made no move to defend himself.

Green light flashed and Wildfire's point was forced up into the air. A wall of power encircled Father Jorrus. Arrin bounced off it and slammed shoulder first into the wall. The opposing motions—Arrin's sword point ricocheting upward while he was thrown to his left—jarred Arrin and separated him from Wildfire.

He found himself on one knee, his back against the wall. The green light of Jorrus's shield that had flashed visibly upon impact no longer shimmered, but Arrin could still feel its energy around Father Jorrus. The prince had no idea how to circumvent the wall of energy to reach the cleric, with or without his sword.

Free us, Jorrus!

The voices in his head spoke in unison now, their collective presence joining to a reverberating through him with a loudness and intensity that made his head pulse with pain. The safeguards—provided to Jorrus by the Child of Az whom Jorrus had believed to be Artus—had abandoned him, just as the Child himself had abandoned him. The souls he had imprisoned now had unfettered access to his mind. Their hatred and despair flowed through him as if they were his own emotions; his own pain.

Arames was to his left, down on one knee and holding his head with both hands. Jorrus knew that Arames had sought to disable him, and that it had somehow backfired on him. He also saw the monk's companion leaning against the wall before him, dazed.

Jorrus! You bastard!

It was Gretta. Her physical vessel was expiring once more, and her soul had entered the staff once again. The insanity of her living form did not affect her soul's clarity in the least.

If I can prolong her transition, I can get the information I need. Jorrus pulled on his staff with all his strength, ripping the metal teeth from Gretta's still-beating chest. She couldn't die just yet.

Are you there, bitch? Nothing. *You can wait. First I must punish the unbelievers.*

Jorrus released the staff's power, extinguishing the wall of energy that had protected him from Arrin's charge. He felt the river of magic all around him and thought of the seamstress's *song. A channeler! Ha!* Jorrus chuckled—Sarah Tremaine and her *song* would bring about the deaths of the very people she had sought to help. He breathed deeply, drinking from the River as fervently as a thirsty horse at a desert oasis. The young warrior had reached his feet. Brandishing his staff before him, Jorrus called on the power of Artus.

Holy Fire, burn these disbelievers! Jorrus silently called down flame from the heavens and gestured to cast it before him, fully expecting it to consume Arrin whole.

Nothing happened. The boy stared at him incredulously, his gaze drifting warily between the priest and his staff.

Free us, Jorrus!

Jorrus growled. He shouted, "Artus, I walk in your footsteps! Protect me from those who block our righteous path!" He raised his staff and brought it back down at an angle, a motion meant to release the spiritual spear of Artus.

Again, nothing happened. Then Jorrus heard the voice, not so much in his head as from a distance: *Poor Jorrus. So dedicated.* Even though the voice had been his constant companion for so many years, he now recognized the voice's owner for the first time. Jorrus's eyes widened in shock.

FREE US!

The shout reverberated within Jorrus's skull. With one hand he involuntarily let go of his staff; his open palm made it halfway to his forehead before he realized his mistake.

⚜

Arrin's gaze was fixed on the spiked staff. Considering Jorrus's threatening stance, Arrin suspected that the sphere of power that had bounced him into the wall of the room no longer enveloped the cleric.

Arrin balanced on the balls of his feet, ready to dodge an attack.

The cleric's eyes went wide in horror and he let go of the rod with one hand. Arrin dove forward and tucked into a roll; Jorrus regained his grip on his weapon too late to strike the prince. An awkward swing of the staff passed harmlessly overhead as Arrin tumbled toward his sword.

The prince's aim was true. As he completed his roll, Arrin found himself on one knee, Wildfire's hilt resting under his left hand. With no time to find his target, Arrin regained control of Wildfire with his off-hand and swung it behind him; the force of his swing spun him around on his knee to face Father Jorrus.

⚜

The boy's blade sliced into Jorrus's left leg just above his knee, striking bone, but the impact did not knock him from his feet. Even the shock of discovering that it was not Artus that had been guiding his hand all these years had not lessened the power that the spirits provided him. The wound pained Jorrus, but he shifted his weight to his other foot and prepared his counter. Holding his weapon near the blades that still dripped with Gretta's blood, Jorrus swung the rod at Arrin's exposed head.

The holy symbol swung over Arrin, the prince easily ducking underneath the slow, off-balanced attack. The force of Jorrus's swing also dislodged Wildfire from the priest's femur. Jorrus, his weight all on his right foot, could only watch as Arrin whirled again, sweeping his right leg around, cutting Jorrus's legs out from under him. Father Jorrus fell, landing hard on his back.

⁂

The unfettered emotions of the souls eased from Arames' consciousness, fading like a dream. Free of Doppin's influence and Jorrus's mind, Arames could now see what was going on around him.

A green glow rose from the edges of the room and a cackling laugh filled the air. Arames tried to call out, but found he had no voice. Though Doppin had fled from Jorrus, the Child of Az still presided over the room. Arames knew he could not move—he did not need to try. Doppin had given this task to Arrin; he wanted Arames to watch, and see where his choices had led them.

Arrin had regained his footing; Jorrus had raised himself onto his remaining good knee. As Father Jorrus lifted his staff, Arrin brought down his sword.

⁂

Father Jorrus felt the boy's longsword slice through his left arm just below the wrist. His left hand hung in the air for a moment, still clutching his weapon. As he instinctively pulled his arm back toward his body, the hand that was no longer his loosened its hold on his staff and fell to the floor.

Tears of pain flowed down Jorrus's face. The cleric watched Arrin effortlessly bring the sword around and up until his hands stopped at eye level, sword point nearly touching the ceiling.

Jorrus now fully realized Doppin had fooled him all these years, yet the cleric still felt empowered. His actions had been justified; his deeds in the name of Artus were as true as ever. He still held onto the rod of power with his right hand. The blood flowing freely from his left arm added to the stains on his soiled robes. "*Dul-Kali Tourim carenna! Artus carenni du Krat!*" Jorrus spat on the ground. "Do your best, BOY! I knew you would be of use to me in the end—" His voice trailed off, his eyes focused on Arrin's weapon. Jorrus heard the *whish* of Arrin's blade through the air and the *sccrick* as it sliced through his neck.

Father Jorrus had decapitated many a creature during his life, and he only found it slightly unnerving as it happened to him—he had just enough time to appreciate the sharpness of Arrin's blade. Jorrus managed to blink once, then again, after his head separated from his body, and then he felt a wave of happiness wash over him.

The bliss was not his own, but that of the souls finally escaping—from him, and from the unholy weapon Doppin had chosen for him.

Arrin stared down at Father Jorrus's vacant eyes. Blood still sprayed from the cleric's neck, but Arrin couldn't tear his eyes from Jorrus's own. The priest's head had fallen to Arrin's left as his body slipped to the ground to Arrin's right. The head had landed with a thud and had rolled once toward Arrin, coming to a stop face up. Much of the cleric's hair, which at one time had been waist-length, had been shortened greatly by Arrin's death blow. Long strands, bloodied during the fall, lay matted against Jorrus's head and face. But the eyes remained unscathed and exposed.

Arrin felt the heaving of his chest and did his best to slow his breathing. The grunts and groans from just past Father Jorrus's fallen body finally broke Arrin's lock on the cleric's face.

Gretta! Arrin lashed out, kicking Father Jorrus's head away from him. Arrin jumped over the cleric's body and landed just in front of Gretta.

"Gretta! Miss Platt! Please, you're going to be fine now. Jorrus can't hurt you anymore." Gretta flailed involuntarily, her moans weak. Arrin grabbed one of her arms as it came toward his head, only to protect himself. Touching her, he realized that his first impression of Gretta's physical condition had been a trick of the light. From the other side of the room it had appeared that some skin hung from her arms, legs, and torso. Now, Arrin found that the strips of flayed skin that still hung from her were indeed the only skin that remained below her once-beautiful face. Arrin's grasp closed on raw nerves, and Gretta threw herself back against the wall, pained. The impact drove her into unconsciousness. She slumped forward against her chains, suspended off the ground.

Arrin looked back at Arames. The monk stood transfixed, unmoving. Beads of sweat trickled down his face, a grimace twisting his features. Arrin didn't understand what manner of psychic struggle Arames waged, but to the prince it appeared Arames was losing the battle.

Arrin lifted Gretta's head gingerly, looking into her soiled and bloody face. Father Jorrus had left Gretta's face almost completely undamaged—when contrasted against the rest of her, it only added to the horror of the priest's acts.

Arms shaking, Arrin raised his sword until Wildfire's blade rested against Gretta's neck, just below her chin. Holding Gretta's hair with his left hand, Arrin slid the blade, slicing into Gretta, through skin, through muscle, into bone. The prince released Gretta's hair and stepped back to avoid the spray of blood as much as possible, but in doing so he slipped on the pool of blood around Jorrus's body and fell backwards to the floor.

Tears filled Arrin's eyes as he watched Gretta die for the last time.

RULER OF THE KNOWN WORLD, REVISITED

"Knowledge is Power"
"... So says the man on the gallows."

—The Death of Magic, by Baldric Wincet

ARAMES ONCE AGAIN STUDIED the balcony that overlooked Avedon Manor's great hall. Six archers stood along the overhang that ran around three walls of the room: four on the east balcony and two more along the west. Four of the guards had crossbows, while the remaining two had short bows, and all weapons were trained on him and Arrin.

Since they had entered the manor's great room, Lord Avedon and his oldest son Richard had controlled the conversation, which suited Arames just fine. Most of the particulars had been related to Lord Avedon by Richard and Sarah Tremaine. Sarah sat at the great octagonal table in the hall, recovered somewhat from the concussion that had knocked her out in the basement of the temple.

As soon as Gretta had died, Doppin had released Arames from his paralysis. Ignoring his pain, he had removed Gretta from her chains, carefully wrapping her in a blanket Arrin found in a nearby room. Arrin had carried Sarah in his arms; Arames had carried Gretta's corpse over his right shoulder. Thus burdened, they were met outside the temple entrance by Richard, Tanner, and several townspeople Arames recognized from the fire at the library. The men stood above Paris, who had collapsed outside the temple, felled by Sarah Tremaine's blade.

Arrin had filled Richard in on the way to the manor. Arames had remained silent, conserving his waning energy.

Lord Avedon projected his voice so all in the hall could hear. "So, Jorrus killed both Gretta Platt and her mother because of his belief in some grand conspiracy of vampires and moon-beasts?"

Frustration had etched Arrin's face since he had stepped out of the temple. Now it was tinged with fear. The bravado that had served him well in the caves outside of town and in the temple had abandoned him completely.

Arames took two steps forward, playing the opening move of the game on which their freedom depended. "Yes. And as you know, Lane Niccols had deceived Jorrus for years, hiding her nature from his senses—a vampire, living under his very watch. That, along with his other stresses, drove him insane.

"Over the last few years, Jorrus recruited Ulrich, Roc and Paris in his battle against the undead. All of them came to believe in his holy war. And eventually, Jorrus found someone to blame for his own failures: Gretta."

Lord Avedon frowned. "Gretta was killed days ago, yet the men who took her from you state the body was warm to the touch."

"Jorrus had an artifact. It was not only the weapon that killed Gretta and Gloria Platt, but it was also the method by which he returned Gretta to life. Jorrus believed Gretta knew the identity of the vampire in Avedon Hill. He brought her back to torture her for that information."

"And what did he discover?"

Arames considered his words carefully, his ambiguity conveying the answers Lord Avedon wanted. "Either she did not know about any vampire, or she was stronger than Father Jorrus realized. Gretta carried any secrets she may have had to her death—to several deaths."

Tears filled Lord Avedon's eyes. He waved Arames forward, and the monk approached the dais.

Lord Avedon lowered his voice to a whisper. "So, Brother of Aarron, what do we do now?"

"No one need learn about Edvard, and Gretta's murderer has been brought to justice. We also know that, unless your son attacked someone we do not know about, Edvard has not tasted the blood of man. You have the King's Crown potion?"

Lord Avedon shook his head. "Carin and Marrissa sit at Edvard's bedside, waiting for Richard and me to join them."

"And you know what must be done if the potion does not work."

Lord Avedon closed his eyes for a moment. "Marrissa created a second potion. If Edvard is not… cured, we'll give it to him." He opened his eyes again, and tears rolled down his face. "It will… I was going to say it would kill him, but he's already dead."

"I hope it does not come to that, Lord Avedon. Why did you not tell me that Louis was your brother-in-law?"

"It wasn't important."

"If I had known it, he might still be alive."

Both men seemed to be ignoring each other's statements. "Since my wife's death, Louis never wanted to be treated as family—by me in any case." Lord

Avedon looked past Arames at Sarah Tremaine, continuing only when he was confident she could not overhear. "He suspected something from the very beginning. I used every method at my disposal to keep Louis from discovering Edvard. But with or without your help, Louis pieced enough together and he stormed into Edvard's room. I had just taken Louis downstairs to explain everything when Cletus informed us that Lane had returned. Louis, in his anger, ran off to confront her about Edvard."

Lord Avedon wiped at his face. He cleared his throat and said loudly, "I thank you for your efforts, Arames Kragen. You have given Gretta back to us. She can be returned to her family's mausoleum... and join her mother."

Arames allowed himself a small smirk. *Wait for it.* "But... "

"But... I cannot allow you and your companion to leave Avedon Hill."

Arames knew that all the guards' weapons were trained upon him. If they loosed their arrows and fired their bolts simultaneously, he knew he would not be able to block them all—not in his current state. Sarah Tremaine protested, "Lord Avedon! This man just saved—"

"Enough!" Lord Avedon's voice had regained some of the authority it had possessed in Edvard's room the previous night. "Miss Tremaine, I appreciate your closeness to this matter. I didn't realize how... important Louis was to you. But this is not your concern." She stood, and Lord Avedon raised a finger. "Not one note, Sarah."

Sarah closed her mouth and sat back down in her chair.

"The murders of Talik Bore and Gloria Platt, the fire and subsequent explosions at the library, while not directly attributable to the two of you—" Lord Avedon paused, searching for the appropriate words. "Nevertheless, we must determine whether these deaths may have been a byproduct of your action or inaction." He seemed to like the sound of that, and smiled. "You will be moved to the town garrison until the matter is resolved."

Arames kept his voice low. "Lord Avedon, I hope you will reconsider. After I discovered the true secret of Avedon Hill, I took the liberty of writing a letter—"

Lord Avedon raised a finger and glanced once more at the archers, who had not moved. Richard, standing next to his father, reached behind him and pulled a scroll tube from the folds of his father's chair. "Are you referring to this letter?"

Richard waved a hand to his left. Arames heard movement beyond the door, and moments later another guard entered the hall, pulling Cousin Red along with him. Red's hands were bound behind him, but he appeared uninjured. Arames closed his eyes for a moment but reopened them in time to see a smug smile upon Lord Avedon's face. Sarah began to protest once more, but Lord Avedon stomped his foot on the dais, silencing the room.

"Nothing more from you, Miss Tremaine, or you'll be removed from the manor."

Arames sighed. *It appears I have underestimated at least one member of the Avedon family.*

"Once we learned of Talik Bore's murder, we knew he must have been negotiating with someone in an attempt to," Richard paused, measuring his words, "circumvent the way we conduct business. We sent men to secure the caves and to prevent further bypassing of our town gate."

Arames breathed in deeply and began channeling what little energy he had within him. In his present state, however, he was in no condition to leverage his abilities. His vision blurred from the effort. Lord Avedon stamped his foot against the dais once more. "Don't even think about using your powers here, Arames Kragen. All I have to do is raise my hand, and your cousin and your valet will be dead before you even reach my mind. Can you truth-read that?"

Arames relaxed, his shoulders slumping. Richard continued, "Red was captured in the caves outside Avedon Hill, carrying a very interesting scroll addressed to the leader of the Aarronic Brotherhood. I must say we were surprised by the contents of your missive."

Lord Avedon nodded. "This letter has sealed your fate, Sir Arames."

"This letter will *seal your fate.*" A booming, mocking voice repeated Lord Avedon's words. Arames turned to see Cletus stroll past Sarah and Arrin. He came to a stop at Arames's side. "Lord Avedon, you should refrain from using such an ominous tone. Threats don't become you."

Arames had always suspected that Cletus was more than he seemed, but the transformation of the gatekeeper seemed a surprise to everyone. Standing straight, Cletus was a full six inches taller than Arames. He wore a clean black tunic under a black overcoat with a thin white border. Cletus had cleaned himself up, as well—he had obviously bathed and washed his hair; and while there was nothing he could do about his girth, his attire seemed to have a slimming effect. With a flick of the thumb, Cletus flipped a coin into the air toward the two men on the dais. Richard caught the coin and looked at it. His eyes widened. "Father—the mark of the Council!" Cletus looked down at Arames and smiled.

"*You* are an agent of the Council?" asked Lord Avedon.

"You will release these two men immediately and provide them access to the Olviaran Pass." Cletus tugged at his newly cropped beard, free of food and tobacco for the first time since Arames and Arrin's arrival.

Lord Avedon was nearly apoplectic. "Why does the Council care about this monk? They've never interfered in my family's affairs—"

Cletus held up a hand. "Six years ago, a member of the Council was killed when his sloop was sunk in the bay west of Morning Isle. There were no witnesses, but the evidence made it clear that an explosion was responsible. While nothing directly linked his death to you, I was sent here to keep an eye on Avedon Hill."

"Then you must know I have only sold to buyers approved by the Council." Lord Avedon's statement raised Arames's eyebrow.

"Indeed. But recent events have altered the Council's perceptions of your family and its control over Avedon Hill—Gretta's murder, you and your family's erratic behavior, the presence of a vampire, the fact that Talik Bore was willing to sell the secret of the glow-rocks to the Tourim. The Council has decided that changes must be made. And as for *the monk* and his student—" Cletus's smile now beamed down upon Arames. "Let's just say the Council wants to ensure that no more harm befalls such important guests of Grozh." Cletus's glance flitted toward Arrin, only for a moment. Arames bowed his head slightly.

Lord Avedon was speechless. It was Richard who finally reacted, moving closer to his father and whispering in his ear. Lord Avedon started to protest, but Richard stared him down. Finally Lord Avedon nodded. He slowly descended the dais and left the great hall, taking the door through which Red and his guard had entered. Richard sat at the edge of the dais; his feet dangled just above the ground. "Tomi, release Cousin Red, if you would."

Richard spoke to Arames. "I apologize on behalf of my father. Our... family secrets have brought us nothing but grief these past two weeks. As Cletus said, things have to change."

Arames tapped the side of his nose with his index finger. "Opening the gates to Avedon Hill will only improve things. This will become a thriving town even before you become the next Lord Avedon—that is, of course, if the Council of Grozh allows your family to stay." Arames turned away from the dais, walking toward the large table. "If you play your cards right, Richard, you could become more powerful than any Lord Avedon in history."

Cletus added, "The Council has no intentions of removing your family from power, Richard." Richard nodded and Cletus turned to Arames, who sat in the chair next to Sarah Tremaine. "Sir Arames, the Council does have one request of you. Write a new letter to your brotherhood, requesting an Advisor to be sent to Avedon Hill. When the next Avedon Housemistress begins performing her duties, she will have to learn a new way of doing things."

Richard slid off the dais and bowed to everyone in the room. "Cletus, my family underestimated you, which I'm sure was your plan from the start." He turned to Arames. "You and your companion are free to go. Cletus can provide you access to the Pass—unless you plan on leaving us now, too?" he asked the gatekeeper.

"No, I will be staying, Richard. I like it here." Cletus's tone didn't waver. "You should join your father. Make sure Edvard is feeling better. I'll take care of our guests."

Arames was again surprised by Cletus's understanding of events. But he ignored that—the growling in his stomach was overwhelming everything else. He raised a hand. "If I might make one request, Richard... is Chef Roland available?"

Richard cocked his head to the side for a moment, but then nodded. "Straight away."

The monk placed his uninjured hand on Sarah's right arm. "Care to join us for dinner, Miss Tremaine?"

"It would be my pleasure, Sir Arames."

❦

The next three cykes were a flurry of activity. Arames was tended to by Father Livasdawn. While his right arm would forever be scarred, Arames knew he would regain its full use soon. After the meal, Sarah Tremaine rushed to her shop and returned less than a cyke later with a package for Arames. Two days before, after repairing Arames's clothing, Sarah had decided to tailor the monk a new set of robes. He thanked her and kissed her hand for a long moment.

Arames spent a bit of time with Red. While his cousin might not have found his riches, his future did look bright. As Red left, he joked that his close relationship with the former innkeeper's ale would allow him to carry on that particular Bore family tradition.

Jon met them on their way from the manor door to the Pass, leading two of his horses—Grozhian purebreeds worthy of the Perti royal stable. Arrin, silent since Cletus had arrived at Avedon Manor, thanked Jon profusely for his generosity.

Jon bid them good luck and left for the stables. Their belongings, packed and collected from the inn, were waiting for them, and Cletus waited alongside them. He used a large key to unlock the gate to the Olviaran Pass. "There you go, gentlemen."

"It appears you fulfilled your own claim," Arames said to the gatekeeper.

"Hmm?"

"When we arrived, you said you were the ruler of the known world. It appears that you not only granted us our entry, but now our exit."

Cletus smiled. "Lucky for you, I have a taste for Arien pipe tobacco."

"You recognized Arrin that morning?"

Cletus nodded. "Even though I knew of you by reputation, I wouldn't have made the connection—but Arrin didn't act much like a valet, even though he dressed the part. I'm sure this won't be an issue for you in the future."

"Issue? It appears that your powers of observation saved us."

"The Council wanted to make sure there was no chance of a *political* incident, especially after the discoveries you made these last few days."

"So, are you a member of the Council, Cletus?" *I knew a secret member of the*

Council—once. Not many can say that.

Cletus laughed. "Me?" As when they had first met, he said, "What I am is what I am, Sir Arames—nothing more."

Arames shook Cletus's hand. "Once again, thank you. Be sure to keep an eye on Jilly Hemming."

"She is under Father Livasdawn's care. He believes he can help her control her ability. Hopefully he'll succeed. I don't want to have to deal with the Priests of Caern if they discover a *wilder* lives here."

Arrin led his horse a few strides down the slope, past the gate.

Arames turned from Cletus and walked to his horse. "You have your hands full. Will you continue on as the gatekeeper?"

"Leilah wants Red to take over as cook and me to take over as innkeeper until she is savvy enough to run the place herself. It will be a good place for me to keep an eye on visitors."

"And will give you an opportunity to bathe more often."

Cletus pulled at his beard. "Yes, there is that."

"I wish you well, Arames Kragen—and you as well, Prince Arrin."

Arrin Perti bowed his head slightly, then continued into the tunnel. Arames turned from Cletus and introduced himself to his new horse, locking eyes and stroking its nose. "I have an apple for you somewhere We should walk a bit before we eat, though. Your friend seems to be leaving us." Arames climbed upon his horse and waved once more in Cletus's direction. A few moments later, as Arames caught up to Arrin, he heard the gate to the Olviarar Pass close behind them.

⚜

"Why do I have these dreams, if I can't change the future?"

Arames had let Arrin stew in silence for nearly a cyke. "What do you mean?"

"The destruction of the library, Talik's death, even Lord Avedon's archers. I dreamed all of that, yet there was nothing I could do to stop it. I still believe the only reason we survived our meeting with Lord Avedon was that I didn't say a word once I saw the archers on the balcony."

Arames shook his head. "Your dreaming touches the past, present, and future. In just a few nights you have learned enough to control elements within your dreams. While this is a step to becoming a powerful walker, it adds another level of complexity to what you do. There are an infinite number of possible futures, more than there are stars in the heavens. If you see time as a straight line from past to future, affecting events during your dream-walk can move you further from that line. The dream-walk may be taking you north, but if you consciously force events to the east, what you see while walking the bridge may or may not take place in your future—and most certainly will not happen in exactly the same way it did in your dream."

"But why? Why me? Why is this a Perti legacy?"

Arames measured his words. "Magic, no matter its form, flows from Az. The abilities you are beginning to discover are connected to Az as well. While the clerics of Caern's sects develop their powers through their spiritual connection to the river of magic, and while the powers that I and many other Aarronic Advisors possess are directly attributable to our connection and service to the Land, other examples of magic are directly linked to the Children."

Arrin pursed his lips. "Meaning?"

"Meaning that when avatars of the Children live their lives on Caern and have families, some of their power can sometimes be passed on to their progeny. Some of these abilities become diluted over time, while others become more powerful with each new generation."

"So you're telling me that there's a Child of Az in my family tree?"

Arames nodded. "Two actually—that we know of."

Arrin twisted the leather reins in his hands and clenched the muscles in his arms and legs. Arrin's mount, a dark-colored horse Arrin had already named Shadow, shook its head and reared once, slightly unnerved by his new master's agitation. Arrin soothed the animal. "I hate this. I killed Gretta during my first dream-walk. I set her ablaze and watched her burn to death. Even armed with that knowledge, I couldn't change the future."

"No, Arrin—Jorrus murdered Gretta Platt before we ever arrived at Avedon Hill. Your act was one of kindness. You released her."

Arrin's face twisted in a mix of anger and fear. "That's the problem. I understand exactly what you're saying. I did what I had to do—what I was meant to do. And I don't know if it's because I experienced Gretta's death during my dream-walk, or because I've taken so many lives over the last few days that I suddenly have a different view of the world—but my reaction in the temple wasn't over killing Gretta Platt. I knew I had to finish what Jorrus had started. The horror I felt—it's because I don't feel any remorse at all." Arrin kicked his heels gently into Shadow's sides and rode on ahead, leaving Arames behind him.

Endings

Iberian will stand with Kalin and Doppin at the Last Day.
He has known the end since the beginning of time.

—The Last Prophecy of Iberian

Arames started to call out to Arrin, to tell him it was shock that he had felt, not a lack of remorse. But he let Arrin go. He thought about Doppin's words: *So begins the true education of Arrin Perti.*

Arames pushed the Child of Az from his mind; he was immediately replaced by thoughts of Arrin's mother.

✦

"You must promise me something, Arames."

As he always did, Arames listened intently to Serena and wondered what events from her dream-walks had brought her to what she was doing and saying. "If it is within my power, you know you will always have my promise."

Serena's smile was over in an instant; she had no time for pleasantries. "You're heading into danger. I've seen this. But I need you to promise me you won't do anything to remove Arrin from the perils you will face. You cannot hold him back in any way, even if it seems the only way to protect him."

Arames scowled. He had reluctantly agreed to come to Castle Pen on his way to Kith-Karn at Serena Perti's behest. She had begged him to take Arrin, to be his mentor and guide, even though he had long since retired. *But this?* "My primary function as a member of the Aarronic Brotherhood is to protect Caern and its peoples. Are you asking me to disregard this?"

Serena Perti had a wild look in her eyes. "You haven't seen what I've seen. Events are transpiring that neither you nor I can... affect. Arrin will play a part in these events. He must be prepared."

"Serena, your family's ability to walk the bridge has always had its limitations—"

"There are forces at work that have the ability to swallow Caern whole, and no magic we or any priest possesses will save us. But there are three living today who will save Caern."

Iberian's last prophecy. "Serena, you are incorporating your knowledge of Iberian's prophecies into your dream-world. It is influencing you, shaping your—"

Serena slapped Arames hard across his face. He recoiled, never more surprised in his entire life. Arames had known Serena since she was six years old. She had never raised a hand against him.

She did not ask forgiveness. "I've never been more sure of anything—ever. Arrin has to be equipped for his part in this. You are the one to teach him. If he dies, then he's not one of the three, and I will have lost my youngest son. Please... please, do this for me—for all of us."

Arames's face burned. He reached out, gently probing the edges of her mind. Serena's eyes widened for just a moment, but then she closed them, symbolically inviting him in.

Her mental walls retreated, but did not vanish. Arames was proud to see how much control Serena had, allowing him access only to what she wanted him to see. In fact, Serena used her own abilities to push the images and emotions into Arames faster than he could interpret them. In moments, Arames recoiled for a second time, severing the connection. He had seen more than enough.

Arames looked into her tear-filled eyes. "You may lose your son."

"If I'm right, I've already lost him."

Arames bowed his head slightly. "I will do what you ask, dear one."

<hr />

Arames Kragen scratched the end of his nose and sighed. He reached into one of his saddlebags and was happy to find it filled to the fold with fruit, a parting gift from Jon Avedon. Arames pulled out two apples. *One day you will discover what we have done—what we are doing. And you will never forgive us.*

The dangers of Avedon Hill were behind them. But each day would take them closer to Kith-Karn, deeper into Grozh—closer to those who would kill Arrin if they even suspected he was a Perti. Arames clicked his tongue against his teeth and his horse quickened its pace. He rode forward until he was next to Arrin, and offered an apple to the prince.

"What about Edvard?" Arrin asked.

"Either he has been restored, or he has been destroyed. Lord Avedon will do what he must." Arrin's brow furrowed. Arames continued. "Besides, Cletus understands the situation. He will ensure that Lord Avedon keeps his promise."

Shadow faltered on a rock in the road, but recovered. Arrin patted the horse's neck, then leaned forward to offer the apple tc Shadow's muzzle.

"Rough road..."

Arames pulled his hood over his head, suppressing a shiver. "Yes, my prince—a rough road, indeed."

AUTHOR'S NOTE

While attending the University of Virginia, P.G. Holyfield majored in Religious Studies, focusing on the belief systems and myths of the Eastern world. His love for mythology led to the creation of the fantasy setting named the Land of Caern.

A gamer for most of his life, P.G. has spent almost twenty years creating content for the Land of Caern. In 2006 P.G. began producing the *Murder at Avedon Hill* podcast novel. After over half a million episode downloads and two years of production, P.G. completed the podcast novel in 2008, and *Murder at Avedon Hill* was a finalist for Best Audio Drama at the 2008 Parsec Awards. P.G. is currently producing a short story podcast anthology called "Tales of the Children," with stories by P.G. and other authors, all set in the Land of Caern. Both podcasts, along with additional content and information, can be found on his website: http://pgholyfield.com

P.G. is hard at work on the next Chronicle of Arames Kragen, tentatively titled *The House that Time Forgot*.

P.G. lives in Charlotte, NC with his family, and probably spends way too much time on Twitter (@pgholyfield).